Unending Nora

Unending Nora

a novel

JULIE SHIGEKUNI

RED HEN PRESS | Los Angeles, California

Unending Nora
Copyright © 2008, 2019 Julie Shigekuni

ISBN: 978-1-59709-122-0
Library of Congress Catalog Card Number: 2008926882

The California Arts Council and the National Endowment for the Arts partially support Red Hen Press.

First Edition
Published by Red Hen Press
www.redhen.org

Acknowledgments:

This book was a long time in the making, and along the way many people have contributed generously toward its realization. For reading early drafts, I thank Madalyn Aslan, Julia Hunkins, Margaret Mayer, the many wonderfully talented and just plain wonderful students at the Institute of American Indian Arts, graduate students I had the good fortune to work with during my year at Mills College, Matthew Wilks for his medical expertise, and Officer Wesley LaCuesta of the Foothill Precinct of the Los Angeles Police Department.

For their reading and generous comments on later drafts, Julie Mars, Frances Sackett, Nancy Barrickman, Christie Waszak, Kathryn Landon, Helena Brandes, Norman Bay.

And always, my husband Jonathan Wilks, for the pleasures of work and home.

For *Kiyomi, Emiko,* and *Issa*

A baby calms down when you rock it, a city
calms down from the distance.

—Yehuda Amichai

Book One

Chapter 1

A HEAT WAVE set that summer in motion. For twenty-two days record-breaking temperatures created a broad stripe that connected Los Angeles to Chicago, and while they knew the weather was not directly to blame, years later the heat wave of '95 still triggered everyone's misgivings about Nora. Don't want to risk losing the bougainvillea, Reverend Nakatani would say shaking his head, looking for early warning signs in the heart-shaped leaves while hovering over the bush with the garden hose. This had become his after-dinner activity, which he returned to every summer since the heat wave, as soon as the weather began heating up. Remember how the grass turned brown overnight? Can't get it back once that happens. Aiko left the watering to her husband. Not wanting to be faulted for an act of God, she stuck to what she knew best, remembering fondly a time when she could yank the crabgrass up by the roots. Now her arthritis prevented her from making a tight fist, but thankfully there was no need to make Christmas roast beef anymore. Her daughters, and even her daughter-in-laws, could cook. And since all four of her children lived nearby with their families, she had taken the old carving fork outside where it worked just fine—maybe better than ever—on the weeds.

Even with her ears tucked under the brim of a straw gardening hat, Aiko knew what her husband was talking about. It was impossible to keep anything alive under so much sun. How many triple-digit days did they have in a row?

What could Nora possibly have been doing out there in that heat?

It began in July, mid-summer. Oblivious to the heat that had taken over a hundred lives, Nora had been walking since early afternoon, overcome by all there was to see and just how nice everyone seemed to be. A newcomer to Pacoima, she had no information to tell her that people in this neighborhood were not generally on such friendly terms with each other. What she saw was the bond the sticky heat created between neighbors and how easily conversation came to strangers. A radio perched on the top shelf of the 7/11 announced the Civic Center temperature at an even one hundred, which in the Valley translated to at least a hundred and five. "How you doin' in all this heat?" the store clerk asked when she set the bottled water on the counter to pay.

Hearing *heat* and seeing the old man's large white teeth, Nora touched her chin to her shoulder to catch the perspiration beading down the sides of her face before reaching into her shorts pocket for change. Easier to focus on the teeth than to meet the man's eyes where she expected to find impatience or perhaps even ridicule as her hand slowly made its way down to the coins. She chastised herself for not stopping at the back of the store to retrieve the money before approaching the cash register. Seconds spread out as the water sloshed then settled inside its clear plastic, waiting to be drunk as her fingers seized upon the first coin, then two more nestled in a tight corner where they had migrated as she walked, and the pain she had been anticipating unfurled then roared like a waking beast.

"Too damn hot for words," the store clerk said, either oblivious to her discomfort, or politely trying to ignore it, and realizing that she had not responded the first time she'd been spoken to, Nora's attention returned outward. "I'm just fine, thank you," she said, glancing up at the teeth and marveling at their wonderful evenness before looking back down, this time at a wet spot that shone up from the countertop. Had it dripped from her chin?

As she pushed her body against the glass door and made her way back to the sidewalk, the store clerk's eyes on her back made Nora self-conscious of the effort each step required. The black asphalt had begun to melt. It stuck to the soles of her shoes and smelled like charred meat, and when she looked down she could see salt stains flowering beneath each of her arms. Was this the reason the old man stared? Or had he thought she'd been signaling him with the coins?

This was the fifth afternoon in a row that Nora had been walking, and along the way she had convinced herself that it wasn't that hot. She had worked hard to find beauty in a neighborhood that most people were convinced contained none. Until a week ago, Pacoima had been nothing more than a port of entry to church, a half-hour car ride from Sherman Oaks where she'd grown up with her two friends Melissa and Caroline. As professionally manicured lawns, expensive boutiques, and outdoor cafes became block homes scattered between junk shops and bodegas, Nora gazed out the window fascinated at how a half-hour car ride could so thoroughly change the world. But even as a child, she'd sensed how little you could know a thing by observing it from behind glass.

Nora delighted in the purple and hot pink flashes of climbing jacaranda that blossomed along Penny Lane, the star jasmine whose tiny white blooms and sweet scent could be found only along one short stretch of Braxton Street, the delicate fortnight lilies whose stalks blistered like chives. Though the area lacked the obvious advantages brought about by money, she admired the small things people did to personalize their yards. The owl whose right ear was one day missing and the next replaced with a stone, only to be knocked off again, the reindeer left out from Christmas, and the flamingo whose fat body had acquired the blanched pink of cotton candy. She wondered about the sensibility of people who would treasure such items, and decided that a willingness to take in what others had abandoned and make them one's own was an endearing trait, and one she wished to share, along with the patches of shade where she'd stop beneath the occasional tree, grateful for the leaves overhead that suggested coolness. While resting in the shade on her sixth afternoon of walking, she accepted the realization, so long in coming, that the ache in her hands might never go away, and that she'd wound up in a world in which nothing might again be as it was. The understanding that proceeded from the life she observed on foot came with forceful clarity, her attention rewarded with a kind of hopefulness that was new to her.

It was evening when she arrived at the church. She was re-lieved to find the outer gate open and the row of lanterns that led to the sanctuary lit. Worried that Reverend Nakatani might see her from the rectory, she did not follow the lit path, but hur-ried instead to meet the line of darkness that fell against the outlying building. Though condemned in the '70s after the new sanctuary was constructed, the outlying building had been the original structure, occupied by a local farmer and his wife, set on a two-acre plot, and purchased by Valley Baptist in the late '50s when the couple traded their land for a condominium. But rather than tear down the old sanctuary once the new worship hall was in place, the congregation chose the simpler task of erasing it from the landscape by the magical act of not looking at it. Families coming to church parked along the front gate and walked straight up the steps to the new building as if the older, dilapidated structure did not exist. It wasn't that people pretended not to notice; they simply *didn't*, allowing the build-ing's lack of usefulness to banish it from their sight. Still, Nora remembered stories about how the holy ghost dwelled in the ramshackle building that had been the congregation's sanctuary, and before that, a home. Twenty years earlier, she and her friends Melissa and Caroline had played inside, and the rotting wood and dust had remained pleasant smells, nostalgia replacing for Nora what had once felt mysterious.

On a day when it seemed as if they'd visited every part of the church worth exploring, Nora had been the one to pry open a loose window and let herself into the old building. Using a discarded hymnal to clear a path through cobwebs, she'd made her way to the bolted door and after unlocking it waved Melissa and Caroline inside.

"We shouldn't be in here," Melissa had warned, her footsteps creaking over the rotted floorboards.

"It's dirty," Caroline had said. "And creepy."

"It's where God lives," Nora insisted. "You shouldn't talk that way about God's house. Of course we should be here."

"God lives everywhere," Melissa argued.

"No, Mel," Nora said. "Jesus lives in the new church, which was built for him. But God doesn't live with him. God lives here."

"Really?" Melissa said, hands rising to cover her face.

Melissa's problem, Nora considered, was not that she lacked originality, but that she was satisfied with partial truths, and could therefore convince herself to pass other people's abstract ideas off as her own. "He lives in there." Nora pointed to a closet door left slightly ajar.

"You're scaring me," Caroline said.

"Don't be scared," Nora said, taking her friend's hand less to comfort her, than to ensure that Caroline would not bolt.

The seconds that her friends stood staring at the door gave Nora an opportunity to marvel at the fear she had created and now controlled, and time to think up what came next.

"Open it," she said to Melissa.

"You open it," Melissa said. "I'm not opening it."

"What are you scared of?" Nora asked, wishing to use Melissa's curiosity, and her weakness, to her own advantage.

"Ghosts," said Melissa.

"Spiders," said Caroline.

"Okay, I'll open it," said Nora. She thrust the closet door open sending a visible spray of dust into the sunlit air. At first they saw nothing, too shocked by the current of stale air coming alive and by the rapid beating of their hearts to notice the shoes.

Melissa collapsed in a fit of sneezes and recovered with an observation. "Look," she said, pointing.

"I didn't know God wore shoes," Caroline said, moving closer to inspect the pair of men's dress shoes. They were black under the layer of dust, well worn, and vaguely familiar looking. When she turned them over to examine the soles, a spider escaped from the foot hole and began crawling up her arm, causing Caroline to fling the offending object across the room.

"What's that?" Melissa said, startling at the thud, then following the shoe across the room with her eyes.

Nora moved closer to examine the white mass that had rolled out of the shoe. "What are *these*?" she said, pinching the sheer nylon and tossing the fabric into the air.

"Underpants!" Caroline shrieked. "I think they're my Baachan's."

"What would God be doing with men's dress shoes and your Baachan's underpants," Melissa questioned, seeming genuinely puzzled.

"Go ask Nora," Caroline said, pointing an incriminating finger. "It's her game."

They didn't laugh at what might have been a funny prank, or rehash what had happened later. Nor did they enter the old building again. But the incident engendered a new activity, and with it a ritual that had continued into adulthood. The next time Melissa began complaining of boredom, Caroline wagged her finger in Nora's direction and lent the diversion its official name. "Go ask Nora."

Over the years Caroline and Melissa continued to play "Go ask Nora." Caroline was the one to consult for tips on make-up, clothing, and boys, and Melissa had unlimited access to practical information. But Nora was the spiritual advisor. They came to believe in the privileged relationship she had with God and were fascinated at the way their friend understood things—as if from the inside out. The truth was, having found no place for herself in the world of appearances, Nora was the natural ruler of the world that existed beneath the surfaces. She gauged emotions readily and was always ready to laugh and be surprised. Nora's gifts had made her their leader, but what had happened to change things?

Seated in a rickety pew in stifling, dark heat, Nora remembered the underpants and wondered about them. How had she and her friends managed not to find their discovery bizarre? Old lady underpants stuffed into the minister's shoes? At what point had she come to assume that the shoes belonged to Reverend Nakatani? Why him and not someone else? Even if they had been his, might there not have been a simple explanation for the underpants? Maybe his wife had once used them as a polishing rag. Nora doubted this theory. But it did no good to assume otherwise. She wondered if the girls, at nine, had understood intuitively about the objects they had discovered; if perhaps that was why no one had laughed, or brought the incident up again.

Even after the problems with her hands set in, she'd always thought of her life as good. She'd been raised to be agreeable, taught to see the pleasant side of people, and urged to trust God. But the more she thought about it, the more dubious the whole arrangement seemed. If it was God's will that she should live out her life in Pacoima, then that was fine. But what if it wasn't God's will? What if she had taken a wrong turn without God knowing it and was being led not by God's will, but, as she was beginning to suspect, by her own myopic vision? She'd been as guilty as the rest of the congregation of not wanting to see. She'd obliterated the ram-shackled sanctuary from sight as if such an act would cause it to disappear. But the building had not disappeared, and she sat in the splintered pew with her hands clasped in her lap struggling to see something that she could not be certain existed.

Outside the dusty window, the moon lacked symmetry. She watched it rise as if charting her own ascension until she could not remain still one second longer. Emerging from the old building onto the lit path, Nora was wondering if one could tell by looking whether the moon was moving toward or past its fullness when she ran head on into Reverend Nakatani. It was impossible to tell who was more startled as each recited an apology.

"Are you okay?" the minister said, rubbing the spot on his upper arm that had met with her elbow. "I didn't expect to see anyone, and I must have been looking down."

"It was my fault," Nora said guiltily. "I hope you're not hurt."

"I'm fine," Reverend Nakatani said, though he didn't look fine. She hadn't often seen him in layman's clothes, and she noted how his golf shirt and belted polyester slacks didn't seem to hang right. "I didn't even know you were here," he said, as if suddenly curious about what should have been obvious.

"I was out walking—"

"You shouldn't be walking around here," interrupted the minister. "It's not *safe*. But I'm glad you caught me. I'd be happy to give you a ride home."

In all the years Reverend Nakatani had been their minister, it had never occurred to Nora that he drove. She remembered how in her childhood the owner of a new car would raise his hood, a signal for the men to gather for inspection. She'd joined her father on several occasions, impressed by how much there was to look at and admire, and at the same time cowed by the gravity of the information exchanged—as if a car were a living thing, worthy of congratulations and even awe. No man in the congregation was exempted from the ritual because everyone in Southern California drove, yet she hadn't a clue even as to the make of the car Reverend Nakatani owned. "You don't need to drive me home," she said, realizing that he was watching her and perhaps wondering why she was taking so long to respond. "That's not necessary."

"It's no problem at all. Of course, you'll need to give me directions."

"I'd rather walk, really." Wondering how much the minister had been told about her present circumstances, and by whom, Nora felt the drop in her tone. She knew that the minister would interpret her refusal as disrespect. He was probably just trying to be kind, but unable to find language to resolve the impasse, she risked rudeness to make herself clear. "I'll be fine."

"I can't allow you to walk," Reverend Nakatani said, exhibiting a kind of forcefulness that did not feel conversational.

The two stood silently for what seemed to Nora a long while. The field behind the minister appeared dramatic, the backdrop of a stage set rather than the ordinary sight that it was. The four striped PG&E towers spewed steam in the distance, behind them the craggy San Gabriel mountain range, and Reverend Nakatani so close that she could smell his breath. She guessed that the minister's wife packed dinners for him on the nights he stayed late at the church, the odor of fish and garlic drenched pickles pervading the air between them. Had he been running when they'd collided? The whole situation made no sense at all. Not what he or she were doing at the church so late at night, no more what had prompted his fit of paternalism. There had been months before her move to offer assistance. Why wait until now, when she'd been on her own walking for days and had met with no harm. "I'm sure you need to get home," she said. "I don't want Mrs. Nakatani to be worried."

"I always have time for one of my own," he said, signaling a shift in the conversation that took Nora off guard. "We can talk in the rectory if it'd be more comfortable for you inside. Or we can talk right here since the weather is so pleasant tonight."

"Oh, of course," she said, relieved to have finally understood. "I'm glad to see you, but I hadn't actually come to talk with you, or even expected you to be here. So you don't have to worry about accommodating me."

"No?" he said. "In that case, I apologize for being presumptuous."

"You aren't presumptuous." Nora smiled warmly. "I'm sure there aren't too many reasons that someone would be here at this hour if they weren't looking for you."

"No," he repeated. "But let's see this as an opportunity, rather than a cause for embarrassment. Maybe God planned our meeting. What we thought of as a coincidence might just be the perfect excuse to talk."

It was impossible for Nora to articulate to herself the terror she felt then. Ahead of her, the slatted fencing shone in the moonlight, the gate wide open as if to signal her exit. But there was no way to get even that far and no one she would have liked to have a conversation with less than Reverend Nakatani.

"The events of the last months must surely be testing your faith." His voice called her to him as she began walking, refusing to look back. To the left, a small stand of trees near the outbuilding obscured the window she'd left open when she'd fled.

"My faith?" she said, retracing her steps from the side of the outbuilding. Couldn't he have seen her approaching? "What do you mean?"

"When times are good, even a nonbeliever can be faithful. Favorable circumstances provide life's most powerful elixir. It's the hard times that test a person's character. Do you feel that your character is being tested?"

The minister's words recalled what she'd been thinking moments before her path crossed his: She'd never considered that her faith was at stake. Her life felt threatened, but not her faith. She hadn't thought of it that way. "There's no need for God to test my faith," she said. "I doubt myself, not God."

"Of course," Reverend Nakatani laughed, as if he understood her confusion completely. It alarmed her how composed he'd become addressing this topic of faith, his stride lengthening beside her. A slight smile parted his lips, and he produced a ring of keys from his trouser pocket. She watched him fumble with the rectory's locked door, his coffee stained teeth reminding her that he had the upper hand.

"I would never ask God for explanations," Nora said. She wanted Reverend Nakatani's help and was therefore attempting to be as honest as possible. "I'd just like to understand why I've been so delusional."

"I'm sorry. I don't quite understand what you mean," he said, rushing in ahead of her to switch on a light, then indicating the chair where she should sit. "Could you tell me what you mean?"

"How can I blame God when I don't even understand what, exactly, has gone wrong?" Nora sat back, her long frame perching awkwardly atop the minister's hardwood chair. "I thought my life had been going along fine until a year ago, when I began to lose feeling in my hands. But now I think things hadn't been right long before then. I just hadn't seen it that way."

Locked in deliberation, Nora didn't know where to begin. She needed to believe that if she could just get the chronology of her life right, if she could pinpoint the moment when the misstep occurred, then everything could be made right again. And so she continued in her attempt to construct a timeline. For as far back as she could remember her plan had been to pursue a degree in medicine. But the summer between her graduation from Cal State Long Beach and her acceptance at UCLA, she'd taken a temporary position at a law firm and had learned to direct phone calls, type letters, and work the photocopier that leaned against her desk. Her mother having praised the same skills that were lauded by her unctuous employer, Nora felt satisfied when her eye had caught on a newspaper advertisement for cosmetology school. What irony her change of plans would reveal. Ugliness never prevented the peahen from wanting to hang with the peacocks. Wasn't that her mother's joke?

"The past is without end," she declared to the minister, puzzled by how one event couched itself in another in her unending search for clarity.

"The past is where we must look if we are to acknowledge God's mystery."

Across the room, a garment bag hung over the dressing closet door, forcing it slightly ajar, triggering Nora's memory. Hadn't she once squatted in the dark closet between folds of the minister's identical black robes? She remembered their stale smell, and how she'd run her fingers over the limp fabric believing that the silken fabric was like touching Jesus's flesh. But what had she been doing in the dressing closet? Had Melissa and Caroline been with her? She thought not, though looking into the dressing closet left her with an uncomfortable feeling. "Indeed," she heard the minister say, "we are indebted to the past."

"So you understand?"

"Of course. The greatest mystery of all is revealed to true believers as the holy trinity. Without Jesus, the son of God, there would be no salvation."

Nora blinked forcefully in an attempt to refocus her eyes, experiencing the same haziness she remembered from nights she'd stay up late as a student, staring down at words until they blurred on the page, until only a walk outside would clear her vision. Across from her, Reverend Nakatani sat on his green plaid recliner, his fingers laced around a bony knee. By his posture, he seemed intent on exuding comfort, leaning forward slightly at the waist, inviting her to trust him. But he looked like an imposter, almost unrecognizable to her. She was trying to explain to him about her life so that he might help lead her back to a path she seemed to have lost, and he was a stranger, rambling on about the holy trinity. She supposed there might be a connection, though she had no idea what it could be. "I'm sorry," she said, giving up. "I must be very tired because I'm having trouble concentrating on what you're saying."

"It's understandable," he said, unclasping his fingers and chuckling to himself. "The foundations of Christianity provide a paradox that isn't easily understood, even on a good night's sleep. I'll drive you home now. We can speak more about this subject later—any time you're ready to talk."

"I don't want to offend you," Nora said, rising abruptly and edging her way to the door. "But I don't need a ride."

I'd rather kill myself than sit locked in a car with you, she thought, surprising herself. She'd spent her life in the church, a devout believer, a good Christian. But the nature of her faith was changing; she felt it as she fled across the field. Like a snake after shedding its skin, she felt light, almost like she was floating. Past the outbuilding illuminated by the moon and through the gate before the headlights of Reverend Nakatani's old Corolla could even make the turn. Though her rational mind had temporarily shut off, her body was not tired. Blocks from the church, the streets came alive with traffic and neighbors sitting along the curbs and on the hoods of brightly colored cars, taking in a breeze that offered one night's respite from the dogged heat.

Back at her apartment, she worried that it might take a while to relax, and was therefore surprised to fall off into a deeper sleep than she'd experienced in weeks.

Chapter 2

THE SAN GABRIELS rose in the eastern sky with an unsettling sharpness. They were a familiar sight, reliable witnesses to Nora's growing up in the Valley, yet, on her seventh afternoon walking, she found the crags and deep pockets of shadow that clung to the mountain range daunting. At the same time, the fact that the mountains had always been so close and yet she had no memory of ever setting foot in them seemed regrettable. She thought she might have traveled to the mountains as a child, for a family outing, and she marveled at the way events and feelings could disappear without a trace. Why did her mind settle on such peculiar objects for its musings in the first place, and how could the complicated facts of her past lay for so long hidden from her?

For no apparent reason, the heat had finally caught up with her. Her body had begun to sweat profusely and to tremble, making her conscious of how her hands hung at her sides like a monster's claws, or bones off a corpse, stiffening into casts of hideous deformity. She tried to reassure herself with the scenery, rationalizing that if she could not make the pain go away she could still pick the objects of her attention, like apples from a tree. Or she could choose to walk away. She was looking around her for something that might allay her increasing discomfort when her attention was drawn outward by the feeling that she was being watched, and her panic instantly shifted. She was more aware of being stared at than most; she knew what it was like to be regarded as a foreigner, a cripple, someone to despise. She knew how not to notice, or at least pretend not to. Even so, this was the second time in two days that she had become the object of attention, and it was not self-consciousness or fear that made her turn to look, but sudden curiosity as to how she might appear in someone else's eyes.

She didn't see anyone right away, noticed first a planter of red impatiens that hung over a shaded porch, then a three-step stoop not commonly found on the west coast leading to a nondescript brown house that guided her eye to its focus: the dark man bent over himself. Shaded by the overhang, he wore a green tee-shirt with cap sleeves that pulled tightly against his upper arms, and though he sat several yards away, she could feel his eyes fix on her.

"Hey," he said, thrusting his chin out in her direction.

Having been recognized, she was suddenly too embarrassed to speak, let alone stare back. She had wanted to see his face close up, but as punishment she turned away, creating in her mind as she walked a picture of what surrounded him. The bright red flowers, a screen door framed in cracking wood. The five books whose bindings she could not read, stacked beside him instead of open on his lap because he'd put them aside to wait for her. He'd take them and her inside, pressing the pages flat for her to see. In her mind's eye, she could see the books clearly. But what had he looked like? By the time she arrived back at her apartment she wondered whether perhaps the stranger had not existed at all. Had she invented him out of a perverse imagination? It was then that her greatest fear asserted itself: that neither her presence nor absence made a difference to anyone.

But the stranger had been real. She knew this because she had deduced at once that he was exactly the type of person her mother and friends would label as dangerous. The dark skinned stranger with the kind smile practiced as a deception. He'd be poorly educated, have little money; most likely he wouldn't even be Christian. And so it was with mounting anticipation that she retraced the route she'd taken home. Striding up the three-step stoop, she watched through the torn screen as the stranger took shape out of the darkness. Brown skin, tight tee-shirt with a yellowed-V across the chest, smooth, muscular legs. As he approached, a slight breeze escaped from the house and a dense, bitter odor filled her lungs. Satisfied by his presence, she stood facing him. Without hesitation she allowed herself to be surveyed while he raised his eyebrows and squinted.

"You're the mute Chinese girl, aren't you," he said, cocking his head.

Such a comment might have caused another person to run away, but, having spent years clarifying her race to others, Nora responded without thinking: "I'm Japanese-American. And as you can see, I'm not mute."

"So you speak English then," he grinned, and after unfolding his arms from around his chest he pushed at the screen door. "Come in," he said. "It's too hot to stay out there."

She was both surprised and comforted to see the layout of the house behind him. It reminded her of her grandmother's, with a narrow kitchen attached to the front room, and through another doorway a hall leading to the back. The low Formica-top table in front of the couch looked like one that had occupied her room as a child, except its legs had been sawed off and that made her laugh a little—the weird recognition of seeing that table together with the collection of children's toys stuffed under it and half-hidden in corners. She took comfort in the folds of a red, nappy couch, letting her finger caress a threadbare patch.

"So what can I do for you?"

His smooth voice called her out of her reverie and made her know how mistaken she'd been to see connections where none existed. He took a seat on the low tabletop in front of her, so close she could smell his breath, and he held out his hand. "I'm Joaquin."

She pictured the Joaquin Valley, which she'd passed through once on a car trip. How the miles of flat desert led her to anticipate the slightest curve or dip in the road and to imagine water glimmering just beyond the flowering yucca and saguaro. Joaquin. Like the Joaquin Valley. Like she'd been dying of thirst when he appeared and he carried her inside. "I'm Nora," she said, staring down at his hand purposefully until he dropped it into his lap.

"I'm glad you decided to stop by." He spoke in a welcoming tone, like he already knew what was inside her.

"I've been walking a lot since I moved here."

"Oh?" he said, "When was that?"

"That I moved here?"

"Yah, when'd you move here?"

She had to count back days in her head to remember, and the answer made her feel foolish. "Just over a week ago. Maybe you'd want to walk with me sometime."

"Nope. I'm afraid I'm not much of a walker."

The sharpness of his response caused her to leap up, his voice trailing her as she headed for the door. What could she do but accept his rejection of her? "It's all right."

"You don't have to leave. I mean, you can sit back down if you like."

"Really?" Having long ago realized how people crave others to talk to, she'd needed his invitation to tell him how she'd found her Braxton Street apartment on a flyer in Ralph's market. She would never have come to the idea to live in Pacoima on her own, but once posed, the cheap rent and proximity to her church had made it irresistible.

"So you're a religious person." What might have been a question came out instead as an observation uttered aloud, and Joaquin sat back on the couch clasping his fingers across his stomach.

"You're Christian, too?" she asked, becoming animated to think they might have something important in common.

"No," he laughed, tilting his head back to a bent ray of sunlight, and she looked up to note that his brown eyes had lightened a shade so that his large pupils glowed like a cat's. "In fact you could say there's bad blood between my people and the church, but I knew a minister growing up. He was nice to my mother when she needed help, so I've always felt friendly toward Christian people."

"I'm glad to hear that," Nora said, her tone becoming serious. "Christians have a duty to help other people. If they don't, then they're not following God's plan."

"That's interesting—what you're saying," he paused. "I like how certain Christians are of things I can't figure. Must be nice. So what's God's plan for you?"

"Me?" Nora had not anticipated her words coming back at her in such a way. "Well, it was supposed to be medical school," she said, "at least that's what I thought."

The day her acceptance letter arrived, she'd finished her daily dormitory lunch of salad and saltines and gone to her mailbox, sensing somehow that good news awaited her there if only because it was early spring and she'd been enjoying that morning the hint of warmth in the air. She'd walked straight from her mailbox to her car and without a thought to the three classes she'd be missing that afternoon, driven down into the Valley, the white sheet of stationary catching the sunlight on the passenger seat beside her the entire way home.

Her mother sat under her sewing lamp fastening a button to the cuff of one of her father's shirts, not seeming at all surprised to see her even though Nora never visited her parents on weekday afternoons. They must have exchanged greetings, but in Nora's mind she'd passed the letter to her mother's hands in silence and watched from across the table while the contents were absorbed. Yukari was not the kind of person to jump up with hugs and effusive congratulations, but Nora had expected a reaction other than what had followed.

"Very good, Nora," she said, recalling her preschool years when Yukari had spoken her approval across the table to Nora's simple arithmetic equations.

"Thank you." Nora spoke with an exaggerated lilt, hoping to signal a response of at least equal excitement on her mother's part.

"What's wrong?" she asked, when instead of enthusiasm she got silence.

"I thought you had classes all day today," Yukari said, looking quizzically down at the white shirt she'd been working on.

"I did." She smiled. She'd discovered the reason for her mother's upset. In all her four years as an undergraduate she'd never missed a class, a fact she suspected her mother knew; she was disappointed that her daughter had ruined her perfect record.

"I'll have to talk this over with your father," she said, staring not at her daughter but at a spot behind her on the kitchen counter.

"Mom," Nora complained, rising to check the counter and rinsing the cup and plate left out, talking now with her back to Yukari. "I'm not missing anything that can't be made up."

"How much is tuition? The letter mentions the amount of your scholarship but it doesn't say the cost of tuition. What part of your expenses do you think will be covered?"

Nora was glad at that moment that her mother could not see her expression. Having received a full scholarship to complete her work as an undergraduate, she'd never considered the expense of medical school. Nor did she know about student loans and other resources available to graduate students. But even if she had, finances were not the issue that should have preoccupied her mother. Her parents had plenty of money, saving their whole lives for some disaster that loomed not in the future, but in the past. It was not simply her mother's ostensible response that upset her, but the feeling she had then that she had misunderstood the fundamental direction her life was to take. As if years ago, through some unspoken command when Yukari had said, *Go right*, she had erroneously taken a left and arrived, finally, at a wasteland.

Besides the unwashed dish and cup—most likely her mother's since Eugene and Ken were away at school—the sink was spotless. With no stain to scour from the porcelain or crumb to wipe off the countertop, she returned to the table to face her mother.

Nora tried to hide her disappointment, though she was sure Yukari could read it. Rather than exacerbate the unease growing between them, Nora excused herself, claiming she'd be late for whatever course it was she was missing, and she fled back over the hill. She never told her parents outright about her decision not to pursue medicine. Instead, she'd enrolled that summer in cosmetology school, ensuring when she did so that her parents would find out.

In hindsight, Nora knew that medical school had never been right for her. It had been the unspoken destiny that followed her through the matrix of classes she completed as an undergraduate—organic chemistry and biology giving way to other, more complex courses—but medicine had held no real interest for her.

"Until recently I worked as a manicurist," she spoke across the darkened room to Joaquin. "I liked my job, and I'd still be there, but while I was busy working on other people's hands, my own hands gave out."

Joaquin nodded, as if to acknowledge that they both understood something about irony without having to speak.

It was true that Nora had enjoyed the leisurely pace at Parson's. She took great pleasure in the salon's chrome fixtures, glass, and high dome ceilings, and in keeping with the pristine setting, she kept her cart of colors clean and well organized. She liked to think that the fine motor coordination involved in doing her job well required no less skill than a career in dentistry, or even arthroscopic surgery. While the prestige and salary were nowhere near comparable, neither was the stress. The loss she experienced when her hands prevented her from keeping her job had nothing to do with reputation or not being able to make-do on tight budget. The work itself had given her life meaning, and after twenty-nine years of struggling, she felt bereft.

What had happened first was a loss of sensation, which she realized the day she cut open the tip of her index finger. Having sliced it with an emery saw, a fat drop of blood caught in the saw's motion and disseminated through the air. The incident might not have been noticed at all had the client who came every Wednesday afternoon for a hair treatment and French manicure not shrieked, mistaking Nora's blood for her own.

Nora did not respond immediately, her delay caused first by the fact that she had not felt the cut, and then by shock at her error.

"Are you okay?"

It had been Ana, the wife of a prominent neurosurgeon. Nora remembered because the woman had worn one of her favorites, No. 23, Opalessence. The perfect choice for her skin tone, the color glistened like river stones. For special occasions Ana preferred No. 27, Pearl Dream. Once she'd tried No. 16, Indian Corral, but she'd regretted that. The elegant woman's face read concern, and Nora followed her gaze down to the spatter of blood on her smock. It took a second for her blood to seep into the porous fabric. "I'm so sorry," she said at last, grabbing a tissue and applying pressure to her fingertip. Until that afternoon her hand had never slipped. Never a cut or scrape; clients marveled at her speed and precision in shaping, and her ability to polish each nail with three exact sweeps of the brush.

For several weeks following that incident, sporadic tingling replaced the numbness in her fingers. She would not have minded this minor annoyance, except that in the days that followed, the unpleasant sensation spread up her hand and wrist and gave way to pain so debilitating that within months she was forced to leave the salon. Her mother made it clear what she thought, that the fumes from the polish and other trade chemicals interfered first with Nora's capacity to reason, and, ultimately, with the nerve endings in her wrists and fingers. But Nora refuted this theory. The ordeal of the last year had given her reason to doubt her most long held beliefs, and in hindsight two images remained: the leaves that traded their dull green for intense shades of yellow, announcing the sudden arrival of fall, and then the blood, seeping into the white smock while she sat staring, dumb to what such a clear sign might suggest. She had at first been able to rationalize that her pain resulted from the sudden chill of early autumn mornings. She'd gone to bed with her windows open and awoken chilled. The ache would be gone shortly, she was sure of it. Everything would be fine because what had ever gone wrong that could not be fixed? But the cut in her finger had loosened knowledge held in the body, of which the malfunctioning of her hands was undeniable proof.

Her parents had initially been kind, paying the first month's rent, then a second. But they had not offered a check for a third, and pride would not permit Nora to ask for money. She knew Melissa and Caroline would have offered whatever they could. They'd been her two best friends since childhood and so felt her predicament as her own, and she waited for an offer from them. But while she saw herself as a child in need, they had made the change to adulthood and appeared too engrossed in their own lives to wrestle with hers. They called often to admonish her and offer their advice, but lately she'd grown resentful of them and what felt like their bullying, and her need to look on the bright side, as her mother would say, had never been greater.

Following her move to Pacoima it had taken a full three days to muster the courage to leave her apartment. When she did, she had been surprised by her own response to the outside world. The paranoia instilled in her by her mother and friends demanded that she scrutinize the habits of her neighbors and pay close attention to the setting they now shared, but her response to what she saw had not been fear. Walking affirmed how like her neighbors she was. The children who played in the streets unsupervised, the parents who appeared at nightfall with their paper cups of coffee and cigarettes purchased from a nearby bodega to cluster and reprimand in languages that were not English the dogs that no one seemed to own. Talking to Joaquin, she emptied her head of everything—of things she hadn't even known were on her mind and even if she had she couldn't have explained to herself, and it seemed like he was a kind person because he didn't stop her once, except when he excused himself and came back with a beer. And then he asked her if she wanted one, too.

Upon his return from the kitchen, he planted himself in the middle of the floor, stretched out his spine, and tilted the brown bottle back, exposing a maze of veins that ran up and down his throat. "I guess some people go fishing, others go for a walk," he said. He'd given her a chance to observe him from across the room, and from her position on the couch she'd been forced to admit to herself that she liked what she saw.

She tried to settle the noise that was growing huge in her head even though it was clear that neither of them were saying anything. Then she began to see bits of fishing trips she'd gone on as a kid—too many to count. How her father and brothers could spend hours in the shivering cold with their lines in the water, not saying a word except to remark on the size of the fish they brought in. "You fish?" she asked.

"No. Plenty of opportunities where I come from, but I never could stand cutting open a live thing. Let alone eating it afterwards."

She laughed, having never thought of it so graphically. She understood exactly what he'd meant. She'd turned down the beer he offered her, but the heat had left her thirsty. With the back of her hand, she wiped the sweat from her lip, and then for a second she looked up from the floor when he sat beside her. His eyes were the same color as hers, and maybe because she'd been imagining water, she could see water in his eyes, collecting behind valleys ridged by bone.

"I used to go trout fishing with my family," she told him. "Summers up at Kern River and June Lake, one time even as far north as Klamath. I gutted and cleaned every fish we caught. I don't think I could do it now, but back then I didn't mind. It was waking up early and freezing to death out on the lake before the sun was up that I used to hate."

"My son was always after me to take him fishing," he smiled.

She checked back beneath the table to see the red truck and ladder she remembered. Across the room, propped in the doorframe, the darkened outline of a baseball bat caught her eye. She didn't know why she imagined without questioning that he lived alone.

"My son's not here," he volunteered, following her eyes. But that was all he offered.

When she stood up to leave she could see that the room was almost completely dark. The things she remembered had become shadows of themselves, forcing her to follow close behind.

"Be seeing you, Nora," he said, holding the door open for her.

On the way home, she knew she hadn't been wrong about what she'd seen. He'd introduced himself, and she'd told him she was Nora. And then he'd wanted to know everything. That was why she'd told him about her walks, and as she talked he made her think of things she'd forgotten for years, like those fishing trips, having to wake up at the crack of dawn and then gut and cook fish for days on end until the scales stuck to her hands like bits of stardust and fish membrane permeated her skin, reached down into her pores until her bones locked the smell and substance into their marrow.

Quite possibly she'd revealed too much. Blood rush to her cheeks and the heat of the day rose up from the asphalt beneath her feet. It had all happened so fast! But he wanted to see her again and that's what mattered. Be seeing you, Nora, she said aloud to herself. *Be seeing you.* If he didn't expect to see her, if he didn't *want* to see her, why would he have said that?

Until she saw him again she had his name to hold on to. It belonged to her, and she turned it over on her tongue, let it float into the hot summer night.

Chapter 3

Joaquin was a man with a house, a son, and an occupation. He drove the No. 163 bus, the route that cut crosswise through the Valley traversing landmarks that he had, like her, committed to memory. She trusted the things he said, about why he had to leave the place he called home, which was a small fishing town on the California-Oregon border, which was where his son still lived. She trusted what he told her: He didn't belong here, away from his son, in this house so close to the city (he said he recognized her because she didn't fit in either).

She trusted him when he led her past the front room on a shadow-walk through the hall to the room where he slept, which was cooler than the rest of the house, and dark. He left her alone to feel what it was like to occupy a strange man's bedroom. From the spot beside the bed where she stood motionless, she listened for him and to the beating of her own heart until he called to her. "Wanna beer?"

This time she took one even though she'd never had more than a sip in her life. She knew from memory to plug her nose, but even then the thick, acidic taste filled her throat, and a wave of foam frothed over the top of the can. When she looked up, he was staring at her the way you'd check a piece of fruit for worm holes, which made her think she was crazy. Then she forced herself to remember how her brothers always dared each other to do things. Her mother said that's the way boys were, and this was just a silly dare. She took another sip and let air out through her nose.

"You like beer?"

"Mmmm." The bubbles made her eyes burn, and she tried squeezing her lids shut against them.

He smiled as if to say he hadn't been fooled. "Drink a lot of beer?"

"No, not a lot." She was gaining courage. "Do you?"

"A lot?" he said, wiping at his grin with the back of his hand, "Not a lot. Maybe not enough."

The room was dark and smelled a little like fish, which made her remember how she'd never caught one. It's no wonder that she was the kid who had to be yanked from bed. And how one morning she'd leaned over the edge of the boat hoping to *see* a fish through the glassy black water and had seen her own ugly face instead. *Keep your face in the boat*, her father, who didn't like to talk when he was out on the water, muttered under his breath. Maybe she would try fishing sometime with Joaquin. She took another swallow of beer. It and the heat had the effect of slowing things down, making the connections almost palpable. His dark, thick arms and shoulders shiny with sweat; she alive in his skin.

But the toys peeked out from their corners, false emblems that reminded their owner only of a life he did not have, and she began to suspect that no child had ever lived in his house or perhaps even visited. She could see that things were not as they should be, and hear, too, her mother and best friends warning her not to trust what she felt; still, when he smiled she could see in his face the son he talked lovingly about, and when he stripped his clothes down to shorts and a tee-shirt and pulled back the bed covers to expose the spot where he slept, her body longed to join him there. Did it count that she didn't take her clothes off, or that when he climbed on top of her she barely moved, even to breathe?

She spent the entire afternoon in Joaquin's bed and left with the moon hanging low in the half-lit sky. In a daze of exhaustion and excitement, she returned to her apartment and almost passed her mother's car, parked in the middle of the long narrow driveway.

From inside, Yukari called her name, an arrangement of sound she didn't immediately associate with herself, but rather with a slow and sad song.

Then the locks clicked and the driver's side door opened exposing a diminutive, more delicate version of herself to the fading light. "Nora, I'm glad you're back," she said. "I was just about to leave."

"Did you forget about Caroline's rehearsal dinner, Nora? You didn't forget, did you?" How could she have forgotten? For over a year, Caroline had involved everyone in the planning of her wedding; the first of a series of events they'd taken such great care to imagine was about to come to pass, might well have taken place without her had her mother given up and driven off a few seconds earlier. A visual reminder of a life that was not Nora's own, Yukari stood with her arms crossed over her chest as if to illustrate an important point about modesty.

"I'm sorry, Mom." Apologies began spilling reflexively from her mouth, but even as she spoke she knew she didn't mean any of them. Caroline had long ago handed Nora a role in the drama of her engagement, which she'd gratefully accepted as a concession to the romance she didn't have. The sight of her mother should have made her nervous. She knew Yukari intended to intimidate her into submission, but she could smell her own scent mingling with Joaquin's in the hot evening air and her mother, standing so close to her, did too. Even if she could not identify it. Nora would attend Caroline's rehearsal dinner and the next day her wedding, as planned, but not as the person anyone thought she was.

With her arms still folded around her waist, Yukari looked Nora over from head to foot, and Nora wondered then what her mother might know. Could she, in some remote part of herself, sense a change? "I guess we're going to be late," she said, waving her toward her apartment door. "But don't take forever."

Standing naked in the bathroom, Nora could hear through the closed door water trickling in the kitchen sink, dishes clattering, stockings brushing the linoleum floor doing their best to get the job done fast. She'd always thought her mother's hyper-efficiency a character flaw, but she could appreciate the need to make things clean. At the very least it meant she could take her time getting ready, and she allowed her thoughts to wander back to Joaquin and the part of the day so quickly gone. In the mirror she moved her arms over her head and examined her face, which, if not pretty, she could almost believe was not ugly. Then her eyes caught on tender spots that ran along the underside of her arm, over her chest, and down her legs, and what she saw there made her gasp. Purple and black marks across her stomach, between her thighs. Pear-shaped thumb prints under her jaw and along her cheeks.

"No-raa," her mother's voice sang from behind the door. "Where do you keep your broom?"

Eyes closed, she tried to remember: his brown torso, her wrists clinging stupidly to his back. Tried to forget. "I'll be out in a minute," she said, conscious of the flatness of her voice.

"It's not in there with you, is it?"

A long wooden pole poked out from behind her back and she turned from the mirror to see it standing beside the tub where a nest of black hair lay threaded white with powdery dust. It seemed a miracle she hadn't gone bald, given the amount of hair she lost daily. She reached her hands up to her scalp half-expecting what was left to have loosened itself. Then, turning back to the mirror, she remembered her mother. "It's not in here," she said, noting how the tenor had returned to her voice, the lie, concealed within it, slipping like soap from her mother's dishrag.

"Where is it, then?" her mother's voice possessed knowledge she couldn't have had, knowledge that incriminated Nora before anyone had even seen the bruises. Or had Yukari seen them? A thread of spittle dangled from her open mouth and landed in the tangle of hair at her feet. Brushing a palm across her mouth, she discovered that her hands had gone numb.

"Forget it, Mom, I'll be out in a minute."

She would have to move quickly to conceal the bruises, and she hummed as she dug through her make-up bag. Beneath her jaw she applied concealer to the soft spot beneath the chin, under the cheekbones, at the temples. She considered what she'd learned in cosmetology school, how make-up can have the effect of drawing attention to or away from certain prominent aspects of the face. The problem read like a palimpsest: layers of sweat, lust, maybe already betrayal. In the heat of a summer evening, she covered her arms with a creamy white blouse, her legs with loose-fitting black silk slacks, and after intoning a brief apology to God, she let herself through the door.

She did not need her mother to remind her that they would arrive nearly a full hour late. Riding beside Yukari through the familiar Valley streets, she considered how different from her friends she'd become, and her thoughts returned to the rectory where she had sat with the minister two nights before, and to an event that took place years earlier that she had not acknowledged to anyone. That Sunday, Melissa had chosen the leg space under the minister's desk—close enough that Nora could hear her breathing and then Caroline's footsteps and Melissa's shrieks that told her she'd been found. Her heart throbbed in her ears with the anticipation of being next. Melissa had seen her moving the robes aside then pulling the sliding door shut, leaving her in total darkness; Nora wished she could be trusted to keep her hiding place secret from Caroline.

On the other side of the wall, low, heaving sighs from the organ signaled the minister's message as the mother's dug in to their seats, preparing themselves for another long one. From the floor of the closet she pictured her mother sitting beside Caroline and Melissa in their Sunday dresses. She could almost hear the soft sound their legs made when they rubbed together through panty hose, the way they would when the lids fell over their eyes and their thighs parted into Vs.

When her friends did not come for her, she assumed that Melissa had led Caroline away from the closet as a way of keeping her hiding place secret. But her thighs burned along the line where they pressed into her calves until all she could think about was straightening her legs. Back into the rectory she crawled and then stood, momentarily stunned by the morning light pouring through the window. Once her eyes had adjusted, the first thing she saw was Caroline. She was walking along the low stone wall with her arms outstretched; a bit farther off Melissa swung from a tree branch to which they enjoyed monkey jumping from the wall. The scene was like countless others, with her two friends involved in play, and yet the moment did not seem like life at all, but rather part of a dream in which the images are clearer than they possibly can be. There, while she navigated the wall, Caroline's loveliness first became apparent, and it took Nora's breath away and caused her to stay still and stare. Her beauty was so overpowering that Nora did not immediately notice that another figure stood close by, or recognize the girl as Melissa. These were her two friends whom she had known for as far back as she could remember, and yet they were strangers. She didn't know whether it was disbelief or recognition that called her closer. Made up of vertical slats of glass, the window had a lever on the bottom that opened the panes like shutters and she rotated the crank and waved to her friends with her free hand. When they didn't look up she figured they hadn't seen her, and so she positioned her mouth between an opening in the slatted glass and called to them. "Caroline, Melissa. Over here!"

A warm, dry breeze typical of summer mornings in the Valley blew in through the window. It carried traces of laughter, which seemed directed at her as she stood watching them, until, looking down, she caught her own reflection fractured in the sheets of glass that tilted up at her, and the recognition she felt then cut into her. In the dirty glass, a chin creased into a thick neck, and, on another pane, eyes that might have belonged to a rodent beneath thick, black brows. Her hand still on the lever, she turned the crank in reverse and the window shut with a clap. She desperately wanted the girl in the glass not to be her, only it was unmistakably her image that congealed in the shut panes. Turning away from the window she ran from the rectory past the stone wall where her best friends played, through the heavy doors of the sanctuary, presenting herself to her mother who blinked several times then wrinkled her brows into a frown.

"You should be outside playing, not in here," she whispered in Nora's ear.

"Can't I stay?" she pleaded.

"Shhh," Yukari whispered, and then, taking pity on her daughter, she shifted slightly away from Melissa's mother who responded by edging toward Caroline's mother. Without a word, the entire pew parted making room for her to sit.

She had been prepared to have her wish denied, and for the abyss that she half expected to open and swallow her up. But that morning it didn't happen. In the small space allotted her between Yukari and her best friends, Nora was beloved, ignorant for the moment that anything in her life might go wrong.

A wave of fondness for her mother rushed through Nora in the wake of her remembering. Between them there existed no space for Joaquin, not for his existence or for the events that had earlier in the day taken place. Sitting beside Yukari in the car, she could be sure that nothing had or ever would come between them.

With that same surety, the evening that was to follow could not have been more enjoyable. An image crystallized in Nora's mind, of Caroline and Melissa, their powdered faces pressed together for photos, the smell and feel of their hair on her cheeks, damp either from having been recently washed or from the excitement of the evening. If it hadn't been evident before why the event held such importance, it would soon become clear. After that evening they would never be the same. Caroline would give her life over to Wade in the intractable terms of a marriage, so that one of them would be gone forever. For her there would be children and all the ensuing events that accompanied the fulfillment of a life. The toasts and other gestures served merely to solidify the fact that she was well on her way. Melissa would soon follow suit, and perhaps, she felt hopeful remembering

Joaquin, she would, too. But for that one, last evening, they were still Caroline, Melissa, and Nora, their names uttered by all the guests in a single breath. Melissa, Caroline, and Nora, the triumvirate that throughout their childhood their mothers called three peas in a pod. They were sisters who all happened to be born in the same year. They liked the same things and were still able to finish each other's sentences because they knew each other's minds as well as their own.

That night reaffirmed a quality which for years she'd tended to overlook: What she loved about her two best friends, what she'd always loved, was the part of them that was the same, their souls—the place inside each of them that the minister told them only Jesus could see—which were exactly alike. Perhaps her two best friends no longer saw what she saw. Loving as they did the part of themselves that was different, they had been patiently nurturing certain idiosyncrasies since adolescence. Caroline her physical beauty, Melissa her self-righteousness, and perhaps, too, her darkness. But Nora? Her future had not been foretold the way Wade had clarified Caroline's, and Mark would soon speak for Melissa's. Still, it seemed inevitable that what was different about them would continue to grow until eventually those differences swallowed up their friendship. They would, in passing, remain friends eternally; likewise, the substance of their love for each other would evaporate over time, causing them with the ebbing of memory to wonder how they'd managed to be friends in the first place.

But on that night Wade was not yet quite the appendage hung at Caroline's side, Melissa and Mark had not yet set a date, and the uncomfortable gap that ordinarily accompanied Nora's name had begun to close.

Nora's mother said very little at the banquet, or while driving her back home afterwards. She simply watched the events unfold, letting Nora know with her eyes that she had seen everything. Before leaving the dinner, in a rare gesture of affection, she kissed Caroline on both cheeks, and when she let Nora off she kissed her, too. Inches away, Yukari's meticulous eyes noted each mark on Nora's face and body and how she had tried to conceal it, and with all the silence bred into her through the generations, she held her tongue.

Chapter 4

THE DAY OF Caroline's wedding, he was sitting in front of the television when she knocked. He motioned her in and she sat on the couch, close to him but not touching. It being even hotter that day than the one before, neither of them had the energy to speak. The television screen flickered images silently into the darkness, but when a woman rushed across the screen carrying a child with half its face shot off, he reached across the coffee table to change the channel. "Ooo that's bad," he winced, waving his arms across his eyes. "Can't watch shit like that."

"Like what?" she asked. "The war?"

"Nah, not the war, the children. I've got one myself, you know."

She knew, but she was shocked to be reminded of this fact of his life, and the toys, scattered like stones across the floor, reappeared in her line of sight.

"You don't have kids?" he said after a time.

"No." This was a question no one had ever asked, and not a thing she'd ever considered as a point of curiosity. "How old is your little boy?"

"How'd you know I had a boy?" he asked, suddenly defensive.

"You've mentioned him." She spoke reassuringly, staring down at the fire truck and figuring the heat had made him confused.

"Yah?" He smiled as if pleased that there were no secrets between them. "My old lady and me, we're divorced."

Then he leaned in to increase the volume, and she listened as a newscaster reported that the death toll had risen to over a hundred in Chicago since the onslaught of the heat. She doubted the temperature in Chicago was any higher than in L.A. True, Valley heat wasn't humid, but it wasn't a stretch to imagine suffocating from it.

"You remind me a little of her." The volume was up loud enough that she thought she might not have heard correctly. Then he gripped her kneecap between his thumb and index finger and squeezed until she flinched.

As a child, she used to practice holding her breath in the back seat of the car on the way home from church. Her parents forced her to sit between her brothers so that they could talk in the front seat uninterrupted. She was their human blockade, positioned strategically for the pleasure of their conversation. It was from the back that Nora learned how Mr. Takara's sister-in-law lost her life's savings to an investment scam; how Mrs. Nakanishi's mother was dying slowly of liver failure; how much trouble the Oniki couple went through to find reliable daycare for their retarded son Ben. It wasn't the way they talked that piqued her interest, for they tended to sensationalize, and to end their stories with a simple reminder that all things happened to glorify God. From where they sat they couldn't have known that she was already formulating the conclusion she had since come to: that anything at all might happen and for no good reason. Nora felt overwhelming sympathy for her parents' friends. She'd think of them while she was being pummeled in the back and hold her breath until her parents' voices were indistinguishable over the knuckles poking her ribs, her heartbeat throbbing until her head felt like it would burst. Next to Nora, Joaquin had pulled his shirt up so that she could see his bare stomach rise and fall into a kind of conversation not otherwise being had. Every so often his belly would bounce, as if in exclamation, though not to anything she said, and she thought that perhaps he wasn't even aware of her presence.

In the beginning, holding her breath and counting was a way of both trying to escape the back seat torture and of trying to feel the suffering of people like old lady Takara, Mrs. Nakanishi, and the Onikis. For that reason she regretted having to give up in the thirties. You could never really know someone else's suffering, even those close to you, yet she saw her inability to hold her breath as long she would have liked to as a failed test of endurance and felt unsatisfied never to be able to get even to forty, except by accelerated counting, which was cheating. Even as a young child, she had wondered at the mind's tendency to be tricked, and to will the body into succumbing. Alone in her room, she had tried without success for a count of fifty until, frustrated, she began devising ways not to be tricked. Her mother's silk scarf had lain in her room since its use for pin the tail on the donkey at her seventh birthday party, its softness deceptive because of its strength. She found that by tightening it around her neck she could get to fifty, and once she even made it to sixty-eight. The thrill of this victory led to other discoveries of an even more clandestine nature. Locked in her room, she devised a platform from which she could let her body go limp. By lifting her legs she could in an instant block the passage of air and experience a sensation of true exhilaration that she speculated might also emulate suffering. In performing these experiments, she found that her body had volition of its own, one minute dangling as if inert, the next wrenching back into life. She knew that what she was doing was dangerous, and she was careful always to let her legs down or release the knotted scarf before losing consciousness. Sitting beside Joaquin, with him so close she could smell the sweat dripping down his neck and under his arms, she felt a pang of longing coupled with the kind of invisibility she found unbearable. She was close enough to confirm that she'd ceased to exist for him, but when the debacle of the world was interrupted by a commercial, he scooted near enough that she could feel the heat of his naked thigh inside her thigh and then the heat of his palms on the back of her numb hands. "I want you to do something for me, okay?" His eyes beamed familiarity, and she nodded.

Slowly, without taking his eyes off her, he unzipped his shorts and slid them down around his hips, all the while talking in a low, easy voice. "I'm not gonna do nothing to scare you, okay? I just want to see if you like this.

"Do you like this?" he asked, pulling his penis out and placing it between her fists.

Then his palm was on her cheek turning her face back to him, asking her with his touch to look.

"It's okay, Nora." Her name sounded good coming from him. "You seen one of these before, haven't you?"

She'd seen one, yes. A magazine tossed aside and left open? Somewhere that she couldn't think, and her head throbbed in anticipation. "My hands," she whispered.

"Don't worry about your hands, Nora. Just turn your face around here and take a look."

When she did, it was standing straight up, brown and stiff and not unlike she thought it might look. He was working it with one of his hands; with the other he cupped her chin, then slid his fingers around the back of her head through her hair and pushed his fingers into the soft spot on the back of her neck.

"Open your mouth Nora. You like me, don't you?"

How could she respond, and how protest? She should have felt revulsion, but it was a pleasing sensation to take him in her mouth. The soft hairs tickling her chin, the burning in her eyes, and the smell of him all around her like standing in a field of onions.

He lowered her head until her nose pressed into his flesh, speaking softly to her all the while. "That feels good, Nora. That's the way, just like that."

As his size increased, it filled her mouth completely and lodged inside her throat, blocking the passage from air. A pain shot from the tip of her left index finger through her wrist all the way up her left arm to her shoulder and her mind conjured a memory of heat. The silhouette of a lovely young woman, her implacable, inscrutable mother, standing in the door frame, and a tightness gripping her chest, followed by impossible heat. And then the release, the sweet, ether-like dissolve, and waking to the smell of her mother hovering over her, the fabric she'd unfastened from around her neck a snake trapped in her palm. But as suddenly as Yukari had appeared, she was gone, replaced by sweat and saliva and the thrusting of Joaquin, struggling to release himself inside her. Giving in to a reflex to swallow, she relaxed beneath him, willing her body to go limp while he worked. With her eyes open, she took him inside her until the room around her spun and went black and the next thing she knew she was lying face up on his couch with only the light from the television to tell her where she was.

Chapter 5

PRACTICAL CONSIDERATIONS KEPT Nora from returning to her apartment for three days following Caroline's wedding. She blamed the sweet coconut frosting for turning a tooth bad, which led to a root canal. And as if the expense were not a big enough worry, the pain in her mouth was excruciating.

It was her mother, however, who convinced her to stay. Yukari said it would be more convenient that way because she'd be the one having to drive Nora to the dentist's office; she knew Nora wouldn't argue, but she couldn't have known how frightening Nora's visit would prove to be. The room she grew up in had been changed into her father's study and bore no trace of her ever having lived there. Her father's huge oak desk occupied the space where her bed had been; from across the room on the fold away couch, it reminded her of a tombstone. *A terrible thing,* she woke up thinking, *not even to be dead.*

Yukari had not consulted her before giving away bedroom furniture—white wicker dresser, hutch, bookcase, and headboard—which she still remembered fondly. She imagined her things decorating the room of some pretty little girl and wondered if the secret drawer where she had hidden away her most personal belongings had ever been discovered. There was the Mickey watch stolen from Diana Plunket in the first grade, an assortment of baseball cards from John Stalinger, a black rock, a red plastic hair band, a fake gold ring, a retainer, a pair of gym socks—nothing of tremendous value to its owner, though worthy of being missed by another and coveted by her.

The Mickey watch was the first item she ever stole. She remembered the day Diana came to school wearing it, so proud of Mickey's moving hands even though in the first grade she still could not tell time. She didn't deserve it, yet there she was at recess with her friends around her admiring it. Of course no one had noticed Nora's new Mickey watch when she'd worn it several months before Diana got hers, the day after her birthday. That day she'd made sure to raise her left arm—the one with the watch—in class, and she'd walked with her arms outstretched pretending she had wings. After school on her walk home, she'd taken it off and smashed it with the heel of her shoe, taking the flimsy Mickey from the wreckage of sharp glass and shiny sprockets, and pulling apart his paper ears, his smiling face, his too big feet and hands. The morning Diana appeared at school wearing in fact what should have been hers, bragging and showing it off, there was nothing to be done but to endure her humiliation because Diana did not take the watch off even once. But the next week, when the class was given a painting assignment and Diana had red in her hair and green and blue up to her elbows, she took the watch off her wrist and placed it in her desk, giving Nora the only opportunity she needed. A twang of pity shot through her when Diana screamed and cried, along with a thrill. The teacher suspected Derek Swanson. Not Nora. That night, when she put the watch on in her room, she felt deeply satisfied that what had been Diana's favorite possession belonged once again to her. The next day she wore the watch to school beneath a long-sleeve blouse. She wore it the next day and the day and week after that feeling privileged all the while, and then occasionally, in the years to come, she stole other things. Stealing fostered her sense of justice, though she noticed as the years followed each small victory how nothing kept its value for long.

Nora did not need to join her parents for dinner or wander through the house to hear the familiar sounds of home, her father's after dinner belch, chairs scooting back from the table, and plates clattering in the sink. When her father entered his study, he did so without knocking. Perhaps he believed she was asleep, or else he'd forgotten she was there. As she lay across the room watching him from behind, she could see the white that had outstripped his once blue-black hair. He wore it short, exposing his large ear lobes with wire frame glasses tucked behind them, and a shiny patch of scalp showed through where his hair was thinning. Still, he was a dignified man, even from behind, with his posture erect and his shirt spotless and neatly pressed.

Lying motionless for what seemed like hours, she realized she'd never actually seen her father at work. Even though she'd known for as long as she could remember that he was a scientist, it seemed a different matter entirely to witness him jotting figures and notes before her eyes. "After careful observation, the derivative remains unknown." She had completed her undergraduate education poised to attend medical school and still she had no idea about him. Having asked him questions about his work when she was younger, she even remembered his answers: "A scientist looks for negatives because in each answer there exists an error."

"Remember," he once said, "it's the flaw that leads you forward."

He'd revealed a powerful truth, but the problem remained. In asking what he did, what she'd really wanted to know was about him, what it was like to be *him*, and the answers he gave never made things clearer. He set out to teach her a method for dealing with unknowns, which had not been enough. She had stopped being a child many years ago, and had managed to live her whole life without any real idea about him.

That he could not feel what she felt came that night as a startling and hurtful revelation. Her tooth pain meant nothing to him from where he sat: so close, yet wholly disengaged. And of more lasting impact, her entire life had amounted to nothing. Even back when she supposedly had a promising future—what had that meant to him? And now that she walked the streets of Pacoima, her body no longer her own? What an irony to have a man who devoted his career to the careful observation of life and its details as her oblivious father.

Still, Nora knew that Yujitaka was, at heart, a reasonable man, and she had always admired her father's willingness to test his faith against principles rather than impulse. She liked too that she could count on him, and perhaps for lack of familiarity, she'd been afraid of him in a way she had never feared her mother. It wasn't that he was ever stern with her—he was a kind, gentle father, yet the thought of displeasing him had once sent shivers through her body. She'd earned good grades so that he would be proud, just as she'd stolen from her friends with the secret hope of being found out by him. Sometimes, lying in bed at night, she imagined his face reddening to the ears, his hand shaking as he raised it to strike her. But of course she managed to be as good at stealing as she was at school, denying her own fantasies from ever coming to pass.

It had never been for her the way it was for her brothers Eugene and Ken born three and four years behind her. They were babies. They were *boys*. In her parents' eyes, their biology separated her from them inviolably, but in her eyes they were simply knots at opposite ends of a rope. She did not retain memories of either of them, except that Eugene came out with thick black hair that always looked matted, and Ken was bald with a big, round head. They were inseparable as children, tugging daily at each other until, as the years passed, they matured; then they believed that they hadn't much to say to each other. Neither could see what was obvious to the eye, that along the way each became what the other once was—Eugene's hair pulling too soon away from his forehead, and Ken in need of a good cut and styling.

She loved her brothers as much as anyone in her life, but she did not love them nearly as much as either of her parents loved them, each showing abiding patience with the boys. The thought of Eugene and Ken intensified the pain in her mouth until her whole body shook with heat and listlessness. She imagined an iron searing the skin on her stomach and all the pain seeping out through the wound there. With the desk lamp turned out and her father gone, the space reverted to her childhood room, and the air conditioning unit bespoke a memory: how as a child she had wandered out her door and down the hall in the darkness, standing just inside her parents' room, captivated by what she'd discovered. Her father's buttocks, gleaming white in the darkness, pressed together and pushing into her mother who, gripping a white sheet tail between her teeth, squeezed her eyelids together and softly groaned. Even knowing she should not be seeing this, she couldn't not see. The rhythmic breathing, heavy and excited, became tangled up inside her. She felt dangerously close to knowing a secret that might save her life when her father fell limply on top of her mother, and she, scooting out from under his weight, stood up fully naked and spied someone there, still occupying the same spot.

Yukari guided one hand across her forehead while the other reached nervously down to her genitals as she attempted to ascertain the identity of the intruder. Then she shrieked. "Nora! What are you doing? Shame on you—out of here. Get out!"

The way she addressed her daughter, Nora might have been an errant pet, or less—an annoying insect, scuttling backwards, spinning as her shoulder hit the doorframe, and diving onto her bed. It was not what she'd seen but her mother's voice that had left its mark. Even then she had understood her intrusion to be an innocent one: She had meant no harm. Yukari knew this, her response to Nora precipitated not by the breech of privacy, but by her daughter's ungainly birth seven years earlier. Nora had not been the child her mother had wished for; instead a mistake from which she hoped to be exonerated each year, until, waking up in her parents' house, she recognized herself as full blown and ludicrous. This sudden understanding of who she'd become in her mother's eyes was the first of many she would have about Yukari and the place she occupied in her mother's life. Without knowing precisely how, she knew her mother to be someone who had been harmed by the world, and as if to compensate for Yukari's lack of feelings, Nora refused to love her mother any less. She understood that feelings could not be helped or held back, and she did not wish to shield herself from the truth.

The sound of Nora's beating heart rose over the whir of refrigerated air circulating through the vent, and as the sweat on her forehead dried she noted that something inside her had changed. In the cool quiet of her own room, she placed herself above judgment and took solace in the knowledge that what had been lost could not be damaged. The next day she would return to her apartment, and to the life Joaquin and she could now begin.

Chapter 6

NORA COULD NOT wait to return to Pacoima and to the apartment she'd come to see as her only true home, but, when she finally arrived on Wednesday, disappointment lay in every direction. The heat had not broken and the air trapped inside was stifling and still. Her belongings, which littered the bed and floor, offended the senses. The place needed a thorough cleaning, and she would have gladly put it in order had it not been for the heat and the pain that extended from her jaw to her fingertips.

The dentist had prescribed pain medication, which she had until then refrained from taking. The mood in her parents' house had been bad enough that she had not wished to contribute to it the hallucinatory effect pain killers often had on her. Now she dropped two white pills onto her tongue, tossed her head back, and waited. She'd been told it'd take twenty minutes for the medication to begin working, and after placing the remaining twenty-eight pills in the pocket of her shorts, she slouched against the wall with her eyes shut and tried to let her mind go numb. It was hard to let the sight and smell of her apartment go, and when she did, a wash of crimson, which she identified as the gown Caroline had made up for her to wear at the wedding, flooded her vision. It was, she decided, an unreasonable color, and she waited for it to vanish, and for the odorless white of daylight to return before opening her eyes once more. Then she headed into the street, careful to lock the door behind her.

In her three-day absence, Pacoima had lost its glorified familiarity. A dirty brown netting clung to everything touched by the sky, exposing decay in crevices she hadn't even noticed so that cracked sidewalks and crumbling stucco buildings loomed hugely and grotesque. Had she not been forced to sell her car, she would have chosen that moment to speed away—windows up, air conditioner pumping full blast on her face. But as if to inform her that such a fantasy was not worth having, a horn sounded when she stepped off the curb prematurely, and the exhaust breeze of the car that brushed past her left her to reflect that this was the only life she had, and that she would have to do a better job of paying attention. Having in her parents' house witnessed her departure from the world, the past had closed behind her. Now Joaquin was the destination against which she judged her surroundings. Each action she took pleased or displeased him, and as she moved toward him a purposefulness marked each step she took. Absence had not dulled her memory, rather it had heightened her anticipation to an almost unbearable pitch.

As she turned from the congested street into the quiet block where Joaquin lived, the air felt slightly cooler and she believed she could smell his presence and that perhaps he could feel her approach. It was late afternoon, and though trees were not plentiful in the neighborhood, the withering blooms of crepe myrtles blew through the air, and the tremoring shadow of leaves cast delicate patterns on the pavement. Still, as she neared her destination, she had to stop several times to wipe the sweat that accumulated on her forehead and each time she raised her hands she was made acutely aware of the fact that they had gone numb.

She'd been gone three days, but somehow she'd failed to imagine that Joaquin might not be home, that he might be in a place other than reclining on the stoop or just inside the open door waiting for her. The possibility of his absence did not occur to her until she stopped in front of his house to observe that something had changed. The walkway, longer than she remembered it, seemed to dare her to cross, and fear rose in her throat as she approached the door, which she somehow did not expect to be solid when she swung open the wire-mesh screen, or expect when she knocked then tried the knob for it to be locked.

Okay, she said aloud, drawing in her breath. Okay. He'd probably gone to the store. Could be at work, might be any number of places from which he'd soon return. Sitting on the stoop the way she'd seen him do, she feigned an attitude of nonchalance. From her vantage point, she surveyed the crab grass her mother spent the summers battling, noticed how (in a solution that would have horrified her mother) he'd trimmed it down and used it as a lawn. Which made her think he couldn't be far away.

Then, turning over her shoulder, she saw that the red impatiens had wilted. There could be no mistaking what those limp petals signified. She searched frantically for a spigot and filled a plastic container with water. The possibility of being seen by neighbors, so close on either side, unnerved her, but what was she to do? Once the flowers had been watered, she allowed herself to sit back on the stoop and reassess. She had no plan save to remain on the stoop watching the traffic pass, to examine the neighbors' yards, to see the world as if through his eyes. And from where she sat she concluded that only a person with a serene heart, someone intent on staying awhile, would keep a yard the way Joaquin kept his. If the landscaping lacked color, at least he'd taken care to hang the impatiens, and to plant flowering ground cover along the walkway.

The shade broadening over the porch reinforced her dread that he might not be returning any time soon and she realized as she waited that she would have to look for a way in. She was not averse to playing detective, but as she circled the house peering through windows for clues as to where he'd gone, she realized that she had no idea how things were supposed to look. She thought she had paid such close attention, yet clearly many important details had gotten by her. Having come full circle and landed back on the porch, she knew only that the impatiens had gone beyond revival, and that Joaquin was not where he should have been. Still, she would not be stopped short. Curiosity drew her once more around the house until she found herself at the back door where she could see through a set of frayed white curtains a washing machine topped with grey lint balls, and shirts hanging on the doorjamb and piled on the floor, which was where her eye settled.

Without another thought, she gave the knob a twist, and, to her surprise, the door opened and the house spread out before her.

Chapter 7

As Nora made her way through the dark house stopping to examine each object, she believed she might finally understand what Reverend Nakatani had preached her whole life about the Kingdom of Heaven: modest, but overwhelming all the same. The low table in the front room, the fire truck and ladder underneath, these items, all of which she'd seen before, now defied her contemplation of them, and so, before touching anything or coming to conclusions, she made it a point to revisit each room. Stacked high in the kitchen sink were plates and cups, thick rings of debris showing where liquid had evaporated. He had, from the looks of it, been gone for quite some time. He had not left much behind in the cupboards and refrigerator: three eggs, a stiff tortilla, and half a jar of strawberry jam.

She was hungry, but she did not eat.

At least not that first night. To compensate for her uninvited entry into Joaquin's house, she gave careful consideration to each move she made. And while it was true that her presence in the house fell out of line with her beliefs as a Christian, the other truth was that her moral nature had taken a degenerative twist long before this act of breaking and entering.

Standing in the laundry room with a handful of shirts pressed under her nose, she found a thrill beyond any she'd ever known. She felt alive in Joaquin's house, viewing from the inside the place where she would live in happiness. She felt his presence in her stomach; breathed his scent into her lungs; let the colors play behind her eyes before exhaling, and moved up and down the hall circling each room like a cat until she felt certain she'd seen enough of everything to understand that the house contained more than would be needed for a life together. It was excess that finally caused her to act. With only Joaquin and her there would be no need for more than two of anything, and this fact became most apparent in the kitchen where stacks of unmatched dishes littered the countertops and cupboards. Brown palm frond patterns, yellow daisies, two green ivy (a motif, perhaps, but not really) plates, and an ornate gold design on white. She would have chosen the daisies, emblem of a happy, carefree life, or the gold pattern, but the white was irreparably stained. Only the ivy made a set of two, and so she set the others aside. To her delight she was able to match two of everything: bowls, dishes, glasses, flatware. Everything, except for coffee mugs, of which there were four, and none of them the same. She shifted the contents of the sink to get a better look, hoping that perhaps a matching one hid there, and when she did not find it resolved that if Joaquin and she were forced to live without mugs, they at least had glasses. Gathering the dirty dishes from the sink, she began piling them into a used grocery sack and, when she'd filled the first bag, tied the plastic into a neat knot. Regret begged her to reconsider, but the knot proved impossible to undo, and in the process of her fumbling with the bag, a dish fell from the counter and shattered at her feet—the yellow daisy pattern broken in three parts where the stems connected to the flowers. Three uneven pieces might have been glued back together, but around them the tiny shards meant trouble. For an instant, guilt far out of proportion to the worth of the dish overwhelmed her.

Standing in Joaquin's kitchen, she responded to the unmistakable sound of something shattering that would never be put back together again. With consideration to her life with Joaquin, she spared exactly what they'd need, and fearless of the consequences should a neighbor report the clatter to the police, she began smashing everything Joaquin and she would not need. Shards of dishes and glass cut into her fingers, and her eyes teared even as the destruction continued. But no one came. In the end, she collected the dish shards into a single plastic sack, double lined.

She took her time setting the house exactly so, in ways that would be both pleasant and comfortable in the long term. All that first day, she straightened, cleaned, and dusted, even stopping to fix the pull on the blind in the living room so that the shade would lift in a perfect horizontal. She felt exhausted at the end of the day, but lying in Joaquin's bed, she could not sleep. Her stomach nagged and the past loomed too closely.

In the bedroom, a single, irregular bar of light shone through a gap in the pull down shades. She had used that light to navigate from the front room with its low table and television back down through the hall, and she stared at the patch of light while she contemplated her life. Sometime well past midnight, her meditation focused itself on Mr. Weissgarten, the fifth grade teacher whom she had once adored. Aside from him, her social life had consisted exclusively of the members of the church, and so it had been difficult for her to know how to respond to a teacher whose ideas and practices were so different from what she'd been accustomed to. Mr. Weissgarten who reserved a full hour each morning for the students to write random thoughts in their notebooks, and who read to them every day after lunch. She looked forward to making up stories that would please him and savored the early afternoons when he would shut off the florescent overhead lighting in favor of the shadows that filled the room with mystery. Within weeks of entering the fifth grade she'd become hopelessly enchanted by Mr. Weissgarten's languid tone and by his person. She liked the dark, curly hair that he wore long, pulled back in a tight ponytail so that his wire-rimmed glasses accentuated the sharp angles of his face. In the darkness, while he stared down at the pages of a book, she memorized his face.

One afternoon he began a story about a young girl whose family was forced by the American government to evacuate their home. She had heard the word *evacuate* only in the context of emergencies: bomb threats, fire drills, earthquake. She did not understand the story fully but sat spellbound and self-conscious, too, of the mix of fascination and horror that it stirred in her. Yoshiko being a Japanese-American girl, she felt somehow implicated. Then, that same afternoon, Mr. Weissgarten pulled her aside after class to ask if her parents had been interned in relocation camps during the Second World War. She had no idea whether they had or hadn't, but since it did not seem appropriate to answer in the negative, she nodded blankly, hoping that her oblique response would satisfy her beloved teacher.

To her dismay, she was instead given the task of interviewing her parents and then of spending the week recording her thoughts in her notebook. While Mr. Weissgarten informed her that this assignment was optional, offered as a suggestion that she should undertake only insofar as she wished, she was no stranger to unspoken commands, and she took on her assignment as solemnly as she would a severe punishment.

For reasons she could not identify, her response to Mr. Weissgarten's suggestion caused an ache in the pit of her stomach that when she got home she described to her mother as sickness. Believing her daughter completely, Yukari felt Nora's forehead then sent her to her room. And perhaps she really had become ill, because when Yukari came to inquire as to whether Nora was well enough to help with dinner she found her asleep. She would have stayed that way, letting the evening pass into morning, except that it was her job to help with dinner and so she roused herself from bed.

Seated on the stool where she worked across the counter from her mother she could feel the sickness return. She could not formulate her question into words and instead watched Yukari, her expertise evident in each pop as her hands worked the ends off a pile of long beans. A fly buzzed overhead, annoying her as she swept the stray hairs from her face with her wrist. When the long beans were ready to be cooked, she carried them away to a pot of water that boiled on the stove. Then, returning to the counter where she sat, she clapped her hands together over her head, plucking the fly from mid-air and startling Nora out of her thoughts.

"What did you learn in school today?" Yukari asked, as was her habit.

"Nothing," Nora shrugged, the question she needed to ask still refusing to gather words in her head.

"Then you should pay better attention." Her mother dismissed her, returning to the stove where steam rose from pots of various sizes.

"Mr. Weissgarten told us a story about a girl whose family was *evacuated*," she said at last.

"Ah," Yukari smiled. "You're learning about history."

"Yes." Nora returned her mother's smile cautiously. "Mr. Weissgarten said I should interview you and Dad about the relocation camps."

"Let me tell you what I know about history." Yukari began unexpectedly, and enthused that the conversation that she had so dreaded seemed to be going well, Nora awaited the thing that her mother, who did not ordinarily tell stories, might say.

"Where I grew up in Hiroshima, there was a zoo," she said, and then she stopped.

Nora sat up straight and perched on the edge of her chair to show her attentiveness. Yukari eyed her before launching into her story. "The zoo was famous in the area because back then there weren't very many zoos around. But during the war, the military were ordered to kill the animals. There was no one left to take care of them and what food there was could not be spared. So one by one the innocent animals were slaughtered until, finally, the only ones left were the elephants.

"The elephants, as you might guess, had been the most popular attraction, beloved by everyone who visited them. They were also massive animals, and even men who had been specially trained as soldiers did not know how to kill one. So, as it happened after protest by the townspeople, the military decided to let them live. They didn't have the heart, so, in the end, guess what happened?"

"What?" Nora asked, bemused.

"In the end, the elephants wound up starving to death."

Nora did not know how to respond to this strange story her mother told, but perhaps she had not been listening. Intent on getting what she needed for her notebook, she was concerned only that the information she sought did not appear to be forthcoming. "I thought you were going to tell me about getting evacuated," she said at last.

"I *am* telling you," Yukari retorted. "I'm telling you that it was wartime, and that horrible things were happening everywhere."

She had nothing more to say. Earlier that semester, Mr. Weissgarten had mentioned the word *ambivalence*. He said it was about two opposite and strong feelings existing side by side, and though she had forgotten the definition, the word popped into her head as she sat and watched her mother put the final touches on their dinner.

She did not take Mr. Weissgarten up on his offer of a special assignment for her. Or perhaps she did. Perhaps she made up some story that she could no longer remember. It was the year she learned about ambivalence, and it was a year of irony, and too betrayal. Her mind was becoming sharper and she was becoming acquainted with its proclivities. She knew she liked orderliness, and that she craved beauty. But her body was daily growing out of control, summoning volition of its own, which was not a pretty thing.

It wasn't long before Caroline and Melissa's circle expanded to include boys from the church. Boys like fat-cheeked, greasy-haired Ronnie Higa who one day became Caroline's strapping boyfriend. Though the shift was abrupt, the fact that she was the only one who thought it absurd alarmed Nora. But her need to fit in was as strong as—maybe stronger than—her friends', and might account for why as the only date she would ever have, she once went to a matinee showing of *Terms of Endearment* with Doug Nakatsu.

She was appalled when Caroline told her she'd set her up. On the way to church, in the back seat of her mother's car. She could still see her mother's Dodge Dart, it's pale blue interior, the waxy feel and dirty smell of the vinyl seats when Caroline leaned against her, whispering. "You *have* to go," she'd pleaded. "Maybe you'll even get your first *kiss*."

Nora's eyelids squeezed shut in embarrassment so great she would have hidden beneath the car seat had she fit there. Patterns in her head vibrated with each bounce of the car, forcing her to open her eyes and look out the window where a hazy sunlight seemed to blur the passing streets. The news of a possible date—even if it was with Doug, even if he'd only agreed because Caroline had asked him—evoked terror that felt also like excitement, and she tried to distinguish the violent twisting of her stomach from the linear movement of the car; it did not help that Caroline sat poised and fragrant next to her. Too many feelings joined inside her resulting in a sensation of carsickness.

In a feeble gesture to relieve her discomfort, she rolled open the car window. Through the diffuse light and evening breeze, she examined the delicate shape of Caroline's eyes, their curves exaggerated by lashes so dark she wondered if she were wearing eyeliner, Caroline's eyes pulling her into their gaze, her lips full and serpentine, the darkness between them causing her fingers to rise to her own lips, if only to hide her breath coming in short, quick gasps.

Nora had often wondered over the physical impulses Caroline awakened in her—whether her reaction to Caroline was practice for what it felt like to be in love. Silly as it seemed. She worried intensely over her inability to control the responses of her body, and perhaps as a result decided that what she was feeling was not connected to a bodily function at all. She did not *desire* Caroline, only wanted to *be* her, to evict Caroline from her body and permanently occupy the premises as landlord. What she wanted, simply, was to wield the raw power afforded by ownership. But somehow, rather than satisfy, this half-hearted conclusion made her very sad, and in the end all she felt was anger, directed at Caroline. How could someone who clearly did not know the meaning of despair understand her need for hopefulness? As if conceding to Caroline's power and retreating to her more natural position as imaginary tenant, Nora told Caroline she'd go on the date, which was destined to be a disaster.

She would willingly have overlooked Doug's shortcomings, including his aversion to her, except that she wept uncontrollably when the character played by Debra Winger died, and Doug turned out to be no more concerned than the armrest that separated them. Even during the sex scene—how could he not wonder what it'd be like to do in the dark what Debra Winger does with John Lithgow? Not that she wanted Doug to notice her breathing heavily and flushing in the seat next to him, but when she got up the nerve to turn sideways, he was staring stone-faced at the screen, not wiggling in his seat at all. That's when Nora realized it was John Lithgow she'd been imagining all along, not Doug, and even at thirteen there was no going back on a realization like that.

It was in this way that her childhood passed. Then Joaquin came into her life and she became thirteen once more. His room held a single piece of furniture, his bed stripped bare, blankets and a top sheet tangled in a heap at the foot. In the middle of the bed she detected a slight round curve, an indentation made by his flesh.

Having surfaced as the thing she'd been taught to despise, Nora would inhabit his form like a ghost, press herself into the space made by his flesh, become invisible, like him.

Chapter 8

ON THE SECOND night it was not enough to occupy the shape Joaquin had left behind on the bed. The perfect oval did not pretend to hold her imperfect form, the pull down shade served only to illuminate a shadow of itself, shedding no light into the rest of the room in which the air had all but run out. In this way the house that had been her haven became her prison. She thought of her parents, trapped in their childhood by the barbed wire fences that held them in and would not let them go, and she remembered how in her childhood she dreamed of being detained behind bars and narrated nightmares to her mother who claimed she never dreamed.

Nora knew that she could, if she chose to, have picked up the phone and called her mother. She was reminded of that fact once when the phone rang and she sat paralyzed not even daring to breathe. Did Joaquin have a mother, calling to check on him? Or perhaps it was his son wanting to say good night. But she could not allow for such thoughts.

On the third night, the waiting became unbearable. That night her period came, causing fat droplets of blood to stain the white sheets, and she rose from bed needing to eat. Making her way in the dark to the kitchen she had worked so hard to clean and set for two, she realized she could no longer survive without food. In the two nights and two days that had passed, she had eaten nothing, convinced that Joaquin's return was imminent, but now she warmed the tortilla on the stove top and ate it with jam and two eggs, which she scrambled for herself in a frying pan.

What remained when she had eaten her fill, washed the frying pan, and reset the table for two, was a single egg. She would, she had already decided, keep it in the refrigerator to celebrate Joaquin's return. But instead she took it from its carton and held it in her fist recalling how Reverend Nakatani had once spoken of the egg as a symbol of God's perfect love. She would never eat the egg, nor, she decided, would Joaquin. Seated at the table she'd set for two with the bowls inside dinner plates and on both sides matching flatware and glass tumblers for juice, she placed her egg in the ivy bowl and staring down at its perfect form realized that the egg might be all she had to look forward to in life. Joaquin, who had had sufficient time to return had obviously fled his home, abandoning the impatiens to die in the heat and abandoning her, too. The egg, her companion, was all she had.

Collecting it in her palm, she took it with her from the bowl where she'd set it in the kitchen to the bedroom where she waited for Joaquin and slept. And when she woke in the darkness, she took the egg from the pillow and welcomed it into the place where the blood flowed inside her. She put it there, in the tunnel that led to her womb, and experienced the ecstasy of holding God's perfect love inside her body, in the secret place she wished to share with Joaquin.

That night she prayed to God for Joaquin to come to her. To return home and find inside her the perfection of God's love that she would release from her womb and share with him as a life created between them.

The egg made the hours she spent alone productive. She let the heat of her body warm it and she could feel what Reverend Nakatani talked about, the smooth roundness pressed against her womb when she squeezed her legs together, safe and good inside her like a flower, like she was a flower holding inside her the gift of God's love. That night passed without dreams, her sleeping in the shape Joaquin created, holding the perfect egg inside her. It passed in rapture and peacefulness into morning when a dull object thrust against her shoulder caused her to rise up with a start.

He stood hunched over the bed rubbing his chin while she let the surprise of seeing him sink in. "I didn't think you were coming back," she said. "I mean, I knew you had to come back some time."

"Well, here I am." He held his arms out, but not for her to fall into. He was angry, and she had not seen anger like this before. "I'm sure you have some kind of good explanation for me, don't you? I mean, this *is* my house."

She wanted to tell him everything, give words to what had been building in her head and heart during her time of waiting. But looking up at him, she could think of no explanation to offer. The man standing over her did not resemble anyone she had ever known. Frightened by his anger and by the unusual circumstances in which she found herself, she sunk her elbows into the mattress and rose to leave.

"Uh-uh, sorry," he said. "You don't just come into my house and make yourself at home then leave when things start to get sticky. You sit back down there because I'm not done with you yet." He pinned her shoulders and didn't stop there. "I'll let you know when I'm done with you."

He wanted to scare her, but she didn't feel scared.

"You know," he pushed her back on the bed, "in a situation like this I got every right to call the cops, let you tell *them* your story, and they'll lock your ass up for breaking and entering, but I'm not going to do that to you. So what am I going to do with you?" He unlatched his belt and as he slid it through the loops of his jeans a sharp little cry came out of her.

She could hear him in the kitchen shifting the contents of the cupboards that it had taken so long to straighten. A cabinet opened, then shut, and he returned with a bottle, carried it by the neck.

"Okay," he said, tipping the bottle to his lips again. She headed down the hall and hid behind the couch, but he lifted her by the arm, the anger rising in him all over again.

"Please," she said, her face turned away her eyelids pressed together to keep him out.

"Please what?" He spit into her face and she smelled the liquor on his breath mixing with the heat of his body. An early morning breeze drifted in through the open window, and with it the wail of a little boy and someone calling after him. "Mi'jo, you get back inside right now!"

It was dawn, and the eerie florescent of a streetlight shone a streak of white into the room. He had her down under him with his knees pressing into her ribs and her wrists held high on her back with his forearm.

"Please don't hurt me," she said, and she turned her face around and looked in his eyes—brown like hers, but not like her.

"Ah shit." His arm came down and he crumpled into a ball. "Get out of here."

Book Two

Chapter 9

LIKE THE LANDSCAPE that lay hidden beneath a thick layer of smog, all that could not be said at the airport ceased to exist as the car began its descent into the Valley. Seated as the passenger beside her mother, Elinore could make out only the crude outline of landmarks, and even with the air conditioning pumping full blast, the air felt stale and incredibly humid, harder to breathe than to imagine what she would say to Hideko. Forcing a blink to brighten her eyes, she felt the sting as her throat pinched closed, recalling long afternoons of a childhood spent at poolside. "I think the smog has gotten worse," she mumbled, not daring to take her eyes from the front windshield to face her mother.

"What we need is a good wind," Hideko said in an upbeat tone.

"That's right," Elinore agreed. "Blow the problem on out to Bakersfield. And why on earth is it so hot? I don't remember Los Angeles being this hot."

"The heat wave." Hideko turned sideways for longer than seemed safe to indicate her stupefaction. "Didn't you know?"

Elinore shrugged. "How would I have known?"

But alluding to a problem only increased the awkwardness. Naoko, who could charm any car ride with her incessant babble, refused even to hum, making the tension between the two women immaculate and complete.

"Spring was beautiful this year," Hideko finally said, summoning her favorite subject. "The perennials bloomed early, like winter never even came."

"How's the weather in Santa Fe?" she asked, extending an invitation to Elinore to join her in pleasantries. "I noticed in the paper that the nights are still cold."

"It gets chilly," Elinore admitted, pleased to know that her mother had kept tabs on her. "I like it that way."

"I don't like the desert," Hideko said. Unable to hold to her offer of lighthearted conversation, she scrutinized Elinore with a sideways glance.

"It's the *high* desert," Elinore said. "Meaning 7000 feet above sea level." Offering back her own correction, she flashed the smile she knew by heart, angry at her face for the tightness that strained the sides of her mouth.

Two brief but unsuccessful exchanges served to warn both women against further conversation, and for the rest of the car ride each remained silent. As Hideko's luxury sedan eased its way up the steep hill that led to the Shimizu house Elinore was brought back to her childhood, and she couldn't help but wonder what her young daughter would see. Notwithstanding the heat, the world appeared greener here than any yard Naoko had ever been in, greener than even Elinore remembered it. Planted along the driveway, huge peonies pressed their faces against the car windows, and thorns from the overgrown rose bushes rasped against the sides of the car. Colorful blooms crept over the rims of planters and decorated windowsills. More than any one color or variety of plant, the abundance itself begged a response. As if to underscore the frivolity of it all, a fat squirrel watched their approach from the shingled rooftop. Naoko followed it with a finger as it scaled the gutter and plunged into a nearby willow. The garden had overtaken everything in its path, obscuring the driveway and dwarfing the house. Elinore feared the changes suggested by the chaos, changes in her mother whose steady hand had once manicured the shrubs and placed smooth, oval-shaped black rocks along the driveway in perfect symmetry toward the house.

Turning to her two year old, she expected to find an expression of horror, for if the child understood any of what Elinore had told her about her grandmother's house, she would feel utterly deceived. But Naoko, who did not take to strangers, had at the airport already accepted the grandmother she'd never before met without tears or even a glance in her mother's direction. As Hideko slowed the car to a stop, Naoko rallied for her grandmother's attention, pointing at the many colorful attractions offered up by the garden and wiggling gleefully to be released from her seat and carried inside.

"Are you hungry, baby?" Hideko asked. "Grandma's been up since dawn making some *oishii tabemono*, and it's inside waiting for you."

"Where's dad?" Elinore asked as she struggled to hoist the heaviest piece of luggage over the threshold.

"He's away."

Elinore rolled her luggage from the marble entryway down the carpeted hallway, too tired to care about the wheel tracks that snaked out behind her. She didn't know why the luggage should feel so impossibly heavy, or what more she expected. Having grown up accustomed to her father's extended absences, she hadn't thought much about Jun in the time she'd spent away; still, she wished he'd been home to meet Naoko and she could have used the extra help toting her luggage. She noted the fine layer of dust that had settled on the framed rims of photographs that lined the hall and even on the bathroom mirror, and the deep grooves that showed where furniture had been moved or taken away. Past the empty room once occupied by her grandmother and another that had been hers, the long hallway spread not in front of her but lingered behind, leaving Elinore to wonder how she could have managed not to anticipate the changes wrought by the preceding decade.

"Just put Naoko's things in his office," Hideko said, frowning down at the tracks. "I'm sure he won't mind."

Elinore pretended not to notice her mother's disapproving look, satisfied instead to note the careful way Hideko set Naoko down beside her and sank into a conspiring crouch from which she began counting toes, tickling each one, recalling for Elinore the prickly, callused fingertips of her childhood. Satisfied to have accounted for all the digits, Hideko pulled the barefoot toddler back in for an embrace. "You're just too beautiful," she gushed. "Yes, you are. I can see right away that you're going to be grandma's pride and joy!"

Having not eaten since breakfast, Elinore didn't know whether it was hunger she felt, or sheer fatigue. After shutting the door quietly behind her, she perched on the edge of the day bed and clamped her hands between her legs to steady them. With Hideko tending to Naoko, there was time for a short nap, which she knew would be interrupted by her mother's announcement of food. Even so, she scooted the bedspread off the foot of the bed, the essence of her mother's housekeeping rising in the sweet smelling sheets. She felt glad to remove the floral patterned bedspread for plain, white sheets. But still the flowers appeared everywhere. Climbers peeped through windows and sprawled out of control in the yard; prints of cut flowers bordered the walls; red, pink, white, yellow, and orange roses sat stuffed together in vases scattered across the nightstand and dresser. Too much color for the eye to take in, their profusion imparted, rather than vivaciousness, a sense of gloom. With her eyes shut, Elinore considered the circumstances that had brought her home, the sadness she carried onto the plane that had since been pushed aside by a different kind of heaviness. Perhaps it had always been that way, the forcefulness of her mother's personality filling the house and subduing anyone who entered. She focused her attention on the whir of cool air cycling through the ventilation unit and, through the wall, took in the faint hum of Naoko's questions and explanations offered by her mother. Despite the changes, Hideko sounded exactly as Elinore had remembered her, and, drifting off, she did not rise again until the next morning.

She knew her mother had woken before her by the coffee maker, which had been set to brew, and the bowl of cereal and fruit laid out at her spot on the round breakfast table. Hideko had cleared away her own place setting, save for an oversized envelope, which reminded Elinore of the sweepstakes her mother always loved to play.

"Feel how heavy it is!" Hideko said when she'd come in from watering, and grabbing at Elinore's wrist she balanced the envelope on her daughter's palm.

"It's going to be a good one," she boasted, removing the thick cardstock, reminding Elinore how happy her mother had always been to attend parties. Leaving Elinore to linger over the excitement, she retreated to the refrigerator.

"Who is Caroline Ikeda?" Elinore asked. After rubbing sleep from her eyes, she fingered the name printed in embossed flourishes and stared at the script, so fancy that it might have contained a coded message. *It's tacky*, she thought to add.

"You know Caroline?" Hideko poked her head from around the refrigerator door.

"No." Elinore shrugged. "How do you know her?"

"Who?"

"Caroline Ikeda!" Elinore flicked the name printed on the invitation, then, worried that she'd wake Naoko, quieted her voice. "What's wrong with you?" she whispered. "Are you not even listening to me?"

"There's nothing wrong with me. Caroline is Teru's daughter."

Hideko must have known that this bit of information clarified nothing, but she seemed not to care. Pulling an orange from a drawer in the refrigerator, she dragged a bar stool from the counter and sat cross-legged beside Elinore, who watched as her mother expertly pushed a thumb into the orange's bottom and proceeded to peel one long spiral. "How do you do that?" she asked, holding up the hollowed out rind into which her mother had crafted a facsimile of an orange.

After breaking the core in two, Hideko placed a stringy half in front of her daughter before popping the slice she'd been waiting for into her mouth. "Ah fa-gat to take 'em out," she grimaced.

"What?"

She pointed behind her at the empty fruit bowl and Elinore quickly connected her mother's wincing to sensitive molars, remembering how Hideko always took three oranges out of the refrigerator each evening: one for breakfast, another for an afternoon snack, and a third to eat at night while watching T.V.

"You've never met the Ikedas, have you."

"No." Exasperated at how difficult it was to get the simplest bit of information from her mother, Elinore turned away.

"Well, when the invitation arrived your father thought he'd be back in time for the wedding." Hideko called her daughter's attention back, having suddenly arrived at her point. "But this is perfect because you can go in his place. You're not doing anything, so you and Naoko should come with me."

"I'm not invited." Elinore held up the envelope, addressed to her parents.

"Two guests attending," Hideko tapped the card stock and Elinore looked down at the dried orange pulp that creased her index finger like flaking skin. "Two people invited, two attending. What difference should it make to them which two?"

"Actually, with Naoko there will be three," Elinore said, realizing that despite her protestations she'd already agreed to go.

"Everyone knows babies don't count," Hideko said.

Having finished her half of the orange, Hideko reached in front of Elinore and took her daughter's portion. Elinore watched her mother chew each slice in deliberate silence. "I'm sure it'll be okay," she said when she'd finished eating. "She'll share your dinner so it won't cost anyone extra."

Chapter 10

THE WEDDING WOULD be a large affair, maybe three hundred people packed into hard-back pews in hundred-degree weather. Seated at the rear of the church, Elinore scrutinized the backs of heads recalling human genetics and biology lectures she'd sat through in graduate school. An examination of alleles would indicate an increased risk of multiple sclerosis. On the other hand, the occurrence of sickle cell anemia would be non-existent. She wondered how many present still bore traces of their Mongolian birthmarks, and in what shapes. The black hair, common to everyone in the room, suggested a set of phenotypes that carried genetic predispositions, but her musing was, she knew, a way to ward off the uncomfortable feeling that had come over her upon entering the church.

At a quarter past six, the ceremony had still not begun and the waiting felt interminable. As if Elinore and her mother had made some miscalculation by showing up on time, guests continued to make their way down the aisle, one middle-aged woman stopping her bent-armed escort to chat with Hideko, then greeting Elinore and Naoko loudly by name.

"Is your friend deaf?" Elinore whispered to her mother afterward, unable to think of the question she should have asked instead, like who this stranger was. But relief settled over the restless audience as soon as the organ music began. Conversations turned to inaudible murmurs and attention focused on the aisle where the wedding party, followed by the veiled bride, made its way to the front of the church.

Naoko, perhaps feeling a tremor on her mother's lap, turned her face up to Elinore's and wiped at a stray tear with her finger. "Watch the bride, baby." Elinore gently pushed the toddler's cheek away. "This is a special moment you don't want to miss. Isn't she beautiful?"

"*Booo-tifool*," Naoko pointed.

Elinore was glad that her two-year-old's attention could so easily be redirected on the bride. Ashamed that her daughter had caught her in an unguarded moment, she hoped that no one else would notice her tears. The weeping was not anything she'd expected and it troubled her. Even if it was acceptable to be seen crying at a wedding, she was not comfortable with tears. She had not wept at the death of her grandmother, nor at the birth of her child. She did not weep at movies, and certainly not at weddings where a person's emotions were in plain view. Yet the formal occasion provided a gateway into her emotions, eternity projected by the minister into the tenets of a relationship, the naive beauty of the bride yet untested by time and failure. Elinore witnessed it all like white slats in a gate beyond which her own life could be seen in the gaps.

The spring she met Saburo had been her final semester of graduate school. She'd been lingering over coffee in the campus bookstore, not quite ready to vacate her seat by the window, and stressed about her upcoming exams. In a phone conversation the night before, her mother had told her of her grandmother's cancer, and the news had thrown her. She'd talked to her Grandma Rio just two nights before, and she'd said nothing—of the tests that were being run, or of the symptoms that necessitated them. Three thousand miles from home, Elinore suddenly had a hint of all that had gone on in her absence and by comparison her life as a graduate student in New York seemed meaningless. What did it matter if she arrived late to Molecular Genetics, or even if she failed to show up to the final exam? Having focused on the assurances that had always governed her actions, she was busy warding off remonstrances by her mother: Don't disrupt your busy life when there's nothing you can do by being home. But why had she not questioned Hideko's logic, even when she knew it to be flawed?

That morning, she had watched the world outside rush by, numbing herself against a sense of foreboding when she noticed Saburo's shrewd but kind eye scanning a display of books; what seemed like moments later he appeared at her side. Even before he spoke, he seemed familiar. A relative? An old friend? She'd pulled a chair out for him to sit and he'd taken her coffee mug, held it under his nose, and wagged his head almost imperceptibly. "Italian," he'd said.

She'd shrugged, slightly put off by his odd manners. "Are you a connoisseur?"

"Yes." He'd grinned enigmatically. "I love coffee."

"It's better at the café up the street," she'd said, wrinkling her nose at her half finished cup, which he'd placed back within her reach. If he asked for directions, she decided her line, after giving them to him, would be, "I need to get going anyway," because she was now more than ten minutes late for class. But he made no motion to leave. Later, when he told her that he was wandering around New York for a couple days, en route from Jakarta to Santa Fe, which he called home, she'd thought he was kidding. In appearing precisely at that moment, he offered the interlude she needed to put her life aside. Two nights and a day later, when she put him in a cab to JFK and he told her that if she was ever in Santa Fe she should look up Saburo's Fresh Roast, she'd imagined that *fresh* referred to fish instead of coffee.

Then, early that summer, following the news of her grandmother's death which came far too quickly after her mother's word that nothing could be done, she packed up her car and headed west. Having made it two-thirds of the way home, across a country she'd previously seen only on maps, the sixty-mile detour off Highway 40, up I-25 to Santa Fe, didn't seem like a big deal. With only five hundred miles to Los Angeles, she could reach the Valley in a day if she drove straight through.

What she hadn't anticipated after the flatness of Texas and Oklahoma was the sight of the Sangre de Cristos when her car crested La Bajada hill—the starkness of thunderheads painting the clear blue sky, casting their shadows on the foothills, lumps of black pinons dotting the honey colored backdrop. Rolling down her window, she breathed in the thin, clean air, and combed her fingertips through her hair wanting to release the scent into her bones. At the motel, she found *Saburo's Fresh Roast* listed in the phone book just beneath *Ryder Truck Rentals*.

How impulsive she'd felt driving to meet him. Grabbing the first bag of coffee she could find, she carried it to the register and was delighted when Saburo rushed out from behind the counter before she could even speak. "What a nice surprise," he said, wiping black flecks of ground coffee onto his apron and offering up a hand. "What can I get for you?"

She'd played the lines out in her head and knew what the right one should sound like, but the way he'd squeezed her hand had emboldened her, and in the end she couldn't stop herself from blurting out the truth. "I came to see *you*."

"Well, then, I owe you dinner. Tonight?"

The smell of coffee followed her as she drifted out into the glare of the street still feeling the warmth of his hand in her palm. Minutes later, he rushed after her with the bag of coffee beans she'd left behind. Did he know that leaving something behind meant you wanted to return?

She couldn't remember what they ate, or much of anything that followed dinner. The drive back to his house, or the bottle of wine on the windowsill that cast a tall shadow over the bed when she opened her eyes and sat up. Each morning of her drive west, she'd arisen to the whir of highway traffic in her ears and the musty odor of motel bedding that scratched at her body and caused nightmares. She still felt disoriented from the shock of her grandmother's death, disbelieving where the news had taken her. Staring down at the man half-asleep beside her, she felt the need to make excuses and mumbled the only thing that came to mind. "Before you, I'd never been with a Japanese American man."

"I'm not Japanese American." He spoke with his eyes still closed, his left cheek bearing a crease from having been pressed into the pillow.

"Oh my God," she said, surprised that he'd heard her, then thinking Chinese, Korean? Unable to imagine, with a name like Saburo, what other options there were, she lay back down beside him, breathing in the stale air he exhaled, examining the dark passages up what she considered unusually broad nostrils, his short straight eye lashes, the almost invisible pores in his smooth, almost girlishly flawless complexion. When physical indicators revealed nothing, she wished for his eyes to open, for him to tell her what he was talking about, but replaying his words in her head, she heard traces of an accent.

Why had it taken her so long to detect it? Rising from bed, she set off to explore his house wondering what other clues she'd missed. But Saburo had very few possessions by which to judge him, and subsequent conversations revealed pitifully little. He was Japanese, just not American. He was born in Japan, educated in London, and had spent most of his adult years in Santa Fe, New Mexico. She'd never met anyone with a background like his, and the information he divulged about himself seemed always to get lost like stray coins sucked into a vacuum bag, never to be retrieved. Had he said his mother was alive, or passed? Was his brother in New York older or younger? Married? Things she could swear he mentioned she couldn't remember; they were, like someone else's dream, without context. Still, with the graduate program over and her grandmother dead, she wasn't in a rush to return to the Valley. Having grown up with her grandmother, she couldn't imagine a life without her, and in Saburo she'd found the excuse she needed to postpone her return. She was in love almost instantly, and for two months that seemed enough. Beyond excitement she didn't know what she felt about him. She disclosed little about her close-knit family; and he seemed content with her answers.

"What made you say you didn't like Japanese American men?" he asked one night after they'd made love, on a night when she'd felt for reasons she couldn't explain preoccupied and even queasy, wanting to hide, perhaps unsuccessfully, her lack of interest in their lovemaking. "Or did you just say that you'd never slept with one?"

"Yes," she ventured, then corrected herself, "no. There weren't a lot of Nikkei where I grew up. I only dated one, and he always seemed to have something to prove."

"Who doesn't?"

"Maybe you're right," she conceded, feeling misunderstood but acknowledging to herself that perhaps she wasn't as clear as she'd thought she was on the subject of men.

"The Japanese in California, weren't they sent away to camps during the Second World War, interned—?"

"Yes," she told him. "My father and mother both were. But they were just small children at the time."

"Even so, I'd think an experience like that would have its effects even generations later."

She assumed that what he'd said was true. But then one of them had changed the subject, or perhaps they'd fallen asleep. That same week she found out she was pregnant with Naoko.

She no longer recalled how she and Saburo reached the decision that she would give birth to Naoko, though she would never acknowledge what she suspected: that had she been more certain of Saburo's feelings toward her, she would have aborted the pregnancy and held off on considering whether or not to have children. Even if his kind and playful gestures bespoke genuine affection, how could she trust what had never been spoken? He had never declared his love for her, never asked her to marry him or spoken a simple I love you. Even though she had felt loved by him, the unspoken words still bothered her. But then again, had her grandmother not become ill and died so suddenly, she might not have made the detour that became her life with Saburo. Watching the bride and groom exchange vows, she marveled at how one story became another. The sudden death of her grandmother led her to Saburo, and who could tell where Naoko's birth would lead. But what she remembered was that Saburo didn't seem surprised by the news of the pregnancy. Or if he was he hid it. Seated between her mother and daughter, the early days with Saburo came to her like someone else's life, not her own. Waking in the pitch dark at four-thirty when the alarm would ring and he would rise from bed, leaving his warm smell behind on the sheets for her to sink back in to. The sound of running water as he splashed his face before heading out the door, and then the immensely quiet mornings she spent alone in their modest house.

Steering her mind expertly away from the sadness that led her to Santa Fe, she cleared a space instead for what pleased her. How he'd come home by six in the evening smelling like coffee. Then after twelve hours of heavy lifting and painstakingly menial work, he'd shower and cook dinner, which they'd often eat in bed. It was a carefree existence, he never mentioning any aspirations beyond coffee and the pleasure it gave him, and she in a kind of lull that came from being in love with him and pregnant. Maybe it couldn't have lasted that way, except that the year Naoko was conceived and all the way through her daughter's first year of life she felt happy, as if the caffeine from the beans was somehow being absorbed by her blood, taken in through her skin in the places where Saburo rested his hands.

"Can't you sit still, Elinore?" Elinore felt her mother's glare. "You're much worse than the baby." Yet despite considerable effort, she couldn't stop moving.

"What are you doing?" Rising to excuse herself, Elinore dropped back into the pew when Hideko grabbed the back of her shirt.

"I'm taking Naoko outside," she said. She needed air, a warm breeze and patch of horizon lacking from inside the crowded church.

"No," Hideko said sternly. "It's not safe outside."

With no choice but to remain seated, Elinore attempted to distract herself. Through a long rectangular window, a field of dirt collected patches of weeds and gave way to an old clapboard house with peeling white paint and an open window that suggested someone still lived there. A caretaker? A ghost? "Who lives there?" Elinore asked, gesturing with her finger.

"Where?" Hideko whispered, following Elinore's finger to what she didn't immediately see. "No one lives there," she said angrily. "Why aren't you watching the wedding?"

"Right." Elinore forced her attention back to the ceremony.

Caroline Ikeda had a noteworthy face if you liked demure, girl-next-door, picture-perfect ordinary. For lack of interest, Elinore shifted her gaze to the groom. His features seemed fine enough, but his hair, short on the sides and longer on top and in the back, made him look immature. "What's with the haircut?" she whispered to her mother, but got back no response. Strange, she considered, because he wasn't bad looking otherwise. Looking from the bride, who appeared wholly immersed in her role in the ceremony, to the groom, whose mind might well have been elsewhere, she attributed his seeming lack of focus to bad hair.

"What do you know about the maid of honor?" Elinore whispered, wanting a story for that pretty young woman.

"How would I know anything about her?"

Elinore noted Hideko's accusatory tone and assumed only that it meant she should stop talking. Following her mother's unspoken command, she silently considered the other bridesmaid who turned out to be both taller and less attractive. In fact, every thought seemed written across the woman's face, the sum total of which bespoke misery. Given the wrong body type, crimson taffeta moved from bad taste to abomination, Elinore decided, staring at how the puffy sleeves and tight bodice, flared at the hips, accentuated what a kinder dress was supposed to hide.

Turning her attention to the minister, Elinore wondered what kind of advice an officiant might have offered her and Saburo: Remember to talk to each other, and use condoms or another reliable form of birth control. Anxious for the ceremony to end, she decided her best bet for entertainment was still her mother. Elinore knew the fake smile plastered across Hideko's face meant she wasn't paying attention to the ceremony either. Besides, despite the admonishments, her mother enjoyed gossiping.

"So tell me something you do know," Elinore whispered giddily.

Leaning over to offer Naoko a candy, Hideko whispered into Elinore's ear, "I think the second bridesmaid is Nora Yano, Yukari's girl."

"Nora?" Elinore spoke a bit too loudly, the reverberations of her voice causing several heads to turn.

Hideko raised a palm and nodded apologetically to anyone who might have been offended by her daughter's outburst, then emphasized her unwillingness to engage in further conversation by angling her back against Elinore's shoulder.

By the time the guests were finally allowed outside, the daylight had softened and the atmosphere felt almost festive in contrast to the stifling interior of the church. Women welcomed the slight breeze by lifting the hair from the nape of their necks and men removed their jackets and blotted at their foreheads. There was movement everywhere, with sheer, brightly colored fabrics rippling like an ocean current and Naoko testing her balance as she maneuvered through the crowd by grabbing knee caps. But no one seemed to mind. People who had seemed quite unfriendly or intrusive inside the church came alive in the breeze as if to say that all they had needed to be happy was a bit of elbow room.

When the bride and groom trotted down the church steps holding hands, rose petals flew and the scene felt very much like ones Elinore had seen in the movies. The crowd followed behind the wedding party, tittering about who would drive with whom, and before long each guest had been accounted for and the cars traveled caravan style across the Valley floor causing Elinore to wonder what had made her feel so tense.

"It's just like in the movies, isn't it," she remarked to Hideko.

"The ceremony?"

"No," Elinore guffawed, "the ceremony was horrible. I mean the rose petals, the cake-top bride and groom, traveling in a line of cars to the old steakhouse high on the hill. I rather like being part of a procession."

"You do?" Hideko eyed her suspiciously.

"Yes, I don't mind being part of a group, especially when I can do so inside a car, with my own mother and daughter." And with that, she reached across the front seat and tapped a few times on the horn.

"What are you doing?" Hideko wrestled her arm away, clearly abashed.

"It's a wedding, isn't it?" But turning to the car behind theirs, Elinore noted wide-eyed alarm fading to chastising unease. To this, Elinore reached back over the passenger seat and waved Naoko's hand, smiling.

Not finding her daughter funny, Hideko slapped Elinore's wrist, the car veering slightly to the right upon impact. Outside, though darker by the minute, heat continued to ripple up from the pavement and coat the Valley air.

"What's that?" Hideko pinched at the loose skin on Elinore's elbow.

"Ouch." Turning her arm over, Elinore discovered a quarter-sized red welt. A mosquito bite? Even though the pinch hadn't hurt she noticed in the silence that followed how itchy the bump became.

"So Nora didn't look too good, did she," Hideko said after a while, as if trying to undo the pinch.

No longer in a celebratory mood, Elinore refused the invitation to pacify her mother with gossip. "Was Nora the ugly one?"

"That's not nice," Hideko scolded, but her mother couldn't resist the opportunity to tell what she knew. "Evidently she hasn't been able to get a job since she lost the one she had working at some nail salon in Sherman Oaks. I heard she was so bright. She was a college student, you know. But then something went wrong. Isn't it scary how life works that way? She developed a rare, neurological problem in her hands. But her mother says her problems may also stem from depression.

"I heard she's moved close to the church and that she walks every-where. It's not a good neighborhood to live in let alone walk around.

"Such a sad case," she heard Hideko say.

With wedding guests arriving one after another, the parking lot filled quickly, and people Elinore recognized from the church scattered into the night clutching evening wraps as if for protection. "How do you know all these people anyway?" Elinore asked, suddenly curious about the acquaintances her mother had made in her absence.

"*Ikebana* club." Hideko dismissed her daughter without looking up.

Inside the banquet room, round tables created a forced effect of symmetry amidst a Valentine's Day color scheme. The décor felt overblown and contrived, except for the pair of perfectly folded paper cranes perched Japanese-style on red lacquer chopsticks beside each place setting. Going for the only item of interest, Naoko crushed in a second the *origami* someone had obviously taken great care to create. "Don't let her do that," Hideko intervened, pushing her own cranes aside, then checking the room surreptitiously for signs of disapproval.

She was right to scold, Elinore had not responded quickly enough, but the toddler's behavior through a long afternoon and evening had been otherwise exemplary, and what else was there for someone her age to do? Shoving a dessert spoon into Naoko's fist, Elinore pretended to admire her reflection in the shiny stainless, then covered parts of her face in ways that made her daughter laugh. But, fortunately their seats had been assigned with the older crowd, who seemed delighted to play peek-a-boo with dinner napkins and coo admiringly through much of the dinner, and just when they were all becoming annoying, the band started up; Hideko disappeared with Naoko and the rest of the couples wandered off to dance.

Removing herself from the festivities, Elinore figured that it had been nearly twenty-five years since she'd eaten at the steak-house—the last occasion a party to celebrate her grandparents' wedding anniversary. She remembered little of the event, except that there, at the balcony, her grandfather had lifted her onto the railing, pointing off in the distance at a solitary light he identified as home. Now, both her grandparents gone, the Valley floor shone in a solid mass of lights so that it was no longer possible to tell where, precisely, home lay. But even then, Elinore recounted, the light her grandfather had pointed out could not really have been their porch lamp. It unnerved her a bit to think that such a realization had taken almost twenty-five years to come by, and while trying to sort out her directions, Elinore was taken aback by movement coming from the row of bushes behind her, rustling that turned gradually to weeping.

"Is everything okay in there?" She thought at first that someone might be hurt, but remembering how she and a boyfriend had once hidden themselves outside a high school dance to kiss she guessed she'd been wrong. She was about to return to the wedding reception when the bridesmaid presented herself. Elinore connected the face to her mother's talk in the car, though the crimson dress was now snagged in a half-dozen places. "My goodness. You're not hurt, are you?" Her hand extended, she had already decided upon a scenario. "Did you fall?"

"No." Nora grimaced, refusing Elinore's gesture of a hand.

The question of what she'd been doing in the bush loomed, but no longer seemed appropriate in light of the bridesmaid's upset. "I'm Elinore," she said, retracting her hand. "You must be Nora."

"How did you know?" she asked, surprised.

"My mother is friends with the bride's mother, and we talked on the way here."

"Did she say I was a freak?"

"No," Elinore said defensively, recalling her mother's gossip along with her own mean spirited comment. Standing face to face with Nora, she regretted having made fun of the woman's appearances. "You're scratched up pretty bad," she pointed to her arm. "And bruised."

"No." A look of relief, almost gladness, swept over the woman's face. "I've been seeing someone."

"Someone who gave you those bruises?" Shocked that a stranger would reveal such personal information, Elinore guessed she'd misunderstood.

"They don't hurt. I think I must just bruise easily."

"I can't imagine bruises that aren't painful," Elinore said dismissively.

"Are you Wade's friend?"

Standing close enough that Elinore was aware of her breathing, the woman seemed not to understand that her question had already been answered. "I'm playing stand-in for my father," Elinore laughed uncomfortably. "I'm here with my mother and my two year old."

"That's right," the woman said, examining Elinore's face from only inches away. "I thought I recognized you."

Elinore was about to ask how it was that the woman might have recognized her when their conversation was cut short by the bride and her maid of honor. "Nora?" A shrill voice called out and Elinore looked up to see heavily lined red lips, tense and illuminated by foot lamps. "Thank goodness we finally found you." The bride evidently saw no need to introduce herself. "It's time for cake."

"This is Elinore," Nora said, her freakishly mellow expression contrasting sharply against the other two women. "Elinore, meet Caroline."

Before Elinore could offer a hand in greeting, the bride dismissed her with a perfunctory hello and turned back to Nora. "Are you coming?"

For an awkward moment, Nora remained where she stood, her hands tracing shadows of bruises as they slid patiently up and down each arm, and when that gesture went unnoticed by her friends, the hands moved down to the dress, where she smoothed snags and brushed away flecks of dirt.

Aren't they even curious? Elinore wondered. "Nora had a mishap," she said, volunteering information that no one had asked for.

The bride raised an eyebrow rather than respond, and even though the evening air remained sweltering, the maid of honor wrapped her arms around her waist as if chilled.

"A fall," Elinore clarified, "into the bushes."

"Are you okay?" The maid of honor reached out an arm, stopping just short of touching Nora's hand, and Elinore thought she saw a smile play at Nora's lips.

"What were you doing out here anyway?" The bride's tone was condescending, yet her obvious aggravation felt more honest than the other woman's gesture of false sympathy; her desire to move back inside fueling each word.

"I left my purse in the car and I came out to get it."

The story seemed plausible, except that Nora held neither car keys nor the forgotten purse. "What a lovely evening," Elinore exclaimed, glancing into the bushes, wanting the conversation to play out a bit longer so that she could figure things out. "Your ceremony was just beautiful!"

"Thank you so much." The bride gushed, and a smile—thrown like a sheet over the irritation and puzzlement of moments before—appeared as she turned to leave.

The conversation would have ended there had Nora not decided at that moment to step out of her pumps, thereby relinquishing her duties to the bride and releasing from bondage her crimson dyed feet, replete with their own sour smell. Lifting and rotating each ankle in turn, she revealed holes in her stockings where her big toes protruded, the sight and smell of which struck Elinore as more than a little disgusting.

"I think my shoes are too small," Nora said, her large frame hovering over her two friends. "Or maybe my feet are swollen. Do they look swollen?"

Unable to resist staring, Elinore expected one of the two other women to address the question Nora had posed about her feet and was horrified when she looked up to find Nora's eyes on her. How was she to know what the woman's feet normally looked like?

The uncomfortable silence that followed was interrupted by the maid of honor. "You could use a pedicure," she said, obviously referring to the overgrown toe nails.

"And a hot soak," the bride added, erupting into forced laughter.

"I think you know Elinore, don't you?" Nora said, and Elinore followed her gaze to the maid of honor.

"No," the woman said, "we've never met."

"Well, then," Nora said, "Melissa Hori, this is Elinore... What is your last name?" she paused. "I don't think you told me."

"Elinore Shimizu," Elinore said, extending her hand once again.

"Are you a friend of Wade?"

To Elinore's surprise, it was the bride rather than the maid of honor who spoke to her now, and having finally received that woman's full attention, Elinore could feel her status shift from unidentified to unwanted.

"I came with my mother because my father's out of town," Elinore said, for the first time feeling truly paranoid about her presence at the wedding. Had she used such abominably bad judgment in agreeing to escort her mother to the wedding in her father's stead? Because if at that moment the reason behind everyone's fuss should have been obvious, it wasn't.

"I was just wondering how I knew you," Caroline said.

"You don't know me," Elinore clarified, wondering whether Caroline could guess at the desire hidden by her statement of fact.

Caroline let a few seconds pass before addressing her two friends. "I don't know about you two, but I need to head back inside," she said, making sure to snub Elinore.

"Sure," Melissa said, turning away.

"Do you think I'm bad?" Nora said when her two friends had passed out of earshot.

Confused by just about every part of the conversation that had taken place, Elinore felt that words had been almost irrelevant to whatever else had gone on in the last minutes. What she surmised was that for unknown reasons both the bride and maid of honor resented her presence at the wedding. Beyond that, she couldn't be sure whether Nora's peculiar question alluded to the most recent exchange or to the earlier one, interrupted by the bride and bridesmaid. "I have no reason at all to think you're bad," she said, hoping that her remark would end the conversation.

But Nora refused to let up. "Can I tell you something?" she asked, her eyes suddenly alight.

"Sure." Still reeling, Elinore used Nora's large frame as an anchor to steady her gaze and was shocked by what she saw. Though Nora was a tall woman, everything about her stature suggested lowliness. The corners of her eyes drooped, her cheeks sagged, her mouth trembled, making her by all appearances the saddest person Elinore had ever seen.

"I'm sure you've had boyfriends," she said, "but I haven't. I turn thirty this year, and this is a first for me."

Nora fingered her bruises as she spoke, pointing Elinore's attention back to her arms where Elinore thought she could make out fingerprints.

"Maybe you're lucky," Elinore said, summoning a smile.

"I am?"

"Yes."

"It's not like kissing and the stuff you see at the movies."

"No."

"Do you think there's some secret to being loved?"

"No," Elinore said decisively. "I don't know any secrets. As far as I know, there are none."

"That surprises me," Nora said. "I'd have bet you'd know about love."

What would I know? Elinore wondered, the conversation turning too bizarre to calibrate.

"Are you coming?" Melissa reappeared, her voice beckoning from a safe distance.

Cramming her feet back into the too small pumps, Nora waved sheepishly and Elinore, having watched the woman hobble away in her crimson gown, followed not far behind. But the banquet room did not look as it had when she'd left it. Half eaten bits of cake lay abandoned and couples drifted stiffly to music that felt too solemn for dancing. Elinore scanned the crowded room for her daughter, and not seeing Naoko, she panicked. Then she spotted Hideko leaning in to whisper secrets to a woman Elinore didn't recognize, and

Naoko, slumped over her mother's shoulder, asleep. It was definitely her, but rather than rush in, she lingered in the distance, allowing the sight of her baby, swaying in her mother's arms, its profoundly soothing effect.

Chapter 11

MELISSA HORI WAS heading over the hill into Los Angeles for a day's worth of appointments when the radio announcer's deep voice interrupted R.E.M. to ask who else out there could feel the rumbling. Her first thought was of Caroline, who had always been luckier than a person deserved, sunbathing in Hawaii while California tumbled into the ocean. She couldn't help it. Suspicious of the mountains sloping into the freeway and all the houses stacked on top of them, she felt puzzled, too, that aside from the cars tearing up and down the hill there was no hint of peril contained in the landscape, and she hadn't felt the jolt. Then again, she'd been preoccupied. Having not seen Nora at Tuesday Night Bible Study and unable to reach her for two nights afterward, she had finally resorted to calling Yukari, only to find that Nora had been staying with her parents while she recovered from oral surgery. Shocked to hear the news from Nora's mother, Melissa well knew how hard it had always been for Nora to ask her parents for anything. If getting to and from the dentist's office had been the problem, or if she had needed someone to stay with after the procedure, Melissa should have been the one to offer, not Yukari. But, then, why had she not even known about Nora's bad tooth? There was a time when Melissa knew about and anticipated all of Nora's problems. She knew how Nora spent each part of her day, when she could call and find her home and when she'd be out. She knew what upset her and pleased her, and she could make her feel better—often before Nora could even identify for herself what was wrong.

Hanging up after her strained conversation with Yukari, Melissa had felt shocked, then insulted that she'd been shunned. Retracing their interactions at Caroline's wedding, she guessed that something she'd said or done had upset Nora, which had caused her to go to her mother, rather than Melissa, for help, knowing full well that Melissa would find out and be hurt. But perhaps Nora had made arrangements with her mother without having thought of her at all. It annoyed Melissa that she couldn't guess what was going on in Nora's head. Beginning with the problems with her hands, she'd lost track of her friend whose medical problems had affected not only her body, but her personality as well. It was true that Nora had become a less reliable friend, someone whose behavior was hard to predict or understand. What's more, the move to Pacoima distanced her and compounded the difficulties between them. What was one to do? Pushing her weight back against the driver's seat, Melissa vowed to stop obsessing about Nora, and gradually her thoughts returned to the news of the earthquake.

Not so long ago, the Northridge earthquake had actually thrown her out of bed, but that one hadn't scared her. She had clients who were traumatized, and friends whose homes were destroyed. The damage was all around her, and she felt almost ashamed to say that she hadn't lost even a dish. Maybe she was lucky like Caroline, or maybe the problems she attributed to Nora belonged to her: an inability to feel things. Not just good things, but bad, too. Sometimes it felt like life happened all around her, but not *to* her, and news of the earthquake only reaffirmed her fears. But had she always been this way? She still remembered the big quake of '72, back when she was six. How the neighbors gathered outside in their bathrobes when the morning light was still orange, and she watched through her bedroom window as parents exchanged flashlight batteries and news. Her family had been forced to evacuate when the local aqueduct cracked and threatened to burst. In addition to the Horis, about twenty other families had camped on the floor of the church for what had seemed like forever, with the radio always on in the background playing "We've Only Just Begun" and "Bridge over Troubled Water."

How strange it was to brush her teeth in the bathroom that she'd only ever peed in, standing next to whomever else happened to pass through. Strange and fun and upsetting, too. She remembered the musty smell of the terra cotta floor, the chill that crept up through her sleeping bag, and waking up mortified that her face was six inches from Caroline's. She'd eaten Spam for the first time ever, and played with Caroline and Nora on the pulpit. They told jokes into the microphone and got to hear how their voices sounded amplified like Reverend Nakatani's. It had been great fun to stand on the minister's stage, to touch the keys of the organ, then to look down on the pews where they normally sat. But no part of the sanctuary contained mystery like the baptismal pool, and one morning when they'd run out of things to do, Caroline dared her to lift the beige carpet cover.

They'd all watched with mouths agape as Reverend Nakatani dunked members of the congregation backwards and brought them up wet and sometimes sputtering, imagined from the wooden bench seats what it might be like to be bathed in the blood of Christ. The one good thing that came from the disaster was getting to touch the water. Lying on their stomachs, hanging over the edge of the shallow pool, Nora pointed out how, down at the bottom, the dark blue paint was crumbling, exposing bits of white plaster beneath. They splashed and sniffed at the water and Nora made jokes about how Christ's blood smelled like chlorine. But Melissa knew they'd ventured into sacred territory, a place off-limits for play, and after a while each girl fell into her own private thoughts about being there. With her eyes closed, Melissa imagined what it might be like to be plunged backwards by Reverend Nakatani: Reborn.

Rebirth was such a fundamentally baffling concept when Melissa learned about salvation as a child: the end of the world as it's foretold in Revelations, how Jesus comes down from heaven and saves everyone who believes in Him. She'd listened with fascination and utter fear to every lesson ever told by Reverend Nakatani and her Sunday School teachers. But when she tried to think about it, she'd felt deeply confused about the possibility of her own rebirth. Though it was expected that at a certain point in her life she would be Reborn, she hoped that the blessed event would not happen any time soon. To reenter the world as a daughter of Christ did not appeal to her in the way she knew it was supposed to. She felt perfectly happy having Asako and Bob as her parents. Furthermore, she liked her friends, and she loved coming to church. Secretly, she prayed nothing would ever change.

But the next thing she knew her ankles were being held up over her head and she was sinking. She opened her mouth to shriek when her head hit bottom and gulped water before she surfaced, horrified to find Nora at the edge of the pool wringing her hands, looking miserable. It was Caroline's mother who finally fished her out by the elbows. And Melissa might have been fine being cradled by Teru, her cracked head bleeding into Teru's chest while she sobbed quietly, except that Asako eventually arrived and jerked her to her feet.

Too scared to open her eyes and face her mother's scorn, Melissa could only hear Caroline's explanations of how lifting the cover off the pool had been Roland Yamashita's idea, and how she, Caroline, had immediately gone for help when Jeffrey Higa sneaked up from behind and tossed Melissa into the water. Even in Melissa's sorry state, she marveled at Caroline's ability to fabricate a story, making herself into a hero on the spot. It was something she still thought about from time to time. That, and what a shock it had been to imagine herself being Reborn, and the next second almost to drown.

Then there was the cut on her forehead; it gushed more blood than she had ever seen, and the sight of the blood scared her almost as much as the fall. Years later, when she returned to face the congregation at the baptismal, she was so nervous that she gasped—an audible groan that penetrated the church—when Reverend Nakatani put his hands on her shoulders and tipped her backward. As she was going under she thought how interesting it is that you fall backward into salvation, opposed to forward. She'd been anticipating, half-fearing that moment her whole life, expecting that she'd emerge from the water with a new life, perhaps unrecognizable to the old one. New eyes with which to view the world. A new heart.

When she came up, the first thing her eye caught on was a dark spot on the beige carpet. The stain. It was a sign, she believed, of her new life, and she realized then that her fear had been foolish. Without her knowing it, the change had happened years ago: her blood soaked in and mingling with the clear water of Jesus's.

But how had she gotten to the subject of Jesus? It was strange, Melissa thought, having arrived at the correct address without any sense of how she'd gotten there, how all inquiries led to affirmations of her faith. Belief was such an important part of life. The thing that Nora needed to remember was that being part of the church meant there would always be a place where she belonged. Because of this, there was no reason to act dejected and to be depressed. She had good friends, and she would never be alone. Still, Melissa continued to worry. Driving between clients she felt edgy and had to keep reminding herself: Nothing is wrong. The scary thing hasn't happened. You are safe.

To make matters worse, a minor fender bender on the Hollywood Freeway had slowed miles of traffic to a crawl, ensuring that Melissa would arrive late for dinner with Mark. Knowing he always got to places ahead of time for the simple reason that he hated to be kept waiting, her heart rate quickened with each passing minute. But the tardiness was not her fault, and at least Mark had his books. Lately he'd been so busy cramming for the California Bar, there was a chance he wouldn't even notice the passing time. Rushing in to the restaurant, she could see that she'd been both right and wrong. Mark was seated at the booth under the neon green *Kirin* sign that they picked whenever it was available, his head bowed over a foot high stack of papers while he slurped *gyooza* and rice from a *chawan* held under his chin.

"I don't suppose you want to share any of that," she teased, scooting onto the wooden bench across from him.

"I waited twenty minutes, then I ordered." Mark put down his *chawan* and wiped his mouth without looking up. He obviously wasn't in good humor.

He had a thing about lateness; she knew that. But she felt the same way about manners. Like not starting to eat until everyone had been served, and so she wasn't about to apologize. "I'm not that late," she reminded him, "considering traffic on the 101. I had to drive in from downtown. Remember?"

She accepted his offer of the remaining *gyooza*, but begrudgingly, her preoccupation having turned to anger. She would have waited for him, she felt sure of it, the way Bob always waited for her mother to sit down before starting. "*Itadakimasu*," he'd say, clasping his hands.

Her mother would pull her chair under her so that she perched on the edge, a bird ready to sing. "*Doozo*," she'd say.

Melissa felt fairly confident that her mother liked Mark and knew, too, that she was right to be hesitant about him. It had taken tremendous effort on her part to ensure Asako's approval. Coaching him on manners, trying gently to inform him of her mother's way of doing things without offending him—without offending either of them. If she tended to judge him through her mother's eyes, it was out of respect for their shared values. Things like manners were important to her. If he were Japanese, it might not have mattered so much, but then, if he were Japanese, she figured he'd have good manners. Melissa understood what her mother meant when she said that people were judged by their manners. Manners made a difference. That and the fact that he'd attended their church for so many years. Melissa still remembered how Mark showed up for service with his family dressed in a suit and tie one Sunday when they were both thirteen. How miserably he stuck out. But then it turned out that his Aunt Edith, the wife of his father's brother, was Japanese.

"If we were having dinner at my mom's house you wouldn't start eating until everyone was served, would you?"

Understanding that he was being provoked, Mark finally looked up. "What? Am I on trial here?"

"No, just answer the question."

"What question, Mel? What are you talking about?"

"Just what I said. You're not going to be one of those slouches who forgets his manners once he's married, are you?"

"So you've decided to marry me?"

"Did I say that?" She had to smile because lately every conversation they had turned into a debate about marriage. Just maybe, she didn't want to get married. But the question for her wasn't really *whether* to get married, it was *when*.

"As far as I can tell, I've got the best manners in the room," Mark quipped, and Melissa tried to see the restaurant as he saw it, the black-haired men at the next table talking boisterously and loud, their fashion-conscious wives silently nodding.

"Those couples are from Japan," she whispered. "I'm not talking about the foreigners."

Mark shrugged. "I'll try to live up to your expectations of how a good *American* man should behave at the dinner table. I just never realized manners were that important to you."

She could get angry all over again that Mark had failed to recognize something so fundamentally important to her, but what would be the point? "Just promise you won't embarrass me in front of my mother."

"What?" he said, taking a moment to think. "Your mother has said I have impeccable manners."

"Okay," she sighed, forcing herself not to respond with bitterness to his self-congratulatory tone. "I'm sorry."

Mark rolled his eyes. "I guess I shouldn't ask you how your day was."

"It was fine," she told him. "Three visits to treat foster families, one of which is probably going to return the kid, which I can understand since he's been smearing his feces on the walls, and my survivors of homicide group."

"That's right." Mark was listening now, genuinely interested, which was a trait she loved about him. "How'd that go?" Melissa shrugged. She knew she should relay some small detail to him, something someone said, or a smart clinical insight on her part, but she'd been in a foul mood all day, and she wasn't going to talk about things that could only depress her.

"Okay." He feigned a smile and waved a heavy text in front of his face. "Maybe we shouldn't talk again until I finish reading this."

"Okay." She stared down at the tabletop, unwilling to meet Mark's eye. The fact was that she loved him, and didn't know where her dark moods came from, or why they seemed to strike out of nowhere, the way the night happens when you walk out of an afternoon matinee only to find the sun gone and you can't even remember where you parked your car. No big deal, except that for a minute you feel completely lost.

Melissa feared unhappiness and the potential for unhappiness, which was connected in her mind to Mark. She wanted to think it was because he wasn't Japanese, but she knew that was only part of it. Looking up, she followed the hum over the tabletop to the neon sign overhead responsible for casting Mark in a sickly shade of green. They would have to find a new table. The salty smell of *shoyu* and vinegar drifted in from beyond the parted *arami* curtains, and just as she was about to complain that the service was unusually slow, the same smiling waitress they always had came by for her order. Then the door chimes tinkled to announce the Kumagais from church.

"Hey!" Mark waved his arms in their direction. "Should I ask them to join us?"

"No."

But the Kumagais were already on their way over, and behind them another church couple.

"Why does this always happen when you eat Japanese?" she whispered when they were alone again. "You can't even start dinner without someone dropping by."

"No kidding, if we were going to have a fight we should have had Italian or something."

"Maybe tomorrow night." She sneered, but conceded to herself that Mark's observation had been right.

"What's wrong with you, anyway?"

"Nothing." Not until she'd finished her noodles and Mark had stopped leafing through his papers did she feel ready for conversation. "Okay," she said, placing *ohashi* across the empty bowl. "I think I know what's wrong."

"What?" Mark snapped back sarcastically, and she could tell he thought she meant him.

"It's not what you think." She waved her arm to dismiss him, remembering the earthquake that morning, and being late for her first appointment. But things had gone wrong even before that. For Mark's sake, Melissa ran through her phone conversation with Yukari, and how she'd wound up feeling inexplicably sad for her. "I'm sorry to have worried you," Yukari kept saying while Melissa imagined lines marring her delicate features and the curve of her back as she hunched into the phone. She could picture it all perfectly, which made her think how unsettling the last months, and maybe even years, had been for Yukari. She was a good mother, compared to the ones Melissa dealt with, a great mother, and she didn't deserve the heartache Melissa knew she felt. So Melissa had gone on, saying whatever she could think of to appease her. "You haven't done anything to worry me, I was just checking to make sure Nora is all right, no please don't feel bad that you didn't call me, you couldn't have known that I'd be worried."

"Well," Mark said, "I'm sure it was a relief at least to know that Nora has been with her parents all along."

"That's just it," Melissa said, Mark's miscalculation about her feelings giving her the entry she needed into her thoughts. "I'm worried about Nora."

"Why are you worried about Nora?" Mark stared down at his notes as if the answer might be found there. "What's wrong with Nora—I mean aside from what I already know."

"See."

"See what?"

She tried to answer Mark's question even though she hadn't been able to figure it out for herself. "I've practically lost touch with her since she moved out to Pacoima, let alone I can't believe a friend of ours is living in Pacoima."

"She's your friend—" Mark cut in, but Melissa, thinking she might be on to something, didn't want to stop.

"I been worried about her for a long time, and this morning when Yukari said Nora had to have a root canal, and that she's been staying with her and Yujitaka all week, it just struck me how terribly wrong things have gone."

"Well, have you ever had a root canal?" Mark gnawed the tip of his pencil eraser. "That's pretty serious."

Why was he being so obstinate? "So you think *that's* what I've been worried about?"

"Could be, I don't know." Mark had seen her through more than one hunch and, against his well-trained instincts, he should have known he wasn't going to derail her by arguing.

"I think Nora should come stay with me," she said, surprising herself. "I think we need to do something."

"Okay." A feeling of relief swept over her when he agreed, or maybe it was just gratification that at least he was finally taking her seriously.

"I knew you'd agree," she said, reaching across the table to grasp his hand.

"Not so fast," he said, squeezing her fingers. "Say she does want to live with you. Then what? What about next month and the month after? You know they don't know what's wrong with her hands so it's not likely that she's going to be getting better any time soon. What are you going to do with her a month from now, or a year?

And even for now, do you really want her living with you? That's a big commitment, I'd think about it, Mel."

"I have thought about it," she lied. She didn't know why Mark liked to predict gloomy outcomes. It made him less than pleasant to be around, yet perhaps his skepticism was merited. "Maybe you're right."

This seemed to be the opening Mark had been working towards, a small concession from her. After enjoying a final, dramatic sip of his tea, he reached for his wallet.

"I'll get it." She pulled the check off the table, knowing she owed him something for her horrible behavior. "Besides, I want dessert. Would you like dessert?"

"No," Mark patted his gut, which was pretty much nonexistent. "I'm full."

When the green tea ice cream came, she asked for a second spoon, and, after a bite, slid the silver dish across to Mark. "Sometimes I can't help but see Nora as a symbol."

"A symbol?"

"Yes. Don't you think?"

"No. I think if Nora were here, she'd laugh."

"No, she wouldn't. It's like, all of our friends are pretty well off financially and attractive and happy, right? But Nora isn't like us. She used to be, but now she's not."

"I think Nora was always different."

"Maybe so, but now she's in trouble, and I still think we should do something. I mean, we're supposed to be Christian, aren't we?"

"We *are* Christian, Mel."

"Yes, I know. And doesn't that mean we should do something?"

Tilting the silver ice cream dish to his lips, Mark scraped out the last bit of green liquid. "Mel, doing something was your idea, not mine. Besides prayer, which we've been doing, I'm not sure what anyone can do to help."

"Well, then, it's just depressing. It's why I'm in a bad mood."

"I'm surprised at you. You see depressing things in your job every day, don't you? And you don't let them get to you."

"No, but I have a professional relationship with my clients. This is personal. It gets under my skin."

"I don't know, Mel," Mark shrugged. "Or I'm not sure I see such a difference. Sometimes I think you've got this picture in your head of a perfect life, and anything that isn't part of that picture you can't deal with."

"I hardly think anyone would consider Nora's life perfect."

"You know what I mean."

"No." She stared straight back at him to let him know she was serious. "I don't know what you mean."

"I hate these talks," he said, finally. "They make me feel our relationship is doomed because I'll never know the right thing to say."

"Maybe you're right," she said, knowing she should ease up.

"Okay," he waved his arm, "do you think the Kumagais or the Miyoshis or for that matter any of the other couples in this restaurant have happy lives?"

"Yes," she answered emphatically, having no idea what he was talking about. "Of course they do."

"I don't know what makes you think so. I know for a fact that most people are pretty miserable and *not* happy, and I also know that it's not something I'm going to spend my days grieving over. That's just the way life is."

"How could you say that?" The pitch of her voice rose and she could feel her pulse beating at her temples. Mark was making observations based on his own family—how his mother's job had always kept her life separate from his, how the Powers didn't even eat dinners together most nights. She'd heard so many people talk about how unhappy their childhoods were; she felt sad for them, and lucky to have grown up completely happy. Not that it had been easy for her mother. For a time it had been only the two of them. But Asako had a knack for anticipating her daughter's needs. She'd even remarried a man she didn't love just because she knew he'd love Melissa as his own. It was because her mother had cared for her all her life that she felt obligated now to choose someone Asako would approve of, and to provide comfort for her mother in her old age the way she'd provided for Melissa as a child.

"Maybe happiness is not what you think," she said suddenly. "It's not just a state that you can summon out of nothing. We have an obligation to each other, to make each other happy. That's what I think. And if you don't think you can make me happy, maybe we shouldn't get married."

"Calm down, Mel." Even though she hated being patronized, she felt comforted to hear in his voice the same alarm she'd been feeling. "Maybe we should just talk about Nora, go back to where this conversation began."

Checking her watch, then looking around the restaurant and seeing that all their friends had left, she had a different idea. "I think we should stop talking," she said, not wanting to point out that there were only seventeen minutes until the time Asako would call to check up on her. She'd have to hurry to make it home, couldn't bear to be the cause of yet another person's upset. "It's late," she said, careful not to reference her mother. "And I'm tired. I think we should go."

Mark concurred. "Well, okay then. I'm sorry, okay? I didn't mean to upset you."

"Yeah, okay," she said. "I know."

Though things didn't make any more sense than they had when she arrived, neither she nor Mark had anything left to say. She carried the check up to the cashier to pay and Mark followed her out the door. And as was usual when they took separate cars, he walked her to hers. After she unlocked her door he craned his neck for a perfunctory kiss, but she pulled him in and kissed him deeply.

"Call me tomorrow?" She smiled, feeling the success of having measured his affection for her.

"Yes." As if sensing he'd been duped, he pulled back.

"Study well," she mouthed through a slit the car window.

"I will," he appeared to say. "Don't worry."

"No, you're right," she reassured him. "I won't worry."

She planned to do exactly what Mark suggested. After a brief check-in with her mother, she would sleep, try not to worry about anything.

Chapter 12

FROM THE HOTEL room where she stayed with Wade on Waikiki beach, Caroline felt the roar of the waves. Even at two blocks away and twelve stories up, the pounding surf shook the building on its foundation, and at night when the heavy curtains were drawn against the sky, the rumbling moved inside. She slept restlessly, and three nights in a row she had the same dream. In it she was wearing her white bikini and floating in the deep end of the pool while boys she'd known in high school paraded across the decking in wet suits. One by one, they tumbled backward, as if in slow motion, and disappeared. She could not see them underwater but saw instead the bubbles that escaped from their black skin and disbursed into the air and felt the water slap against the tiled edges of the pool. Tilting her chin to her chest, she saw the outline of her darkened stomach, which had grown as round as the moon. The water sounded peaceful and she knew she could sleep, but she felt pressure, then the slurp-like sound a diver's mask makes when it's sucked from the skin, and she startled awake. In this way, Hawaii turned into a fifty-foot kidney shaped swimming pool while she floated in the middle, poised for something to happen. For the third morning in a row, the disturbing, sucking sound had woken her up. Her eyes opened wide in the dark room, the only sunlight beating through a slit in the drapery; a week had been enough time to find the atmosphere achingly ordinary, only this morning Wade was gone. When she turned over, she could feel that the spot where he'd slept wasn't even warm. She imagined him getting out of bed, dressing, and leaving while she dreamt she couldn't sleep, and, for the first time, she felt the strangeness of her married life.

But the epiphany lasted only a second. She knew Wade would return shortly with a newspaper and a cup of coffee, perhaps two. Without it, there was no point in getting up. Turning sideways, she assessed her image in the mirror fastened over the dresser, letting her hair hang off the edge of the bed, pleased with its lofty sway. Two more inches and it would reach the floor. The last time it had been this long had been in junior high school. But she had been right to grow it out for the ceremony so that it could be braided and wound with forsythia. The pictures would most likely be ready by the time they returned, and she reminded herself that she should call the photographer, then grimaced, hoping such a phone call would not be necessary. The photographer had been so difficult to deal with, his reputation built perhaps on his bone structure and musculature rather than quality of his work. Still, she lay wondering what in her had brought out his brusque nature and how she had compared to other subjects he'd photographed when she glimpsed the red Hawaiian print of the shirt she'd picked up at a beach front shop and scrambled upright. She couldn't read Wade's grin, but felt embarrassed by what he might have observed. "Where have you been?" she asked, her tone accusatory from having been startled from her thoughts.

"I needed to make some phone calls," he told her, "and I didn't want to wake you up."

"What's wrong?" she asked, her eyes traveling to his face, reading trouble.

"There's nothing wrong," he told her.

Opening the shade and moving the bedspread to the floor so he could sit, he urged her to dress, said he had a surprise for her on this, their last day before heading home. A short flight to Maui, then a drive to Hana, to see the seven sacred pools. He'd already reserved two seats on a small plane and rented a car. She'd go along with him even though she found his behavior suspicious. Edgy and irritable since the honeymoon began, she'd gladly spend the day anywhere, not because of Wade, but because the end was close in sight.

They arrived in Maui just past noon and picked up their rental car so that they could begin the long journey. Mile after mile of windy roads, some in desperate need of repair, sometimes edging perilously close to cliffs that led straight down to the sea, still Maui proved every bit the paradise that people said it was. She didn't know why she should feel bereft. But maybe she viewed the landscape the way she saw herself. Beautiful beyond reproach, and, sadly, misunderstood. After months of planning followed by the few hours the vows and ensuing party actually took, she felt, somehow, let down. Like the result of so much activity should have added up to something more, or at least different. She wanted to say that the difficulty was in slowing her pace. She'd been moving so fast for so long: it was inertia. But that wasn't quite it. She thought of the porter she'd become friendly with. How he stood ready to greet them every afternoon when they arrived back. The courtesy nod he gave Wade, and the special look he gave her. She knew he lingered over the glances she cast his way. A smile from her meant something to him, his worth gauged by her reception. Like the waiter who doted over them at dinner the night before and so many others she'd met. She couldn't help but imagine her impact on their daily lives. Not like the people closest to her who regarded her with disdain or disaffection. She wondered if the contact that made a person knowable was also what made them dull. She wished there were someone to whom she could explain her feelings, but then she wasn't sure she could describe them, even to herself. Wade sat behind her, soaking in the local scenery, only a camera separating her from him. He'd come to escape life, not to dwell on it, and he could not be brought down. There were Melissa and Nora, with whom she'd always talked, but it wasn't the same for either of them. In the end, it felt like bragging to say that her beauty defined her in an untenable way: that the thing that distinguished her made her lonely and totally vulnerable.

"Everyone treats me like an object," she'd observed not long ago to Melissa and Nora.

Melissa dismissed her complaint, but Nora seemed to consider what she was saying. "I think I know what you mean."

"You understand, then."

"Yes, of course. I've always been treated like garbage."

Go ahead, laugh, she wanted to say. It wasn't so different because how they appeared prevented them *both* from ever being loved, but Melissa added a sarcastic observation, which had ended the conversation.

What would Nora have seen, looking out the car window, the late afternoon breeze blowing off the ocean, the ancient and hideously beautiful land spreading out like claws. Her mother would admire the splendor of this day, and she laughed to have conjured Teru's kind face. How it would please her to be here in Hawaii, this close to the ocean!

"You're too temperamental," her mother liked to accuse her. "Why can't your nature be as beautiful as your face?"

"It's *your* nature that's the problem," she'd fumed. "You see a face you recognize and are incapable of looking beyond it!"

A simple woman, Teru's only response had been to point out the obvious. "I don't need to know more than I can see," she'd responded defensively. "Isn't it enough to be treasured?"

It had never been enough. But perhaps the real mystery was only how such an ordinary woman could wind up with a daughter like Caroline. Teru, who was all softness, her doughy flesh reflecting the person inside, someone with a malleable, easy nature, capable of taking everything in. Teru loved everyone. Treated Caroline like Melissa like Nora, as if they were interchangeable, each one as good as the next. She loved sloppily, indiscriminately, so that in the end her love hardly mattered at all.

It was evening by the time they reached Hana and its seven sacred pools, the sun moments ago having vanished beneath the horizon so that what lay before them was an impenetrable mass of darkness. "I guess I'll have to be content just looking at you," Wade said, turning toward his wife for a kiss.

Caroline sighed, biting at his lip as she listened for the movement of the sea.

But fortunately the journey back passed quickly and Caroline woke early the next morning feeling ready to go. With seven sleepless nights finally behind her, she felt happy to pack up and settle in. As the plane that would carry them home ascended into the sky, she kicked her shoes off and rested her feet on the carry-on beneath the seat in front of her, feeling through the bulges the *omiyage* and dozen rolls of film, proof of a trip that might otherwise have felt unreal.

"Did I tell you Melissa called?" Wade said out of nowhere, the jet's motor hum, like a device used to induce sleep, dulling his voice.

"I don't think so." Caroline didn't move. She knew he was aware of his omission and couldn't think why he'd chosen this moment to tell her. But she assured herself that if the news were bad, he would have told her sooner. Making her senses alert to him, she'd play along, a smile curving one side of her mouth. "Did you?"

"It's about Nora," he said, finally, staring past her out the window. "No one seems to be able to find her."

"What?" Alarmed, she braced herself in the cramped seat, and in the minute it took to focus wished she were anywhere but pressed against Wade. Why had he found it necessary to withhold this information from her till now? As Wade made excuses, she imagined the panic of not knowing where Nora had gone, but perhaps he was right to assuage her because she couldn't quite feel the horror she had anticipated. Nora would probably have turned up by the time their plane landed. The consolation of being so far away was not to have to get caught up in the hysteria of the moment.

As the plane leveled off, her thoughts settled on the Tuesday afternoon not long ago that Nora had called her, asking to be picked up early for Bible study. Arriving at her friend's apartment, Caroline had been surprised to find boxes blocking the entryway.

"I'm moving," Nora had announced, smiling over a short stack of cardboard like a proud child.

"What?" Caroline stammered. "Why on earth would you move?"

"To be nearer to the church." Nora responded with an answer that sounded rehearsed.

There were many questions she might have asked, each underlying a genuine concern. But, rather than say anything, Caroline picked up a box, relieved that at least Nora didn't expect her to do the packing. With her wedding less than two weeks away, she had no energy to spare for details that were not part of her own planning. "How did you do all this by yourself?" she asked, her shoulders folding forward from the weight of the box.

"If it's too much trouble—" Nora began, having perhaps anticipated her friend's agitation.

"It's not that." Caroline sucked air into her lungs and held it there. "We'd better get going—I mean, assuming you still plan to make it to Bible study tonight."

Caroline had never thought of Nora as secretive, but a Nora she'd never seen had begun to emerge. The apartment Nora rented was a dive. One room, dark, in a section of the Valley no one would live in by choice. When Caroline asked how she'd found it, Nora mumbled something about getting a phone number from a flyer posted in the supermarket. It was all too strange. Then, on the way to church, Nora offered even more startling information: "Did I tell you I met someone recently?"

"What?" Caroline turned her attention briefly from the road to Nora, which she knew was what Nora wanted. Nora loved to make people turn, to take notice of her. And Caroline knew it was especially *her* attention she was after, her attention that made Nora feel desirable. Behind the steering wheel, she bit at the inside of her upper lip, holding back words. It was a habit of hers, to appear ready to say something, then to say nothing, and she used the silence to convey her disapproval. It wasn't a nice thing to do. But she'd been irritated by Nora's presumptuousness. Caroline could see her friend's eyelids shut, as if trying to locate something inside herself.

"Do you have a headache?" she asked, after several minutes of uncomfortable silence.

Opening her eyes to the heat and diffuse sunlight of late afternoon in the Valley, Nora refocused on Caroline, but did not speak.

"Are you going to tell me who you met, or not?"

"Just someone when I was out walking."

"You met someone on the street?"

Nora sat up a little straighter. "I met him when I was walking."

"A man?" Caroline gripped the steering wheel, irritated at the way her knuckles bulged white like teeth.

"Yes."

"Walking isn't safe, Nora," she'd said, trying to relax. "It's one thing to walk in Sherman Oaks, but walking in Pacoima can get you killed." The thought that her observation might have proved prophetic was too much to consider; easier to examine Nora's part in their conversation. "You don't need to worry," she'd said.

"You know, Melissa or your mother or I can drive you wherever you need to go. Just call us if you need to go out." Caroline reassured herself that she'd given the proper admonition. "So what's his name?" she asked when Nora had again fallen silent.

"Whose name?"

"The man you're seeing."

"Oh." Nora sounded surprised. "No name, not yet."

"What are you talking about, Nora?" she scolded, offended by the sudden realization that Nora had been making up a story just to annoy her. But with the admission of the lie, Nora appeared deflated, as if air had been forced from her lungs. "Have you lost weight?" Caroline asked. "You look thinner."

"Maybe," Nora said. "I haven't been very hungry lately."

"Well, you look good," Caroline lied, pausing to remember her point. "If you haven't been out walking, and you're not seeing someone, what have you been doing, Nora?"

"Just thinking," she said. "What else is there to do?"

"There's plenty else to do," Caroline said defensively. "Are you taking your pain medication? What are the doctors saying about your hands?"

"I don't need medication and there's nothing new," Nora said, listless as she gazed out the window.

"Things will get better." Caroline followed Nora's gaze to the church's steeple, which glowed white through a cluster of tall trees. "You just need to trust Jesus's plan for you. I'm glad tonight's Bible study. We'll pray for guidance."

"That's nice of you." Nora directed the air vent away from her face and used the back of her hand to brush hair out of her eyes. From the side, her face had lacked any discernable expression, but Caroline didn't like the ironic edge her friend's voice had taken on. "Are you okay?" she'd said, pulling the car up to the church entrance and parking. "What's happening to you?"

High over the Pacific, Caroline closed her eyes to nap, certain that she'd asked, but unable to remember Nora's response. When they'd gotten out of the air conditioned car, she'd felt stunned by the oppressive heaviness of the air, even with the sun nearly down. Maybe Nora had commented on the heat, or, more likely, she'd said nothing at all. But, in hindsight, the conversation seemed eerie and somehow significant. And the thought of where Nora had gone off to unnerved her.

Chapter 13

BACK IN THE Valley less than twenty-four hours, Caroline watched through the open window as Wade steered the car out of Sherman Oaks, which, early on a Sunday morning was deserted, the shops and restaurants showing no signs of life inside. When the heat left the Valley it had done so like a thief, causing Caroline to reason that if one had to mourn the disappearance of the best days, at least one could expect that the worst were gone, too.

As they headed east, her eye caught on the four PG&E smoke stacks sending white clouds into the otherwise clear sky. She wondered what kinds of toxic emissions were being spewed into the sky, and yet she was glad to see the towers; having been visible for as long as she could remember, their presence off in the distance provided a clear assurance that she'd arrived safely home. At the corner donut shop, she stood in line for coffee and two hot glazed, and she ate her breakfast while Wade pumped cheap gas at the busy station where he stopped every Sunday. She sipped her coffee and licked flakes of glaze from her fingertips amazed that life could be so much busier on this side of town: what were all these people doing on the street at this hour on a Sunday morning? The shops were still closed, only junkyards and barred up businesses tucked between rows of box houses—the life here too different from hers to imagine.

Having returned to the church Caroline had attended for as long as she could remember, she found it hard to believe that just one week had passed since her wedding. It seemed telling that the subject of the morning sermon was renewal: "This is the Day the Lord Hath Made," and Caroline took holy communion doubting the world would ever match God's good intentions for it. This wasn't the right attitude, she knew it, and when she walked from inside the dark chapel into the sunlight, she looked guiltily up at the sky and thanked God for giving them such a glorious late summer day to come back to. The slight breeze signaled the Santa Ana winds that gusted through the Valley in the fall, and she blinked a bit of dust from her eyes remembering how Melissa, Nora, and she had once stood on the church steps with their mothers, hanging on to pant legs and purse straps with their stomachs grumbling and eyes closed to keep the dust out, begging to get to have lunch together.

Caroline looked for Nora and Melissa in the crowd that gathered outside, wanting to be reminded of her lovely wedding, to be admired for her suntan, and perhaps even to think of pleasant things to say about Hawaii. But unable to get what she'd come for, she felt anxious to leave and perhaps try to sleep off the sadness that had been mounting. It was jet lag, she complained when Mrs. Yamamoto asked if she felt all right, and she steered Wade to the car wishing to be back home. "I don't think I can stay standing one minute longer," she said, using his arm to prop herself up. "I'm just too tired."

"I'm tired, too," he confessed. "But didn't you say we were going to the Yano's for *gochisoo*?"

"What?" she said, suddenly remembering the invitation to lunch, extended a week before the wedding. "I can't believe we agreed. Can't we tell Yukari we're just too tired."

"It's up to you," Wade sighed, knowing he wouldn't be the one to make the call.

In the car, Caroline's irritation settled on Wade, whose only concerns were football and lunch, both of which could be had whether they wound up at the Yano's or at home. She'd be so grateful if he'd make some excuse for them both. But she knew he wouldn't. And perhaps he misunderstood her wish, because he steered the car toward the Yano's house without speaking a word.

Walking up the flagstone steps that led to the Yano's front door, Caroline's ambivalence about the day manifested suddenly in renewed interest in the news Wade had mentioned on the plane. Why hadn't it occurred to her to worry when she'd not seen Nora at the morning service? But surely, she thought, grabbing at Wade's arm when her heel caught on a soft spot between steps, Nora had shown up. If there had been a problem, a genuine reason for concern, an announcement would have been made, wouldn't it? Because that was how problems were always handled. Rev. Nagatani would say what was the matter, like when Chieko Ono's father had a seizure, which led to the discovery of a tumor in an inoperable part of his brain, or even when high school students were waiting on acceptance letters from colleges. It was true that when Nora began having problems with her hands, the congregation had prayed for her. But then no announcements had been made when she'd lost her job or, when she moved to Pacoima, no public mention of how her personality had begun to change for the worse. That was because a problem had to be identifiable as an event in order for people to pray about it. A thirty-year-old woman losing touch for a few days didn't qualify. But Caroline knew that wasn't true. Everything about Nora's life qualified as problematic, and the reason people had stopped praying for her was that there was no way to talk about what was wrong without stirring up everyone's feelings of guilt. Yukari felt blamed, Caroline herself felt blamed, and so the best course of action had always been for each person to quietly endure the pain Nora's problems caused, and to try to do the right thing. But Caroline knew that wasn't right either. She hadn't done the right thing, and rather than not talking about Nora because of any guilt she felt, she'd simply forgotten.

"Well?" Wade said, and Caroline looked up to see her husband staring at her questioningly.

"Well, what?" Caroline said, stomping dirt from her heels as she waited on the doormat. "Maybe they're not home."

"I didn't ring the bell, did you?"

"No," Caroline said, turning to press the ringer that had been hidden behind her shoulder.

"Yujitaka woke up with a migraine," Yukari said to Wade, appearing confused when she greeted them. "That's why we weren't at church this morning. But his medication is probably working by now. He should be out soon."

Wade wandered off to the T.V. room to watch football and Caroline watched his back, angry at his sarcasm and his unwillingness to help her navigate her feelings about Nora, though his predictability at least made him easy to please. The house seemed unusually quiet, and dark. The doors to the back section, which usually allowed light to fill the long hallway, were shut, and she eagerly followed Yukari into the kitchen, knowing that that room would be less gloomy. The kitchen had always been the most comfortable room in the house, with the large window over the sink and everything in perfect order. But upon Caroline's inspection of it, Yukari didn't seem ready for lunch at all. Her hair, usually pinned up and sprayed, hung below her shoulders, and the stove where at least one pot always simmered was bare.

"Did Wade and I get our dates mixed up?" she asked, surprised that Yukari seemed unprepared for the visit. "Maybe today isn't a good day for lunch."

"No," Yukari raised a hand to her mouth. "To tell you the truth, I'd completely forgotten. I'm so sorry."

"It's okay, really," Caroline offered, sensing everything was not okay at all. Something was wrong, she was sure of it, but Yukari's lack of decorum scared her, and Caroline wouldn't bring up the subject of Nora without being invited to do so by her host. "We can do lunch another day."

She turned toward the T.V. room to collect Wade, but Yukari's brows came together, and Caroline could see that she'd compound Yukari's upset with embarrassment if they left. "I'm glad you're here," she said. "Please stay. I can fix something simple. And then Yujitaka and I can hear all about Hawaii."

"If you're sure," Caroline said, settling herself at the counter. Watching Yukari cook, she remembered coming to Nora's house as a child, the constant noise of Nora's brothers who were both so spoiled. And how Yukari would set up little projects in the kitchen for her and Nora. She'd always admired Yukari's economical gestures combined with her expediency and grace. Everything she did seemed deliberate. Not like Caroline's own mother, who often forgot what she was doing, and so had to return to the task later. She enjoyed Yukari's company, and watching the older woman prepare lunch, Caroline allowed herself to relax for the first time in days.

"You got such a nice tan. So beautiful," Yukari said, not even needing to look up to see Caroline's image, held perfectly in her imagination. "I've always wanted to visit Hawaii."

Picking her favorite *arare* out of the pretty ceramic bowl that Yukari set out, Caroline felt Nora's absence like something solid between them, and she wished that circumventing it didn't feel so impossible. Maybe if she'd asked her mother, or called Melissa and plied her for information when she and Wade got home, but she'd been exhausted. Assuring herself that if something were wrong she wouldn't be expected to know, having just arrived home from her honeymoon, she broke her silence. "Nora's coming, isn't she?" she said, deciding it best to feign ignorance, in order to see what information Yukari would offer up.

"I don't think so," Yukari said. "You haven't talked to her since you've been back, have you?"

"No," she said, the hopefulness in Yukari's voice letting her know that she should have considered her question more carefully. "Wade and I didn't get in until late last night."

"Yes, of course." Yukari turned to greet Yujitaka who'd come to the kitchen looking for beer. "Lunch won't be too much longer."

Lunch was simple, just the four of them sitting awkwardly around the large oval dining table, as if waiting for the others to show up. Watching Yukari ladle hot rice into each of their bowls, Caroline remembered the first time she had dinner at the Yano's. How Yukari had filled her bowl first, before Nora's and the boys', even before Yujitaka's. It was, Caroline knew, a signal of the deep connection she'd always felt with her. Only today, without Nora, the sentiments implied by Yukari's swift movements were hidden even to her.

"How's Eugene liking M.I.T.?" Wade asked politely

"I guess he's doing fine," Yujitaka grinned. "If he weren't, I'm sure we'd have heard from him."

"My father said he saw Ken when he went by Gross Opticals."

"Ken's a hard worker."

"Play any golf this week?"

"You should have invited Nora." Yujitaka finally looked up from his conversation with Wade to scold Yukari.

"I'm sure I told her to come," Yukari said. Then, turning to Caroline, "Did you notice how red the Chinese maples at church are turning?"

"No." Caroline frowned, trying to recall the trees that lined the front of the church.

"Already! And the chill in the air this morning. Fall's coming early this year. Pretty soon the *kaki* will be ripe." Caroline followed Yukari's gaze out the window to the old persimmon tree, its branches drooping from the weight of the globular orange fruit.

"Yujitaka, neh, we'll have to remove some fruit soon or the branches will break."

"Huh," Yujitaka sounded annoyed, but Caroline didn't know if it was from the request implied by Yukari's observation, or because he was still thinking about Nora. "The first fruit will be ready next week, then we can remove a branch or two."

Yukari scooped more rice into her husband's *chawan*. "I hope the tree can make it till then."

"Lunch is good," Wade said, even though he hadn't stopped to consider what he was eating.

"Yujitaka," Yukari placed her *ohashi* across the top of her bowl and drew a deep breath. "I went by Nora's apartment this morning to pick her up for church and she wasn't home."

Yujitaka grunted, as if digesting the information along with his rice. Then he turned to Caroline. "Off with one of her friends then?"

This time not even Wade dared to speak. Yujitaka could be so out of touch. For heaven's sake, Caroline wanted to shout at him, what friend have you seen Nora with lately? Or for that matter, ever. All her life he'd been so protective, practically dictating her every move. To be fair, she let him get the best of her. But it was only because she'd been so eager to please him. It was no wonder Nora had never had a boyfriend, let alone a life of her own, or that she'd moved to Pacoima. But sitting across from her, Yujitaka looked old and tired, and she knew it was unfair to blame him.

Caroline saw the sweat collecting above Yukari's upper lip, visible even in the half-light of the dining room. Who would build a dining room with no natural light source and how could anyone stand to live in such a depressingly dark house? The lamp over the table cast everyone in a yellow glow, and the way Yukari stared down at her jaundiced hands made Caroline want to cry. Nora was almost thirty years old, a grown woman. She should have known better than to worry her mother.

But of course it wasn't as simple as that, and fear never played out in life like it did in the imagination. Perhaps sensing this, Yujitaka attempted to comfort his wife. "She'll show up," he said. But just when everyone believed he might be right, everything would be fine, he interrupted the conversation again. "Maybe it's best to call around, just to be sure."

"You're right," Yukari said, pushing her chair back from the table. Without even finishing her lunch, she disappeared down the hall to Yujitaka's office, where even through the walls the worry in her voice was audible. Caroline moved the dishes from the table to the counter, washed them, and even put them away before Yukari returned. "I'm sorry about this afternoon, neh," she said.

"You don't need to apologize," Caroline assured her, trying her best to hide her anger over having waited for nearly an hour in Yukari's kitchen alone. "Did you call Melissa?"

"Yes," Yukari said. "She hasn't heard from her either."

"I'm sure she'll show up," Caroline said, still unwilling to acknowledge that something might have gone seriously wrong.

"You're like a daughter to me," Yukari said, placing her unsteady hand over Caroline's, and Caroline allowed her anger to dissipate. Behind them, an old china cabinet held European style stemware next to traditional Japanese teapots and ceramics, and Caroline remembered the gifts Yukari had given her each year to celebrate her birthdays: a miniature tea set, a porcelain doll, a gold bracelet and charm. The gifts would be signed from Nora, but then Yukari would say, "Nora doesn't like this kind of thing." Or she'd say, "Nora doesn't appreciate fine things the way you do." Each box came wrapped in a fancy gold or pink bow, and inside would be something incredibly beautiful and feminine. Treasures she'd one day hand down.

"You're like my daughter," she said. "So I'll tell you, I'm scared. I was going to go to church this morning, even without Yujitaka. Partly because I decided I'd pick Nora up, but she wasn't there."

"She could be anywhere, Yukari," Caroline said, looking sweetly into Yukari's eyes. "I wouldn't worry."

"No." Yukari's lip began to tremble. "She made me a key to her apartment, so I let myself in. I thought, I'll just sit and wait for her, but I'm pretty sure she hasn't been there in days. There was a musty odor; it was horrible, even out in the hall."

"Her bed was unmade. I looked through her closet. I even opened her shower door hoping maybe she'd be in there."

Yukari's desperation now apparent, Caroline didn't know why she hadn't felt it earlier. "Nora has an African violet. I bought it for her when she moved, and when I saw it shriveled up over the sink, I sat down and cried. The leaves were limp, like something you'd cook in a soup.

"But you want to know the thing that really worried me?"

"What?" Caroline hesitated, not sure she wanted to hear.

"The prescription bottle. I saw it on the counter under the windowsill. I got her those pain killers after she had her root canal, and when I saw the vial out, I thought to myself, that's a good sign: it means she'll be coming back soon, she can't have gone far. I thought I'd just wait there for her. But when I picked up the vial, it practically flew into my hand. I pried the white cap off and shook it. I even turned it over to make sure. But it was empty. That's when I panicked. I ran from her apartment, and I've been scared for her ever since."

Yukari's story didn't make sense. Caroline wanted to say that nothing Yukari said proved one way or another that Nora wasn't just fine. But she didn't know what to say. What she hadn't realized was how essential Nora's presence had always been to her feelings about Yukari. Nora's jealousy of her, always feeling slighted and overlooked, in a way that had made Caroline self-conscious, even resentful. Caroline couldn't imagine feeling close to Yukari without her.

Chapter 14

How nice of you to call, Melissa thought to say when she heard Yukari's voice. It wasn't often that she missed Sunday services and she would have attended that morning had she not overslept. She'd felt a little embarrassed to admit it, as if fatigue pointed somehow to a character flaw, but better to tell the truth than to say she was sick. "Melissa, I was just wondering—" she listened for a signal from Yukari to tell her exactly what to say, and in the silence she felt certain Yukari had something else in mind.

"Ano ne," she said, and Melissa noticed that her own hands were trembling.

"Have you seen Nora recently?"

She had no answer. The afternoon sun brought out stains in the beige carpet, and what she saw was the mess that her apartment had become. When she took a deep breath she could smell old pizza in the empty cardboard box, see milk rotting in the ring etched on an empty glass, and feel apple cores browning beneath her in the crack of the couch even though there wasn't a scrap of food in the apartment. Melissa sat on the floor, leaned back bent-kneed against the box spring, and closed her eyes. "Yukari," she said, trying to clear her head and convince herself of what she knew, "when I called you Friday you said Nora was staying with you."

"Yes. She was here until Wednesday, then I drove her back to her apartment."

"I told you when I talked to you that I hadn't seen Nora since Caroline's wedding." Melissa hadn't meant to raise her voice, but she had panicked. Yukari's tone seemed to implicate her when what she'd needed was to be exonerated. She realized her panic might be misinterpreted as anger, but then, suddenly, she was angry. To regain composure, she cleared her throat and spoke in a practiced tone she used to question clients. "So you haven't seen her since Wednesday?"

"No, Melissa I haven't. But I'm sure there's nothing to worry about, I just thought I'd check with you."

This was not the answer Melissa sought. If, at that moment, Yukari had indicated her concern or taken responsibility for her uncertainty, Melissa might have been able to respond rationally. But Yukari was shutting her out, denying there was a problem while offering false assurances, and the dangerous façade she'd constructed caught Melissa off guard. "We've had a terrible misunderstanding," she explained. Holding the receiver to her ear with an elbow, her chin resting on her kneecap in a contorted pose, she felt close to tears. "I thought Nora was with you. I thought you told me when I called you that she was staying with you."

"She *was* staying with me, Melissa."

Melissa tried to tell herself that Yukari was only passing along information, but she could feel Yukari's exasperation narrowing in on her, making her believe that whatever had gone wrong for Nora had happened because of her. "She had a root canal, and she stayed overnight here until Wednesday."

"That was four days ago." Having made the mistake of raising her voice in anger, Melissa attempted to modulate her tone.

"So you haven't heard from her?"

"No."

And there it was, the lie. True, she had no idea where Nora had gone off to, but Melissa *had* heard from Nora. She'd felt sick about the phone call and, as a result, rather than call Yukari immediately she'd told no one. Now, in her persistence, Yukari threatened to expose her.

"Mel?" Once Melissa had accepted the charges, Nora used the nickname Mark had taken from her, an endearment she herself hadn't used in years. "Did I wake you?"

"No," She'd tried her best to hear, but Nora's voice had been muffled and contrary to what she told Nora, she *had* been sleeping. It sounded like she said, "Did I make you—?" followed by something else she couldn't hear. "Where are you anyway?"

"Let's see," Nora began. There was a brief pause filled with a honking horn and two male voices arguing. "I'm outside the 7/11 on Glen Oaks."

"Okay," Melissa said, having no idea where that was. "What are you doing there, Nora?"

"I don't really know," she said.

Her thoughts turned to the conversation she'd had the night before with Mark, how he'd warned her about Nora and her problems and her need to extricate herself from them, or at the very least to exercise caution in her commitment to help. "Are you okay?" she asked, trying not to sound tentative.

"No," she said. "Yes, I am. I'm fine."

"I'm worried about you," she confessed. "I've been worried about you."

The interference on the line increased, and in it Melissa thought she heard *I'm sorry.*

It took a minute to respond, lost as she was in her thoughts about what to do. She'd wanted to invite Nora to come stay, she knew she should have, and she'd hesitated. Perhaps that was not what Nora needed anyway. Perhaps Nora had called for something else entirely. Melissa heard the bass beat of music nearby and human noise from a life that seemed so distant she couldn't place it, and she thought again of Mark and of his convincing argument that offering Nora a place with her would solve nothing, and before she could respond the line went dead.

"Melissa?" Yukari's voice cut in. "So you haven't seen her or heard from her at all?"

"No." Melissa's response was subdued, almost inaudible, the deep and conflicting emotions of moments before having left her enervated. She should have done something about Nora's phone call, but in the ensuing days she'd told no one, and so she'd been forced to lie and had created for herself a conundrum. Now, rather than correct her misstep, she sat back, entrenched in her belief that what had gone wrong had happened to her, not to Nora. Nora's life had been headed off track for a year, maybe even longer, and nothing anyone could do would save her. It didn't matter that Melissa had reached this conclusion erroneously, and too late. To offset her enormous shame, she vowed to make everything right. "You should call the police," she heard herself say. "Or I could come over and call for you."

"No, that's not necessary. I'll keep calling around. I'll be sure to let you know when I find her, okay?"

You're not going to find her, Melissa wanted to say, but said instead, "You're not going to find her on your own." Melissa hedged her bet that Yukari hadn't the slightest idea what needed to be done. "You need some help," she said, conveying her urgency to Yukari by letting her know that she would be the one to take charge.

"We don't know that anything's wrong."

"Look," Melissa said, calmly walking to the cabinet where she kept the East Valley phone book and jotting down phone numbers for the Foothill Police Station and Serra Memorial Hospital. "I talk with the police almost daily as part of my job. It's something I do and I'm good at it. So let me handle it."

"Well, if you think so."

"I think so," she told her. "I'm going to hang up now. And I'll give the police your number and call you back myself if I need more information."

But what Melissa didn't anticipate was how awkward it would feel to be calling the police. Since Yukari had mentioned Nora's name, Melissa's hands had not stopped trembling. She gripped the receiver with both hands, noting when the desk sergeant picked up how accusatory his voice sounded. "Foothill Precinct. How may I direct your call?"

"I'm trying to find a friend who seems to be missing."

A child turning herself in for a mistake, she wanted forgiveness, but the voice on the other end was brusque, refusing even to acknowledge her upset. "Hold the line while I transfer you."

She had to fight the urge to hang up. "I'd like to report a missing person."

"When is the last time you or anyone you know saw this person?" The perfunctory tone, so comforting when she dealt with the police at work, now unnerved her. The fact that her inquiry could not have been the desk sergeant's first call of the evening seemed to verify that what people said about lotteries was right—the odds didn't change: the chances of finding Nora were random. But if she believed instead that God had already determined the outcome, then why did every word, every second that passed, matter?

"She missed Tuesday Night Bible Study," Melissa blurted out, realizing it had been a while since she'd heard the question. Melissa reassured herself that even though Tuesday Night Bible Study meant everything to Nora, her nervous pause meant nothing to the person gathering information. "No one's heard from her for at least four or five days," she corrected herself, attempting to respond not as a friend, but in her professional capacity as Yukari's envoy.

"Name of the person you'd like to report?"

"Nora Yano." She took a breath. Police hate crying. She did, too. She counted the eight days since Caroline's wedding, knowing that things had been spinning out of control for much longer than that.

"Spell it."

"N-o-r-a Y-a-n-o."

"Your name?"

"Melissa Hori. H-o-r-i."

"Okay, Melissa, what is your relationship to Nora?"

"She's a friend."

"That's right. How were you two friends getting along the last time you saw her?"

"Fine." The word *friend* prompted a defensive response that made it difficult for Melissa to see which details were relevant, which not.

Had the officer understood her lack of contact with Nora to be a contributing factor? Was her need to justify her actions irrational? But, more importantly, what had caused Melissa to know before anyone could possibly have known that something had happened to Nora, something *bad*?

"Does Nora have any medical problems?"

"Yes. She's disabled. She can't use her hands." Poor Nora. Talking about her hands with a stranger seemed the ultimate betrayal.

"Does she drink?"

"What?"

"Does she consume alcoholic beverages?"

"No, she doesn't drink at all."

"Is there anywhere you know that she might have gone? For instance, with other friends or relatives."

"No, she doesn't have a lot of friends, and I was just on the phone with her mother who's as worried as I am."

"What kind of behavior was she exhibiting the last time you saw her?"

"Last Sunday we were both at our best friend's wedding, and she seemed happy." Reflecting back to the wedding, Melissa knew she'd offered yet another half-truth. Nora had worn a dress identical to hers, but the picture in Melissa's head refused to come out whole. Instead she saw Nora's head, oblong and distorted like in a funhouse mirror, her black hair flying in all directions, then the bridesmaid's dress bloody and clinging to her body like fur on a wet cat. "What I mean," she cleared her throat, "is that there is certainly no connection between last week's event and Nora's disappearance."

"Would you consider her to be suicidal?"

Even though Melissa knew that the officer was simply trying to piece together a story based on facts that were common to other scenarios in which someone had disappeared, his question still irked her. Nora, a Christian, believed as Melissa did, in redemption through Jesus' love; no, suicide was out of the question. "She's not suicidal."

"Okay. It would be helpful if you could come down to the station and give us a physical description. A recent picture would be even better. And we'll need you to make a statement and sign the report."

"Okay," she said, suddenly curious what the wedding photos might reveal.

"When we get everything we need, we'll log the information into the NCIC, a national computer base that keeps track of missing persons. We'll also send teletypes to local stations to be on the look out. You can stop by any time. Do you know where we're located? You might also try calling hospitals in the area."

It was just as well that the line at the Yano house remained busy all evening because Melissa couldn't bear to hear Yukari's voice again. But that didn't stop her from trying to get through. In between she called Mark, who wasn't home at ten or eleven or even midnight. She pictured him at the library studying, oblivious to her need to tell him how this was her fault. She'd known all along that something bad was happening to Nora.

When she finally reached Mark, she'd remind him of that, and of how she should never have listened to him.

Book Three

Chapter 15

NORA LET THE first one dissolve on her tongue while still standing on Joaquin's stoop, pausing to consider even before she'd left that she wouldn't be returning. The taste leaking into her gums made her mouth weep and her cheeks pucker like when she used to eat Lemon Heads, except it was better. Or maybe just bitter. Joaquin didn't want her. His *get out of here* stung the inside of her head. She wondered if he'd ever feel sorry he sent her away. Perhaps one day he'd see that what she did was for him. For the life together that now they would never have: there would be no life together. Not ever.

The thought invited a second pill, which she crushed with her tongue as she walked away. The saliva flooding her mouth bathed it like a seashell being brought to life by the tide's pulsing and noting the heaviness in her throat she swallowed on the count of three. It wasn't a bad thing not to be going back. Not bad to be outside again where the air felt ten maybe even twenty degrees cooler than it had been in the house. She had two things to be thankful for: her feet could still take her wherever she wanted to go; and while it might have been pleasant to have someone to talk to, it was also fine to be alone.

Alone again, and the street lamps hung down from tall silver poles lighting the way into morning. Her throat felt dry. After the second pill the wetness was gone. Her eyes took her to the sides of houses where spigots attached to hoses conjured up her brothers, how they would squirt each other, catching the drops of hose water that always burned and then ran cold. Water coming up from the ground. It wasn't right to be so thirsty and so close to water but none for her to drink.

At the end of the block the church spire shone over the roofs of houses and on top of it the cross like bones. Walking, she wondered why she'd never before noticed how like a skeleton it looked. Or why she should approach such a fleshless symbol of dehydration expecting water. Or be surprised to see a chain and padlock hanging from the gate. Closed. Come back again Sunday. What day was it about to be? No matter. There was too much dryness—the plants inside the gate dying, the cross parched.

The metal bars screeched for lack of moisture when she leaned against them. Closing her eyes, she reached into her shorts pocket for two more pills, which she placed under her tongue, summoning water. With her gaze turned inward, she could feel the neck of her womb closing around the egg. She, who had always had a problem with symbols, felt the everlasting love rotting inside her, and the locked gate leading to the church cool against her forehead. Instead of prayer, she stuck out her tongue and imagined cupping her hands under a faucet of running water, letting the wetness spill between her fingers and rush down her throat. Opening her eyes, she could see beyond the locked gate the field between the outbuilding and the sanctuary still lit by the moon, which was setting behind the mountain range with brilliant clarity. Or perhaps the sun lit the area where Melissa, Caroline, and she once played as children, pointing to the overgrown weeds where they made scissors out of wheat grass, until the day Eugene lit a fire with a magnifying glass and burned the field. At the far end the broken swing set cast its crooked silhouette against the morning sky, dizzying her to think how many memories could be held by a place. Quickly, and without thinking, she recited the Lord's Prayer and John 3:16 and her favorite Psalm then looked out at the landscape once again. She wished she knew the words that might please God and that there were some way to test the effect of her words, yet aside from the scripture she had memorized, she had never known how to talk to God. Still, she hoped that God would be pleased by her tribute to him because she could not remain standing in front of the church much longer. It would not be right to die at its locked gate.

As she walked along the mesh fence, sticking her fingers through the holes, she imagined the barbed wire that held her parents in as children. Not just hers, but Melissa's and Caroline's, too. Life went wrong for them all when they were carted off to internment camps and detained for reasons no one could comprehend. The grandparents spoke to no one of their crime; what was there to say? They had lost too much. Along with their homes and the rewards of a life's work, other intangible possessions, subjects of a conversation no one dared speak. Fear and uncertainty weighted their faces. They had been set apart because of their likeness to the enemy, a presence they were told might have resided within them, and because of this, they regarded each other with suspicion. Locked in and locked out, they became the same. Yukari would emerge with a new identity. Superior, more exacting, cruel. Nora remembered standing beside her mother, listening to the wartime story of the elephant that starved to death at the Hiroshima zoo. Stuck on the poor elephant's suffering, she had not understood the story at all. The powerful effect of the protests, the threats made against the zookeepers who didn't have the conviction necessary to carry out murder, or the right weapon.

The grey elephant, great symbol of indifference, with its big heart and still bigger stomach required more food than anyone had to give it. Dressed in a red checker-board dress, she could feel the broad bow stretched taut around her midriff, her mother's eyes regarding her with disgust, her own wandering to the mirror where she saw reflected back an upended picnic table. Horrified, she could see that the elephant's starvation was emblematic, yet less significant somehow than all the suffering combined, and mitigated by a story that had been kept alive for fifty years in the imagination.

Once she had reached the mountains, the sharp ridges and gaping fissures so prominent from a distance smoothed into open expanses where along the foothills strawberry plants hugged the ground and tomatoes climbed vines planted in long, even furrows.

She looked from the ground to the clouds that had amassed into a haze so that the sky seemed to hang low above the warming earth, severing the four red and white striped smoke stacks that jutted out of the murky southern sky. The smoke stacks displayed the entrance to heaven like flags at an amusement park, then became her parents and two brothers begging for attention, disseminating steam from their angry tops. Forever disturbed by the sight of them, she felt comforted as she turned away.

Alone in his bed, Joaquin would be waking with a headache, cursing her as he walked through his house to assess the damage, seeing her in the broken plates and overturned furniture, the table still set for two. She had no compunction, yet knew enough to see that he should not be made to suffer. In the distance, a neon blue light revealed a telephone. It wasn't hard to know who to call. Reliable Melissa could be made to see that Joaquin had committed no crime. Melissa, who could be counted on for her need to make reparations.

"Nora?" she'd sounded relieved.

"Hi Mel."

"I've been worried about you."

In the gaps between words, strange shapes appeared through the haze. A wrecking shop displayed headlights in the front window along with a chrome fender and side door painted metallic red. Nora stared at the loose parts troubled by the disasters that had caused them to wind up looking like new. Even closer, a row of gas pumps clustered together like fat old men. The smell of coffee drifted out from the 7/11, though she no longer felt her thirst.

"I'm worried about you," Melissa said again. "Are you okay?"

Nora hesitated, having never been able to bear her friend's sadness. "Yes."

"I'm sorry," she said, unable to find the right words to tell Melissa about Joaquin.

"I can't hear you," Melissa said, speaking, it had seemed, to herself. "Are you still there?"

Talking didn't need to be so difficult or painful, but perhaps Melissa no longer remembered. Nora wondered what Melissa would say if she'd called back and reminded Melissa that she'd been the one who'd shown her how to kiss. The night before her date with Doug Nakatsu, when Nora's intense anxiety led her to believe she'd pass out, Melissa had assured her that there was nothing to kissing. "Shut your eyes," she said, "it's easier that way." Holding Nora's face gently in her palms, she'd brushed against her lips, then run a tongue playfully over her teeth. "See," Melissa had said, quickly blurring a moment unlike any Nora had experienced.

A year earlier, anticipating their maturity with great enthusiasm and worried that their breasts weren't developing on schedule, they'd lifted their shirts for weekly checks, examining the possibilities contained in the bathroom mirror. "Your *chi chis* are the biggest," Caroline had said of her.

"It's because she's cold," Melissa had said, in defense of her own competitive spirit. "I can make mine do that," she'd said, running a finger over her nipples to make them stand up.

"That feels good," Caroline said, licking a finger and making hers stand up, too.

Too young to be embarrassed by their sexuality, they'd shared a bond, clutching hands tightly together and pinching eyes shut against the tears that leaked down their cheeks when Melissa's dog had bolted down the road and been hit by a car. Nora had spoken for the group, praying to Jesus to please take the pup into heaven, though she and Melissa had later agreed that the puppy, who'd died instantly, could hardly be expected to have a better life up there. Had Melissa forgotten even that?

What was left to remind them of what they'd been to each other? Assessing what remained of her life, Nora remembered their initials CI, MH, and NY penciled inside the Ikeda's broom closet, a hidden reminder of what they'd once been. States adjoined at the borders; land no longer occupied.

The year they turned thirteen their parents had sent them away to Camp Evergreen where the girls from Gardena went to repent. They saw the girls like angels enveloped in beautiful halos of light and wanted the mystery for themselves. All three of them, at vespers.

That day they couldn't wait for the blazing heat to lift so that they could gather around the fire circle in the dark and with bowed heads ask Jesus to enter their hearts. They could smell the ash in their hair. They were ready.

Nora smelled the soot in her hair as she walked on, shaking the remaining pills into her palm, counting them before tilting her chin back to swallow one last time.

"Do you feel different since we've been back?" she asked Caroline the weekend they returned from camp, when she and Melissa were staying overnight.

"Different like how?" Her best friends exchanged furtive glances, their eyes already beginning to roll.

"I don't know," she shrugged.

Caroline began to laugh, but Melissa quieted her. "What do you mean, Nora?"

"I mean because we're special now."

"We're not special," Caroline laughed. "You think too much, but that doesn't make you special." She turned onto her flat stomach, and tilting her chin to her chest, gulped from her can of Tab.

"We *are* special," Melissa argued. She lifted her soda to her lips in much the same way that Caroline had, but she wasn't smiling.

"I think you two have both forgotten something," Caroline scolded. "Isn't the point of accepting Christ so that you won't have to suffer? Jesus suffered so that we won't have to. So let's just try to be thankful for that, okay?"

Nora had not said what she'd been thinking, that Jesus's suffering could not have been greater than hers. Her friends lacked humor and would certainly have considered such a remark blasphemous. They would not have understood how she could equate her suffering to Jesus's. "Are you going to get baptized?" she asked. *Baptized*. The word, once articulated, sent a chill up her spine.

"Melissa's getting baptized," Caroline said.

Nora's interest piqued, she sat up, accidentally flinging an elbow into Melissa's side, causing the can of Tab next to her to release its contents on the floor, thereby ending the conversation.

Now, the four smoke stacks reemerged out of a brightening sky to mock her, and a name escaped through parted lips: Nora. Followed by another name: Elinore. Drawn to the part of her own name contained in such a strange assemblage of sounds, she repeated it. Elinore. A face followed the name, though one she barely recognized. How ironic that a stranger should be the keeper of her intimate secrets. The night had been clear and beautiful, lit by thousands of shimmering lights that shone up from the ground like stars. Having long feared being forgotten, would she be remembered by that small moment?

The crisp air had cleared, fooling her into believing she could see to the coast as her thoughts dissipated on the ocean's surface, a dingy with nothing to do but float. Matters of a temporal nature had ceased to be a concern. Time could no longer interfere with her thoughts. Her mother, once the great keeper of the clock, had lifted the crystal face so that its springs and fittings lay exposed, painful memories tossed aside, springs bouncing into the air before mysteriously disappearing. Squinting into the glare of light so bright it stung her eyes, she stumbled over an upturned tree root and slid down a low hill on her knees. She felt it inside her, then. Like the crush of dead leaves crackling in her ears, wet heat penetrating her body, the egg cracking open, its yolk oozing from between her legs along with its profane stench. Upon standing, she could feel the thick mustard yellow drain with the blood from her gashed knees. Not far off a car radio announced that the afternoon temperature would rise above ninety, the warm breeze already piercing her flesh. She would need to stop walking soon; just beyond a ravine, the stand of olives trees where leaves fluttered defiantly against the heat lent in their dappled shadows a resting place.

Book Four

Chapter 16

IT FELT SIMILAR to watching a boat's wake—tiny crests that danced like flames on the water's surface, the mind playing tricks. Love that had begun in the imagination now took shape in its failure. Naoko would grow up not knowing her father, she missed him at night and her wailing rattled the thin wall that separated the bedrooms, forcing Elinore to perform her magic; the baby's cry a snake charmer's flute causing the mother to rise into her skin, to coil around what was perfect and invisible. Elinore knew her mother anticipated the drama—the tears that signaled her exodus into the garden. Hideko had always hated sorrow and, too, its consolations. It might have been different had she been the mother, Elinore's tears once propelling her into action. But her daughter's failings were not something she could face.

The way Elinore saw it, Naoko's difficulty adjusting was to be expected, and controllable to the extent that energy and patience allowed. But Hideko's retreat felt unbearable. Once quiet had been restored to the house, Elinore stood over the kitchen sink watching through the window for signs of movement in the garden, imagining bamboo reeds jutting into the sky to be her mother until one night, staring into the fading light, her eye lingered on the sego palm in the ornamental clay pot. It sat near the pond in the spot it had always occupied, but its sharp fronds seemed spindly and thirsty-looking. Opening like a yawn, they pointed at something just beyond reach, which was how she located him. Jun stood beside the palm, the slight stoop and bald patch in the back giving him away, and Elinore bolted from her spot at the kitchen window, leaving the sliding glass door open behind her as she ran the length of the stone path to greet her father. "What a nice surprise!" she shrieked over her mother, who held the garden hose, running water over a droopy stand of ferns near the fish pond. "When did you get in?"

"Your mother didn't tell you?" He looked at Hideko, perplexed as the water that leapt off the stone path caught his pant legs. They'd always been such a secretive couple, her parents, existing for months with lives that seemed not to conjoin at all, then managing somehow to fall back into each other's company.

"I told you, Elinore," Hideko scolded.

"Mom!" Elinore glared at her mother, not knowing what she was talking about, then wondering if the perceived omission wasn't just a simple miscommunication.

"I've been looking forward to seeing you for days." Jun cocked his head sideways, sending a secret signal to Hideko before facing Elinore with a grin that beamed his pleasure.

"Let me turn this off," Hideko said, and Elinore watched the hose water spilling over a planter as her mother disappeared behind the house.

"Why didn't you come inside and meet Naoko?" Elinore asked, hurt that her father who had taken so long to get home hadn't yet made it inside to see his granddaughter.

"I'll wait until morning," he said, "when she wakes up."

Elinore knew that her father and she had never seen eye to eye when reading events and their importance. Called to the site of disasters, he spent his time trying to restore order to the lives of victims. But in his professional capacity, she'd seen him assign deep psychological impact to simple things, and dismiss momentous events as trivial. Where her daughter was concerned, she felt sure he had his reasons for waiting to meet her, but whatever they were they weren't good enough, and her happiness over seeing him turned quickly to resentment.

Hideko reapproached, stumbling over a tangle of hose and breaking the silence between them. "You should feel honored, Jun," she said, "Elinore hasn't come out to the garden at all since she got home."

"Really?" he said. "Your mother has been working so hard to keep it watered. I'm surprised to hear you haven't been helping her!"

Could it be true? Elinore retraced the path that had led to her conclusions. What if her mother's leaving the house each evening was not a way to stand in judgment of her; what if Hideko had merely needed to tend to her plants? She wondered whether her mother's observation had been intended as a reprimand, or whether she'd simply meant to dispel the tension mounting between Elinore and Jun. She knew she could go on wondering about a lot of things, but looking out at the pond brought a peace beyond what she imagined she might feel. The garden, though nothing like she remembered it, really was beautiful—a perfect retreat. In the silence of nightfall it seemed especially so, the sun leaving behind warmth that rose up from the earth to meet the cooling air overhead precisely at the spot where they'd gathered. Why had she waited so long to join her mother? Making the connection that had eluded her, she shuddered: the landscape was linked inextricably to her Grandma Rio, the last of a generation, a part of Elinore's heart gone with her. The garden had belonged first to Rio's parents. Long before the war, it was ten acres purchased by her great grandfather on which the Shimizus grew and sold roses. They worked hard and made a passable living, surrounding themselves and their daughter with the roses, which kept their home always colorful and sweet smelling. The acres of roses that encircled a pond of fancy carp, imported from Japan, which her great-grandfather designed for his wife. When the war came and they were told to pack up, they had been forced to leave it all behind.

It wasn't the same after that. The roses gone. The house vandalized beyond recognition. The pond dried to a fraction of its size. But swimming in the stagnant, green water, a pair of carp had survived, magically, without food. Elinore's grandfather saw them as a flash of gold through the murky surface of the pond. He saw them like a mirage and rebuilt his family's livelihood around them, first moving the fish to a smaller, safer pond, then using the soil fertilized by the fish that had died to start over.

Elinore's eyes settled on her mother, so still that she appeared in the approaching darkness as a sizable rock, unthwarted by all of history.

"The garden *is* beautiful," she said, having let go of her anger, wanting to acknowledge instead how well Hideko had taken care of the garden.

"You should have seen it when your grandmother died."

Hideko flatly rejected the praise her daughter hadn't quite figured out how to offer, but Elinore was no longer thinking about the garden, remembering instead a comment her mother had made on the phone when she'd called to say that Rio's kidneys had failed. She said, Don't come. I'll call if you need to come home. "You told me not to come."

"Even when you were a child, I could never force you to do anything."

Hideko spoke so softly that Elinore wondered if she'd misheard. "You told me not to fly back," she said.

Deciding it best to ignore her mother's reverie, Elinore turned her attention to the funeral service held without her. Had Hideko deliberately misled her when she'd said not to come, and then expected her to attend the funeral despite her urging not to? In hindsight, she couldn't forgive her own stupidity, or underestimate the sway of her mother's command. She'd lived away from home for years, even given birth to a child, but she'd never gone so far that she couldn't be yanked back instantly on her invisible lead.

"It was a beautiful service," Jun mused. "Your mother made sure of that. She picked roses and used them to line the casket."

"Not just roses," Hideko said. "Every flower in the garden. After the funeral there was nothing left."

Elinore imagined the garden, bereft of its brilliance, a palpable image of absence and all that she'd missed. Hideko destroyed the garden, a tribute to her mother-in-law with whom she'd lived for thirty years. Yet in doing so, she'd inadvertently created room for new growth, and as a result the garden thrived, transformed once more.

Things change, just not how anyone would expect. When Elinore thought of home as she had constantly, it was her grandmother's face she saw alongside, often overlapping, her mother's, and having not responded when she heard of the cancer, having not witnessed Rio's death or returned for the funeral, she'd expected her grandmother to be waiting, there to greet her upon her arrival home.

"So tell me," Jun smiled, taking control of the moment. "Why didn't you bring Naoko home sooner?"

"I couldn't believe I was pregnant. And once Naoko was born it seemed too late."

"I'm sorry," she said.

She'd spent months avoiding the question her father had just asked, and yet she'd been so preoccupied by her mother's story of the funeral that the response and its attendant apology had slipped out effortlessly. Why had Hideko waited so long to tell her about the flowers? Perhaps for the same reason that, upon returning, she had not asked. Hideko was the holder of information, storing it away like a cache of food to be used in an emergency. Through an unspoken imperative, she'd instructed her daughter not to examine what had been left out, but to concentrate instead on what was pleasing. Elinore sensed her participation in a dangerous gamble, this game of omissions that claimed the comfort of ignorance as its prize. Wasn't it, in fact, the same bluff she'd played on her parents in keeping Naoko's birth a secret? She'd followed her parents' example, and they therefore had nothing to complain about. Smiling enigmatically back at Jun, Elinore felt the guilt of the past year leaving her, satisfied instead with her newfound knowledge.

But there was Naoko to consider, and, realizing this, her contentment lasted only a moment. Elinore had clung to her grandmother's promise made in the stories she'd told, about her passage into the Valley and about her love of the land she had worked. Recalling how nice it had been to grow up with her grandparents, to be surrounded throughout her childhood by them and their stories, Elinore had returned home with her daughter vowing to do her best to replicate her childhood for Naoko. But what if Naoko asked Jun and Hideko for memories of when they were young the way that she had asked her grandmother? What stories would they tell their granddaughter? How the land and the people who occupied it succumbed to a hiatus of memory? Standing beside her father, whose face read skepticism, she admitted to herself that she hadn't kept track of life well enough to know what the story should be.

"Well, we're just happy you're here," Hideko said. In what was clearly an attempt to placate her daughter, Hideko offered up a reward, but having spent weeks with her mother in her father's absence, Elinore heard only how quickly one person became two.

"Thank you." She wanted to express gratitude to her mother for letting the subject of Naoko's birth drop, but she knew if she didn't limit her words, Hideko would fall back into anger.

"How did you decide to name the baby Naoko?"

Jun, on the other hand, would not let the subject of his grand-daughter drop, and in that instant Elinore knew what he wanted: his question an indirect way of asking about her relationship with Naoko's father.

"Her father chose the name," she said, smiling.

"It's a good name, I think," Hideko said. "And hopefully she'll live up to it."

"What do you mean?" Elinore asked, bracing herself.

"You don't know what Naoko means?"

"I thought it was a nice name." She wanted to say yes, of course, she knew, but she wanted to be told. She refused to humiliate herself by admitting she didn't know. "I liked the sound of it. I didn't know it had to mean anything."

Jun shrugged. "All Japanese names mean something."

"Yes," she said, "I know."

"The baby's father is Japanese, then?" Jun inquired openly.

"Saburo."

"Saburo." He wrinkled his brow. "You lived with him in Santa Fe."

"Yes."

Now it was her mother who spoke up. "But you were never married?"

Elinore shrugged, misinterpreting her mother's comment as moralistic. "You're hanging out with the church women too much."

"No," Hideko laughed. "I'm just trying to get the story straight. My friendship with Teru has nothing to do with needing salvation."

"Saburo was born in Japan," she offered, happy if she'd misunderstood her mother's inference. "His family left when he was five and moved to London. He was educated there, and then came to the states on his own."

"So he's not American born Japanese."

"No."

"I see," Hideko said confidently. "Now, I see."

"What?" Elinore demanded, wondering what Hideko could possibly glean from such a cryptic conversation.

"You can't trust Japanese men from Japan," Jun said, responding for his wife. "They're arrogant. They haven't been persecuted like the Nikkei men here have. They don't know about suffering."

"Oh?" Elinore dismissed her father's remarks. "How about the bombing of Hiroshima?"

"You interrupted me before I could finish," Jun said, punctuating his thought with a long pause before he deigned to continue. "On a personal level, Nikkei men have been emasculated."

"And for your information," he stated abruptly, turning back to the house, "Naoko is the one who fixes things. Makes them right again."

Disregarding her urge to follow him inside, Elinore remained with her mother by the pond, needing to reconstruct what, exactly, had passed between her and her father. But a moment later Jun reappeared with Naoko in his arms.

"Is this your mommy?" Jun asked the baby, who squeezed tears out of her eyes with her fists.

"Mama," Naoko cried. Seeing her mother, she held out her arms.

"Baby." Elinore took her daughter from him, not knowing whether to feel grateful or upset. "Were you crying for mama? I'm sorry I didn't hear you. That's your grandfather," she whispered into Naoko's hair, damp with tears. "Did you know that's your Grandpa Jun?"

Shouldn't he have known better than to pick up a toddler he'd never met? Even if he *was* the grandfather—especially since he was the grandfather. Breathing in the moist, warm heat of Naoko's scalp, Elinore whispered into her daughter's ear, "That's right, that's your Grandpa Jun," trying to turn fear into excitement, or at least to convey why she would have allowed a stranger to take her from her bed.

Naoko buried her face in her mother's neck. Trading one incident for another, perhaps she'd picked up on the adults' tension, and Elinore prayed her daughter wouldn't ask questions. Let Elinore stand quietly with Hideko and Jun on the flat black stones, her fingers forming a blanket around bare feet. Hideko pulled a heel of bread from her shorts pocket and gave it to Jun who, reading her silent instructions, handed a piece over to Naoko along with a handful of grain pellets. Within seconds the sleeping fish rose to the surface, splashing and making suckling sounds like infants.

"Say," Jun said, too caught up in his own thoughts to pay attention to Naoko. "Did your mom tell you what happened to the koi?"

"During the war?" Elinore asked. "The story Grandma Rio used to tell?"

"No. After you left, they began to disappear."

"These koi?"

Jun waved his hand over the surface of the water causing the feeding fish to scatter in flecks of red, gold, and white. "We noticed one night that grandpa's prize fish was missing and we figured he'd jumped, like they sometimes do. When we couldn't find him we just assumed a cat or raccoon had carried him off."

"How sad," she said, generations of koi having inhabited the pond for as far back as she could remember.

"About a month passed and we noticed a few more missing and your grandma said she'd seen a raccoon in the yard. They're smart, you know, so we baited a cage.

"Then one night we came home and as I was coming out to feed them, I saw a kid dart away with a fishing pole in one hand and a bucket hanging from the other."

Elinore imagined with horror some teenage boy taking a koi home and trying to keep it alive in a bathtub. How it would suffer, the scales turning grey, the fish floating unevenly on its side, the gills gaping, the eye losing its shine.

"I think the children were eating them," Hideko interjected. "That's the only thing I can think."

"These fish are all new," Jun boasted.

Elinore examined the new fish, along with the guard railing that had been installed around the pond complete with a placard posted by an alarm system manufacturer—all the changes she hadn't noticed until they were pointed out to her. What other signs had she ignored or misread?

"More," Naoko said, holding a hand out to her grandmother, wanting to see the colorful fish feed again.

"It's time for them to sleep now," Hideko said sternly. "We'll give them more food in the morning,"

"Grandma's right," Elinore said, turning away from the pond. "It's way past your bedtime."

Chapter 17

JUN'S HOMECOMING CHANGED everything. Hideko appeared transformed, attending to her husband's every need in favor of Elinore and even Naoko. Elinore wanted to tell her mother to stop, or at least to slow down. But so much activity wasn't all bad. Having had the opportunity to observe her mother's solitude, Elinore decided that Hideko appreciated her husband's presence as much as she did his absences, for unlike her daughter she could listen to Jun's ramblings endlessly, without a loss of attention or a hint of sarcasm.

As a child, Elinore had often wondered why her father took so much pleasure from talking about other people's misfortune. But now, as an adult seated on the periphery of her parents' conversations, she could see that her assessment of him, in addition to being unfair, had been inaccurate. It wasn't that he enjoyed other people's misery, only that he seemed most alive when talking about his work. She wished he could regard Naoko with the same care he relegated to the abstract; ask him for his impression of his granddaughter and he became tongue-tied, a serene smile ensnarling his words, but about his latest stint in Philadelphia he couldn't say enough.

With the baby still asleep, Elinore marveled at the father whose overblown public presence had embarrassed her as a child, and she attempted to understand his theory regarding the effects of wartime internment and the resultant success of his newest lecture series.

"Japanese-Americans who were interned have in common that their lives are shaped in fundamental ways by personal tragedy," he said.

Elinore wondered what Jun would say about the misfortune that had shaped *her* life. "Do you think your theory lends itself to other situations as well?" she asked hesitantly.

"Of course," he waved her question away. "People need to tell their stories." And for the next half hour he obsessed through breakfast and the appearance of his granddaughter over the *issei* he'd met in Philadelphia and what they'd experienced during the internment. "To think that people have held their stories inside for years. It's so important to be able to *talk* about these things. What a shame that they've had to wait for so long. To have the opportunity only now—at the end of their lives."

Was his interest in others merely a projection of his own personal desires, his own needs mistaken for the needs of others? How else could it be that Jun could talk tirelessly about story, but never manage to tell one of his own. "What about your life?" she asked politely, as much for Naoko's benefit as her own, as she cracked an eggshell and scooped the warm yolk up for her daughter. "Tell us a story."

Naoko waved her hands in excitement, a gesture Elinore recognized as her father's. "More," she said.

"Just a minute, baby," she said, shifting her attention from her hungry daughter to her relentless father.

"The hardships that these people have gone through is unimaginable to people who have never had their rights taken away from them."

Jun's body language made him appear animated, and yet there was a flatness to his expression and in it Elinore recalled what Saburo had once said about the internment camps. *I would think that an experience like that would have an effect, even generations later.* In her father's presence Elinore felt as superfluous as a specter, and yet she knew he meant by his talk to judge her, and not wanting to be judged, she found her thoughts leaving the table, returning to Santa Fe and the call that came while she was still asleep. There had been an accident, and the halting tone of Marina's voice issued warning: Saburo had been badly burned. He was at St. Vincent Hospital, in the emergency room. He would be brought by helicopter to the Burn Center at the University Hospital in Albuquerque. If she wanted to see him before they transported him, she needed to get to St. Vincent immediately.

The only thought Elinore had when she dropped the receiver into its holder was *Go.* Get Naoko changed and dressed. No, don't dress Naoko. Just go. Tears trickled down her face. So many that she stumbled through the wide space between her bed and the baby's dresser, and before doing another thing sat on the floor with her head in her hands and cried. Perhaps she knew then what she could not have known; perhaps she was just getting it over with as best she could. When she stopped trembling and could stand, she grabbed Naoko in her thick infant blanket and ran from the house in slippers.

"Hayashi," she yelled, pushing through the heavy blue doors of the emergency room. "Saburo Hayashi, I'm his wife." It was a lie, but a considered one. She'd worried as she navigated the still-dark streets that hospital policy might prevent her from seeing Saburo and had decided then that she should say she was his wife. "I'm his wife," she'd practiced, it being the first time she'd ever referred to herself as a wife, the word always before seeming derogatory, like an insult you'd hurl at someone you didn't like well enough to name.

Her father had always referred to her mother as his wife. And she'd watched her mother, a capable woman, structure her daily life around both his demanding presence and painful absences. She'd vowed long ago never to become a wife, but hearing the authority in her voice she wondered if she hadn't missed something. As the doors parted and hospital personnel rushed to her side, she knew they'd remember her later as the wife. They didn't care about her slippers or the bundle in her arms that was Naoko. She would be in their minds the wife, poor wife. Clearly, that single word carried with it certain advantages she hadn't considered, and as she made her way down the wide, sterile corridor, she vowed to follow through. In her rush to imagine, she pictured an elaborate ceremony—white dress, rose petals, seven-tiered cake—if Saburo recovered.

"It's his wife," a nurse's aide spoke quietly to the blue smocked group gathered around the gurney. The room seemed too small for all the activity. The life-size machines and doctors moving rapidly, grunting in code to each other, blocked Saburo from her view. She wanted to push them aside, demand to see Saburo at once, but perhaps it was just as well that they stood huddled around him administering to him, protecting her momentarily from the sight of him, for those seconds signaled the gravity of what she would see.

Saburo, naked and oozing, his clothes cut away, his eyes encrusted with ointments and turned inward, his body spasming in shock. With her free arm, she reached out for him and his skin peeled away leaving behind a shiny pink circle where she'd touched the back of his hand. "Saburo, I'm sorry." She cried, and turned to curse the doctors who'd let her touch him, and demanded to know what had happened. But the doctors continued on with their work as if she didn't exist, and she stood back paralyzed, breathing in the red-black of iodine and other antiseptics, and an even stronger smell hovering in the room. Amidst the chaos, she rocked Naoko and hummed a song Saburo had made up: *Green beans smell like fresh alfalfa, burnt beans smell like burnt toast.* Saburo. Burnt beans. Why at times of crisis was the mind unstoppable? It was the worst sight anyone could ever see. But it was not Saburo, she told herself even as she looked on and could not stop looking. The skin stripped back from the body, the body laid bare to air and infection in ways no one should ever be. Black specks of roasted bean and ash stuck in the wounds needed to be removed before the skin could be disinfected, and the doctors worked assiduously with tweezers and gauze, oblivious to anything but cleaning out the wounds as best they could. Standing at the gurney with Naoko in one arm and Saburo inches away but wholly beyond reach, she thought: It doesn't get any worse than this.

But of course it did. Life changed so that what had come before the accident seemed like a life as distant as someone else's, and she glimpsed the past reticently. Like a burglar pulling up across the street from a house he had robbed just a few days before, she felt the irresistible pull of memory.

"So what is your opinion?" Across the table, Jun folded the morning paper and stared across at her in light so bright it stung her eyes.

"My opinion of what?" she asked.

"All this affects you, too, you know. Studies are beginning to show the impact internment has had on subsequent generations. Did you know that the children of internees present problems that are many times analogous to, if not worse than, those experienced by the survivors?"

"I didn't know that," Elinore said, flummoxed.

"You seem a little down," he said, fingering his coffee mug with a worried look.

"I'm tired," she said, having found little relief in her musings. "It happens when Naoko doesn't sleep well."

"You certainly have your hands full," he said, reaching across the table to pat Naoko on the head. "But isn't it more than that?"

"Your mother has been worried about you," he whispered, as if Hideko, who stood at the sink loading the breakfast plates into the dishwasher, should not hear.

"There's a lot to think about." Elinore smiled, wondering what Saburo would say to her father. If he were seated between them, would he engage Jun? Probe for information of a personal nature, or add insight based on his observations? Or would he find her father a hopeless bore? She refused to take her father's concern seriously, but neither could she dismiss him. There was, after all, the selfish question to consider, of how his theories might lend themselves to *her* life. When he was training as a social worker, were there special topics classes, like Disaster, Race, & Ethnicity? Disaster in the Family? Disastrous Love? Or did they eschew the particulars, claiming that tragedy should bring people together regardless of race and circumstance. She let herself remember, and responded out of an intuitive sense that if she wanted him to stop talking she must give him something. "Really," she assured him, "I'm just fine."

Chapter 18

ASAKO HORI LIKED Mark because he had good manners, he was training to become a lawyer, and he was handsome: for a man, that was more than enough. Melissa was still a baby when her father left. Not even walking yet, she was young enough to ride on Asako's hip. She remembered the way her mother stood in the doorway to the bedroom she shared with her father, watching him take his socks and underwear out of their shared dresser and fold them into his bag. The luggage became huge, like a living thing, swallowing everything whole so that he had to keep feeding it until all his drawers had been emptied and nothing remained behind. She'd wondered if it wasn't a trick, aimed at entertaining her. Or, she considered with horror, perhaps she would be next. Clinging to her mother, she buried herself in Asako's protective arms, not knowing whether extreme vigilance would save or end her life.

Asako spoke not a single word to her husband or to Melissa, that day or for a long time to come. What Melissa remembered was silence, and what her mother liked to say: that she talked late. While Melissa sat listening in silence, the doctor asked her mother if it was that she couldn't understand what Melissa said, or if Melissa said nothing at all. Thirty years later, Melissa wondered what would be the difference.

She told her mother what she remembered. But Asako believed she didn't remember accurately, that she'd been too young to understand. What Melissa knew was that her mother never really loved

Bob, her second husband, that she married him so that Melissa would have a father. She did it for Melissa's sake, so that her daughter would talk to her. But, knowing how Asako didn't like to hear things, she had never shared her observations with her mother. Nor did Melissa find it ironic that Asako enjoyed their nightly telephone conversations precisely because Melissa kept to herself what her mother wouldn't want to hear, concentrating her talk instead on everything good she could remember about her day. Full disclosure was the term Asako had coined to refer to their phone conversations. They often laughed about it, yet on the day Melissa had been questioned by the police investigators, anticipation of her mother's call left her stomach in a knot.

"No," she told Asako, having decided what to say beforehand. "I told you there's nothing wrong."

The tension Asako heard in Melissa's voice was the result of guilt that had been reawakened by the day's events, doubts she would not reveal to anyone. Still, the unspoken policy of not telling her mother things Asako didn't want to hear worked only when Melissa was able to hide her negative emotions, and in light of what appeared to be Asako's genuine concern, she was forced to weigh one type of upset against another. "Okay, I went down to the Foothill today," she explained. "The detectives called me in to answer questions about Nora."

"Why would they want to talk to you?" Asako asked naively.

"I'm sure they're talking to everyone," Melissa said in as casual a tone as possible.

"Of course," Asako said, "that's right. It's only that your mention of Nora took me by surprise."

The interview had taken Melissa by surprise as well. Not the request, which she'd known would come, but the fact that she couldn't keep the events straight in her own mind, so that when the detective had asked whether she were connected in any way with Nora's disappearance, she had trouble at first parceling out her response. "I was her friend, so of course I take responsibility for whatever bad might have happened to her," she'd said.

"Were you involved in any way, directly or indirectly, with her disappearance?"

"No."

"Do you have any information that could help us find your friend?"

"No," she said regretfully. "I wish I did."

The lie she'd told Yukari had been magnified a hundred times in the days following Nora's disappearance. With the same trust she placed in God, she knew that the truth about her error of judgment would eventually come out, and so the threat of her lie bringing shame on her mother felt inevitable. Until then, she had no choice but to suffer silently and do what she could to make the truth more palatable. "I think we need to do more to find Nora," she heard herself say.

"You don't think the police are doing a good job?"

"I don't know whether they are or not. But I'm going to make a flyer and talk to people on my own." In the same way that she'd always known the break-up of her mother's marriage to her father was her fault; it might not have been possible, but she wanted to make things right again, and for the first time in years she found herself thinking about her father.

After he left it was understood that he would never be her father again. He would become someone else's father instead. Sometimes she thought she saw him with his new family, though most likely any man with black hair and a child her age would have been him. Once she actually did see him in the deli section of the Alpha Beta where her mother used to grocery shop. He was holding a cellophane packet of turkey breast and a salami stick, pretending not to see them as Asako pushed by with Melissa in the wire front basket of the shopping cart. That he looked away was okay, and not as scary as years later at Tower Records, where she'd gone with her parents to spend her birthday money. That day, unlike the first time in the Alpha Beta, he acknowledged her mother. "Hello, Asako. Bob," he nodded. Then he turned and it seemed to Melissa that he looked right through her, as if she didn't exist. As if her presence were so inconsequential that even hello would have been too much to offer. She remembered the exact spot where he stood, with the glass storefront behind him showing the parking lot where all the car fenders glared silver against a big orange sky. Time stopped on that moment. Even though it was a busy point in the day, the cars didn't move and the sun hung in the sky refusing to set. It was a static image, a flash photograph that fueled her, like drawing upon a reserve that never went empty.

The eve of her eleventh birthday, all the albums she'd dreamed of owning turned out to be slightly more than the dollar value of the gift certificate. Not wanting to make Asako feel bad, she lingered in the aisles, as if to say the choices were endless, thumbing more than once through the popular titles under 'Rock.' She wondered as he turned and made his way empty-handed back out to the parking lot whether he remembered that she'd been born exactly eleven years earlier. Picking up a discounted copy of James Taylor's Greatest Hits, she followed her mother to the register thinking how even if she never listened to James Taylor she'd gotten the present she needed, just not in the form she'd expected. She would never allow herself to go invisible, and she'd spent the ensuing years making sure of it, until Nora became invisible. Maybe she tricked herself into accepting Nora's disappearance because she recognized that Nora had been disappearing for years, except what Melissa hadn't figured was that Nora's disappearing meant *she'd* been left behind. And what she felt seeing her father in the record shop was like her mother and grandparents in the camps—the fences that would let them go no further, with nothing left behind them and nothing in the future. She knew she'd become a social worker because what went wrong for her was forever, and it shouldn't have to be that way.

And so when her father had called to ask for a favor, she'd been sucked in immediately by the sad story he'd told about Elinore.

Chapter 19

MELISSA DROVE FROM her eleven o'clock appointment to lunch feeling the same giddy kind of dread she associated with dates in high school. Until her late twenties, Jun had not contacted her at all. Then it had happened by chance that the two were asked to present together on a domestic violence panel. She'd worried beforehand: What was she supposed to say to the estranged father who'd never attempted to contact her, a man she had no inclination to know? Perhaps out of allegiance to Bob, whom she called Dad, there wasn't a place for Jun in her life, and, to her relief, their brief meeting had produced nothing more than the cordial type of exchange you'd expect between strangers. They were professionals, social workers collaborating around a cause. Because of that, Melissa had not stammered when Jun called her at her office. Neither had she been terribly surprised to hear from him.

Jun's need to disguise his request under professional auspices had been understandable to Melissa. After living away from home for a number of years, Elinore had returned with a child; she was depressed, and in the throes of a spiritual crisis. The root of the problem, which of course he hadn't mentioned, was that he hadn't been a good father. Melissa felt lucky to have escaped the man's parenting; she also knew she didn't owe him anything. The task as she saw it was to help Elinore.

But as she neared the restaurant, the compensatory glow having worn off, she realized that the questioning and not knowing brought about by the prospect of a lunch with Elinore had exhausted her. Arriving ten minutes late, she tried to exude confidence as she made her way through the crowded restaurant. The scenario had already been ordered in her head, but upon discovering that Elinore wasn't there, she hid herself in a booth and wept. It was all too much. Nora's disappearance coupled with the reemergence of her father after a life lived without him. It wasn't Elinore's fault, and Melissa tried to convince herself of that by fixing her attention on the six-year-old she'd just left. The girl had been a miserable child, difficult to be around, destined for unhappiness later in life—Melissa's job being to help work it out. But maybe Elinore had left before she arrived or, worse, maybe she'd never intended to show up. Melissa had resigned herself to eating alone when the familiar-looking woman slid into the booth across from her. "I'm so sorry I'm late," she said, asking for forgiveness without looking up.

"That's okay," Melissa said, suddenly understanding the annoyance Mark felt when he saw her after she'd kept him waiting.

When Elinore did look up, her gaze was disarming. She was more beautiful than Melissa remembered from the wedding, and Melissa set to work comparing their features, finding Elinore's to be more symmetrical, somehow, more gentle and pleasing. Less than a year separated them, but Elinore looked younger, causing Melissa to feel protective, and jealous, too.

"Is there something wrong?" Elinore asked, made nervous under Melissa's scrutiny.

"No," Melissa lied. "Why would you say that?"

"Are you angry that I'm late?" Elinore asked. "It's the first time I've left Naoko in quite a while, and I didn't realize how much time it would take to drive over the hill. Traffic has gotten much worse since when I grew up in the Valley. I really am sorry, but I didn't want to leave with the baby crying. I woke up early this morning and got everything ready hours before I was supposed to leave. But you know how you always think you have more time than you actually do?"

Elinore's attention shifted to a server carrying a pitcher of iced water and menus across the room giving Melissa time to decide on a different approach. "I'm glad you could meet me for lunch," she said.

"My father says he's worked with you on a couple of panels," Elinore said, the mention of Jun as her father making it impossible for Melissa to establish rapport. "You must be very busy."

It was obvious from Elinore's words that Jun had not been entirely honest. But why should she have been surprised? He wasn't trustworthy. Wasn't to her mother thirty years ago, any more than he'd been with her. It occurred to her to tell Elinore just that. But maybe it didn't matter that Jun was the connection between them, in the same way it had never mattered that Jun was the thing missing between her and her mother. Smiling at the woman across from her, she wrapped both hands around her teacup and stared down at the churning leaves. "It's a busy week, but I'm glad to have lunch with you," she heard herself say, proud of the lack of ambiguity in her tone. "Lunch is nice. It breaks up the day."

"Are you engaged?" Elinore asked, holding her hand out to admire Melissa's diamond.

"Sort of," she smiled.

"Oh?" Elinore smiled back. "Is it someone from around here?"

"I've known Mark since I was thirteen."

"He's the man you came to your friend's wedding with?"

"Caroline's wedding?"

"Yes."

"That's right, I'd forgotten you were there," Melissa lied. "Are you friends with Wade?"

"No," Elinore said rather curtly. "I went with my mother because my father was out of town."

"Oh." Melissa frowned, feeling Elinore's unease coupled with her own confusion, trying to sort through the gaps in what each was supposed to know about the other.

"He's handsome," Elinore said.

"Mark?" It was strange to hear Mark's looks complimented by a stranger. But was she a stranger?

"Tall, thick brown hair, strong nose?"

"I guess with those features he wasn't too hard to pick out of the crowd," Melissa said, finally finding a way to enter into conversation.

"No," Elinore laughed.

"But enough about Mark," Melissa said, her mind returning to Jun's phone call and his plea that she help Elinore through a spiritual crisis. "Tell me about your life. Jun says you've traveled a lot."

"Not really. I went to school on the east coast, lived in Santa Fe. My daughter was born there. Now I'm back in the Valley." Elinore shrugged, the bones around her eyes hardening into a frown. "There's nothing really interesting to tell."

"How old is your daughter?"

"Two," Elinore said, holding up two fingers like a child.

"What does your husband do?"

"Oh," and for the second time Elinore's eyes met hers, "Saburo and I were never married."

"It must be difficult for you," Melissa said, thinking of all the single mothers she'd heard talk, and recognizing at that moment how outside the church Elinore lived.

"The difficulty isn't that I wasn't married," Elinore laughed.

"I didn't mean to imply—"

"But you judged me just now, didn't you. Even though you know nothing at all about me."

"I don't let my beliefs interfere with how others live their lives," Melissa said defensively.

"I'm sorry," Elinore said. "Of course you don't. Maybe I'm just touchy about Saburo."

"Your baby's father. Is he still in Santa Fe?" Melissa asked, sensing that if Jun had been the least bit honest with her about Elinore being troubled, she'd be getting close to where the problems lay.

"You want to hear about Saburo?"

"Sure," Melissa said, feeling like she'd gotten herself caught in a spider's web, "I'd love to hear."

"I met Saburo when I was a graduate student in New York," Elinore began. "He was passing through on his way home from Indonesia, and I moved to Santa Fe to be with him."

"Sounds exotic," Melissa said.

"Really?" Elinore looked puzzled. "Actually, I was passing through New Mexico on my way back here. My grandmother was ill. But then she died and so I didn't really have a reason to return. I knew immediately that I wanted to be with Saburo."

Melissa nodded, wondering if the grandmother was her grandmother, too.

"You know how sometimes you just know?"

Melissa wondered if she'd ever *known* anything. Having met Mark as a teenager and dated him for almost three years, she longed—even sensed that she owed it to Mark—to have that moment of knowing with him: the feeling of being able to trust him, to feel confident that she'd made the right choice. She often fantasized about what it might be like to desire him intensely, perhaps that moment had come along earlier in their relationship, and passed, and she'd failed to recognize it. She wanted to ask Elinore how anyone could know anything for sure. But maybe it was her fear rather than a question she needed to articulate. She'd take command of the situation, tell the woman sitting across from her what she knew: that outside of her mother, she'd never really known—never trusted—anyone.

"We were perfectly happy," Elinore continued blithely, setting her *ohashi* down and smiling at some point over Melissa's shoulder. "Then the coffee roaster at the store Saburo owns exploded. It was a freak accident, and he was badly burned. Over fifty percent of his body, covered in second degree burns."

A silence descended out of nowhere, and Melissa rode it, self-conscious suddenly to be surrounded by so many strangers. Perhaps she'd misjudged Elinore. "So he died?" she said, hoping to end that portion of the conversation. If her conclusion, however hasty, were correct, if Saburo were dead, then she could be generous in her feelings, beneficent—she could *like* Elinore.

"What?" Elinore looked puzzled, as if suddenly made aware that she wasn't alone.

"Is that why you came here?"

"Everyone thought he'd die, but he didn't."

"They had to cut deep into his body to remove the burned sections, then they took patches of his skin from areas that hadn't been burned and laid them over the fresh wounds. But there wasn't enough skin to go around. When they ran out, they used cadaver skin to fill in. Yards of it."

Pushing her bowl away, Melissa wished Elinore would change the subject.

"It was amazing," Elinore said, suddenly looking up, "what they did to try to save him. I might have found it sickening, but for months I felt nothing at all. I never asked what his chances for survival were, and I didn't allow myself to be comforted.

"There were countless surgeries, and skin grafts. They began almost immediately. Then one day, while I was waiting for him to come to after a long surgery, I realized that he'd survive. I don't know how I knew, but it was as if the thing I had most feared had come to pass. I remember that moment precisely. There was a large window above his bed, and through it I could see that evening was approaching and a light snow had begun to fall. I knew it would be hours before he'd be fully conscious, that I should leave and head back up north before it began really snowing and the highway got shut down. I knew I needed to get back for Naoko. But for some reason I couldn't leave. I stayed with him for as long as I possibly could."

"How horrible," Melissa said, unable to think what she was being called upon to offer. "I'm so sorry."

"Yes," Elinore said dismissively. "I thought that was the worst of it, but it was really just the beginning. Once it became clear that he'd recover, the hospital stay seemed to end fairly rapidly. I'd spent most of my waking hours sitting with him, or driving to see him, or driving back home, or taking care of Naoko in his absence, and at night while she was asleep, I did what I could to get the house ready.

"He was horribly scarred," Elinore said, staring off into space.

"I can imagine," Melissa said, now genuinely sympathetic.
"It was awful."

"But you say he made it," Melissa said. "That's incredible."

"Yes," Elinore agreed, dubiously. "Everyone said that."

"You wouldn't believe the pains I took to get the house ready. I had it in my head that if he could just not see himself, he'd recover quicker. So I took down all the mirrors. I began with the one over the bathroom sink, unscrewing it and carrying it out to the storage shed. Then I dealt with our dresser, which I wound up selling because its backsplash mirror couldn't be unhinged. Those were the two big items; the others were less trouble. But Saburo became depressed. Despite his doctor's saying that he could expect a full recovery, his energy didn't return.

"Fortunately, there was Marina, a clerk who had a lot of experience running the store. He relied on her to cover for him on the days he didn't make it out of bed. While Marina ran the store, he'd eat lunch in front of the T.V. and sit around all afternoon in his underwear.

"I'm sorry to be telling you these details," she said, suddenly seeming embarrassed. "It's just that he became unrecognizable. He'd always been hardworking, and so capable. But he let himself go. He lost his confidence."

For a moment Melissa wondered whether Elinore's telling was guided by a need to be heard, or a need for *Melissa* to hear. But perhaps it didn't matter. The strange story was like watching a film you could get lost in; while it evoked unpleasant feelings, she rather liked the experience of it. How else to understand the sensation that had overtaken her—a tingling in her chest, her limbs so light that her body felt suspended, as if she were both part of the conversation and hovering above it. Realizing that the woman had stopped talking to stare at her, she spoke: "Go on."

"One night when Naoko was asleep in our bed, he came up behind me while I was finishing up the dinner dishes. He put his arms around my waist and kissed my ear in a way he'd never done before.

"Maybe you don't want to hear this," she stopped.

Made self-conscious by Elinore's warning, Melissa wasn't sure what she wanted, and she comforted herself with the assurance that the explicitness of Elinore's telling wasn't so different from stories she heard all the time. "Please," she said, the word escaping through pursed lips. "You can tell me."

"Okay," Elinore grimaced. "You really are good to listen. I don't know why I'm telling you about Saburo. Do you think it's because you're a social worker?"

Was she being made fun of? The thought occurred to her that perhaps Elinore was distorting the real story; she could even be making parts up. But why do such a thing? She tried to recall Jun's exact words. Elinore was in trouble, and could she please help out? I know you're a good person, he'd said. I've been thinking of you for a while now, and I wouldn't ask you if I didn't think it was important. For a fleeting moment, Melissa allowed herself to believe that the story Elinore was telling could be important to them both.

"I wanted to pull away," Elinore was saying, her features grinding, then setting into a frown. "But I had my hands in a basin of dirty dishwater. So I closed my eyes, and I just let him touch me. I tried to imagine Saburo, and to remember. It was autumn, and the cool breeze that blew in from the window smelled like smoke from fireplaces and the sagebrush outside. It reminded me of when I'd just arrived in Santa Fe, how Saburo used to light fires for us every night. But I could feel my fingertips wrinkling under the dishwater, and instead of love, I felt his gut brushing my back, and he must have felt it too, because he sucked in his breath and walked away.

"I was brushing my teeth for bed that night when the same thing happened. He wrapped his arms around my waist, and this time I turned around to face him. The room was dark except for a sliver of moonlight through the curtains because the bathroom led into our bedroom and Naoko woke with the slightest bit of light, but I could see the outline of my daughter. I'd been astonished how seamlessly she'd adjusted to her father's disfigurement. She liked to stroke the new skin. To her it was soft—never grotesque. I admired her courage, which I didn't share. I like to think of myself as a kind person, but I seem to lack qualities she possesses inherently.

"The next day Saburo told me he'd been thinking about something important. He said it in the morning, bending over me while I was asleep, and I woke up seeing that he was already dressed and shaved. 'Let's talk when I get back,' he said.

"Of course I couldn't go back to sleep after that. I had no idea what Saburo would want to talk to me about. So I fixed a pot of coffee while I waited for Naoko to wake up, and that's when it occurred to me that Saburo was going to ask me to marry him. And I knew I couldn't do it.

"I had never discussed my feelings about Saburo's condition with anyone," Elinore confided. "Santa Fe is such a small town, and everyone either knew firsthand or had heard about the accident. I don't think anyone wanted to see Saburo, or me, as anything less than courageous.

"But after the accident I began to feel that I didn't really know him at all. I worried that I'd find myself in a marriage destined for troubles from the start, and yet I had Naoko to think of."

"Yes," Melissa interrupted, able to relate completely to Naoko and her needs. "Of course."

Elinore smiled politely, but Melissa read annoyance in the woman's response to her, which, having listened patiently, she couldn't help but resent.

"Saburo breezed into the house later that morning smelling so strongly of coffee that there was no need to ask where he'd been. It scared me that I could guess what variety of beans he'd been roasting. I was thinking I should congratulate him on getting back to Fresh Roast when he cut me off from my words.

"He said that he'd asked Marina to help me with Naoko. She'd come on weekends or any time that was convenient for me.

"But even after his declaration, which was maybe only intended to free up my time, it didn't occur to me that Saburo had spoken the thing he'd mentioned wanting to discuss with me. I had been working nonstop since the accident, running myself down without a thought to how such a frenzied state might end. So I thanked him, and suggested that I could work the counter in Marina's absence. That way he wouldn't have to train another employee.

"Marina showed up the next morning bright and early. Her new job was to help me, and my new job became her old one.

"Pretty strange, huh?"

Melissa's thoughts had begun to wander. No longer listening to Elinore, she had cast Nora in the role of Saburo. The poor man's disfigurement had come out of nowhere and had changed everything for him. Under those circumstances, wasn't Elinore obligated to care for him? Perhaps she was Elinore, wanting to do the right thing for Nora, but failing. Or maybe she was Marina, the worker who took care of everything but was, when push came to shove, expendable, being outside the family unit. Yes, she was definitely the outsider.

"I didn't see our reversal of roles as ironic," Elinore's voice cut in. "For the first few weeks, I was happy to be out of the house busying myself with the running of Fresh Roast. Saburo had personally managed the shop for a dozen years and had tons of loyal customers, and I took pride in the fact that despite his extended absence the business continued to thrive.

"But when the workday ended, I didn't feel like going home. It'd be getting dark, and I knew that Saburo and Naoko would be waiting for me, but I couldn't make myself return. So I'd walk to the Plaza instead. By that time, most of the shops and galleries were closed, but that didn't seem to matter. I was content to stand outside, looking in through the windows. I'd stop at each storefront and just stare until one night it occurred to me that I wasn't actually seeing anything, that it wasn't the objects inside the windows I was looking at, but my own reflection I wanted to see posted back at me.

"I don't know why it should have come as such an epiphany, but it did. By my own doing, I was living in a house without mirrors, but Saburo had never needed me to protect him from the image of himself. I needed to protect myself from the image of him, and yet I saw him everywhere.

"It's so confusing how the mind works. I guess I thought I could purge myself of memory, but I realized that night that I was failing Saburo, and fooling myself. I couldn't remember the last time I'd really looked at Saburo, but I saw him in windowpanes, and in the chrome bathroom fixtures, even in doorknobs. I'd constructed a funhouse of sorts, where the darkened and distorted images of Saburo were more frightening than Saburo himself.

"That night I pulled my car into the driveway and sat back in the dark with the lights off and engine running, still refusing to go inside. I don't know what I was looking for exactly, but I watched through the front window of our house, and it was as if I were catching a dramatic performance in mid-act. I saw Saburo enter from the back room and take a seat on the couch, then Naoko whirling circles in Marina's arms. The window was waist high, so I couldn't see the floor beneath them, and in my mind's eye Naoko seemed to float, held by music I couldn't hear or feel, and behind them all the colors and warmth of the house that no longer felt like home.

"That's when I decided I had to leave. When I told Saburo, it was as if he already knew. I know he loves Naoko as much as I do, but he took our leaving in stride. He's a proud person, I'd always known that about him.

"And I guess I am, too."

"Yes," Melissa said. "I can see that." She'd been wrong to confuse Marina's life with her own. She'd come to the same painful conclusions that Elinore had come to, only about herself and Nora. Like Elinore, she was the proud one, and also the one who'd needed to save herself, perhaps at the expense of someone she loved deeply. "I'm sorry," Melissa interjected. "I was just thinking about my friend, Nora, the one you befriended at Caroline's wedding."

"What?" Elinore quipped, her eyes darting to a corner of the room as if the connection could be found there.

"Nora and I were the bridesmaids," Melissa said, calling her back. "At our friend Caroline's wedding."

"I remember," Elinore said.

"Well, then, you should know she's gone missing." Melissa knew it wasn't right to drop important information in this way, but she didn't care. Elinore had taken up time with her story, though she hadn't seemed to regard Melissa's time. In the end Melissa felt violated; now it was her turn.

"Nora's missing?" Elinore reached for her glass of water, but held it just shy of her lips.

"Yes." Scooting to the edge of her chair, Melissa lifted her tea cup, letting the steam open her pores as she inhaled. "She's been gone for over six weeks now," she said. Was it the hanging of posters and talking to people, mostly strangers, who might know anything about the events that led up to her friend's disappearance that had left her feeling overwhelmed?

"What happened?" Elinore asked, biting at her lower lip, still playing coy.

Melissa felt sure that Elinore knew more than she was letting on. By now everyone knew something about Nora's disappearance, and she wondered what, exactly, Elinore was hiding. "I only brought it up because I was going to ask if you knew anything. It's what I've been asking everyone."

"How soon after your friend's wedding did she disappear?" Elinore asked.

"It was almost two months ago, the week after Caroline's wedding. But I still can't believe it's happening."

"Really?" Elinore asked, casting herself in further suspicion. "I'm not surprised, somehow. I mean, she seemed like such a sad person."

"Nora?" Melissa had a hunch that Elinore knew something had been wrong, but suddenly she didn't want to hear what Elinore might have to say. For all she knew, the woman was a compulsive liar and had been making things up all along.

"Do they think it was a suicide?"

"Of course not," Melissa said sharply.

"Why not?"

"She had no reason to want to kill herself. She's Christian."

"So what?" Elinore said, as if to prove her ignorance with a cheeky remark. "When's the last time anyone heard from her?"

"She stayed with her parents because she had to have oral surgery, then her mother dropped her at her apartment and no one's heard from her since." Melissa debated herself for a minute before answering, then hated Elinore for how the story wound up sounding. But perhaps it wasn't Elinore's fault that an agonizing week could be condensed into one utterly meaningless sentence. "Actually," Melissa said, her tone becoming matter-of-fact, "that's not exactly true.

"She called me," she said, shocking herself with her admission. "I think it was the same night she disappeared. She said she was outside a convenience store. I haven't told anyone."

"Why not?" Elinore asked, leaning forward.

Melissa looked down, unable to face being judged. But when she looked up again, Elinore's face read only curiosity. "I don't know," she said. "I lied to her mother and then to the police. I didn't think it was important. I felt guilty. She called me, and I should have done something to help her."

"What did she say?" Elinore asked. "I mean when she called."

"I couldn't really hear her."

"Nothing?"

"Not really." Melissa pulled a flyer out of her handbag and wrote her home phone number on the bottom. "Please call me if you happen to hear anything, or if you think of anything that might be useful."

"What's this?" Elinore asked, holding up the sheet of paper.

"Nora," Melissa said, as if it were obvious. "Don't you recognize her?"

"Honestly?" Elinore said, "no."

"I thought it was a nice photo of her." Melissa shrugged, eyeing the empty two-top tables on either side, noting that the lunch crowd had cleared out. "I've got to go."

Melissa watched as Elinore stuffed discarded napkins into water glasses, picked up pairs of *ohashi* and empty wrappers, and stacked the bowls into one neat pile. "I've made you late, haven't I," she apologized, for although she seemed to recognize the problem, there was nothing she could do to remedy it.

"I have an appointment downtown," Melissa said, checking her watch.

"I enjoyed having lunch with you," Elinore said, but her face did not read enjoyment.

"Can I meet Naoko?" Believing that the woman might cry, Melissa spoke before thinking. "Maybe the three of us could take a trip to the zoo."

"Yes, fine," Elinore said. "That would be nice."

A big mistake, Melissa thought as she rushed out of the restaurant. But steering her car through the parking lot, she couldn't help checking for Elinore in the rear view mirror. How odd it felt to know so much about someone else's life—and yet to be strangers. Speeding away, she rolled down her window, and as the aroma of *teriyaki* mixed with the dry, dying smell of late autumn circulated through the car she wondered if such distinct odors made everyone feel melancholy, and what about them should remind her of her childhood.

Chapter 20

ELINORE KNEW HER mother. Speeding away from the restaurant and down the hill into the Valley, she pictured Hideko: anxious to be relieved of childcare duties, she'd have tidied up Naoko's messes made from an afternoon full of activities and would be pacing the halls with a very tired baby, ready to see her daughter back home. Even so, Elinore would have to disappoint her. Lunch with Melissa had dislodged the misfortune of a year ago somewhere inside her; she felt it in her stomach as nausea and in her head as dizzying stupefaction. Deliberately missing the turn that would lead up the hill to her parents' house, she continued west on Ventura Boulevard instead, along the strip she'd once cruised with boyfriends after football games and dances. The afternoon traffic plodded along the wide-lane streets carrying BMWs with paint so shiny they appeared surreal. Such were the trappings of life in the Valley, which, having been away for so many years, she felt glad to know existed.

"How many?" A stylishly dressed teenager approached, bearing a stack of menus like a script.

She had once played hostess at a fancy restaurant and now, a teenager no longer, delighted in ignoring her former self as she made her way to the bar. Instead, she'd be a customer, one who expected prompt service and a stiff drink.

In no time, the bartender was standing in front of her. "What'll you have?"

The rows of glass bottles and colorful beer pulls left her speech-less as she stretched her legs and tapped her heels against the brass footrest.

"We have a good selection of wines, and you get a dollar off any beer we have on tap until four o'clock."

"Beer sounds good," she said, wishing to seem less out of place than she suddenly felt. Stretching her arms over her head, she attempted to ease the tension from her body, wondering as she scanned the bar what prompted people to drink alone in the middle of the afternoon. As if on cue, a tall, curly-haired boy scooted in to the stool next to her and without being asked told her about his recent graduation from a local two-year college and how he'd taken on freelance work at an ad agency.

When her beer arrived, she produced the wadded cash her father had given her from the front pocket of her jeans, but the boy put his hand over hers. "This is on me," he said. "Pretty girls shouldn't pay for their own beer."

She guessed he couldn't be more than Twenty-three, and flat-tered by his generosity and naivety, she stuffed the money back down into her pocket. Let him have his fantasy. She could be whomever he thought up. What did it matter?

"Are you from around here, or visiting?" He faced his drink as he spoke, and looked at her out of the corner of his eye.

"I grew up less than five miles from here," she said, swiveling on her stool to face him and raising her glass for another gulp.

"Let me guess. Chinese? Japanese?"

Elinore laughed uncomfortably. "I'm American. My parents' parents immigrated from Japan."

"I was right," he said, setting down the empty beer stein half off its coaster and wiping his mouth with his forearm. "You're a JAP!"

Elinore bristled, the lightheaded feeling of moments ago gone. Her father had once asked over dinner if anyone had ever called her a Jap at school. Seated across from her, he'd appeared enormous, her chin level with the table as she focused on the cup-shaped chest pocket of his dress shirt. It had seemed an important question the

way he'd asked it, putting his fork down in anticipation of her response. She had wanted to answer correctly, but having never heard
the word and not knowing what it meant, she responded honestly
instead. No, no one had. Jun did not explain what Jap meant, only
said that she was to tell him or her mother if she ever heard anyone
use the word. Of course, what seemed like the very next day, someone
did. A boy stole her hopscotch marker and called her a "Jap," as if
the expletive justified his action. It had only been a ponytail holder,
not worth a chase or the attention of the teacher on playground
duty. She'd thought about the incident all afternoon, but she didn't
mention it to either parent, the way she'd been instructed to do—
fearful of what, she couldn't say. She no longer recalled how she
came to know the word's meaning, or knew why hearing it should
cause the stony feeling to return to her stomach, yet having gone
to the bar to forget she felt the irony of wishing she were back with
Melissa. Seeming to understand he'd offended her, her drinking
mate attempted to explain himself. "C'mon. No one's ever called
you a JAPANESE-American Princess?"

Elinore scooted hotly down from the bar stool, put her feet on
the ground to test her balance, and turned her gaze to the doorway
where an explosion of afternoon light stunned her senses.

"I dated a girl in high school who called herself a Jap," he said,
prepared to defend his remark. "She thought it was funny."

"It's not," Elinore said, finding she lacked the energy she'd hoped
for, and realizing he had no idea.

"Sit down," he coaxed. "Don't go yet. "If it'll make you feel better,
you can call me a kike."

Did it make her feel better to know he was Jewish? Leaning
against the barstool, Elinore laughed at the absurdity of her predicament. The routine of her life broken, her thoughts so far from where
they'd been only an hour before, she was in no shape to drive, and
she had no desire to return to the life she'd somehow managed to
leave behind.

The boy waved his arm to signal another round, and Elinore
raised the glass mug to her lips, her hands trembling even after the

anger had left her, her feet seeming not even to touch the ground when she followed the boy out of the bar and walked with him along the busy boulevard, turning up a quiet side street. A full head taller than she, the boy might have been anyone walking beside her with his hands in his pockets, stepping gingerly over bumps in the pavement where tree roots grew up, ducking to avoid low branches. It was a pretty street, with its many trees and bushes that protruded onto the narrow sidewalk causing her to lean into him more than once. With the sun on the horizon, a chill penetrated the air, making distinct the smells of vegetation and the sound of sprinklers spraying water in the distance.

Elinore felt sure she'd driven down this residential street, having grown up less than a mile away. Perhaps a friend from childhood had grown up on this block, though she didn't recognize any house in particular. Then the boy stopped in front of a three-story apartment complex, unusual for this part of town. "This is it," he said, gesturing with his arm. "Home away from home."

Elinore stared up at the flat roof and small, modular spaces with resignation. If the prescribed sameness of it all felt prison-like, potted flowers resting on low metal tables lent a smattering of color and casualness, as did the beach towels slung over several balconies, which suggested their nearness to water. She'd never set foot in an apartment in the Valley where the people she'd grown up around lived in sprawling, luxurious homes. This was unfamiliar territory, which carried a sudden thrill, and she took in her surroundings, staring up into the boy's eyes in the shadowy light, without a care to the possible danger of following a stranger home, trying instead to decide whether the boy's irises were green or grey.

When he kissed her, her thoughts turned to Naoko and she reflexively pulled back. "I need to go," she said, feeling his arms tighten around her waist.

"No," he said.

He took the side stairwell, and she let herself be led by the steady grip that pulled her up two flights of stairs and promised excitement, and lulled, too, by the inaudible murmur of his voice calling back to her. If the crucifix hanging over the television should have alarmed her, it did not. With her back turned and eyes closed, she willed the world to disappear and was surprised at how effortlessly it obeyed.

His bedroom window faced west, filling the space with light, allowing heat from the setting sun to warm the room. The beer smelled pleasantly sweet on his breath, and she didn't turn her mouth away the second time he kissed her. The promise of sex was not nearly as satisfying as the act itself, but it was what she had wished for. He held her wrists over her head as if to ward off a possible escape. He worked with his eyes closed, concealing beneath his lids a fantasy she would never know. His movements were sharp and forceful and seemed to implore her to give him something of herself, though her body refused to yield to the plea. He climaxed into her and rolled away, his breath deepening beside her—a bear, slumbering after a full meal. With her eyes open she allowed her senses to re-enter her body.

It was nearly dark. Her panties had gone missing and she missed her daughter. A tear escaped the corner of her eye and her head throbbed, causing her to wait for the pain to subside before picking what was hers off the floor and quietly making her way out the door. Back on the street, she turned over her shoulder to see if she could tell which apartment she'd been inside, but she didn't have a clue. Walking along Ventura Boulevard back to her mother's car, she became once more the mother of a small child and quickened her pace to the anxious thudding of her heartbeat in her ears. The boy was gone. It was understood that she'd never see him again, yet the thought of who *she* was horrified her. As darkness cast shadows over the street and a steady line of cars sped by carrying commuters home, she was, to anyone who might have noticed her, nothing out of the ordinary. But her life was assuming a kind of shape she could not have imagined. Her mouth felt painfully dry and a sudden wave of nausea caused bile to rise in her throat. Back at Hideko's car, she pointed the remote and watched as the lock popped open, allowing her to take her seat behind the wheel.

Welcome to the Valley, her mother had said to Naoko six weeks earlier when they'd descended the hill on the way home from the airport. Hearing Hideko's voice in her head made her task of the moment clear—get home quickly and, if she could, slip unnoticed into the shower before greeting her mother and daughter.

Chapter 21

As if to taunt her, Jun called over the back of the couch before she could even see him. "Hi, baby," he sang cheerfully. "Did you have a nice time with Melissa?"

"Yes," she said, eyeing the room for her mother.

"Mom is putting Naoko down," he said casually. "She got a little fussy there at the end."

"I'm sorry." Not sure whether to be reassured or disturbed by her father's nonchalance, she decided to take her cue from his calm. "I think I'll just take a shower then, while I can."

"Okay with me," he said, closing the book on his lap to indicate his desire to talk.

"I won't be long."

"So you liked Melissa?" he smiled, ignoring her.

"Lunch was fine," she said, taking the rumpled twenty out of her pocket and flattening it before handing it back. "Thank you."

"What did you and Melissa talk about?"

"Nothing." It didn't matter that she'd spent the late afternoon doing everything she could not to think about her lunch with Melissa and trying to avoid her father's inevitable questioning of her. If she walked away, she knew he'd pursue her, probably even follow her to the bathroom, until she relented. "She was very nice."

Frowning, Jun handed the money back to her. "I thought if you intended to stay here, especially with Naoko, you might like to become more involved with other *Nihonjin* women in the area."

"The thought never occurred to me," she said, taken aback enough to sit down. "Is that really why you wanted me to meet her?"

"When I grew up, there were only a handful of *Nihonjin* in Los Angeles. Even though the area has grown over the years, sometimes it seems like that's still true. Did Melissa mention the church? Her family belongs to Valley Baptist where a good many of the Japanese-Americans who settled here still go."

What was his point? Smelling her sweat mixed with traces of the afternoon's intimacies, she scooted as far away from Jun as the couch would allow, wondering how to end the conversation before her mother, or worse, Naoko, appeared.

"Nora Yano's family attends that church. Did Melissa mention the memorial they're planning for her?"

"She said that Nora's gone missing," Elinore said, suddenly interested in what her father might have to say. "Is she dead?"

Jun shook his head and averted his eyes to the floor. "No one knows."

"Well, then, isn't it premature to be planning a memorial?" Elinore asked, wondering why everything that had to do with Nora seemed bizarre.

"Maybe they're saying it's a prayer service or something," he said, waving away her question. "They might not be calling it a memorial. But that's what it is. A way for people to commemorate her life and move on with their own lives."

"That's sad," Elinore said. "People can't stand uncertainty, can they?"

"No," Jun laughed. "You're right about that."

"What do you know about Nora?" she asked, curious that people seemed to have such different opinions about the woman and how they should feel about her disappearance.

"Yujitaka and Yukari Yano and Bob and Asako Hori have lived in the Valley for as long as I have. I met Yujitaka and Bob just after the war."

Why was it, Elinore wondered, that neither of her parents could ever respond to the question being asked? "But have you heard anything about Nora?"

"I'm going to the memorial to express my condolences to the family. It's a terrible thing for the Yanos, to have their daughter missing like that."

Like what? Elinore wanted to say, the mystery of Nora's disappearance looming larger with each unanswered question. The wedding, now almost two months in the past, had taken place just a day after Elinore had arrived in the Valley. She'd barely had her feet under her then, unsure about almost every connection in her life when she'd met Nora. She was the stranger who appeared out of the bushes with bruises up and down her arms to ask for advice about love. But a different Nora had surfaced over lunch with Melissa—a Nora Elinore would not have connected to the person she'd met, and who didn't much resemble the photo being shown to those looking for her. None of it made sense. And now there was the business of the memorial service, which her father of all people planned to attend. How was it that a stranger should become the center around which the events of the last months converged?

"Do you think there's any chance that they'll find her?" she asked her father. "What do you think happened to her?"

"I don't know," Jun shrugged. "But her parents seem to think she was murdered."

Murdered? Remembering Nora's bruises and the casual assurances she'd given, Elinore fell silent.

"So things must have been pretty bad between you and Saburo for you to leave with Naoko," Jun said, changing the subject.

"What?" Elinore said, still thinking about Nora. "What are you talking about?"

"He wasn't hurting you, was he?"

Suddenly, she understood what her father had been getting at. Sexual Abuse. Domestic Violence. Of course. "No," she said, seeing the connection he was attempting to make between Nora's disappearance and whatever had happened to her. Cautious that her vehemence not be viewed as denial, she tried to appear calm. "That's not why I left."

"Well, that's good," he said, clearly not believing her. "So why did you leave?"

"So I could be here. So you could meet Naoko and she could get to know her grandparents." Irritated with him, she could hear her voice catching in her throat. She hated that he'd drawn conclusions about her relationship with Saburo without ever having asked for the facts, couldn't understand why since she'd arrived home her father and probably both her parents had been drawing conclusions, neither having bothered to check with her first. She could certainly be accused of omitting important information, but she refused to take all the blame. Her mother had betrayed her and undermined her affection when her grandmother, the person she was closest to, had died, and after Rio's death, her life was not the only one that had spun off on its own trajectory. Jun had speaking engagements scheduled a year in advance, and with Elinore away and Rio gone, Hideko had ferreted out for herself a bizarre social life.

Elinore could have told Jun how she'd listened more than once to the sound of his voice recorded message, or that her reasons for returning home were none of his business. But there was no point in defending herself against the accusations he'd hurled at her—or Saburo. She knew he'd believe what he wanted to believe, regardless of the truth. The real problem was Naoko. She doubted Jun had spent more than an hour getting to know his granddaughter since his arrival home. The way when she was growing up he was oblivious to her, his limited responses based on ideas about people rather than actual relationships. That people were unknowable based on his theories was a given, but outside of his convictions, Elinore wondered whether she had ever known him.

Famous for his scenic Sunday drives, Jun loved to find shortcuts to familiar destinations. Elinore still remembered the afternoon Hideko had stayed behind, leaving Elinore to navigate alone, how from the backseat her trepidation had grown with each passing mile as the unfamiliar roads turned in and out of each other while the fantasy that Jun was abducting her became so real that she'd decided to hurl herself out of the moving car. That day her recognition of a landmark was the only thing that saved her life. Now her childhood was repeating itself for Naoko. Ultimately, even though the answer her father had come up with was absurd, she knew the question itself to be a good one. Why hadn't she stayed with Saburo? Sitting with Jun on the couch, Elinore was forced to consider why she hadn't anticipated her present predicament before she arrived. Fingering the pink spot on the armrest where grape juice had spilled years earlier, she tried to reimagine her life with Saburo.

"You're misunderstanding me," he said. "Of course I'm glad you've brought Naoko home. I want you to stay. That's why I tried to make a connection for you, with Melissa."

"Well, as busy as Naoko keeps me, I don't have time to make friends," she said, still angry.

"I just thought—"

But Elinore had stopped listening. When Jun reached across the couch to hug her she quickly stood up. "You don't need to worry about me," she said looking down at him, already feeling guilty. Jun, though tenacious in his beliefs, wasn't a bad father, and she knew she'd hurt him.

Across from her, his smile had turned beguiling, his painfully sweet demeanor making her wonder why she'd thought such an innocent looking man could cause damage. "I do worry about you," he said.

"I know."

He nodded, but was no longer listening. His sweetness having disappeared, he was scheming, she felt sure of it. "Did I mention I had a conference in Oregon?" he asked, leaning toward her again. "It starts Friday night, but I'll go late to be at the memorial."

"Okay," she said, sitting back down.

"I'm sorry," Jun said, looking penitent. "I know it's hard on everyone for me to be away so much."

"Don't worry about it," Elinore muttered, rising again, and this time turning away. "But I want to go with you to the service for Nora. I want to hear what people are saying about her."

"Okay with me," he said, picking his book back up. "I'll tell your mother you're home when she comes out."

But Jun wouldn't have a chance. Elinore's shower was cut short by Naoko's wailing, followed by her mother's placating tone ringing through the tiled wall. Hopping into the low bed with her hair still dripping, Elinore wrapped the toddler in her arms, whispering a quick 'thank you' to dismiss her mother. "Hi, baby," she said, "Mommy missed you."

Naoko watched the door shut behind her grandmother before turning to face Elinore, dejected and more sophisticated than a two-year-old should be. "Where were you?" she demanded.

"I told you I was going out, remember?" Flipping the child over, Elinore cupped her own body around her daughter's small back, feeling her fragility along with the ultimate safety she offered.

"I'm sorry I was away so long, but I had a very nice lunch today," she said, deciding it better to win Naoko's interest than confirm her anxiety. "Melissa, that's the person I had lunch with, she asked if you might want to go to the zoo. Would you like to go to the zoo?"

Rather than respond with words, Naoko flung a fist over her shoulder, catching the corner of Elinore's eye.

"Ouch!" Elinore shrieked. "Don't hit." She was impatient to be back in her own room, yet she understood the penance required by her absence. "The zoo will be fun," she whispered, tickling Naoko's armpit, wishing to turn her heaving gasps to giggles as quickly as possible. Brushing her nose along Naoko's earlobe, she chanted, "You can see lions and tigers and bears, oh my!"

"Elephants, too?" Naoko asked, her sobbing apparently over.

Elinore laughed at her daughter's unlikely choice of a favorite. "Yes. Elephants, too, but only if you go to sleep. Close your eyes and dream of all the wonderful animals you'll see. The zoo in Los Angeles is very big. I know because I used to visit it with your grandma and grandpa when I was a little girl."

"Really?" Naoko said, her breath lengthening.

Back in her room, Elinore felt desperate for comfort, and closing her eyes was surprised how quickly her thoughts settled on Saburo. She'd once taken pleasure from his body, and she missed how good it felt to be pinned beneath his perfect strength. At some point during the course of the day, a spot had opened inside her making it possible to re-imagine her past. Forced to acknowledge the bleakness of a future without him, she let the tears drip down her face knowing that by his mere presence he could help her make sense of her life. Though it had once seemed clear, she no longer knew why she'd left, and now, needing to tell him how much she missed him, she punched into the phone the sequence of numbers she knew by heart.

Holding the receiver snugly against her ear, she felt enormous relief to hear ringing on the line. Saburo would already be asleep, she supposed, turning over to locate the telephone with his eyes closed, the room so dark that it wouldn't make a difference whether they were closed or opened anyway.

"Hello?"

Elinore recognized the groggy-sounding woman's voice immediately. "Marina?" she said. "It's Elinore."

"Saburo's not here—"

Coward, she thought, disconnecting without a sound. *Liar*. On the other side of the wall, as if sensing distress, Naoko began to cry, beckoning Elinore to comfort her when all she felt was numb. Had Marina been what was wrong between Saburo and her? She'd always dismissed the woman's presence as too insignificant to be a problem for anyone, but now, cradling her daughter, she wondered why her response, rather than despair, should be renewed curiosity. Quite possibly she was more like Jun than she'd imagined, giving herself over with abandon to ideas about people without regard for the truth. The idea occurred to her in the moment before sleep, and she awoke feeling thickheaded. Without any sense of how much time had passed, she tiptoed out of the baby's room and nearly collided with her mother in the hallway.

"What are you doing still up?" Hideko asked, sounding as surprised as Elinore felt.

"I was just going to my room to sleep," Elinore said groggily. "Thanks for watching Naoko today."

"No problem," Hideko whispered. "She didn't give me any problems."

Elinore moved past her mother as she talked, smiling. "I'm glad."

"Was it nice to get away?" Hideko asked, not yet ready to let the conversation end.

"Yes," Elinore called over her shoulder before letting herself into her room.

"I was thinking," Hideko said the next morning over breakfast. "You should go out more. There's no reason I can't take Naoko on Friday afternoons. That way you can have some time to yourself."

"That's a nice idea," she said—meaning if only you knew.

"I like spending time with Naoko," she said, "I'm glad you're home."

Elinore smiled. Hideko's presence had made her homecoming inevitable, and it was as if her mother had known she'd return to her all along; Hideko's faith, even in Elinore's absence, complete.

Hideko smiled back. "I have no plans for next Friday, so we can start then."

Chapter 22

THE STREET OUTSIDE the Yano's house had already filled with cars, forcing Melissa to park almost a block away after fighting the urge to turn around and head home. The memorial service had been a disaster, just like she sensed it would be, and she wasn't in the mood to see anyone; but even more than that, she didn't want to be seen. From a safe distance, she sat back with her car windows up, following the raindrops that amassed and bled down the windshield.

She had been present the morning Reverend Nakatani's Sunday sermon "Planning for Jesus's Birthday" had bombed. She'd noted his purposeful stride as he approached Yukari and Yujitaka after services, and had thought it odd that he'd shaken their hands. Why did he, after so many years, greet them as she would a stranger? The Santa Ana winds had left the air chilly and the San Gabriel mountain range exposed, as if to lend extra attention to the minister's plan. "A special service," he'd called it, "to commemorate Nora's life."

"Do you mean a memorial?" Arms wrapped around her waist, Yukari appeared very small. Still, her voice carried sharply in the breeze.

The minister might have ended the conversation there. He could easily have turned to another subject, thereby saving face, but Yujitaka clamped his hand down on Yukari's shoulder. "So you mean," he paused, "I'm sorry, what do you mean?"

Reverend Nakatani rubbed his chin, eyes cast downward. "For the last months we have all felt Nora's absence. But we shouldn't forget what Jesus said in Matthew: 'Consider the lilies of the field, how they grow and do not toil. Seek ye first the kingdom of God.'

"With the coming celebration of the birth of our Savior, I think we should take the opportunity to remember Nora. Rather than dwell on her absence, we should offer each other strength through a celebration of her life."

"Of course, whatever you decide is fine," he said, having made his point to a silent audience.

Melissa had watched the way he spoke almost exclusively to Yukari, most likely in deference, since she was the mother. But in directing his questions to her, Melissa perceived that the minister had been afraid of Yujitaka, as if he knew what Yujitaka was going to say when Yukari cut him off. "Everyone has been so worried about Nora. I guess we owe them something."

"What do you think, Yujitaka?" she asked, having made up her mind.

It should have been obvious to her that Yujitaka didn't think it a good idea. "Yukari, I have discussed with you what I think about Nora," he began. But maybe he knew that his opinions would not stand up against the minister's or his wife's planning, or he simply didn't have the energy to do anything other than accept what Yukari had already decided upon. Still, Melissa couldn't help feeling disappointed when he had conceded, "You know my thoughts, and so I will leave it up to you." Even if Melissa didn't like it, she understood the minister's misguided logic, and, too, its power to convince Yukari that the memorial was necessary. But why had Yujitaka refused to intervene? Perhaps she was to blame for not stepping in and encouraging him to speak his mind. She had, after all, witnessed the fiasco being set in motion.

The event having been doomed from the start, it seemed fitting that the Sunday morning chosen for the service should have arrived with an onslaught of winterlike weather, everyone showing up wrapped in raincoats, donning umbrellas wrinkled from having been hidden away for too many seasons in closets. Even though it couldn't have been much below sixty, Melissa noticed how the younger women all wore gloves, some even trekking across the field in brightly colored plastic boots to protect their nice shoes from being ruined by the sodden grass, but also because what other chance would they have to wear them?

Among the faces were people she'd known all her life. Gossips, prima donnas, people who would never have talked to Nora outside of church, there were at least twenty young women her age in the congregation, and she hated how willing each was to take her place, like a friend.

Even with her oversized black umbrella, an occasional raindrop beaded down the side of Melissa's face as she watched Eugene and Ken, who seldom came to church anymore, standing on either side of Yukari, who wept openly. Usually the paragon of strength, she seemed for a moment to be admitting to the only thing Reverend Nakatani had refused to say: her daughter, only thirty, was missing with no sign of return. When her dark-stockinged legs collapsed beneath her, Eugene and Ken held her in their arms and led her away, leaving a gap to Yujitaka's right that no one made any movement to close. Melissa had been scared of him then, such a proud man, looking so sorry for himself over the daughter he should have loved better and longer. His face, turned to the sky, caught the rain on closed eyelids, but looking closer she was surprised when it wasn't sorrow she saw, but anger.

Standing at the edge of the crowd, Jun had looked ruinous, his hair thinning and caught up in the weather, his stature not grand enough for the beautiful daughter flanking him. Despite her envy, she'd smiled, and Elinore had returned the gesture, oblivious. Melissa rationalized that it wasn't Elinore's closeness to Jun she resented as much as her distance from all the anger. There was much to be angry about, too much to keep straight, and standing shoulder to shoulder among the others in the circle, Melissa thoughts settled on Mark. He had called the memorial a ridiculous charade, and she had defended it in a knee-jerk reaction.

"People need a way to think about Nora's life," Melissa had said, inadvertently quoting Reverend Nakatani to counter Mark's conclusion.

"People need for life to be simple," Mark had said, "for there to be closure where there is none. After three months people are ready for it to be over—end of story."

Melissa hated the indignation that edged its way into his assertions. Why did he have to be so stalwart, so unmoved by people's need to feel comforted. They had argued over what the memorial represented and to whom, and why Yukari and Yujitaka had agreed to the minister's plan to hold the service at Hansen Dam Park. In the end, she had to agree with Mark. But she resented him, too. His principled decision not to participate had left her unaccompanied, a solitary dot in the circle occupying the wet playing field, and the tears she wept mingled with gusts of frigid rain on the way down her cheeks.

Reverend Nakatani could not have known the bitter emotions his event would summon, nor could he have imagined worse weather. Wind crackling through the leaves, rain that left everyone wishing to cover their frozen ears. And what was there to hear? The minister preached from inside the circle, its self-proclaimed locus, occasionally waving his arms as if to remind everyone to keep their eyes on him. Clearly, he failed to see himself the way everyone else did—his service like watching an old movie in which the gestures are exaggerated, the dubbed sound making it impossible to catch more than the occasional sentence: "We are gathered not to mourn. . ."

What could they do if not mourn?

He ended by saying, "Nora's disappearance makes us appreciate our lives. We should be thankful for that."

When the minister bowed his head, everyone followed by bowing theirs, and a muffled prayer passed through the air. Melissa normally followed benediction with closed eyes, but scared to face her own thoughts, she had stared beyond the crowd at the huge cement bridge sticking up over the edge of a deep ravine, the crest of Hansen dam spanning the horizon. Farther to the east, the red and white PG&E smoke stacks rose like stoic witnesses, contributing a sulfurous odor to the misty morning air.

Now the house where Nora had grown up stood apologetically in the distance. Still the drab tan exterior with dark brown trim, the roof missing a few shingles that the wind had blown off, carefully pruned plants filling up only slightly more window space than they had the last time she'd looked. Melissa had been a baby the first time she'd visited Nora, too young to remember, and she glared at the house, squinting through the rain spattered windshield and fidgeting with her hair, willing the bland façade to offer up a memory. Perhaps of her mother, carrying her inside? Her well being seeming to hinge on her ability to recall some forgotten detail, she felt relieved when she finally landed on something.

The Yano house had always been dark inside; as a child she'd been afraid to stay overnight. Though Yukari was a meticulous housekeeper, she was no match for her sons' unsanitary practices and foul smelling experiments. As a result, a sour smell emanated from each room. Nora was responsible for cleaning the bathroom she shared with her brothers, which meant that she'd wet her finger under the faucet and wipe away their stains and globules of dried toothpaste left behind in the sink. "Remember the seat," she'd warn after the time Melissa forgot to put it down and fell backwards into the toilet. Melissa still laughed when she recalled the look of alarm on Nora's face. Alerted by the shrieking, she'd rushed in without knocking. "You have a lot to learn," she'd scolded, trying to suppress a smile, referring to life with brothers, which Melissa experienced only at the Yano house.

Nora's room was the safe haven. No boys allowed, she kept it tidy but filled with mementos. Glass sculptures that relatives had given her, stuffed animals left over from her childhood, every piece of artwork she'd ever made, photos from magazines, soda bottles bearing flowers that had long ago dried up. Made curious by her memories, Melissa left her car for the rain and ventured up the block to join the other guests, all of them hurrying for cover with their umbrellas up. At the entryway, warm air smelling like rice vinegar and shoyu rushed through a small crack in the kitchen window, frosted with condensation, and for the second time in less than a month Melissa had to fight to control her emotions. Bending to take off her shoes, she distracted herself by imagining that the gathering was a party at her mother's house. She placed her shoes in line with the dozens of others all faced in the same direction and noted their position in the foyer for retrieval later. Upon looking up, she was not surprised to see the large assortment of food. Women from the church stood outside Yukari's kitchen armed with their best *sushi*, *chirashi*, pickle and potato salads, Kentucky fried and *teriyaki* chicken. Counters overflowed as Caroline's mother cleared the contents of half-empty platters onto smaller ones, and her own mother stood over the kitchen sink, a dishrag thrown over her shoulder, washing the cookware that was no longer needed. Having recovered from the service, Yukari rushed from room to room to gather coats and tell each guest how glad she was that they could come. Her graciousness set the mood, told everyone how they were supposed to feel, asked the guests to treat this occasion with a festive spirit.

It was a sham, an ill conceived attempt to offset the sadness everyone felt, and glad that she'd no longer have to endure her contemptuous feelings privately, she was relieved when Caroline finally arrived flanked by Wade.

"How come you weren't at the service?" she asked after a hug. "You weren't there, were you?"

To Melissa's surprise, Wade stepped in front of Caroline, inserting himself between them. "Caroline wasn't feeling well," he said, warning Melissa not to pursue the subject.

Looking more closely at Caroline, Melissa was forced to concur with Wade. Her cheeks were pasty and colorless. But so many bodies brushing past made them all a little uncomfortable, and perhaps the commotion had interfered with her interpretation of Wade's meaning. "You're not pregnant, are you?" Melissa blurted out, unable to retract her indiscretion.

"Oh my God," Caroline gasped, raising her hands to cover her face. "How could you have possibly known? I wasn't planning on telling anyone yet, and this is definitely not the right occasion. I should leave."

"Don't worry about it," Melissa told her, and from the corner of her eye she watched Wade slink off toward the television room, no doubt glad to get away. "I'm happy for you. When's the baby due?"

"Mid June."

"I feel bad about missing the service," Caroline confided to Melissa, "but I haven't been well lately, and I just couldn't bring myself to go."

Had the sadness of the occasion been too much for her? Or, perhaps, the bad weather? Only Caroline could be forgiven for missing Nora's memorial service, though Melissa reminded herself that it wasn't her place to offer or withhold forgiveness. The living room was crowded with people spilling into any space they found available, and Melissa led Caroline down the hall toward Nora's room, partly to ensure she wouldn't disappear.

The news of Caroline's pregnancy was surprising, but not really, considering how little the two had talked since Caroline's wedding. Before that there had been weeks of preparations, which were themselves the subject of conversation. Melissa was surprised when she didn't see Nora's room as she made her way down the hall. Walking past it, she had to retrace her steps. "What are you looking for?" Caroline said, seeming exasperated at being made to follow.

"Where's Nora's room?" Melissa asked, disoriented.

Caroline took the lead, stopping in the doorway of Yujitaka's office.

"Oh no," Melissa sighed, remembering her only visual locator of Nora from the car. "What on earth has Yukari done with all her things?"

Caroline laughed. "Remember how cluttered her room used to be?"

"Yes," Melissa said emphatically, "I was just thinking about that. I wonder who got the posters of the suntanned teen idols."

"That's a good question," Caroline smiled. "I know Nora didn't take much with her when she moved. Maybe Yukari has her things packed away somewhere."

"I'm sure she threw them out," Melissa said, knowing how Yukari never understood Nora's need to hold on to things.

Caroline gravitated toward the one tangible reminder of Nora, a childhood photo set out on Yujitaka's desk. "She looks pretty, doesn't she," she mused, picking the silver frame up and running a finger over the glass.

Melissa walked to where Caroline stood and turned Yujitaka's desk lamp on to admire the photo of Nora, taken at her sixth birthday party. She could tell from the helium filled Mickey Mouse balloons tied to the lawn furniture in the background. After the party she'd begged her mother for balloons like those and had cried when Asako said they only gave them out at Disneyland. Pressed right up to the camera lens, Nora's smile radiated happiness, with bits of chocolate cake clinging to the sides of her mouth and scraps of wrapping paper littering the background. Melissa had forgotten how much Nora loved getting presents.

"I can't remember seeing her that happy," Melissa remarked, thinking that 'pretty' wasn't really the right word.

"Did you hear the police arrested someone?" Caroline asked, using both hands to place the silver frame back on Yujitaka's desk, then sitting herself on the daybed and smoothing the bedspread with her well manicured hands.

"What are you talking about?" Melissa demanded.

"A man Nora was seeing was arrested on unrelated charges. But the police are thinking he was involved in her disappearance."

"She was seeing someone?" Shocked, Melissa lowered her voice, not wanting to sound accusatory. "How did you find out?"

"It's a long story," Caroline said, sucking in a deep breath.

Melissa couldn't believe Caroline's nonchalance, as if she were passing along information known to everyone. "Caroline, why didn't you tell me?" She pulled Yujitaka's heavy brown chair out from under the desk and sat with the old photo in front of her. If she stared into it long enough, would she find something else she'd missed?

"I don't know any more than I just told you," Caroline shrugged. "But it's true that I haven't talked to you in forever. How are you, Mel? How's Mark?"

"*Car*-o-line," Melissa enunciated each syllable of her friend's name, exasperated. "Tell me what you know about Nora."

"She was seeing someone, and he was probably the last person to see her. I guess there's a chance that he killed her."

"Did she tell you she was seeing someone?" Melissa asked, truly puzzled and irritated by what she'd not known. "I wonder why she didn't tell me. Why do you think she didn't tell me?"

Caroline paused before speaking, "Maybe she thought you'd judge her."

"Why would I *judge* her?" Melissa directed her anger at Caroline, but imagined that quite possibly others would hear her and come rushing in. Let all the questions moving surreptitiously through the house coalesce in Nora's room.

"See," Caroline said.

"See what?" Melissa yelled.

"It's not easy to tell you things, Mel."

This bit of information had never occurred to Melissa. She'd never considered herself a hard person to talk to. Horrified by Caroline's sudden disclosure, she wondered if her clients shared her best friend's opinion. But Caroline had offered her more information than she could take in at once, and unable to focus on what had been revealed about Nora or herself, stray bits of conversation from the rooms outside filled her ears along with nearby footsteps even though she hadn't seen anyone walk past the doorway to Yujitaka's office. "What do you mean?" she demanded of Caroline.

Lowering her voice when Caroline didn't immediately respond, Melissa tried again. "Caroline, I'm serious, I really want to know what you're talking about."

Caroline bit the inside of her lip looking like she was going to cry. "You've always been the smart one, Melissa, the successful one, the one who knows things. You know that."

"Caroline," Melissa pleaded, her give-me-a-break tone coming out in a screech. "I'm a social worker. I have a master's level degree in social work."

"It's not that," Caroline said, having moved on to bite at her pinkie nail. "I'm sorry to have brought it up. You know, I haven't been feeling well and maybe I'm not thinking clearly. But it's the way you're always so sure of things. Like you know what's right and other people don't."

"I'm sorry you're not feeling well," Melissa said, giving up, "but I honestly don't know what you're talking about." The conversation destined to go nowhere, she vowed to consider her friend's accusations of her later, for they were, at the moment, keeping her from the issue at hand. "So who is this person Nora was seeing?" she tried again.

"I don't know," Caroline sighed. "Nora didn't tell me much. She didn't tell Yukari anything, but one of Nora's neighbors saw her face on the news and called the police to say that she'd seen Nora hanging out at the house next door. The detectives questioned someone, but they haven't had enough evidence to arrest him."

"So why would this person have killed Nora?"

"Didn't you see the bruises?"

"Bruises?" Melissa said, shocked. "She was getting beat up?"

"Mel?" Caroline sighed, clearing a path through the air with her delicate fist. "Hello? You're already coming to conclusions. Some people just bruise easily."

I don't think so—, Melissa was about to interject, but caught herself. "When did Nora have bruises?"

"I noticed them when we were dressing for my wedding. Didn't you see them? Along her arms and thighs?"

"No."

"And she told you someone hit her?"

"No, Melissa." Caroline slumped back against the throw pillows. "She didn't tell me anything, and I didn't want to embarrass her, so I didn't ask."

Melissa sank her weight into Yujitaka's desk chair, trying to calm down.

"Do you remember when Nora started working at Parson's?" Caroline mused.

"Of course I do. Who wouldn't—" she caught herself again. Maybe Caroline had been right to accuse her of being a horrible friend.

"I know everyone thought it was a mistake, but she was really happy being a manicurist. Did you ever visit her at Parson's?"

"When would I have—?"

Caroline looked up from her nails and smiled beatifically. "It's okay, Melissa. I'm not blaming you for anything. I'm just remembering how I used to go for manicures on Friday afternoons. There was a parrot in the window. A macaw, I think. A big yellow and blue bird that perched in the storefront of the pet shop next door and greeted people. He loved Nora, and she liked to tease him. When she first saw him she called him *aloof* and *glorious* and then every time he saw her he said *Alooo gor-g-eous!* and whistled.

"I think she'd still be working there if her hands hadn't given out," Caroline sighed. "She had such elegant hands. Isn't it a sad irony that the most beautiful things are often the most ill-fated. I always envied her hands."

Trying to remember what Nora's hands looked like, Melissa stared down at her own hands, but what she saw was how badly *she* needed a manicure. She'd never *had* a manicure. Her middle fingernail was chipped and the ridges on all her nails were plainly visible, even from a foot away. Suddenly she saw Nora reaching a hand up to brush her hair away from her face, and she thought, *It's not the bones. They were straight. It's the ghosts of the bones that haunt the marrow.*

"You should have gone," Caroline sighed. "If not to see Nora, to get your hands worked on. You know, she gave great hand massages. She'd push her thumb into the middle of your palm and massage outward to the tips of your fingers until your whole hand tingled. She always told me I was too tense."

"Really?" Melissa asked. Watching Caroline emulate the actions she was describing, Melissa believed her friend to be the least tense person she'd ever known.

"She'd lift your fingers to catch the light and you could see her mind at work. In her heart she was an artist," Caroline declared. "She had an artist's eye."

Unable to recognize the Nora Caroline was describing, Melissa wondered how she and Caroline could each be involved in such different conversations. "Did she mention the name of the person she was seeing?"

She was still trying to steer the conversation her way when Yukari's face appeared in the doorway. "Caroline," she said, cheerily. "Melissa. I thought I heard your voices in here."

"How are you holding up?" Caroline asked, casting doe eyes on Yukari.

"All these people are keeping me too busy to think about much."

"Yukari, what's the name of the man Nora was seeing?"

"Joaquin. Joaquin Siler. Why?" she asked, looking Melissa's way, and then as if answering her own question, "We'll talk later, neh. Right now, both of you need to come have some food."

Obediently, Caroline followed Yukari out the door, but Melissa stayed behind. She wrote the name 'Joaquin Siler' on Yujitaka's memo pad and folded the slip of paper away. She knew she should join the others, but the conversation and laughter coming in through the walls made her lonely. Missing Mark and hearing Yukari move from group to group to inquire after the needs of her guests, she suspected how difficult life must have been for Nora growing up in this room with its thin walls that seemed to amplify noises rather than shut them out. From Nora's room, Melissa acknowledged her friend's suffering, along with the awareness that the hole Nora had left in the lives of her family and friends when she disappeared had begun to close. That had been the rationale behind having the afternoon's miserable event, had it not? To begin the process of forgetting.

A chill shuddered through Melissa's body as she rose to leave Yujitaka's office. She'd planned to go after paying her respects to the Yanos, but Caroline's mother stopped her to chat, followed by her own mother. Staying on to help Yukari clean up, Melissa was among the last group of guests to leave. Late into the afternoon, she collected plastic cups and empty food plates as people clustered among friends and socialized, the way they normally did when Sunday service was over.

Chapter 23

EARLY INTO THE morning of November twentieth, while Yukari dreamt she was chasing a young Nora around the backyard of a house she couldn't recognize, a patrol car pulled Joaquin Siler over on Terra Bella, just past the intersection of Laurel Canyon Blvd.

"Are you aware that you just ran a red light?" the officer asked perfunctorily, shining a flashlight on his face, and then over the empty beer cans in the back seat.

On his way home from a bar, Joaquin knew this inconvenience might take a while. It had, after all, been going on for some time, his drinking more than he should, but at ten past two, the delay felt intrusive.

"I'll need to see your license," the CHP officer demanded, and, after scanning it, "Been out drinking tonight, Mr. Siler?"

From behind a flashlight, the cop reminded him of his father, ransacking his room for money when the booze ran out in the middle of the night and snatching up what he could find like it belonged to him. *Fuck you, asshole,* Joaquin wanted to say. He'd have given the old man what he had if he'd asked, but he never did.

After checking Joaquin's license on the computer and finding nothing, the patrolman returned. "Get out."

"You've got nothing on me," Joaquin complained, confident of his innocence.

"Shut your mouth," the patrolman told him, which was good advice, because after failing a breath-alcohol test, he was thrown in the backseat of the squad car in handcuffs.

At the station, just over the desk sergeant's shoulder, a photo blown up to near life-sized proportions caught Joaquin's eye. Seeing it, Joaquin had the scary feeling that Nora was watching him through a hidden mirror. "Holy shit." He winced, momentarily confused. But after wiping his eyes on the sleeve of his tee-shirt, he laughed, remembering the event that had brought him to the station.

To the desk sergeant, Joaquin Siler was just another drunk being booked in the early morning hours, but the DWI arrest provided the detectives with the opportunity they needed to question Joaquin again.

After almost four months, Joaquin had a hard time remembering, but he didn't mind talking about Nora. "She was kind of crazy," he said, unaware of the connections being summoned. "But nice, too."

Drunk and vulnerable to the detectives' questioning tactics, he recalled how he drove the five hundred miles to Klamath for a three-day visit with his son and how his car started to rumble coming down from the Trinity mountains, still a long way off from the Valley. The car had to be towed into Redding, and he'd waited there, a new third-cylinder on order. He'd meant to be back home by Wednesday, and he might have had his car not given out. That was when everything began going wrong.

He'd lost his job for missing two shifts, even though he'd made sure to call to tell his boss he'd be late, but his son's crooked smile, palm held up to meet his in greeting, made him smile as he told the story. He'd given his father the same greeting on the occasions when he'd get to see him as a child. Having a son had changed his mind about a lot of things, like maybe he wasn't just the things he'd always thought he was made of—drunkenness, divorce, meanness—passed down through the generations. Knowing there wasn't a thing bad about his son was what got him through each day. Even if he couldn't live close (he'd seen to that with behavior he wasn't proud of), he was thankful to have a son in the world. It had been hard to return, to see all that he'd missed, his son a little taller than the last time, his gestures awkward, like someone who didn't understand where his body began and left off. That, and the same innocent smile he'd been born with, had made Joaquin stay longer than he'd intended to.

Who knows? Maybe if he'd gotten going when he should have and not taken his son for an overnight on the river, maybe then the third cylinder wouldn't have blown, forcing him to spend two days and a night in Redding, waiting for the parts to come in. Those hours hovered like an omen, too much time to think about how fucked up his life down south had become, and to wonder why he was driving away from the one person who mattered to him. The Valley would never be home. It was a place of exile. Any crazy thing could happen there—things that might never be explained. He imagined returning to find his house ransacked; more realistically, he expected to see his flowers and grass dead. And yes, there was the I'm-not-Chinese-I'm-Japanese-*American* girl he met before he took off. She hadn't been by in the days before he left town, and he wasn't counting on seeing her again even though he'd driven the long, flat highway between Central California and the Valley thinking of her. Sandwiched between so many green fields and so much dirt, he remembered how she told him about her family planting the fields a long way back.

Without air conditioning it had been hot in his car, and coming over the hill and into the Valley with his windows peeled down, he was surprised to find that the heat hadn't dropped even a little. A faint cast of red lit the night sky, and the haze of city lights and desert air blowing in off the San Gabriels made the house seem nicer than it was when his car rolled up the driveway. Things could look all right at night, he guessed, twisting his neck until a crack released the stiffness and noting the flowers reaching up to greet him.

He was pretty sure the neighbor kid would not have watered without being paid; he was probably just seeing the street-lit shadows of flowers and mistaking them for the real thing. But when he saw that the shade had been propped and the window opened a crack he knew that something was up. His ex- come down to greet him with the boy? No chance of that, and everyone else who'd drop by unannounced was still up north.

He'd been drinking. It was true. And he'd been shocked to find Nora. Who wouldn't have been? There was no good way to explain his own behavior, never mind why she'd done what she'd done to his house while he was gone. His thoughts returned to the busted third-cylinder. The only reason he'd come back to the Valley had been because of work. He knew that getting his son back meant keeping a job, but now he'd lost his, and without a job it'd be hard to find work. Wasn't life just like that? Always things around that you didn't want, and never what you needed. If he'd have listened to his instincts, he would have stayed focused on his son, turned around once his car had been fixed, and headed back up north without telling a soul.

Following a night in jail, Joaquin returned home sober, jobless, and depressed. Told by the police to stay in town or to notify them about any plans to leave Los Angeles, he missed his son more than ever and couldn't understand why his luck had taken a turn for the worse. He didn't place much interest in the police's questioning him about Nora; how could he have known that his life had become a story about her? If someone were to have told him he was losing his mind, he might have believed them. But if they had told him he was losing his life and becoming a part of Nora's, he would have tilted his head back and laughed.

Chapter 24

HAD WADE BEEN better able to assess his wife's mental state, he would have recognized that even before her pregnancy Caroline had not been right. It wasn't more time alone she needed, not more sleep. Unable to extricate her needs from his own, he prescribed for her the things he himself could have used.

"Why don't you come with me to Coronado?" Wade coaxed. "You're just grumpy because of the recent surge of pregnancy hormones." Wade's jocular tone undercut the serious problem that Caroline feared, made it sound like the severe mood swings she was experiencing happened to all pregnant women. It was all she could do to get her bags packed, but asked to believe that her problems were generic and therefore remediable, she placed her hope on the therapeutic value of a short vacation. They'd stay at the Coronado Hotel, sightsee in San Diego, and she could stay back on the beach while Wade attended a pharmaceutical conference. So what if San Diego was an uncomfortable three hour car ride and she'd have to spend most of the weekend by herself? The hotel would be beautiful, and everything free, including the beach just outside their suite.

Walking the shoreline, Caroline remembered how the Yanos spent the first two weeks of every June in Baja, and how the summer she and Nora turned eleven she got invited to go with them. Nora carried a blue metal bucket that she'd had since childhood, which she used to collect trinkets from the beach and to torture crabs. She liked to build castles out of the smooth black pebbles and sand dollars, which the crabs would climb, almost to the top of the bucket before they slid back down to the bottom again. At night Nora brought them back to the condo, and while she slept, Caroline stayed awake listening to the screech their claws made inside the bucket. In the morning they would all, of course, be dead.

That June Caroline had gotten to know Nora in a fuller sense. Melissa wasn't there to make them the usual threesome, and away from church Nora became a more carefree person. They'd walk the beach each morning, curious to see what the tide had dragged in, and by noon, when the fog had lifted, they'd let their hair down to trail in the breeze and Nora would begin slathering on the Hawaiian Tropic tanning oil. On the beach in Baja Nora, soon as dark as a shadow, introduced Caroline to the most enormous sea gulls she'd ever seen. They'd save oyster crackers from bowls of clam chowder and toss them at the gulls hanging in the air, their beaks gaping open so wide they could see down their throats. Nora admired their ferocity, and said their endless bickering reminded her of her brothers.

Nora taught Caroline to watch for spouting whales, and to spot the seals leaping on the horizon. "They're like black crescent moons," she'd said. On Coronado Island the rich marine life felt even closer than it had in Baja. Combing the beach alone, Caroline was surprised to discover a conch, remembering how Nora had once held one to her ear, revealing the shell's secret mystery of sound. Asleep in the Coronado Hotel with the conch on her bedstand, Caroline dreamt the same dream she had on her honeymoon: she was wearing a white bikini and floating on her back in the kidney shaped pool, except that this time when she looked down at her round belly and thought, I'm pregnant, she woke up and she *was*. The dream reawakened the misery she'd experienced in Waikiki, and unable to shake the feeling that the dream portended, as it had the first time, catastrophe, she found herself obsessed with her memory of the Baja trip, which she believed had brought the dream on. The time spent with Nora had included snorkeling and long walks on the beach; it had all been nothing short of spectacular, up until the day they'd had to pack up and leave. Five hours trapped in the Yano's station wagon with Eugene and Ken had signaled the end. It had been hot in the old Chrysler, but when Yujitaka stopped for gas in Escondido Caroline had declined Nora's offer to get out and stretch her legs, and the next thing she knew Nora was gone.

Was that the bad thing she'd been after in the dream, Caroline wondered, the fact that Nora had disappeared that summer when they were both still children?

The sun beat through her side of the window bleaching the color out of Caroline's trinkets, stowed at her feet, and though she couldn't hear Yukari and Yujitaka's conversation in the front seat well enough to discern whether it was important, she didn't want to interrupt them to ask about Nora. Besides, Yujitaka was in charge. He knew what he was doing; that's why she'd stayed quiet, watching signs along the freeway to check how many miles they were from home. She felt sure she would have said something eventually, but then Yukari turned to offer everyone apple slices and saw beside her the spot where Nora had been. Caroline shut her eyes like she was sleeping, and opened them again when Yukari said, "Where's Nora?"

In the way back of the station wagon, Eugene and Ken started howling, holding their sides, doubled over. Thinking Yukari's contorted features funny, they laughed so hard that she wanted to laugh too, but of course she didn't. When Yujitaka told the boys to quiet down, the silence that filled the car was terrifying. Caroline could see Yukari looking for an exit so that Yujitaka could turn the car around, and the next thing she knew Eugene was barking out the window: "What an idiot, Nora!"

Nora's brothers saw her before Caroline did, or maybe they saw her at the same time, only Caroline hadn't expected to see Nora walking along the freeway, or anticipated the bright red patch of blood staining the back of her shorts.

When Wade returned to the hotel room for the night, Caroline told him what she'd remembered about how Nora had disappeared that summer in Baja when they were only eleven. "We found her walking along the freeway with a big blood stain on the back of her shorts," she said, feeling more animated than she'd felt in weeks.

Caroline paused to reflect on what she knew about that day. Convinced that her dream had signaled disaster and unwilling yet to admit that the calamitous event had already taken place, she continued, "Do you think maybe I was prescient?"

"No," Wade said. "What made you think she wasn't hurt?"

"It was period blood," she confided.

Wade shrugged. "How on earth did no one notice that Nora wasn't in the car when Yujitaka pulled out of the gas station?"

"I was asleep when her father stopped for gas," she said. "And I guess her brothers thought it was a prank or something." She remembered Ken bellowing, *Did you think you were going to walk home?* And Yukari scolding, *Get in the car, now.*

"Yukari whispered across the seat to Yujitaka, and he drove back to the filling station. Yukari got out first and gave Nora a sweatshirt to tie around her waist, then followed Nora to the bathroom. When they got back in the car even her brothers were quiet."

"Didn't you use the buddy system to go to the bathroom?" Wade interrupted. "I'm surprised Yukari would have let her leave the car alone."

"I didn't have to go," Caroline shrugged. Of course then she realized the error she'd exposed in her story, but by that time it was too late. She didn't know whether she was trying to defend herself or making an attempt at humor when she said, "You can hardly blame me—the horrible way gas station bathrooms smell."

Wade lifted an eyebrow, but said nothing, while Caroline imbued the memory with pity for Nora, for whatever had made her want to keep her period a secret. Why couldn't Nora have gotten a Kotex or tampon out of the vending machine since bathrooms always had them. Maybe she didn't have a dime. But couldn't she have asked for one?

Maybe she did. Caroline imagined Nora working up her courage to ask a stranger for change. She'd wait for the right person, a woman, and then say something like *May I borrow a dime for a phone call, please?* The woman would glance up briefly, just to make sure Nora knew she'd seen her, before driving off. What a nasty thing to do,

Caroline thought, imagining a familiar looking woman with a white silk scarf tied around her long hair, her make up and nails just so.

It wasn't until the next morning, left once more to wander the beach by herself, that Caroline recognized the woman in the car. Her feet planted in the wet sand, she stood over the surf watching the holes that appeared with a subtle crackling sound indicating where sand crabs burrowed. Knowing as the tide came in and the sand ebbed away under her feet that she'd supplied the woman in the car to assuage her guilt for having allowed her friend to be left behind, she wept. What had it felt like for Nora to watch the car with her family and best friend speeding away? Though she might never know, Caroline turned her attention to the part she'd played in Nora being left behind. She'd refused to accompany her friend to the bathroom, which had not been a nice thing to do. Then she'd feigned sleep as Yukari pulled the car away from the filling station, feeling beside her the empty space where Nora had sat. She'd listened to the conversation in the front seat, waited for the boys to say something, but what could have prompted her to remain silent? Nora had not spoken to her afterward about the incident, but had she blamed Caroline for her abandonment? The dream had been a portent, leading Caroline to own up to her involvement in gas station incident in Escondido, but had that incident also been the prelude to whatever awful thing had happened to Nora?

Moreover, why had Wade remained silent when she'd explained to him her part in the gas station incident? Had he simply failed to understand her involvement? Or, worse, and as Caroline saw it more likely, had the knowledge of her involvement not surprised him? The thing that no one had warned her about, the thing that might have soured her on marriage before she'd ever gone through with hers, was that no matter what idealistic notions one might have had, the marriage ceremony ended the romance, for rather than become her soul mate or even her lifelong partner, Wade had thus far turned out to be a stranger. As the afternoon sun warmed the sand and flooded the beach with undiluted light, Caroline attempted to shift her reminiscences to happier times. The church retreat took place every year in spring, the last one just six months earlier, though the temperature on the beach had been roughly the same. As if her life depended on it, she sniffed at the ocean air for the smell of the nearby pine forest, trying to recapture the exhilaration she'd experienced holding hands with Wade and kissing him under the shade of trees. Everyone else had taken the bus, chartered by the church, but having always loved the ocean Wade had wanted to drive down the coast so that they could stop off at the beaches. Even though the water was freezing, they'd rolled up their pant legs and chased the waves. It wasn't a thing she would have thought to do so early in the year, but she'd never had such fun. It had seemed that nothing could get between them or stand in the way of their happiness; nothing to suggest all the good and bad yet to happen.

Wade had worn his green cashmere sweater, the one she adored, and when her shirt got wet he'd taken it off and slipped it over her head. She loved how men could run around in fifty degree weather without a shirt and not get cold. Her fiancée looked sexy chasing her through the waves exposed from the waist up, and his sweater felt soft against her skin, the shoulders hanging half-way to her elbows, the sleeves drooping over her hands. She could have changed clothes when they got back to the car because everything they'd packed for the weekend was in the trunk, but she didn't want the moment to end. So she'd stayed in the sweater, and Wade had put on a fresh shirt and driven them to Santa Barbara for dinner on the pier.

She hadn't thought he'd pick a fancy restaurant, and she'd felt a little uncomfortable at first, wondering if people were staring because she wore a sweater three sizes too large and because they both looked like they'd been dragged in off the beach. "Do you think I should go back to the car and change?" she'd whispered across the table.

"No, of course not," Wade whispered back. "Why would you do that?"

"I'm not dressed right," she said. "People are staring."

Wade took a perfunctory look around at the older couples dressed in their expensive clothing and jewelry. Then he smiled and squeezed her hand. "People are staring because you're the most beautiful woman they've ever seen," he said.

She smiled, believing him.

Wade ordered a bottle of wine, and they ate pasta with crab and scallops and shrimp and she was thankful that it was only an hour drive back to her apartment because after dinner they were both so tired that she had to talk nonsense just to make sure he stayed awake.

When they arrived back in the Valley, it was nearly midnight. Because it had gotten so late, she said he should probably just stay the night at her apartment, which was something he'd never done. He took a shower, and she put blankets and a pillow on the couch for him and went to her bedroom to sleep. Then he came in after his shower and lay down on her bed and they began kissing, and the next morning when he left she thought everything was going to be fine.

That night they'd gone farther than they should have, but a pregnancy seemed out of the question. For heaven's sake, she'd just sent out her wedding invitations, and for what? She hadn't done anything wrong. Wade had just started up his practice and she'd been working as his receptionist to help save money, but in the week she found out she was pregnant it became harder and harder for her to face him at the office. From her desk, she could picture him in the examining room, fingering the black mass on Mrs. Kumagai's back. Pretty soon he'd be calling her in to assist with the cauterization. Mrs. Kumagai would say, "Why hello, Caroline, so nice to see you. How have you been doing?"

"Well, Mrs. Kumagai, I'm fine," she'd say. "In fact, I'm pregnant."

Would Wade's hand flinch? Would his scalpel slip, causing an irregular shaped scar on Mrs. Kumagai's back? Would the wind Mrs. Kumagai had been trying to hold in escape?

For two days, rather than engage in the conversation she knew must take place, she concocted the most absurd scenarios she could imagine. She delayed until the end of the day when she'd finished sterilizing the surgical instruments and everything was in order for the morning. Wade left the office first, she behind him, and while they waited together for the elevator, she said, "I think I'm pregnant."

"What?" The bell sounded and the red down arrow lit up.

The elevator doors slid open and Wade nodded at the five or six other doctors and nurses leaving the building for the night. They all stood quietly facing forward, her feeling the drop and rumble of the hydraulics in her stomach all the way down to the ground. When the doors again slid open, Wade caught her by the elbow and walked her to his car and drove to Savon's, leaving her behind in the car with the engine running and five minutes to imagine what it might be like to have a baby. Even though Wade's practice was so new, with everyone in the church coming in or sending referrals, it wouldn't be long before they were well off financially, able to give a baby everything he or she needed in life. She thought of what fun it'd be to decorate the nursery and shop for all the baby things she'd seen and dreamed of one day having. She was deep into her fantasy when the driver's door opened, and Wade tossed a brown bag onto her lap.

"You scared me," she said, glaring at him.

"Who did you think it'd be?" he said.

Back at her apartment, he waited outside the bathroom for her to perform the test, which she'd already done once herself.

"See?" she waved the stick at him. Even though she'd known for two whole days, she should have guessed he wouldn't really believe her until she offered him proof.

"Let me see the packaging," he said.

"What else do you think a plus sign can mean?" she asked, aiming the box and its contents at his head.

"Is it mine?" he asked, raising an arm to shield his head while he squinted down at the small print.

"Wade," she said, finally, "What do you think?"

Though she'd been far from euphoric about the pregnancy, she had assumed they would keep the baby. Surprised and hurt when Wade had spoken out adamantly against the idea, she'd told him something she didn't really believe, that the circumstances didn't matter, that maybe this *was* the right way, that God had obviously wanted her to have this baby. In turn, he'd surprised her by saying things she didn't think he believed: that conception had not been up to God, that the pregnancy was just bad luck. Then he asked how she planned to wear the gown she'd already picked out, and what about her mother, what about his?

Wade had made her agree to secrecy. She doubted he'd ever understand what a betrayal that was, or how deeply the decision to abort her first pregnancy impacted her. The procedure itself proved less traumatic than all the feelings for which she could not find words. Wade refused to understand how she could have gotten pregnant, and she didn't understand it either. Why it would have been God's will to punish her when she hadn't done anything wrong. Since then, a lot had happened to change things; she knew she should be the happiest person in the world, but she wasn't, and much to Wade's consternation, the vacation in Coronado had done nothing to improve her mood. "You're going to have to pull it together," he explained when, unable to rouse herself, she made them late checking out of the hotel.

"For god's sake, Wade, I'm pregnant," she said.

"You still have a good six months to go," he practically shouted across the car seat.

"Maybe you're depressed," he relented when she began to cry. But instead of going on to offer a solution, he stopped short at the observation.

It seemed likely that Wade had been right about Caroline being depressed, though on her own she had no tools beyond the rough chronology she'd constructed to understand what had gone wrong for her, and to herself she repeated what she knew almost constantly. Then, to contribute to her misery, a detective at the Foothill Precinct had left a message on the answering machine, requesting that she come to the station for an interview. The detective had explained during their initial phone conversation the purpose of her visit, and she'd been anxious to have it over with. "What is it you want from me?" she asked, shaking the younger, overweight detective's hand from across the interview table.

"Thank you for taking the time to come in, Mrs. Noguchi. The reason we asked you for a few minutes of your time is that we've spoken with a potential suspect with regard to Nora's disappearance, and we were wondering if you might know of anyone Nora might have been seeing when she disappeared."

Caroline flinched when she recalled the name Yukari had told her and the story she'd put together. She knew the police who'd canvassed the neighborhood had interviewed a woman who saw Nora sitting in front of the house that belonged to Joaquin Siler. The detectives had reported those details of the case to Yukari, but cautioned her that the evidence, though implicating Joaquin Siler in Nora's disappearance, was still scant and circumstantial; there was nothing clear-cut enough to merit an arrest. "Someone who was responsible for her disappearance?"

"Anyone at all." The older, senior detective finished the younger officer's sentence. "Did she mention a name?"

"She told me there was someone, but no, she didn't mention a name."

"So Nora talked with you about the man she was seeing?"

"No," Caroline said, remembering her conversation with Nora in the car and unable to decide what it had meant.

"Did you ever see Nora with a Joaquin Siler?" the young one asked.

"No," she said, though she'd imagined the scenario so many times that she guessed she could describe fairly accurately how Joaquin Siler would look.

"Well, then, what did Nora say about Joaquin?"

"She might have said she was seeing someone," Caroline said, confused.

"About when was that, would you say?"

Caroline shifted in her seat, looking beseechingly to the younger detective for support. "It was sometime around my wedding. I can't remember exactly when because there was a lot going on in my life at the time."

"Did you notice anything different about Nora at your wedding?"

"No," she frowned, remembering the bruises on Nora's arms and confused as to why a simple story had become so complicated.

"Did she ever say that anyone had been violent with her?"

"No," Caroline said, wondering if she'd heard correctly.

"Okay, Mrs. Noguchi." The detective, appearing distracted, set down his writing pad. "Is there anything else you can tell us that might help us find Nora?"

Satisfied that she'd been truthful thus far, Caroline placed her hands on the table to steady her weight, determined not to enter the colossal mess that seemed to be forming around her. Yet hadn't that been precisely the problem the first time, when Nora had disappeared in Escondido? Had she offered up what she'd known, the reality she'd helped to create, that day would undoubtedly have turned out differently. Ashamed of the meanness that had caused her to turn away, Caroline spoke wishing to rectify her error. "Nora never had a boyfriend before Joaquin, and so she didn't have any idea what to expect from a relationship," Caroline said, her voice full of emotion. "She was desperate to be loved, and to be recognized as someone worthy of attention."

Seeming to recognize potential value in her statement, the older detective leaned in. "So what are you saying, exactly?"

"I noticed bruises on her arms when we were dressing together for my wedding."

"Did you suspect then that your friend was being beaten?"

"When Nora disappeared, she was afraid," Caroline said, dissolving into sobs.

"Did she tell you she was afraid?"

"She was crying at my wedding reception, outside on the deck. Maybe she was scared because she didn't even want to come back in."

"Why didn't you go to the police then?"

"I didn't ask her about the bruises. It was my wedding. I don't know." She paused, then found herself saying, "Nora made me promise not to tell anyone about Joaquin. She was embarrassed because he wasn't Christian. She didn't want her parents to know. She thought she could handle the problem herself."

Caroline was still feeling sad and guilty about her abandonment of Nora two days later, when Yukari called to say that Joaquin Siler had been formally charged with assault. A search of his home revealed blood that matched Nora's on his mattress. Suspicious of the evidence that had clenched the state's case against Joaquin Siler, Caroline didn't think to say what occurred to her the moment she heard about Joaquin's arrest, that the mattress stains were most likely menstrual blood.

Chapter 25

DETECTIVE GOMEZ WAS the one who came for him. "You're under arrest for aggravated assault in connection with the disappearance of Nora Yano," he said, turning Joaquin around to cuff him after flashing his badge.

A rainy Friday afternoon, winter had arrived with a vengeance. It seemed somehow appropriate that the front room of the house was dimly lit and the hall leading to the back almost black. Joaquin's breath reeked of beer, his hair tousled and longer than before. It had taken him a full minute to answer the door. Had he been asleep? The detective reading him his rights was noting the hard-on bulging from his jeans when a woman presented herself in the hallway and the detective's tone changed from brusque to sardonic. She wasn't who he'd have expected, though he didn't know why not. He'd seen all kinds of situations in his line of work, but the woman clinging to the doorframe didn't come around often. Someone he'd consider going out with, she appeared confident. Dressed in a white tee-shirt that she'd hastily tucked into jeans, she looked like a college girl and her presence commanded attention. "What's going on here?" she asked, pulling a mass of black hair off her pretty face. "What has he done?"

"Who's this, Joaquin? You got a thing for Asian women?"

Sgt. Gomez wondered what he might have missed, and Joaquin's involvement with the woman in front of him, clearly not from the neighborhood, tugged at his thoughts.

"Sorry to end the fun, but your friend here is being arrested. If you don't mind accompanying him to the station, we have some questions for you as well."

Noting the woman's hesitancy, his partner added, "It won't take long."

"Of course." The woman looked frightened, sensing she didn't have much of a choice about riding with Joaquin to the police station. "I need to get my purse," she said, disappearing down the hall and returning with a fancy black shoulder bag. Gomez didn't know if he believed the woman's story, that she'd met Joaquin in a bar, that her acquaintance with him didn't extend beyond that afternoon. But what she said would later be confirmed by the bartender of the Tavern, a local bar just off the 101 freeway.

"I thought I told you to stay out of trouble." Recalling Joaquin's recent incarceration for DWI, Gomez stared across at Joaquin who kept blinking like his eyes refused adjust to the light.

"Whatever." Joaquin thought he might recognize the detective, though he couldn't be sure of anything except for the pounding in his head that began the second the cops had arrived, and the dry, pasty feel of his tongue stuck to the roof of his mouth.

"You know, we still haven't found the body." Gomez's partner leaned back in his chair to show that he wouldn't be moving any time soon, pausing to let his words take shape in Joaquin's head. "You could really help us out by telling us what you did with it."

Curious as to what kind of turn the case had taken, Joaquin guessed they'd be explaining it to him, along with a bunch of other crap he'd rather not hear. Dealing with other people's problems was a tedious process, like the time he sat up through the night with his boy at the emergency room, the paperwork and hours of holding his son's limp body just so he could have a stick shoved down his throat and a bottle of pills to take home. But the comparison didn't hold together. A defense attorney was brought in the next morning, just prior to Joaquin's initial appearance in court. "Are you aware of the charges that have been brought against you?" he asked. After holding out his hand for Joaquin to shake, he was all business, flipping through the stack of papers without looking up. "The prosecution is arguing that you assaulted the defendant."

"Aggravated assault?" Joaquin laughed. So he'd fucked her a few times. Now she couldn't stop fucking him. But he knew that that was just part of it. The detectives had wanted to scare him. Thought they could strong arm him, bully him into making their case, show everyone what good work they could do by bringing him to his knees. He'd looked Sgt. Gomez in the eye letting him know that it wasn't going to happen. He wasn't scared of anything they could do to him; his father, the man who heaved cans at the T.V. screen and sent lamps to the floor, had taught him early on about fear. Joaquin had watched the objects, which were not him, hit their mark inside him. He knew those cans, bent at the waist. In the morning, wanting to make things right, he'd picked them up and sold them for a nickel each. They told him what a life was worth and what he should fear. He hadn't been scared of the detectives, but he'd been scared of his father's anger, and after that, his own. When he'd drink, he could feel all the goodness well up inside of him turning angry and mean. The anger was something to fear. It didn't belong just to him, but also to his father, who had once wronged him. They'd had that in common the night before, the beer making him cocky and the adrenaline flowing through him, the love torqued up inside him. But the defense attorney made him feel something different, the anger turning to sadness, which, was one of the things he feared.

Having heard that they planned to keep him locked up until a preliminary hearing two weeks off, he remembered his Uncle Gilbert, who he hadn't thought about in a while. Sweetest man he knew. "Your Uncle Gilbert is your father's younger brother," his mother had told him when he'd asked why they called him 'Uncle.' Still couldn't believe his father and the uncle shared a bloodline. Gilbert was always smiling, give you his last penny if you asked, or even if you didn't. He loved people and didn't give a shit about the trappings of the world. But the police had taken him away in connection with a bank robbery. Took them over a year to find out they had the wrong man, and when he came home, Joaquin couldn't even be sure the man they'd released was his uncle. Gilbert never talked in front of him about what it was like to sit in a jail cell for a year, but Joaquin could guess from the looks of him. Because of Gilbert he'd been scared to death of being locked up. He'd sometimes dreamt of what it would be like to be separated from the people he loved. But that didn't scare him anymore. There was only his son, hundreds of miles away, his home for the time being in the Valley.

At the initial appearance, when they charged him with assaulting Nora, he knew he should have been irate, and he would have been had he remembered what, exactly, had happened. The way the events blurred together in his mind made him think that maybe there was more than what he remembered.

As far as he could recall, he'd only ever seen Nora a total of a half-dozen times. The first time, he'd nodded in her direction, the same way he would at every girl who passed his house. As a kid, he'd spent long hours on the stoop, watching for birds and clouds, and if a familiar face happened to pass by, all the better. She'd given him a cold look, which was not unusual for people in this part of the state, which he would have ignored had she not knocked on his door an hour or two later. That same afternoon. He knew what she wanted. Back home he'd known a couple of girls like her. Lonely, wanting to be loved. So she'd come by a couple times to get laid. Then he'd gotten a couple days off and gone up north and found his son in a funk, which led to the busted third cylinder followed by the over-night in Redding and the long drive home only to find that Nora had let herself in and changed everything around, like the house belonged to her. She'd been wrong to think he'd not left everything exactly as he wanted it. Even if the house had been a mess, it was his to keep as he liked. His wife had done the same thing throughout their marriage. Just a little straightening up, she called it. More like a bitch in heat squatting over your things, then wagging its tail, all happy about what it's done.

She'd been asleep in his bed when he came in. And when he'd woken her to ask what she was doing in his house, she'd gotten upset and left. That was the last he saw of her. He didn't have anger toward Nora; in fact, he'd liked her. She was the shy type, not the pretend to be shy type, but the kind that laughed at your jokes and liked getting it from behind.

But there was more still. Maybe he had been angry with her. When he came home and found her in his house. Thinking about it made him wish he had a drink. Why not? With no job to return to he could forget about getting his son back. He'd lose his house, and his ex- would never take him back—she'd have no reason to. He couldn't blame her. Maybe everything in his life had led to this moment. The girl who came to him for the few visits that weren't altogether memorable and then disappeared leaving him in a world of shit. Alone, in the jail cell, the sadness he'd tried to stave off came down on him. The events had not been random, but prophetic. Maybe it wasn't like he'd thought, the third cylinder fucking everything up. Asleep in the holding cell, he'd fallen out of his bed, something he hadn't done since he was a small child, and he'd tried to piece together his dream. He'd been driving, and there'd been something coming at him in the road, and instead of swerving to avoid it, he'd rushed at it head on and collided full force. The impact had shaken him from bed.

Over the next days the thing blocking the road took shape in his mind as Nora. He could have turned the car around when he saw it, or swerved to avoid it, but maybe that was the thing they had in common. Maybe that's what drew him to her, or her to him. He couldn't get around it, and she had the distinction of being herself the roadblock. And because he'd fucked her, or she'd fucked him, he knew something about her that everyone else had missed, busy as they were trying to look the other way. The detectives and defense attorney had spent their lives looking the other way. He couldn't figure why anyone would want to do that, but maybe the answer wasn't as complicated as he'd once thought. People did crazy things to trick sadness, but he couldn't do them: he had to face it.

Before entering the courtroom on the morning of his preliminary hearing, the defense attorney asked again where he was the night Nora disappeared, and then about the nature of his relationship to her. Believing he'd thought the events through, yet unaware of the danger he faced, Joaquin told his attorney what he left out when the detectives had first questioned him—about returning home from Redding drunk, and finding Nora in his house, how he'd thought about hitting her.

"So you're saying you hit her?" the attorney asked. "My guess is that the D.A. is upping the charges from aggravated assault to homicide once the body is found."

"I didn't kill her," Joaquin volunteered.

The whites of the attorney's eyes shown red like he'd been crying. Joaquin guessed it was for himself and his shitty job. Was this some kind of joke? He made an attempt at humor, but when the attorney only stared down at his watch, he realized instead the value of short answers.

"I hardly touched her," he said, thinking of charges his wife once filed against him.

"It appears that the state's evidence against you is circumstantial. A report from a neighbor who saw Ms. Yano at your house and heard yelling the night she disappeared. A friend corroborates that Nora told her she was afraid of you. Then a search warrant found blood on your mattress that matched Nora's."

"I don't know anything about any of it," Joaquin said, knowing his own lawyer didn't believe him.

"Was the defendant your girlfriend?"

"Is there anyone who can corroborate your story?"

Not wanting to involve his ex-, Joaquin decided it was best to keep her out. The mechanic who changed over his third cylinder might remember him. "My car broke down up north," he said. "I wasn't home the last week in August. And when I got back, I saw Nora for only a few minutes."

That was what the defense attorney planned to argue. It was Joaquin's first time to the L.A. county courthouse—he hadn't even been downtown before. The musty sulphurous smelling air made it difficult to see more than a few feet out the high window. The night his ex- had told him to leave, he'd driven through the night and into the next morning. Had it been bad luck or fate that he'd arrived in this hell?

The courtroom's thick paneling and heavy doors were impressive. He'd never been inside such an imposing building. He knew he should be scared; he would have been if he'd thought the events of the day were happening to him. But instead of fear, he busied himself matching faces to the people Nora had talked about, surprised to find Nora's mother so small and youthful looking.

Far from an intimidating presence, his attorney looked wiry and young in the courtroom. On cross-examination, he leaned toward the mother, all friendly: "Mrs. Yano, did you notice anything out of the ordinary around the time your daughter disappeared?"

Without saying anything, the mother stared into the attorney's eyes, which seemed to call for honesty, and assured her only that it was okay to speak. "She had bruises."

"Bruises?"

"Yes."

"Where?"

"All over."

"Where, specifically?"

"Everywhere."

"Did she say how she got them?"

"I don't know."

"She didn't tell you?"

"She might have told me, I don't know." Joaquin felt sorry for the mother, fragile in ways his attorney was either ignorant of or couldn't understand. "I didn't ask her."

A silence, not unlike the one Yukari experienced the first time she saw Nora with the bruises, fell over the room as his attorney jotted notes.

"Poor Nora," Yukari stifled a bitter cry. "She never had a chance."

The sentimental moment had its intended effect, and suffering through the weeping, Joaquin realized the woman's likeness to his own mother and wanted to asked her: If your daughter was so innocent, why was she walking the streets in hundred-degree weather, looking to get laid?

He was relieved when the reverend took the stand. Growing up, Joaquin had gone to church once or twice, and he'd always respected the pastor, a kind and honest man to whom his mother had turned more than once after his father arrived home drunk.

"In the days leading up to Nora's disappearance, did you notice anything different about her? Perhaps a change in her behavior?"

"Yes," the minister said. "She wasn't herself. I'm thinking of the night she showed up at the church. She said she'd been out walking. She seemed upset about something. When I asked her if she wanted a ride home, she stormed off."

"Did she mention a boyfriend?"

"No. But I'd known Nora since her birth. I married her parents and baptized all their children—including Nora. You can trust me when I say that there was something wrong. And I am certain that Mr. Siler was manipulating her."

Manipulating. That would be who? The minister's testimony sealed the state's case against Joaquin. But without a body the district attorney knew murder would be difficult to argue, and how would they discount reports that Nora had been sighted? According to a grocer at Trujillo's Place, a bodega on San Fernando Valley Road, a woman fitting Nora's description wandered in early Saturday morning, a week after she was presumed to have vanished. The Mexican shopkeeper remembered her because she appeared agitated; it was "kind of weird," she said. "You don't usually see Chinese girls looking that way." The record noted her as a credible witness. If only because her store had been ripped off so many times, she could be trusted to keep an eye on vagrants and possible thieves. The shopkeeper identified Nora accurately, and reported that the woman resembling Nora paced back and forth in front of the refrigerator section, stopping to finger the melons before wandering off without buying anything.

Late in autumn, a high school classmate of Nora's vacationing in Lake Tahoe with her husband and two young children swore that a woman resembling Nora appeared in Harrah's casino. More than a month after her disappearance, at a time when most people who knew her were looking for her, she appeared camouflaged by others with similar features, not easy to spot. No matter that the classmate hadn't seen Nora in over ten years, or that she would not have remembered Nora at all had her name and face not been planted in the woman's head by newspaper stories and rumors she'd recently heard. With news of Nora's disappearance fresh in her mind, she called out to the woman, who smiled across the noisy casino with a look the classmate would mistake for recognition before crossing the crowded floor behind a row of quarter slots.

Farther north, two reports came in from Oregon, one from Washington state, one as far east as Nebraska. People saw Nora buying booze, hitchhiking across Interstate 80, standing in line at a bank. Quite likely there will always be those who spot the missing, the dead, the lost. Thrill seekers, busy-bodies, insomniacs, hopeful watchdogs of the night, the dispirited and disenfranchised, each knowing because of Nora what it might be like to be intimate with the unknown in such a way as to render it almost harmless; to believe that what has vanished has merely left their field of vision.

Book Five

Chapter 26

THE THOUGHT OF handling meat made Caroline sick to her stomach, but she chose a small pot roast for Wade. Wanting their first New Year's Eve as a married couple to be remembered as special, she slow cooked the roast with a medley of potatoes and carrots for color, and she sent Wade to the bakery for dessert and to the deli so that they'd have sparkling cider for a toast. Despite her increasingly dismal outlook, Caroline knew how things were supposed to look, and she worked hard to set the mood—two white candlesticks rising like spires on either end of the table set with the dishes and flatware they'd received as wedding gifts.

Wade plunged a knife into his slab of meat. Then, setting his utensils down as if remembering he wasn't alone, he held up a crystal for Caroline to admire its shape and luminescence in the candlelight. "To my wife, and all the good things to come in our life."

Recognizing the stemware as a gift from Melissa and Mark, Caroline said a silent thank you and touched her crystal to Wade's, surprised by the tears that rose in the back of her throat. Setting the crystal back down she steadied herself, fingering a ridge in the tablecloth. "That's a nice thing to say," she smiled at Wade. "Thank you."

"Looks good," Wade said, knife back in one hand, fork in the other.

"It just doesn't seem fair."

Wade put his utensils down again. This time slightly annoyed that his meal was being delayed, he stared contemplatively down at the steam rising from his rice. "It's not for us to judge what's fair and what's not," he said, sounding smart even though Caroline knew he didn't have the slightest idea what she was referring to.

Lately she'd been remembering events from her childhood with Nora, like how she'd once helped Nora baby-sit her brothers. After spending the afternoon settling petty arguments, making them lunches, even doing their laundry, she'd arrived home with three dollars in her pocket, exhausted and shocked, too, at how much work Nora did at a time in her own life when the only thing she was expected to do was entertain herself. It was Nora, not her mother, who taught her how to separate clothes by colors, and then how to hang and fold them. Sometimes Yukari treated her daughter like a slave, but Nora just kept being her mother's good girl, meaning that she went out of her way to make things look good. Nora made a game out of folding tee-shirts and underwear into neat stacks, then licked the mayonnaise off the top slice of bread before cutting Eugene's sandwich into two perfect triangles, just the way he liked it.

All day Caroline had listened to the pot roast spitting its juices in her oven, disgusted and amazed at how much trouble it had been to cook a simple dinner. By her preparations as a child and by her temperament, Nora had been the one among them most ready to be a wife and mother. "I hope it's good," she said about the pot roast.

"It looks delicious." Wade picked up his utensils again, a grin spreading across his face this time.

Caroline watched him chew, unable to tell whether she'd succeeded with the pot roast or not. "I suppose Nora would be happy for me, and that she'd want me to be happy."

"Yes." He swallowed and took a gulp of cider making her think it was dry. "She would."

"And who knows, maybe she'll even return in time to see this little person born," she said. Hating herself for how falsely optimistic she had sounded, she stared down at the mound her flat stomach had become, not really believing that anything good would come out of it, and knowing that Nora wouldn't be coming back. As if agreeing with her sentiments rather than her thoughts, Wade eyed her with a slow nod that made her wish she could read his thoughts. "What do you think?"

"I can't say what will happen, but we'd better get some food down there. Another toast." He raised his glass a second time. "To the little person down there. Happy New Year."

"Happy New Year." Caroline lifted a forkful of meat to her mouth, chewed, and swallowed. Not bad, she thought, even though she wasn't the slightest bit hungry. "I've been worrying about the statement I gave to the police when they interviewed me," she said when they'd run through the obligatory things to say to each other.

"That was weeks ago," Wade said, clearly troubled by her mention of the police interview. "Why would you still be thinking about it?"

"I've been thinking about it for weeks," she said. "And I would have told you earlier, but how often do we really get to sit down and talk about things."

"Caroline, we eat together almost every night."

"Yes," she said, "I know. I just can't help but think that it's my fault. That maybe Joaquin Siler was arrested because of something I said."

"Well, what did you say?"

"I don't even remember, exactly," she said, which was the truth. The interview itself swirled in her head like a puff of smoke, a hazy feeling of guilt hanging over her head for something she couldn't quite remember.

"I wouldn't worry about it," Wade said. Judging by the genuine concern that ringed his eyes, Caroline believed his assurances to be sincere. But the problem was that he didn't know the whole story, or perhaps he did and was refusing to see.

"I think maybe I'm to blame," she said, unable to hold back her tears.

"Caroline," Wade said, coming around the table and kneeling to cradle his wife's shoulders. "Don't do this to yourself. You're upset, but you're not to blame."

"Yes," she said, "I am." Breathing in the heavy scent of meat she could see that neither of them had finished their dinners, the pot roast providing a centerpiece for their elegant table. "I've ruined your dinner," she said. "I'm sorry about that."

"I don't care about the dinner."

"You're so good to me," she said, and cried some more.

"I'm worried about you."

"You are?" she asked, withdrawing from his embrace and composing herself enough to speak. "Do you remember when I told you about my trip to Baja with the Yanos, how Nora disappeared from a gas station on the way home?"

"The story you told me in Coronado?" he asked.

"That's right," Caroline said, feeling bile rising in her throat, but unwilling to cut the conversation off. "I hadn't remembered until I was telling you that I'd known Nora wasn't in the car when Yujitaka pulled away."

"Sounds like you were complicit in a dirty trick." Wade shrugged.

"No," Caroline said, fury rising in her voice. "It was more than that. Something mean spirited in me that wanted to make Nora disappear.

"It disgusts me to think about," she continued, gagging on what little meat she'd eaten during their unfinished dinner.

"Don't be so melodramatic, Caroline," he said calmly. "You were a kid, you didn't know any better, and now you do."

"You don't understand," Caroline said, not understanding herself.

"For god's sake," Wade said, his voice rising above hers. "I'm a doctor. This type of thing happens to me all the time. An error in judgment, doing nothing when action is required, not doing enough. Being responsible for someone else's life is a complicated matter.

Mistakes happen. You get over it. It's you who doesn't understand," he said with finality. "You need to get over it, Caroline. You need to move on."

The conversation had spun out of control; her guilt coupled with Wade's anger resulted in a fundamental error in Wade's thinking that prevented him from seeing the truth. As a medical doctor, Wade had taken an oath to help people. If he disregarded the needs of his patients, he could be sued, or his license revoked. She knew that any mistakes he might have made hadn't been for lack of effort whereas she'd not only done nothing, but in doing nothing had wanted something bad to happen to Nora—years before she'd wished for the bad thing that had finally happened.

"Promise me you'll stop worrying," Wade said when she didn't respond to his remonstrance. "If not for my sake, then for the sake of that little person," he said, brushing a hand across her swollen belly.

"Okay," she said, biting her lip to keep from crying again. "I'll try."

As a result of her conversation with Wade, Caroline vowed to do a better job keeping what she knew to herself, but her secret knowledge, coiled like a knot inside her, asserted itself each time she looked in the mirror. By February she'd gained ten pounds. In front, her belly finally protruded enough to start wearing her maternity clothes, and in the rear the spreading of her hips caused her to waddle so that even from behind everyone could tell she was pregnant. With little else to do, Caroline spent hours poring through magazines and catalogs to find things for the nursery (pink *and* blue since Wade wanted to be surprised), even driving out to Laguna Hills to shop when she saw a baby in the mall wearing a hand knit sweater she had to have. Still, more often than not, keeping herself busy was a way to stave off dread.

She'd kept to her resolution for nearly a month and was making an inquiry to a catalog company about a stroller she'd seen while out walking when her call waiting signaled an interruption.

"Oh, hi mom," she said, trying to sound cheerful, "Can I call you right back?"

"No." Her mother's answer and curt tone startled her. "Your Uncle Albert is in the hospital."

"What?" Still thinking stroller, she couldn't be sure she'd heard correctly.

"I've been debating over whether to call you or not—"

"What are you talking about?" she demanded, a hand gliding absently over her belly.

"We had some bad news last night."

"Hang on," she said, remembering that she needed to tell the stroller people she'd call back, then dismissing the other caller from her thoughts. "Nevermind. What happened?"

"Your Uncle Albert was involved in a car accident last night."

"You said that," she shrieked, beginning to hyperventilate.

"Maybe I shouldn't have told you."

"Tell me what happened. Please," she said, and hearing her mother mumbling something on the other end, it occurred to Caroline that Teru had never intended to spare her.

Teru's sigh lasted just long enough for Caroline to brace herself. "Auntie Mona called to tell us. Evidently it's pretty bad. His Plymouth was broadsided and overturned. It took the paramedics over an hour to get him out. Now the doctors say he's paralyzed on the left side, and maybe there's some brain damage, too."

"Oh no." The other phone line clicked dead and the baby rolled inside her belly as if to call attention to its presence.

"We're going to visit him tonight," Teru said, "and I thought maybe you'd want to come along."

"Yes, of course, I'll go," Caroline said. Then, remembering she was married, "I'll have to check with Wade, but I'm sure it'll be fine." He'd been her favorite uncle ever since she could remember, always bringing toys and taking time to play with her when he and her Aunt Mona visited.

Wade's new receptionist said he was with a patient, but an hour later he rang back and she repeated the news. "I can't believe this has happened," she said. "We just saw him at Christmas and he was fine, and now this awful news!"

"It *is* bad news, and I'm glad you called to tell me, but at the minute there's a roomful of people stacked up in the waiting room so I've got to get going."

"Oh, I'm sorry, and here I am going on—"

"It's all right. We'll talk more tonight."

"Yes, tonight. My parents are going to visit him tonight and I told my mom we'd go too, but I wanted to check with you."

"I don't think that's such a good idea just now."

"Why not?"

"Many reasons that I told you I don't have time to explain right now."

"Like what?"

"Oh, Caroline," he sighed, annoyed. "Is he conscious?"

"I don't know. I guess I forgot to ask."

"I'm just thinking that maybe he'd rather not have visitors. Maybe it's best to wait until his condition stabilizes to see who he wants in his hospital room. If it were me, I know I wouldn't want people I hardly know hovering over me—after all, I've only met your uncle once or twice. If he asked for you specifically that's one thing, but it doesn't sound like he did, and I don't think it's a good idea for you to go."

"But I told my mother we'd go."

"Yes, well, you can always call her back. It's not as if we won't go at all, just not until we know more about his condition, and we can talk more when I get home tonight because right now *I* have to go."

It felt slightly like a betrayal not to pay a visit, and she resented how Wade had made her beg him. He might have been trying to take care of her, but what he hadn't known was that she'd expected something bad to happen. Her only surprise was that it hadn't happened to her. The bad luck she'd caused had left her scared to visit the hospital, to see the damage done to her uncle, and glad when Wade had said she couldn't go. That night, while Wade slept, she made a pact with God: she'd do everything in her power to live right if he'd not cause any more suffering. When she rubbed a hand over her belly the baby's gnarled limbs rose to her touch, and she tried to connect with the life forming inside her body. She settled on the image of a row boat, swaying under the stars on a clear, calm night, and she rocked the baby under an imaginary sky filled with stars, careful not to allow the fantasy to lull her to sleep.

As a result of persistent nightmares, sleep was something she avoided. Once the baby had sunk to the bottom of a stream while she sat on the mossy bank scooping up rocks and lichen, forgetting it was her baby she was looking for until something black and freakish began wiggling in her net. That night, a baby sprang from her body full grown with thick, matted hair, and she wished that Wade weren't such a heavy sleeper, that he'd wake up when she called to him in the dark so she could tell him how scared she was.

But Caroline had not been home when, less than two months before the baby was due, the phone rang with more bad news. This time Caroline's eighty-year-old grandmother had had a stroke and was in serious but stable condition at a hospital in San Jose. Her speech had been impaired and she was having difficulty using her left arm and leg, but the doctors said she was out of immediate danger and could be expected to recover. "I'm glad it's you," Teru told Wade when he answered instead of Caroline. "I hate being the one to tell Caroline bad news. The poor thing's had more than her fair share lately."

"Yes." Wade glanced down at his watch. "And so have you, Teru."

It was just past noon and Caroline wasn't due back from shopping for at least another hour. The baby, he quickly calculated, was less than two months off, yet the risk of premature labor, were she to fly or take a car trip up north, still existed. "I can have Caroline call you when she gets back," he said.

"Okay," Teru said. "Or you could just tell her yourself. I'll be flying out this evening, and there isn't that much more to say."

"I'm sorry about the news," he said, and remembering to be kind he added, "please give your mother my regards."

The conversation had been quick. When it was over, Wade ran the tap and poured himself the glass of water he'd come inside to get, and after drinking it down returned to the garage where he'd been stationed all morning putting up the old kitchen cabinets for storage. It was mid-afternoon when Caroline pulled up with shopping bags stacked so high that Wade had to scold her for not being able to see out the rear window of the hatchback.

He'd planned to tell her the bad news after he'd finished unloading the bags into the nursery, but then she'd looked tired, and so he'd suggested a nap, and before he knew it, the afternoon had vanished. Unable to wait for her to get up and make dinner, he suggested Italian and by the time they left the house, his thoughts were elsewhere.

The next morning, Teru's absence at church should have triggered his memory. He should have told her in the car on the ride home rather than making her worry when no one answered the phone at her parents' house. He should have heard Caroline's voice in his head demanding of him, How can a person who doesn't remember life-altering details manage as a doctor? But somehow his memory of the phone call eluded him until that night, when Caroline's mother, having returned from San Jose, called with an update.

Caroline was furious with Wade, who stared wide-eyed at her while she pretended to her mother that she knew. It was bad enough to have had to put the news together herself, but why had she felt compelled to protect her careless husband? Sensing Caroline's scorn, Wade retreated to the bedroom, where he sat reading in bed when Caroline stormed in. "Wade," she said under her breath, plopping her pregnant body down beside him and talking into the back cover of John Keegan's *A History of Warfare*. "What kind of an idiot do you think I am?"

"Calm down, Caroline," he begged, genuinely contrite. "I meant to tell you, only I forgot, and I'm very sorry."

"Did you think I wouldn't find out?" She felt too angry to cry. "You're not sorry at all!"

"I meant for you to find out!"

"No, you didn't. You're just like my mom trying to spare me the bad news. For heaven's sake, it was my *grandmother* and I should have been there!"

"Caroline, calm down." He found anyone's anger, but particularly hers, alarming. She knew this about him, and hated the insidious way fear lurked behind his seemingly reasonable facade. *The mole was malignant,* she imagined him saying. *You have about two months—*

"Look," he tried to reason with her when she could not be consoled, "you couldn't have gone to San Jose anyway. The airlines wouldn't have let you fly, and the drive would have been too much for you at this late stage, so you couldn't have done anything."

"Wade!" She yelled, now furious. "I can't believe this. You don't understand at all."

"Well, maybe I don't," Wade conceded. "But I *am* sorry."

"No you're not."

"What do you want me to say to convince you?"

"Nothing." There was nothing he could say.

"I'm sorry," he said.

"You're not," she wept.

"Okay." He would say anything to make her stop crying, if only he knew the right words.

"I never understood your fascination with malignant moles," she spat, "but now I can see exactly why you get along with them so well. I hate you."

She'd have plenty of time later to think back to her childish response, to wonder where it came from, because, gathering the bedding, she intended to retreat to the couch in the living room. But Wade insisted that the couch should be his. Knowing he'd be unable to dissuade his wife from sleeping apart from him, he offered a reasonable alternative, and in the end she gave in.

That night her tears were both justified and self-indulgent. To her mind, Wade's withholding the news of her grandmother's stroke was connected to his handling of her Uncle Albert's car accident, a plot between Wade and her mother because to them she was merely a fancy toy, valuable, but otherwise unimportant. Having forgotten about her pact with God, she hated them both, her mother for her culpable oblivion and Wade for his manipulations. And she hated herself, too. Floating inside her belly, as if sensing its well being is in jeopardy, the baby bunched like a fist in her womb and lay perfectly still. That night Caroline didn't know how it would be possible to go on with Wade or to continue with her life. Lying awake, she found herself thinking about Nora—maybe because she'd come to understand how a person's life could become loathsome and intolerable—and the knowledge of her friend's suffering brought her comfort, which she accepted apprehensively, along with the recognition that the terms of her relationship with Nora had changed. That day in the car, she'd wished for a verification of her superiority. She'd nullified her friend to fulfill her own selfish wish. But this was different. Even if she'd never really understood Nora, over time she'd become her equal, and grief lifted her out of reach of her mother and her husband, and brought her finally down to sleep.

In the morning Wade had a hot breakfast waiting for her, and, still half-asleep, she remembered the night they'd brought in the New Year—all their new dishes and flatware and two candlesticks lit at either end of the table. She ate in silence in blue-grey darkness, the baby fluttering in her belly in the absolute peace of morning. The flames flickered, and in their shadow she saw spread across the table the outline of all the things she loved.

On a full stomach, she tried but no longer remembered why she'd been so angry with her husband. How could she not love this man, who could admit with a kind gesture that he'd been wrong, this man who she'd agreed to love forever.

Wade didn't eat, only gazed attentively at Caroline eating. After clearing the dishes, he led her back to their bedroom and began to undress her. She'd been waiting for that moment through most of breakfast, but for reasons she hadn't anticipated she couldn't stop giggling. To think she'd known Wade since they were children, all the difficulties he'd had to go through to ensure that his practice and his reputation were impeccable.

"Sleep," he told her before heading off to work.

Chapter 27

To celebrate Mark's passing the state Bar exam, Melissa planned a date: the movie they'd been wanting to see, followed by a late dinner. Unfortunately, however, the movie was no longer showing, and they arrived at the restaurant out of sorts, neither of them particularly hungry, for lack of an alternate plan. "So this is the end, and the beginning," Melissa said, fidgeting with the menu, pondering how Mark could stop clerking now and move up the ladder.

"Yes, things are never as they seem," Mark said under his breath. "Should I have the curry, or the miso ramen?"

"Definitely the curry," Melissa said. "It's a relief, isn't it, to achieve your goal after so many years?"

"I'm just glad not to have to cart law books everywhere I go," Mark sighed. "I guess now I'll have to find some other form of exercise."

"Right," Melissa laughed, knowing that Mark, her skinny fiancée, had never given much thought to the condition of his body. "This is a well deserved victory. I knew you'd pass."

"Really?" Mark said. "I had no idea I'd pass."

"Oh, come on," Melissa chided him. "You knew after you took it, didn't you? You said you thought you'd done well."

"You never know," Mark said. "It's all a guessing game."

Waiting for their meal to arrive, Melissa stared across the table at Mark. Between them there had always been something pressing to discuss, and no time to talk at length. The effect was so many things gone unsaid, so much that she didn't have words for, or time to tell. Now the prospect of a leisurely evening frightened her. "You say you never know, but I think you do," Melissa said, attempting to sound more playful than she felt. "Tell me something you know, something I don't know about you."

"What?" Mark said, his eyes widening.

"You know," Melissa said, "like a game. I've known you for all these years, but I bet there's lots you've never told me. Tell me something you know that I don't know."

"Okay," Mark said, clasping his hands together and staring directly into her eyes before speaking. "Do you remember when I first came to Valley Baptist?"

"Yes," Melissa said, "of course. You came with your parents."

"Right," Mark smiled. "But do you know *why* I came?"

"No." Melissa felt her upper lip twitch. "Your parents made you? That's how I first showed up."

"My parents didn't have any interest in attending church," Mark said flatly. "I asked them to go and they took me believing I wanted to find religion. They had no idea I'd chosen that church because I wanted to find a Japanese girlfriend."

"What?" Melissa said, eyes wide. "No way."

"Way," Mark said, clearly pleased with his surprise.

"You were thirteen!" Melissa said, unbelieving.

"Exactly," Mark said. "My Uncle Bill had just married my Aunt Ruby, and I had a crush on her. She made great sushi and let me touch her family's ancestral sword, which hung over the television, and she showed me her collection of *kokeshi* dolls. Plus she always smelled good."

"My god." Melissa scanned the room for her dinner, fairly certain that Mark was having her on.

"Your turn," Mark said. "Tell me something I don't know about you."

"Okay," Melissa said tentatively, no longer sure she wanted to play. It was easy to think of what he *did* know. Like how she could have rescued Nora if he hadn't stopped her, the conversation they'd had in this very restaurant ten months earlier. How dismissive he had been when she *knew* something terrible was going on. It could make her angry all over again to think about it. But maybe, Melissa reasoned, not wanting to be angry, love was born out of the need to forget. She remembered standing with Elinore at the baboon exhibit, how painfully little there'd been between them to talk about. Entranced by the garish baboons, she'd felt embarrassed, unwilling even to acknowledge her connection to her half-sister.

Then Elinore had turned the stroller into the simulated darkness of a cave exhibit. "'Night Crawlers,'" she'd read the sign to Naoko. "This one's got to be creepy."

Melissa knew Elinore was watching as she pulled Naoko from the stroller and boosted her against the glass to see a nest of baby field mice.

"Don't tap on the glass," Melissa had cautioned Naoko when she reached up to touch. "The parents are burrowing. See how they carry the hay into the nest? If you disturb them, they might abandon their babies."

"What will happen then?" Naoko had wanted to know.

"Well, the babies are too young to fend for themselves. So they would probably die."

Naoko pulled her hand away from the glass wall, hugged Melissa, then squirmed out of her arms to the snake exhibit with Elinore chasing after her. Melissa didn't much like Elinore, but she loved Naoko. She'd known it then. Standing at the wall of mice, she'd felt the mistake she'd made in disclosing to the small child a fact she hadn't been ready to hear, but Naoko had forgiven her, and Melissa had stood for a minute still feeling the warmth of Naoko's body against her chest.

"I'm sorry I had to run the last time we had lunch," Melissa had said, transferring her feelings for Naoko to Elinore when they were back in the daylight.

"Don't worry about it," Elinore had said, sounding irritated even though Melissa's tone had been conciliatory.

How little things changed. And, she considered, how much. She'd told Mark about meeting Elinore, but she hadn't told him the full story. Biting her bottom lip, she stared across the table at him, debating what to reveal. "Elinore Shimizu, the woman I met because Jun called in a favor, she's my half sister."

"Get out," Mark said, clearly thinking Melissa's declaration an attempt to one-up him.

Melissa nodded without looking up. Unable to continue, she wished she could retract what she'd said, or say it had all been a joke.

"You're not kidding, are you," Mark said, folding his arms tightly across his chest. "I'm guessing Asako has to be your mother, so that leaves Bob."

Melissa continued to nod. It was a simple thing, a glitch from the past. Once uttered, so simple seeming, and yet she hated herself for telling, and hated him, too, for getting the information out of her. "Promise you won't tell a soul," she said bringing her eyes up to meet his.

"It's okay, Melissa," Mark assured her. "Your secret is safe with me. You should know that this information doesn't make me think badly of you, or anyone involved. If anything, I like your mother more, and Bob, too, knowing what they've been through. No one would ever guess that Bob isn't your natural father."

Melissa smiled; perhaps everything would be okay.

"How did all this happen, I mean, may I ask?"

"My mother never talks about it," she said. "But I remember, or at least I could swear that I do, even though I couldn't have been more than a year old. My father left and remarried Elinore's mother the same year."

"Ouch." Mark clucked his tongue, then surveyed the room with eyes that looked hungry. "That makes sense."

"What do you mean?"

"Well, your mother isn't the easiest person to get along with."

"Mark!" Melissa reached across the table and slapped his arm.

"She's not," he said, relieved when the waitress appeared with their bowls of food.

Quiet as they ate, Melissa watched Mark dig into his curry. "You have to admit," he said, after scraping the last the last bit of yellow chicken and rice to his mouth, "your mother is a very controlling person."

Melissa recalled her mother's delight at seeing her in the fairy tale white gown she'd recently picked for their wedding. It called to mind all the vicarious pleasure Asako had taken in every step of her growing up, graduating from high school, college, graduate school. In an overt way, choosing Mark was the first time she hadn't acted upon Asako's wishes. Melissa remembered how scared she'd been that her mother wouldn't like Mark, certain that Asako would have preferred her to date someone Japanese. Maybe because of the war and everyone of her mother's generation being interned, her parents never socialized with non-Japanese. Granted most of the population in Southern California wasn't Japanese, the church was where they all belonged. "I owe everything good in my life to my mother," Melissa said defensively. "She's the kindest person I know.

"But let's not talk about her," she said, wanting to change the subject before Mark could make a less than ingenuous comment. "Tell me something else about you. This is an interesting game, and it's your turn."

"I don't believe in Jesus," Mark said, not missing a beat.

"What?" This time Melissa felt truly stunned.

"I love you," he said, "but I wouldn't go to the church if it weren't so important to you. I've always hoped you'd grow out of it."

"I can't believe you're saying this." Melissa's voice trembled as she spoke, hot pressure rising under the surface of her face like the aftermath of an internal explosion. Could Mark really have meant what he'd said? "You can't mean this," she said, giving him a chance to retract.

"I don't mean the people," he said, seeming conscious of her fragility. "I know how important your friendship with Nora was. How important Caroline still is, and that's as it should be. But the Jesus stuff. It's like an old shoe. You can keep it around, but why wear it if it doesn't fit?"

"What are you talking about?" she demanded. "What are you even saying?"

"I like Caroline," he said quietly. "I've always liked Caroline. And I've caught her dozing through more than one of Reverend Nakatani's Sunday messages. She's savvy, much more so than she looks. Do you and Caroline talk about Jesus?"

"Stop!" Melissa shouted. It was too much. "I can't believe you're saying this. Any of this. You like Caroline, but not because she's so savvy. You find her attractive and you can't see beyond that. You think you're so smart, such a good judge of people, but you have no idea."

No longer in control of her thoughts, Melissa had lost track of the truth, though her competitive spirit still played the game to win. "Did you know that Caroline framed an innocent man for Nora's murder?"

"What?" Mark smirked, but Melissa knew that she was the one in charge now.

"Joaquin Siler. The man who's going to trial in connection with Nora's disappearance. Caroline is the one who identified him. She gave the police false information."

"How do you know all this?"

Knowing she had his full attention, Melissa took a minute to breathe before responding. "It's a long story," she said, letting the air slowly out of her lungs. Aware she'd used Caroline's words to compose herself, she inhaled again, trying to slow her pulse.

"Nora called me the day she disappeared," she confessed, feeling the heaviness lift from her chest. "It was early in the morning and I was asleep. I didn't think much of it until later, when I found out she'd gone missing."

"So?" Mark said, obviously not making the connection between the phone call and Joaquin's arrest.

"I didn't know Nora was seeing someone until Caroline told me—at the reception at the Yano's, after the memorial. Caroline said that the police had brought someone in, and I wrote down his name. Then I called a connection I have over at the Foothill precinct.

Basically, Caroline is responsible. She pinned Nora's disappearance on the person who Nora was involved with."

"How do you know this person's not responsible?"

"That's a good question." Melissa's thoughts traveled back to games they'd played as children; somehow Caroline had always wound up the hero. "Because Caroline made up information," she said, not willing to tell Mark what she was really thinking. "But I'm also sure Nora called me after she left Joaquin's house."

"I can't believe you didn't tell me this," Mark said, shaking his head in disbelief.

"You were so busy studying for the Bar, I didn't want to bother you."

"You're kidding," he said. "Tell me you're kidding."

She shrugged, blissfully aware of how irrational she sounded.

"Did you talk to the police?"

"Yes, I told you. I have a friend who knows someone at Foothill."

"Forgive me if I'm having a hard time keeping straight what you've said—and what you haven't," he said, as if unable to believe her stupidity. "Did you tell the investigators what you know?"

"No."

"Melissa, why the hell not?"

"They wouldn't believe me if I had. I lied when I said I knew nothing. So who's to say I'm not lying still?"

They sat in silence, Mark absorbing what Melissa had said; Melissa numb to all but her own pain. She'd always felt so unbridelike. They'd chosen September for a wedding date, a year after Caroline and Wade's ceremony and Nora's disappearance, an attempt to keep their wedding day separate in people's minds from both events. When she'd accepted Mark's proposal of marriage, she'd done so because she loved him as much as she'd ever loved anyone, and for lack of a better idea of what to do with her life. But then she'd gone about ticking off the horribly complicated items that went into planning a wedding—picking a date, informing her parents and friends, choosing china, stemware, and flatware patterns at Neiman Marcus, shopping with her mother for a gown, finding the right place to hold the reception. Having seen Caroline finagle hers, she knew how to do everything right.

Her mother attributed her dark moods to the fact that she'd spent too much energy on Caroline's wedding. And Melissa, wanting to diffuse the resentment of Caroline that brewed in Asako, told her mother that, to the contrary, helping Caroline had prepared her. The saleswoman who handled her bridal registry claimed Melissa was just shy. She should know, she said, given the hundreds of bride-to-be's she'd worked with, and Melissa had listened not only to her mother, but to the solicitous saleswoman as well, wanting in earnest to know why she lacked joy, or even ambivalence.

What she recognized now, sitting across from Mark, was that she loved him, and that he might well be the person who could save her. Just like Reverend Nakatani promised redemption in Christ. He was strong enough to transform her—if she chose him. It had never been so clear to her that she had choices, or that the two paths before her were exclusive, each leading somewhere entirely different. "I'm sorry," she said, after trying to think it through and failing. "I can't marry you."

"It's not you," she said. Forced now to explain herself to Mark, she realized that the evening's events would figure prominently into his interpretation of her decision. Staring at him from across the booth, she believed that what she was saying was not really the truth, and yet she didn't know what else to say.

"Mel, if you don't want to marry me, then your decision has got to have something to do with me."

"Okay, you're right," she sighed, exasperated.

He scooted himself out of the booth and stood up to leave, but Melissa grabbed his arm and pulled him back. "No, please," she begged, "please don't go yet. You owe me another minute, or I owe it to you. Please, sit."

Mark slumped back against the hardwood bench while Melissa swallowed down some ice water and cleared her throat in an attempt to keep talking. "I don't understand how any of this started," she confessed.

"Okay," Mark sneered. "I need to go."

"Fine," she said, and when he made no motion to leave she waved him on. "Go if you need to. I'll see you on Sunday."

But rather than go, Mark dug into his seat. "So that's it? We go out for five years, then you break off our engagement and it's *See you Sunday, Mark*?" His mouth gaped open like a big ugly hole in his head, and she hated how belligerent he'd become.

"I don't think anything has to be different. It's not like I want to date someone else; I just don't think we should be getting married right now."

Mark gazed up at the neon beer sign like he was trying to keep himself from putting his fist through the wall. "Melissa," he talked very slowly, with his jaw clamped shut, and Melissa examined the bones sticking out on the sides of his face. "You've made your decision, that's clear. But you can't believe that nothing will change as a result of it. I can't just go on seeing you this way. I don't want to. Maybe there will be a time when I'll want to see you again, but right now I'd prefer not to see you at all."

"Okay," she said, claiming understanding even though she didn't feel any. "What do you see in me anyway?" she asked, sensing that she mostly made him miserable.

"You try to be a good person," Mark answered right away, like he'd been thinking about it, and Melissa noted that his smile appeared both forced and sincere.

"I do try," she said, accepting his compliment and pleased that he'd found it so easy to find something redeeming about her.

"And you've always reminded me of Lucy Liu," he said, and after slapping a twenty on the tabletop, he left.

Melissa didn't know how long she'd been sitting when the waitress stopped by. "Should I take these plates?" the pleasant voice asked, smiling.

Melissa stared down at the empty bowls. He wasn't coming back, and she thought that maybe she understood why she had no words as a child. Maybe it would be years before she'd speak again. Maybe experts would have to hold up flash cards of familiar objects and say words slowly, over and over, until she could repeat them back.

"Well, I'll just bring you a check and you can pay when you're ready," the same voice said, and coming back with a black lacquer tray, the waitress picked up the twenty that Mark had left on the table.

The only thing Melissa knew for sure was that the news wouldn't come from her. Let Caroline's mom tell her, or, better yet, Caroline could do it. Asako would find out either way, but she wouldn't hear from Melissa how she wasn't getting married, or how she'd been abandoned, utterly despondent. Or how much she still loved Mark.

The hardest part, she reflected, had been taking the engagement ring from her finger. When she'd slid it across the booth to Mark the diamond had winked at her, like it was sad to leave her finger.

Chapter 28

HIDEKO'S FRIDAY AFTERNOON out plan aimed at putting Elinore in better humor had failed, to the point where Elinore suspected that not only had she been a bad mother, but that she'd brought irreconcilable problems into her parents' lives as well as her daughter's. Through the wall, she listened to Hideko and Jun argue in restrained hush tones that persisted late into the night, followed by her mother's circumspect, and often accusatory, behavior in the morning.

At the end of the day, after Naoko had been put down for the night, she and Hideko sat together in the den, amidst toys that neither had the energy to pick up. Since Jun's departure the week prior, Elinore had been making her way through a pint of Ben & Jerry's mint oreo chip ice cream by the spoonful while Hideko continued her nightly consumption of oranges, the scent of which had begun to burn in Elinore's throat. The news magazine shows blurred together like a never ending string of commercials humming along in blue darkness until the night that Hideko, with a dramatic wave of the remote, shut down the power.

Using uncharacteristic resolve, she commanded her daughter's attention by positioning herself in front of the set. "There's something I need to tell you," she announced. "Your Dad and I talked about it when he was home and debated whether or not to say anything. Now I think I will."

Elinore sat up, bracing herself. But instead of launching into the rebuke she had expected, Hideko popped a wedge of orange

249

in her mouth. "Boy, the oranges are really tart this year!" she said, grimacing between bites.

"Are they?" Elinore said, figuring it best to go along with her mother.

Hideko made a sour face. "Your father dated Asako Hori for several years, and he had a daughter with her just over a year before we had you."

"What are you talking about?" Elinore looked down at Naoko's blocks whose alphabet letters painted in bold primary colors created a jumble of sounds out of the zoo animals huddled together at her feet.

"It's not anything you have to worry about," Hideko said. "Only a few people know or even remember anymore, but just in case, I wanted you to hear it from me."

The pressure in Elinore's head moved quickly down to her gut and transformed into an ache in her bowels, the information she'd received a moment ago threatening to leave her. "Why did you never tell me this?" she asked, raising her voice and rising to her mother's eye level, then sitting back down again. "I don't understand why you're telling me this."

"I guess I waited too long," Hideko said apologetically, making Elinore instantly sorry for having raised her voice. "Sorry that I waited so long, neh."

Elinore watched the distinct movement of her mother's mouth, masticating orange slices as she spit out words along with occasional bits of pulp and seed.

"Dad's someone else's parent?"

"Elinore, no, that's not what I'm saying at all."

What was clear was not that Hideko had waited too long, but that neither she nor her mother had ever been the person she'd thought they were. Elinore wanted to convey her incredulity, to speculate whether it was possible to trust anyone to be who they said they were, shame Hideko for making her into the real live emperor in Naoko's fairy tale book, parading through life exposed. But she guessed that analogy didn't quite work. The woman standing in front of the T.V. was undeniably her mother, the man off in Kansas City her father. And yet Hideko appeared wholly unperturbed by the notion that for an entire lifetime her daughter's birth origins had been kept a secret by people Elinore didn't even know—and some whom she did. Elinore glared at her mother, who might have hopped live off the television screen, and at that moment realized who Asako Hori was. "Are you saying that Melissa Hori and I are related?"

"Yes." Hideko nodded. Then, pointing to Elinore's lap, she said, "Watch that container, will you? Maybe you'd better put it away before you stain the couch."

Elinore got up and walked the ice cream to the kitchen. Before she put the carton in the freezer she attempted to replace the lid, but it slipped from her hands. Standing over the garbage can she poured out the frothy green liquid and black specks before returning to the television room, still with no idea what she was supposed to do with the information her mother had revealed. "Melissa Hori is my sister?"

"You can't really call her that. It's not as if the two of you grew up together," Hideko concluded smartly.

"My god," Elinore whispered. "Melissa is my half-sister."

But Hideko had already become impatient with the facts. "Are you listening to me at all?" she demanded angrily. "I didn't raise you in that church. I never wanted anything to do with it, or expected that you'd become friends with Asako Hori's girl.

"You're an adult now, so what you do is your business; I just didn't want you to find out from someone other than me.

"Don't worry." Hideko refused to be threatened by Elinore who held out her hands as if prepared to do violence, and instead pulled her daughter in to an embrace. "Like I told you, not many people know, and those who do have probably forgotten by now."

In shock, Elinore buried her head in Hideko's neck and breathed in the sweet smell of her mother's perfume. "You know as well as I that this is not the type of information people forget," she said, feeling the thin, soft tissue of Hideko's earlobe. "At least not normal people."

Then, remembering the look on her father's face when she returned home after her date with Melissa, she pulled back. "Did you know that Dad arranged for me to meet Melissa?"

"No," Hideko said, becoming again her stalwart self. "He didn't tell me until after he called her."

"Why?" Elinore asked, her question directed more at her absent father than at her mother, whose expression radiated control.

"He was worried about you. He thought you needed a friend. Maybe unconsciously he wanted to make amends. You know your father."

"No," Elinore said flatly, "I don't."

Try as she might, Elinore couldn't quite imagine her absent father as the man who'd stolen her mother's heart, let alone wrap her mind around an even more complicated story: Her father, married to Melissa's mother, the father of an infant who ran out on his wife and baby daughter. It made no sense. Or maybe she just didn't want to believe that there was more to Jun than met the eye, or to have to wonder what, exactly, she'd missed.

Seated back on the couch holding a hollow orange peel, Hideko looked ceremonial, perfect, and young enough to be mistaken for someone's child rather than her mother, recalling a story she'd once heard about her parents' romantic beginnings. "I thought you said you met Dad at a Dodger's game."

"I did," Hideko said. "And it was love at first sight just like I told you. I didn't lie to you about anything, I just never mentioned Dad's life before we were married because Asako and her husband Bob and your father and I agreed a long time ago that it would be better for everyone that way. We didn't want to disrupt people's lives."

"Oh right." Elinore paced the room dodging the toys that seemed to leap out at her in the darkness. "So what am I supposed to do with this news?" Planting herself in front of the T.V. screen, she implored her mother to tell her, but Hideko looked through her, as if catching something more appealing on the blank screen behind her.

"There's nothing you need to do," she said dismissively.

"Look at me," Elinore said, calling Hideko's attention back. "Don't you see the mess you've created?"

"It's in the past," Hideko shrugged, refusing to take part in her daughter's drama.

"No," Elinore shouted. "It's standing right in front of you. Is Dad even *my* father?"

Pelting Elinore with her hollow orange, Hideko clucked her tongue against the roof of her mouth, exasperated. "Yes, silly," she said. "Of course he is."

Elinore stared noncommittally down at the orange rind that had fallen open at her feet. "But he's Melissa's father, too?"

"Biologically speaking, yes. But Melissa grew up with Bob. Besides, she doesn't know."

Elinore watched her mother's face as she spoke, attempting to visualize the person Hideko spoke of, but saw instead herself. Her tall nose, thick eyebrows, pursed mouth, and prominent cheekbones were all Hideko, the story about Melissa ludicrous. But on Hideko's face, lines had formed around the mouth and eyes like a secret map of routes. "I'm tired," she announced, suddenly feeling too weary to continue. "I need to go to sleep."

"Okay." Hideko blinked playfully before offering her ritual goodnight. "*Oyasuminasai.*"

"Yeah," Elinore waved behind her back. "Goodnight."

What she needed was to lie in the dark, to listen to the sound the house made in all its silence. There was comfort in Naoko, asleep on the other side of the wall, and even in her mother who hadn't yet moved out of the den, and in her father, away in Kansas City.

Had Jun been lying awake in a hotel room when he'd manufactured the drama that had forced her out of her life to take part in his machinations? She'd left her partner in Santa Fe due to spousal abuse, why not set her life on a new track, introduce her to her half sister, let a relationship develop between them. All the while he'd be gone, far enough out of reach to avoid any fallout if it came to that. But while Jun had been guilty of creating a ridiculous story, Elinore's guilt lay in the failure of her imagination. Jun had been the absent father whom, when home, was prone to meddling. But he'd also lived a life impossibly far from anything she knew. In addition to being her father, he was also the man who'd married one woman and fallen in love with another, and before that a boy, detained in his childhood behind a locked gate.

Perhaps the time he spent traveling was a way of exercising the freedom he'd long ago lost. He was flexing his muscles against a loss that he'd experienced only remotely, on behalf of the parents whose lives he'd seen being wholly disrupted. Now he was doing the same for his daughter.

The truth was nothing Elinore could have anticipated. Irrespective of her father's betrayal of her and her anger with her parents over their long kept secret, she felt glad to know that Jun would leave a marriage that wasn't working, and grateful for the love he'd found for her mother and her. Though she hated to admit it, she rather liked the story blossoming in her head, along with the tenderness it engendered, which she would not have expected to feel for her father.

Chapter 29

ELINORE INVITED MELISSA to lunch, and this time she named the spot: Tommy's hamburger stand on Roscoe Boulevard because she remembered eating there once and it would be convenient for Melissa, whose appointments that day were along a stretch of the 405 freeway in the Valley. The Anheuser-Busch plant across the street contributed a yeasty thickness to the midsummer heat, and Elinore arrived with a sick feeling, like the heaviness of the air had settled in her stomach. It didn't help that the only people at the hamburger stand were workers from the beer plant, and that Melissa was late. Fifteen minutes passed on Elinore's watch before she saw an arm waving out of a down-turned car window as Melissa sped into the parking lot.

"I'm sorry I'm late," she yelled over the nearby traffic as she approached the cement block table where Elinore sat waiting. "Have you eaten?"

"Two chili-cheeseburgers." Elinore patted her stomach facetiously.

"I heard they were great here."

Elinore nodded to confirm the stupid lie that she was too worked up to care about. She had picked Tommy's at the spur of the moment, combing her memory of the Valley's dining establishments for neutral territory and, having done so, she refused to explain to Melissa that she hadn't eaten even one burger in recent history.

"Mind if I order real quick?" Melissa seemed distracted, eyeing the burgers, hot dogs, and fries that appeared out the side door by the armful as men made their way past in grey coveralls.

"Not at all."

Melissa took her place in the lunch line, and from the safety of the cement block table, Elinore scrutinized the woman to whom she was mysteriously related, intent on making comparisons. The paper-thin skin alongside Melissa's tall nose wrinkled when she grimaced at the pasteboard menu, causing Elinore to touch her own nose. She had long legs for a Japanese, but were they longer than Elinore's? Sensing that men in every direction had taken notice of them as the only females around, Elinore imagined conducting a poll. Who was the more desirable of the two, and why? Was this craziness? If she told Melissa they were sisters, would Melissa lie awake fearing that Naoko would want to call her Aunty?

But on re-approach, Melissa's mood seemed to have lightened. She strode confidently back to the table, oil already saturating the orange paper that held her burger, her eyes inward looking and ravenous. "How are you?" she asked, grabbing her burger with delicate fingers and opening her mouth for a bite.

"Fine," Elinore stretched her jaw, forcing a yawn. "You?"

Across the table, Melissa chewed and nodded as if agreeing emphatically to some hidden conversation. "You met Mark, didn't you?" she asked between bites.

"No." Her question surprised Elinore, who guessed Melissa didn't remember asking her the same question the first time they'd had lunch.

"Really? He was at Caroline's wedding, remember?"

"I saw him at Caroline's wedding, but we weren't introduced."

"No?" Melissa, who looked genuinely puzzled, squinted into the glare behind Elinore's head. "I wish you had met him."

"You two are engaged, right?" Elinore said, at the same instant looking down at the empty spot on Melissa's finger where the diamond engagement ring had vanished.

"We're not engaged anymore." Melissa took another chunk out of her burger. "I broke up with him."

"I'm sorry it didn't work out." Elinore shifted in her seat, aware of the hard bench beneath her and that an undesired subject seemed to be edging its way in.

"No," Melissa waved her pity away, recovering. "I didn't really break up with him. Maybe you could still meet him sometime."

"Okay, that would be nice." Elinore lied, angry that the conversation could slip so quickly from where she'd intended it should go.

"What am I saying?" Melissa corrected herself. "Right now he doesn't even want to see me."

"Oh?" Elinore groaned.

"Here's the thing." Slowly, Melissa licked each one of her chili-stained fingers, the slight tremor Elinore had perceived causing her to wonder about a neurological problem. But perhaps the symptom was emotional rather than neurological, or Elinore had simply been looking too closely at the wrong moment for indicators of bodily stress. "I just felt like it wasn't the right time to get married. Do you know what I mean? But I'm thinking I might have made a mistake."

Elinore nodded, not knowing what she was supposed to say, for suddenly Melissa's story had beckoned forth Elinore's own—the history she'd carried back to the Valley when she left Saburo her own invisible flaw. She'd told herself that her leaving had nothing to do with him, that the break-up was her fault, easier to accept responsibility than to look at how Saburo's accident had changed things between them. Ashamed of her revulsion over the red patch on his scalp and the way hair never grew back, the keloids that grew like tomatoes along his neck, she'd turned away unable to bear how he *looked*. But maybe she was running from *him*, from something that had gone bad before the accident, the scarring a physical manifestation of what had gone wrong between them.

"I guessed you'd understand." Melissa offered a conciliatory smile across the table. "I knew you'd understand."

Elinore wondered if Melissa's resistance to Mark was anything like her feelings of aversion for Saburo, but having tried and failed to make sense of her story to Melissa, she merely smiled back. "I'm not an expert on these matters," she said. "I'm single. Remember?"

"Oh, I forgot," Melissa said, orange fingers rising to cover her mouth. "I'm sorry."

"Don't worry about it," Elinore said. "Why would I be offended?" Maybe a part of her had known Marina would take her place, was perhaps taking her place even before she'd given it up. Maybe her clandestine knowledge accounted for the absence of ill will she felt toward the young woman across from her, as if Marina and she had agreed beforehand that Marina would take care of Saburo, as if Elinore's ex-lover were her child rather than the father of her child.

"The Lord works in mysterious ways."

Melissa straightened her posture, as if to appreciate what she'd just said, and Elinore cringed. "I don't think of my life that way," she said, hoping Melissa would stop.

"How do you think of it then? I'm curious."

"I make my own choices."

"It's different if you're Christian," Melissa said with conviction. "Christians place their lives in God's hands. Jesus guides my choices."

"Whatever."

The last thing Elinore wanted was to be witnessed to, and she wondered how she might start the conversation over, or whether it was even worth the effort. The summer sky had turned a murky shade of grey, and steam hung over the beer plant in the shape of a large ugly animal. "So tell me, what's the news about Nora's disappearance? I caught the tail end of a story about her—"

"They found her body." Melissa cut her off.

"Does that have an impact on the murder trial?"

"The body was completely decomposed, but I guess we'll see. The trial's been set for sometime this September."

Along with this news, Elinore's memory of her conversation with Nora the night of Caroline's wedding resurfaced. She hadn't felt terribly surprised to hear that Nora had disappeared, but Elinore remained convinced that Nora hadn't wanted to die. Her expression had been animated, excited about whatever might come next. "Do you still think she was murdered?"

"Maybe," Melissa said. "No. What I can't stand is that she disappeared while we were all right there."

"I'm sorry," Elinore said.

"We should have been paying better attention."

"Yes." Elinore nodded, thinking of Naoko.

"But at least we know one thing: we couldn't have loved her more."

Love? The word stung Elinore's eyes. Of course they could have loved her more. Love was not just a feeling, it was an act, and in this case, an omission. "Is it a relief?" Elinore asked nonchalantly, "to know that she isn't missing anymore?"

"I keep seeing her," Melissa complained. "I can't believe she's gone. I grew up with her. I've known her and Caroline for as long as I can remember. I should have done more."

"It's not about you," Elinore said without thinking.

"You're right," Melissa said, her straight spine sinking into a slouch.

Elinore sighed to indicate her resignation. In Melissa's vindication of her, she felt her own guilt. Melissa was not the only one to have been proved wrong by Nora's disappearance; in Melissa's own way she had been right. Nora's disappearance implicated them all.

Looking like the child who had just been publicly chastised for giving the wrong answer, Melissa hung her head. "Sometimes I can't stand it," she confessed.

"Can't stand what?" Elinore asked, not understanding.

"When I was growing up, my mother did everything for me. She cooked and cleaned house and took me to art and ballet and piano after school and on weekends. She said she wanted me to have a happy childhood. Maybe because hers had been unhappy. Her parents were interned like yours probably were and they never really recovered from it. Financially or emotionally. She had watched her parents suffer and she had been helpless to do anything until the opportunity came to protect me, to give me things her parents couldn't give her, only her good intentions backfired. I've never been carefree. I think I've always just been waiting around for something bad to happen."

Elinore felt she knew what Melissa was talking about. There was something genuine in the information Melissa had just revealed about herself as if by accident, something that connected them and made Elinore want to forgive Melissa in a way that had not before seemed possible. Maybe what Elinore knew was like a secret shared in the blood—this bracing for a disaster like some people plan for the next day's weather. The belief not in what is but in what might be possible coupled with an absolute denial that anything remotely bad could ever happen. In her memories of childhood, the sky was clear and blue, yet the loss of freedom her parents had experienced, events she'd only ever heard about secondhand, loomed like a threatening storm cloud off in the distance. According to Hideko's story, Melissa would be a year older than she, but the way she tucked her hair behind an ear made her look young. Were she to ask at the next table who was younger, Elinore bet the beer plant workers would say Melissa. "I think the bad thing has already happened," Elinore, not entirely certain of her own references, blurted out. "You don't need to wait any longer."

"I know what you mean," Melissa said, smiling.

"You seem so unhappy." Having spoken irrationally, Elinore misinterpreted Melissa's smile as condescension.

"No," she said, "I'm not happy. With Mark and me not together anymore, one of my two friends missing and the other as good as gone from my life, I don't know what there is to be happy about."

Elinore didn't respond. Though she had eaten nothing she felt full, and in her silence, she attempted to give what had just happened a chance to sink in. The conversation, though it had taken a different path from the one she'd hoped for when she arrived, had worked to clarify her relationship to Melissa. "I don't know what to say," she conceded.

"Are *you* happy?" Melissa asked, shocking her.

"No."

Melissa appeared unreasonably satisfied by this answer.

"It's not what you think," Elinore said sharply, wanting to cut short Melissa's satisfaction. "I think it's okay for people not to be happy all the time. As far as I know we're not supposed to be that happy. It's just not—" and she searched for a word, "*realistic.*" An image of Nora's crimson dress flashed before Elinore's eyes, followed by black, like an impassable cave. Grief was the sister of fear, the two existing side by side all along, though never knowing it. Naoko was her protection against the future, her own personal shield, and her defiance of the past. Melissa had inherited her mother's fears, and perhaps Nora had experienced something similar. Maybe it was too late for Melissa just as it was certainly too late for Nora. But maybe the bad thing didn't have to happen at all; it had happened to their parents when they were forced to leave home with their parents, though they were too young to know exactly what had gone wrong. As children denied of memory, they had inherited their parents' grief and passed it along unwittingly. "It's hard to breathe today, isn't it?" Elinore said, stretching in an attempt to shift her mood.

She'd survived the thing she'd feared, but she'd also managed to stray from her point because, given the opportunity, she guessed it would be easier to withhold the truth forever. "There's something I need to tell you," she interrupted herself, surprised by how much like her mother she sounded in doing so.

"Oh?" Melissa glanced up.

"My mother told me something the other night that really shocked me, and I thought you might want to know, too."

"Oh?" A half-smile tugged at Melissa's lips, and in that instant it occurred to Elinore that she knew.

"You know, don't you."

"Know what?"

"My mother told me that we're half-sisters, that Jun is your father, too. You already knew, didn't you."

"Well, yes, I knew."

"Did you know I didn't know?"

"I don't know."

"You didn't know whether I knew?"

"No."

"Doesn't it matter to you?" Elinore asked, pausing first to consider how much it all mattered to her.

"Yes, of course, it does," Melissa said, meaning that it didn't, the lie abundantly clear in her word choice.

"How long have you known?"

"I don't know. I can't remember."

"My god." Elinore began tugging at the roots of her hair.

"Look, Elinore," Melissa said, "I didn't know you didn't know. Or maybe I did. It's just that the people in the church are my real family. That's the way I've always thought of it."

"My god," Elinore said again, and her body flinched involuntarily, as if in response to physical pain. She had the vague feeling of trauma, of not knowing what had just happened, like the worst was yet to come, like how the doctors used pointy tweezers to pick specks of grey matter out of Saburo's skin, trying to clean out his wounds.

"It's okay," Melissa said. "It's what I was trying to tell you before about being Reborn. It changes what you think about which relationships are real and which ones make us a family. It's like getting a new past for your new life. That's what it means to experience Jesus' love—to give up what you thought you knew and who you were, the same way Jesus gave up his life for us."

Elinore watched Melissa's mouth move. Her tone was emphatic, her expression sincere, yet what the woman said made no sense at all. Knowing there was nothing left to say, nothing to debate or even to discuss, Elinore sat waiting for an end.

"The worst thing," Melissa said at last, "is that Mark hasn't been coming to church."

"What?" Elinore asked, having no idea what Melissa had moved on to talk about.

"Since I broke off our engagement, he hasn't come to church."

"I guess he must need some time to himself," she said, but to herself she thought, *He needs to get away from you. You're nuts.* Then acknowledging that the crazy woman and she were related, she began to laugh.

"Why are you laughing?" Melissa looked annoyed. "I mean, if his faith was so weak that breaking off with me could shake it, then I wouldn't want to be married to him, right?

"It makes me sad," she complained when Elinore refused to answer. "All of it." And then, glancing down at her watch, her expression assumed a blank quality. "I'm going to be late for my one o'clock," she said without an apology.

"Right." Disoriented, Elinore motioned her away. "Go."

"Cheer up," she said, leaning in to fake punch Elinore's arm before leaving.

Chapter 30

CAROLINE'S LABOR BEGAN in the middle of the night, a nagging at her insides while she dreamt she was barrel riding down a waterfall at Magic Mountain holding her breath, trying to convince herself that the ride should be fun. The clock read 3:16, but it took a minute to realize where she was. "I think there's something happening," she said, turning over and nudging Wade.

"There is?" Sitting up in the dark, Wade rotated his neck, then, reluctantly, opened one eye.

"I don't know." She stared down at her belly lit by the red glow of the clock numbers. "I think so. Maybe."

Wade disappeared into the bathroom and after flushing the toilet came back to the bedroom holding a stopwatch. A few minutes passed in which neither said anything, and then Caroline gasped. "Eww, that's one."

Wade turned the stopwatch from side to side to catch light from the bathroom, then set it off with a click. Less than an hour later, the contractions appeared to be getting closer together and increasingly stronger, and after returning to the bathroom to splash cold water on his face and pulling on a pair of jeans and a shirt, Wade decided it was time to leave for the hospital. Caroline was ready to go even before him, her overnight bag by the door to the nursery where it had sat for over a month. It held everything she could possibly need, checked off from a list that she'd been adding to for days, upon the advice of her mother and friends. Having heard horror stories of hospital stays, she wanted her labor to go smoothly and comfortably—not unlike her wedding, which had taken a lot of work to plan, but had been a resounding success.

Unfortunately, however, when the triage nurse checked, Caroline's cervix was only one centimeter dilated, which caused an argument between the nurse and Wade, and then between Wade and Caroline, over whether she should be admitted. "The contractions are two minutes apart," Wade explained to the nurse in order to defend his wife. But the nurse's comeback was to attach Caroline to the fetal monitor, and when the sporadic contractions appeared in wavy black lines, even Caroline could see that the activity had subsided.

"I told the nurse they were two minutes apart," Wade scolded while Caroline packed up to leave.

Caroline didn't understand why Wade would accuse her of imagining what she'd been feeling, or why the contractions, so regular at first, should slow down. "I'm sorry, Wade," she said. "I really don't know what happened. But *you* were timing them, remember."

"Well, at one centimeter and contractions five to ten minutes apart the nurse is right. It's possible to hang on like this for days. Let's go."

It wasn't yet light when they left the hospital. Back in bed, Wade fell asleep almost instantly, leaving Caroline to time her own contractions and worry over the progression of labor.

Twice more that week she considered waking Wade. Once the pain was so intense it caused her to double over. But each time she held off, and in the morning was glad she did. In this way, her due date came and passed, and Wade went to work early each morning reminding her to page him if anything changed, and each morning at eight the phone rang.

"Hi, Mom," Caroline spoke into the receiver without even needing to ask who it was.

"Just checking in," Teru said. "No baby yet?"

"You'd be the first to know if there were." Teru's failure to grasp the obvious was annoying, but Caroline tried to be nice, knowing that her mother's excitement about the baby exceeded her own. Besides, she was grateful to Teru, whose daily visits to check on her and keep the house in shape helped pass the hours.

Not the world's most tidy person, Teru undertook light housekeeping as an excuse to visit, the real purpose being to resolve an issue outstanding between them before the baby could be born. "I hope you have a boy," she'd say each time she entered the nursery to dust the crib and refold items from the layette. Teru had wanted Caroline and Wade to find out the baby's sex, and her anger at having been overruled showed in her quibbling over their decorating in pink, which was inappropriate for a boy, and blue, which for a girl should have been yellow.

"Haven't you heard about the studies? Babies who grow up in yellow rooms score ten to twenty points higher on intelligence tests than babies who grow up in pink, blue, or white."

The real issue was not that Teru wanted a grandson. In fact, Caroline believed her mother's preference had been for a girl. The problem was that Wade and Caroline's choice of a girl's name was Nora, and the thought of naming the baby after someone who'd gone missing drove Teru crazy. Never mind that the baby would be named after one of her daughter's two closest friends.

It had been Wade's idea to name the baby Nora if Caroline had a girl. He'd thought of it early into Caroline's pregnancy and the name had stuck. Raised Buddhist, Teru had only converted to Christianity because her mother had had her baptized after the war. The way she told it, a group of Christian women had helped the family relocate from the internment camp where they'd been sent in Rower, Arkansas, back to Los Angeles. The church women had donated food and supplies through the church when Teru's parents left the camps with only one suitcase each to build a new life. According to Teru, the women asked for nothing in return except that her mother, grandmother Kobayashi, attend church, and because she'd felt indebted to them for their kindness, she couldn't refuse. "A Nikkei woman would never have placed anyone in such an awkward position," Teru said, "but these women were *hakujin*, and my mother's loyalty to them was sincere."

Teru's heart had never embraced Christian beliefs, but through the years she'd refused to admit it, claiming instead what her father had always said, that one religion was as good as the next. As proof, she pointed to her husband Tom, who she'd met at Valley Baptist. But the importance of the church could not be denied; it being the place she'd met her closest friends, she'd stayed.

When Caroline reminded her mother that Christians didn't believe in bad luck, Teru wagged her head knowingly. "I know. It's my fault," she confessed. "Still, I can't get over how Christianity moved through our family from my mother's burden to your true belief."

"What do you mean?" asked Caroline, too tired and pregnant to dodge her mother's jabs. "You're Christian, too."

"Not in the same way," Teru said, clamping her lips together as if she found what Caroline had said distasteful.

What, then, did she believe? When Caroline asked, Teru reverted to the position she'd always taken of not wanting to talk about her childhood. "Conjuring up the past is like putting your eye to a keyhole jammed full of spider webs," she said. "What I want now is just a happy life for my soon-to-be grandchild."

"That's why," she added, pointing at her daughter's stomach, "you should find a better name for that baby.

"It's more than just bad luck I'm scared of," she conceded. "You want to be careful what you pass on to future generations: Good genes and manners are important, but the spirit of a person is conveyed in a name."

In part, Caroline was thankful that the baby was going to be late because even tight-lipped, her mother revealed more of herself in the final weeks of her pregnancy than in all the years that had come before. Nights when she couldn't sleep, she contemplated what her mother had said and worried, too, that Teru might consider the long days they spent together the last chance she'd have to tell her things.

When the baby was officially two weeks late, Caroline went in for her weekly o.b. appointment and her doctor insisted that she schedule an appointment for nine o'clock the next morning to have her labor induced. "July third," Caroline reflected while hovering over the receptionist's desk. "Too bad we couldn't wait one day longer and have a holiday baby."

The receptionist offered a quick smile. "Yes. Too bad. But the doctors don't induce on holidays if they can avoid it."

It all felt very matter-of-fact and disappointing, too, that thus far nothing had gone as planned, but Caroline didn't let on that she was bothered. "At least nine o'clock is a convenient time, opposed to the middle of the night," she said to Wade, knowing that night or morning didn't make a difference one way or the other.

"This won't hurt," the doctor said, reaching inside her with a long, sharp hook, explaining as he worked that once the membranes had been ruptured, labor would most likely start up on its own. Caroline grabbed the bed rail when she felt the prick, followed by warm fluid seeping out from her womb. The doctor was right; it hadn't hurt, not really, though he might have warned her about the leaky stuff. That and his dramatic surgical instruments and his white, gloved hand between her legs. She vowed not to watch any other procedures being performed, heaven forbid they should be necessary, and she called to Wade to get her overnight bag because her gown had been soiled.

It took a minute for Wade, who stood at the foot of her bed talking to the o.b., to hear her, renewing Caroline's belief that she was the object and not the person, let alone the *wife* in labor. "Wade," she repeated, sounding more polite than she felt. "Could you *please* bring me my overnight bag?"

"What?" he said, eyes scanning the room. "There aren't any bags in here. Did you leave it in the car?"

"No," she said, aggravated. "You carried it *for me* from the car. And you were holding it when I was admitted. Remember?"

"I didn't carry anything in," he insisted. "What did it look like?"

"Wade," she said, taking a deep breath and biting at her bottom lip, "it's white, with a pattern of yellow and blue cornflowers."

"Okay," he said. "Don't get excited. I think I remember seeing it. It has to be here. I'll go check at the nurses' station."

But Wade returned only to say that the nurses didn't have the bag. Then, after disappearing down the long hall for a second time, he reported back that no one in Admitting had seen it either, though they had suggested he check the Lost & Found. Sitting in her soaked gown, Caroline wondered which would happen first: would her husband find the bag, or would she have her baby, which might happen at any time.

"This is pointless," Wade said into the phone when he was transferred through to the labor room. For over an hour, Caroline had imagined him in the Lost & Found when instead he'd left the hospital and driven all the way to Sherman Oaks (speeding through the Valley streets toward home, thank God he didn't crash along the way), the judgment of which she had to question, especially since he'd still not found the bag.

Unfortunately, this was not the first time she'd worried what impact Wade's temperament would have on their baby and doubted whether the man she'd married would make a good father. But, flummoxed, all Wade could discern over the phone line was that Caroline was crying again. "I'm happy to bring anything from home you can think of since I'm here," he said, trying to cajole her.

"No," she yelled. "There's nothing else. Just for god's sake get back here before the baby's born."

"Last chance before I leave," he sang. "You're absolutely sure there's nothing?"

Wade was beyond being able to understand. She knew he'd say when he returned that the hospital would supply everything she needed. And of course he was right. But that wasn't the point. From her hospital bed, Caroline vowed to leave Wade once the baby was born. The way she saw it, she'd carried the baby past the time most women give birth, she'd done everything right, including making sure she ate the right foods and gained the requisite amount of weight, she'd even served dinner all the way up to last night when *he* had a craving for spaghetti and meatballs. She'd been responsible for more than her fair share when all Wade had to do to help get her through this was to remember one small bag. Granted the bag hadn't meant much to him, if he'd taken the time to look around he would have seen that to her it meant *everything*. She'd pretty much made up her mind when Wade walked through the door, a huge bouquet of purple irises in one hand and a cup of ice chips in the other.

"My favorites!" Caroline propped herself up, opening her mouth for an ice chip.

"I know."

The flowers made bearable the sight of the on-call obstetrician who entered the room behind Wade and began a pitocin drip. "We thought rupturing the membranes might do the trick," he said, obviously in a good mood at the start of his rotation, "but it's not medically prudent to wait any longer."

Before Caroline could acknowledge the latest turn of events, labor came on furiously. She tried to visualize her cervix opening, like she'd been taught in birthing class, to remember that the intense pain didn't mean there was anything wrong. On the contrary, each contraction brought her closer to having this baby.

But the pain proved too intense and lasted for too many hours. At four centimeters she requested and received an epidural. By midnight the bed table was crowded with monitors that flashed and beeped, and lines that poured out of her body and made her think she was a dying person.

"This is not what I wanted," she said to Wade, her voice barely audible after too many hours of pain and no sleep.

Wade clasped her hand in his and kissed it. "No, but you're doing good."

The scary part came when she stalled at six centimeters and the baby's heart rate slowed, indicating the need for an emergency cesarean. Eyes shut, she counted on Wade to watch the baby being lifted from her womb and didn't open them again until the delivery nurse handed her her baby girl, wiped dry and swaddled in a fresh pink blanket.

She'd keep forever the image of her eight-pound baby girl, her sleeping face still wet from the womb, eyes two tight slits with barely any lashes or hair to speak of crowning her red, mottled head.

Caroline held her baby through the night, watching the newborn's expression shift beneath closed lids like clouds parting the moon. In the morning, the baby pursed then relaxed her lips in time with her tiny fists, which clenched and released over and over, until she finally opened her palms, extending the length of her tiny fingers inside Caroline's palm. "Look Wade," Caroline said, seeing something extraordinary about her daughter that brought her startled husband rushing to her bedside. "She has the most beautiful little hands. Look at her fingers!"

"She has your hands," Wade smiled, slumping back in his chair, satisfied. "I think the baby was hanging out, just waiting to surprise us on the Fourth of July."

"Weren't you, baby?" he sighed with his eyes closed, totally spent.

"Why don't you call her by her name, Wade," Caroline scolded him, running fingers through the baby's matted black hair.

Wade took a moment before saying anything, his exhausted mind slow to rouse. Then he opened his eyes. "I think *Nora's* life began as a wonderful surprise."

Caroline's parents were Nora's first visitors. After comp-liment-ing Caroline on her ruddy, wrinkled baby, Teru scowled at Wade. "Do you think you and Caroline chose the right name?"

"It's her name." Wade cast an invitation across the room for Tom to intervene.

Caroline knew how Wade felt; names weren't that important to him. And the situation didn't matter to her father, who smiled and said nothing.

"I guess maybe she does look like a Nora," Teru laughed. "Independence Day Nora."

Chapter 31

AT NIGHT, THE names circled like ravens overhead and Elinore fell asleep counting: Melissa and her parents Asako and Bob Hori, Nora and her parents Yukari and Yujitaka Yano, Caroline Noguchi and her parents Teru and Tom Ikeda, and now Caroline's baby Nora. She'd brought Naoko to the Valley so that her daughter could be surrounded by family, yet maybe what she thought Naoko needed she'd needed for herself—a great gathering of names to siphon her back from the dead.

"Your father and Asako Hori began dating when they were both sixteen," Hideko had said. "Bob Hori, Tom Ikeda, and Yujitaka Yano were all friends."

But Hideko's cursory musings, told without context, were not enough.

Elinore had become insatiable, the way someone who'd lived for thirty years without answers to the most basic questions would be, for Hideko's initial disclosure, rather than offering answers, had given her license to question. Sitting with her mother in front of the television after Naoko had gone to bed, she wanted to know: What had Jun been like? Had he loved Asako? Or, even if he hadn't, how had he gotten up the nerve to leave her? Did Hideko ever think of Jun's other life? Why didn't she go to church? Did she believe in God? Had she been close to her mother?

"Why do you pester me?" Hideko complained, wanting to be left alone with her nightly orange, relenting one sentence at a time.

"Yukari's family, the Fujimotos, they always thought they were a cut above the others."

And the list of names was appended to include the Fujimotos.

Hideko accepted the demands of her daughter for information as compliantly as she took on any of her obligations. She did not mean to be cryptic; rather, the truth had not magically granted Hideko access to stories that had lain for so long submerged.

"I think people can only embrace change if they haven't been excluded," she said one night, in response to nothing in particular, and her statement, in addition to seeming oblique and mysterious, recalled for Elinore similar statements Hideko had made throughout her childhood. As a child, Elinore received frequent quizzes about the children in her classes, their aptitudes and backgrounds. At the mention of a newcomer, Hideko would straighten her spine like a cat, her attention piqued. Once, when a child had a particularly hard time adjusting, Hideko had gone so far as to confer with Elinore's teacher and extend an invitation via the child's mother for a play date. Put out by her mother's strange and intrusive gesture, Elinore had at first ignored the child. "You need to be nice to your company," she'd pulled Elinore aside with a pinch, not caring that her daughter had allowed the child into her room only in deference to her mother. "Think how you'd feel if you were the new child. Try being a good friend."

But Elinore had not thought of the taciturn child as her friend. She'd had no experience living outside the home where she'd grown up in the Valley, no way to know why Hideko should have been so concerned for the welfare of strangers.

A full twenty years later, Hideko still made it her business to see to the despondent, along with the injured. A pair of newborn kittens, abandoned by their mother in a crawl space under the house, had been Hideko's latest save. Their mewling began in the middle of the night, and in the morning Hideko had found them pressed up against the hot water pipes. They were blind and furless, more like rodents than felines, when Hideo carried them inside. Naoko had helped make them a warm bed with cotton and newspaper shavings, and Hideko had brought home from the veterinarian's at considerable expense a newborn feline milk formula, along with a feeding bottle and a half dozen nipples. Even so, one kitten had not lived twenty-four hours while the other had thrived. Hideko could be heard in the kitchen in the middle of the night warming formula, and evenings while she and Elinore sat together on the couch, Hideko would hold the kitten on her lap, cooing to it while she offered it milk. The kitten provided the distraction Hideko had needed. Soon it developed a soft black coat along with a set of razor-like claws, and while attending to it, a fuller story emerged.

"Your father began dating Asako when they were both sixteen. They were married the day Asako turned eighteen because her parents, the Takemotos, had refused to give their approval. Melissa was born not quite a year later and everyone assumed they were perfectly happy together until the Sunday afternoon of that first Dodgers game."

"Ah, the Dodgers game," Elinore said, acknowledging the memory already shared between them.

"I met your father at that Dodgers game," Hideko said, disregarding Elinore in favor of the story forming in her head. "Your dad was there with his friends Bob and Tom. Yujitaka, that's Nora's father, he was the one who'd brought me. The three of them—Bob and Tom and Yujitaka—never took their eyes off Sandy Koufax. I think sports is maybe the one thing that can take an eighteen-year-old Christian boy's mind off his religion, which was a good thing for all of us, because while they were watching the game, Jun and I were falling in love."

In her mind, Elinore juxtaposed an image of her young mother with her long black hair and heart shaped face taken from pictures she'd seen with one of Sandy Koufax, his sleek body a stretch of graceful motion that the men had gathered to witness.

"But the problem was that Jun was already married to Asako, and she was pregnant," Hideko said, stroking the kitten, whom Naoko had named Junket, between the eyes.

"Do you think the stress of her getting pregnant so soon into their marriage was what broke them up?" Elinore asked, calling Hideko's attention back.

"No," Hideko said, holding Junket up so she could admire him one last time before placing him back in his box. "It wasn't that. Your dad and Asako were high school sweethearts. After they graduated, marriage probably just seemed like the next logical step. It might have lasted except that you father was curious about the world, and Asako was as straight as a ruler. Your dad said she was conservative in her thinking even as a teenager."

"So you and dad just eloped?" Elinore asked, doubting she could trust her mother's impression of Asako.

"It's not what you think," Hideko cut in. "Asako had always liked Bob and was thrilled to find her feelings returned. She married him less than three months after you father married me. But the sad thing was that none of the friends could get along after that. What had happened was unholy and couldn't be forgotten until someone was punished. Maybe it was like the way the Jews in the Old Testament made sacrifices to God to get him to forget their sins—only he didn't forget. He merely forgave, and so did all the friends. They politely forgave your father, but since I was the outsider and someone who'd grown up Buddhist, they decided to sacrifice me.

"From then on, your father wasn't welcome at the church, and I was *persona non grata*, left to raise you without the help of anyone." Hideko's voice faltered, and Elinore could tell by the way she averted her eyes that she felt ashamed. "Back then people had community, something you could rely on," Hideko said, and Elinore tried to imagine how hard it had been for her mother.

"I see what you mean," she said.

"No," Hideko snapped, "how could you?"

"I get it, okay?"

"People can only embrace change if they haven't been excluded," she said again. "For someone who's been left out, even when they are finally taken care of they will always feel betrayed."

"At least you had your mother," Elinore said, her grandmother's kindly face projecting itself into her thoughts.

"That's what you think." Hideko wiped her sleeve across her eyes causing Elinore to look away, unable to bear the sight of her mother's tears.

"What are you talking about?" she asked, beginning to panic.

"When I married your father, my parents disowned me. Your grandmother didn't speak to me again until you were five years old."

"What?" In Elinore's memories, her grandmother had always been present. Hadn't she?

Elinore grew up loving her mother and grandmother Mizuno with equal doses of ferocity. When angry at her mother, she'd say she was running away. She didn't imagine going anywhere, but she'd threaten and scream. Hideko would tell her, *Go ahead, go if you're not happy here.* So she'd call her grandmother and tell her she'd be coming to live with her. *You mustn't!* she'd cry. *Your mother would miss you too much.* So she'd stay.

Her mother would say, *Go away!* And her grandmother would say, *Stay!* They were *yes* and *no*; *right* and *wrong*; *left* and *right*; *back* and *forth* like rocking. As a child, she felt their rhythmic motion like the swinging of a door, *open* and *shut*. It was unthinkable that her memories could have deceived her. "Why until I was five?" Elinore demanded.

Reaching for a tissue, Hideko blew her nose. "Because you were so cute," she laughed. "She couldn't resist not being a part of your life."

"I've forgiven your grandmother, but I can never forgive Yukari," Hideko said resentfully, and the ground beneath Elinore's feet began to recede. "Nora's mother was the one. The Fujimotos were founding members of the church, and Yukari Fujimoto thought she was a cut above the others. She told the other women not to talk to me. She said I stole your dad away from Asako and from Melissa who needed him, and what kind of woman would do that?"

Clearly, Hideko still suffered. For a second time, her eyes glazed over, and she glared at Elinore as if she'd participated in her undoing. "Yukari didn't treat her children right either; everyone knew that she favored her boys over Nora, and maybe they remembered from the way she treated me how she liked to turn people against each other. I think Nora suffered because of all the bad luck Yukari accrued through the years—her *bachi*."

"How could you wait so long to tell me any of this?" Elinore demanded when Hideko had fallen silent, figuring it might take years to sort through all the heartache.

"I didn't want you to know at all," Hideko shrugged.

"But why not?"

"Because I wasn't married when I had you. Your father's divorce from Asako hadn't been finalized, and we couldn't get married until it was."

Big deal, Elinore wanted to say, but stopped herself, realizing how much the issue of her illegitimacy still troubled her mother. "Isn't it interesting," she said, seeing the irony of her mother's story unfolding in Naoko's origins, "how history repeats itself?"

"It's what I'm telling you," Hideko said, sounding perturbed to have been interrupted at a crucial moment.

Needing to sort things out for herself, Elinore ignored her. "I wasn't married to Saburo when I got pregnant with Naoko, so aren't our stories essentially the same?"

"Don't think it's so different now," Hideko said, dismissing her. "But Teru Ikeda shouldn't get so riled up about Caroline deciding to call her baby Nora."

"I don't understand you," Elinore said. "How could you be friends with Teru after all the bad blood between you?"

"We were never friends," Hideko reminded her. "I didn't speak to any of those women again for over twenty-five years. But we're adults now. We all know there are more important things to worry about than what happened years ago," she said, leaving Elinore to wonder whether she was aware of the irony of her words.

"I'm only sorry that you had to become involved in all this," she sighed, expressing her sincere regret, letting Elinore know her story was over.

"Then why did you bring me with you to Caroline's wedding?" Elinore asked.

"I didn't want to go alone," Hideko shrugged.

Elinore laughed. To Jun's credit, he wasn't put off by her mother's illogic; maybe he even found it satisfying to have his notion that things were not as they seem confirmed by his canny wife and his attachment to her. Elinore knew her parents had in common the desire not to see—to turn away from complexity that at the same time they desired to create. Forced to reconsider what her mother had meant when she'd said that people could embrace change only if they hadn't been excluded, she wondered if her mother had gotten what she wanted when she married her father. But maybe Hideko, like Jun, was evoking an event that took place long before she'd met her husband and fallen in love. Her life in the camps, or, stretching even further back, the effect the internment had on her parents' lives, an experience outside their control that had left them feeling permanently excluded.

"I didn't mind going with you," Elinore called to her mother as Hideko stowed the box that held Junket away for the night.

"Good." Hideko double blinked, then headed off to the kitchen for an orange.

Chapter 32

RECOVERY FROM A cesarean was more harrowing than anyone could know. Within hours the nurses sat Caroline up and forced her out of bed. When she complained that movement of any sort was painful, they pretended not to hear. One of them even had the nerve to say, "Of course it's painful," leaving her certain that she wasn't cut out for life with a baby.

The scar across her bikini line scared her, though not anything like the much anticipated walk down the hall. She was a mother now, but soon they'd see that she was really still baby, not quite ready to take her first steps and mortified by the wound that everyone claimed would heal just fine. If someone were to have told her childbirth would be that way, she doubted she would have gone through with a pregnancy. But when her o.b. listed symptoms of post-partum depression, then wanted to know if she'd been experiencing any, she dismissed the question as irrelevant.

Reverend Nakatani's wife Aiko sent over a basket of things for the baby and long-stem pink roses for her. Caroline had never much liked the minister's wife, and the roses pointed to why. She knew they'd been given to remind her of the church and how she'd not attended a single service in weeks. She wondered if it were rational to hate a flower, and concluded that her feelings were more properly directed at Aiko who had cast a spell over the flowers, causing them each morning to appear droopier and more neglected, and to emit a stench that was far from fragrant.

Since Nora's birth, she'd seen more friends than in all the time she and Wade had occupied their house. Each came bearing a sympathetic smile and a bit of advice. But she no longer took people's well-intentioned advice seriously. The best advice, she told herself, was not to listen.

Caroline was not with Wade at Tuesday Night Bible Study when the announcement was made that bones that were thought to belong to Nora had been discovered in the San Gabriel foothills but she had heard the rumor that Yukari had not been attending church since she'd heard the news. The following Sunday, soon after Wade left the house for services, Caroline dressed Nora in her yellow sun suit and took her for a visit.

"I'm sorry I didn't come see you in the hospital." Yukari greeted Caroline and her baby at the door looking surprised and at a loss for the right words.

"That's okay," Caroline said, apologetic herself; she understood about unexpected visitors. Though it was past ten o'clock, Yukari still wore a housecoat. She looked awful, but took Nora from Caroline, cooing at her as Caroline entered the Yano house behind her. The couch, a sickening green and yellow floral pattern, all but swallowed the older woman up making it clear how much weight Yukari had lost since Caroline had last seen her.

A foul odor of pickled vegetables or perhaps it was stewed fish permeated the room, and for the baby's sake Caroline got up, hoping they could move to another room where the air might be fresher. But Yukari, disregarding Caroline, only cooed down at Nora. Her long greasy hair loosed itself from its pins and fell over the baby's face, and looking over at her, Caroline realized in horror the source of the bad smell. Attempting to calm herself, she parted the thick drapes and pushed open a window. "That's better," she said, exposing the room to air and sunlight.

But the natural lighting revealed the brown shag carpet, along with stains in the shabby mustard colored furniture. The room looked exactly as it always had, no less depressing now than it had been when Nora was growing up, the ravaged looking woman across from her no stranger. Yukari was the mother of a woman who had been her lifelong friend; as well she'd been Caroline's friend and role model, and Caroline willed her to look up from the baby and declare herself familiar again.

"They found Nora," she said, hugging the baby to her chest. "Just her bones. In a stand of Russian olives, on a nature preserve in the San Gabriel foothills. A medical student made the discovery when she was out running with her dog."

"I'm sorry," Caroline said. "Wade told me."

"The police said all that was left of her was a pile of bones, just off of a hiking trail.

"A pile of bones," she said, rocking the baby, looking herself like a pile of bones. "Just skinless bones, perfectly exposed, piled next to a large boulder."

"I can't believe it," Caroline said, needing more information than she'd been offered. "How did they know the bones belonged to Nora?"

"They matched a tooth to dental x-rays taken when Nora's root canal was performed—after your wedding."

Caroline thought to speak in defense of her wedding, to say something that would extricate Nora's disappearance from her happy event forever, but when she looked up, Yukari was talking about Ken, her younger son who had driven in from Valencia to deal with the coroner's office. "He told me there was nothing to see."

"He said, 'It wasn't Nora. Just a pile of hollow bones. Bones lighter than driftwood.' What good did he think he was doing telling me that?"

"Did the investigators examine the bones? I mean, couldn't they tell anything more than that the bones belonged to Nora?" Caroline asked, for lack of a more subtle way to inquire about the cause of Nora's death.

"There wasn't much they could tell, but they said that her skull wasn't fractured. There were no signs of breaks or knife or bullet marks—no signs of foul play that they could determine."

This was the news Caroline had wanted to hear. But rather than relief, she felt doubt. "Doesn't the evidence point to Joaquin?" she asked, almost begging. "I mean, they should be able to make a case that he dumped her body there, shouldn't they?"

But Yukari wouldn't hear of it. "Caroline, believe me, I asked the investigators. But they say the evidence is inconclusive, and I know what they're thinking, that she just wandered off into the foothills to die."

"That's ridiculous!"

"Yes, but what's really strange is that just days before the bones were discovered, Joaquin violated the order of protective custody. He wasn't supposed to leave Los Angeles, but they found him in a car just outside Crescent City, near the California-Oregon border. Killed in a car crash just last week. The police say he had alcohol in his blood. Now we'll never know the truth."

"They don't know that it wasn't him," Caroline said, her thoughts drawn back into the room when her baby startled and began to cry.

"I don't know what to believe," Yukari said, cradling Nora and rocking her in a forceful sway. "As soon as Ken and his family left, I had Nora transferred from the morgue to the Mizutaki funeral home. That way I could go see her myself." Without warning, Yukari rose from the sofa, taking the baby with her down the hall.

"Caroline, come here," she called through the wall.

With the baby asleep on her lap, Yukari sat under the green desk lamp. In front of her, Nora's photo still occupied the spot where Melissa and Caroline had found it the afternoon of Nora's memorial; she'd been just five weeks pregnant that day. In front of it, Yukari had placed a ceramic box and a heavy magnifying glass.

"Once in the sixth grade when Nora had a fever she stayed home from school and cut her bangs off with a kitchen knife," Yukari spoke. "She flushed the loose hair down the toilet thinking that way no one would know, but for weeks afterwards her hair turned up in the oddest places—out of the cuffs of pants, in the back of kitchen drawers."

Rambling on, Yukari opened the box and unwrapped something from a tissue.

"Let me take the baby so you can do that," Caroline said, nervous at the way the baby, asleep again, balanced precariously on her lap. But Yukari seemed not to hear.

"She was in the second grade when she knocked this tooth out. Remember? On the swing set at church."

Caroline nodded, not remembering.

"There was blood everywhere. Nora was always scared of blood after that."

Yukari picked up the magnifying glass, and used it to compare the shape and color of the baby tooth to the molar. One as translucent as a pearl, the other bronzed with decay, she turned the molar in her fingers then closed her fist around it as if to deny the official conclusion that it belonged to Nora. "If this were Nora's don't you think I'd know?

"Come, look," she said, holding the magnifying lens out for Caroline.

"I'm really sorry," Caroline said, standing over the lens, not wanting to look. What she wanted was to tell Yukari how the baby kept her up nights with her crying and constant need to be fed. The only time she stopped was when Caroline held her, which was probably why her scar wasn't healing properly. When she'd looked in the mirror the other day, she hadn't even recognized the person she saw. She'd thought that if Yukari could see her with the baby she'd see what it was like for her. But the baby slept unperturbed on Yukari's lap, her wrinkled face glowing in the sickly green of the desk lamp. The pregnancy had officially ended, Nora had entered the world. The search had come to an end. Nora was dead.

Yukari clasped the molar inside her palm, her focus strained as if to connect with Caroline's thoughts. "Nora is dead, isn't she?"

Caroline nodded, and Yukari began to weep, a howl that seemed to emanate from deep down in her throat and she clutched the baby against her heaving chest. Caroline knew she should take Nora from her, but sat motionless, enthralled by the woman's immense sadness.

"It's not whether life will go on that I worry about anymore," Yukari said when she'd fallen silent. "It's that it will."

"It will get better," Caroline promised, more to herself than to Yukari.

The truth was that she'd never been more thankful to feel the warm air and sunshine that rushed in when she pulled open the front door, or to know that Wade would be arriving home from church soon and bringing her mother with him to fix lunch. She needed to get home, but Yukari still clung to the baby, preventing her from leaving. "I want to tell you something, neh."

Looking into Yukari's eyes Caroline could see Nora's sadness. "You might think it's strange for me to hold on to Nora's tooth, but I have nothing now."

"No. That's not true." Pressing her body against Yukari's Caroline took her baby and backed away. Quickly making her way down the cement walkway, she was aware of the weeds that sprouted in the cracks under her feet and the paint that peeled away from the house's trim unnoticed, a tangible reminder of its grieving occupants.

Yukari followed Caroline down the path, her hand clenched in a tight fist. "I envy you," she said as she approached.

Caroline fumbled with the baby's car seat then raced around to let herself in, unable to work fast enough.

"You have your new baby, your Nora, but this is all I have."

"No." Caroline wedged her key into the ignition and started the car up. Outside the driver's window, Yukari had opened her palm, exposing Nora's molar that appeared in the sunlight as a dark hole. Unable to face the woman, Caroline looked down at the decayed tooth and then at the wrinkled palm that held it before turning over her shoulder to steer the car down the driveway.

It was the tooth she saw like a sunspot when Wade asked about the visit. "I bet Yukari loved seeing the baby," he said.

"She did," Caroline said, clutching her baby, her eyes unblinking and focused straight ahead.

"Did she have any more news about Nora?"

"No."

From the kitchen where Teru stood fixing lunch, she saw her daughter's blanched face and trembling arms. "Caroline," she looked up from the sandwiches to wag her head. "You can't keep this up. You need to think about that baby."

Caroline watched as Wade, upon hearing his mother-in-law's words, obediently carried his sandwich plate into the living room, and with her husband gone she thrust the baby into her mother's arms and began to cry. Though she knew Teru had never trusted or understood her closeness to Yukari, she could not keep the details of her visit to herself. "I went to see Yukari," she said, blotting at her tears with the backs of her hands.

"I know," she said. "Wade told me. I'm glad you went."

"I wish he would have told me not to go," she said angrily, pursing her lips in an attempt to staunch the tears.

"It's a hard thing to face someone's grief."

"It's made her bitter," Caroline said, relaxing her mouth and wondering if maybe Yukari hadn't always been bitter.

Teru bounced the baby on her knee while Caroline sat across from the two, absently watching. "Look!" she said, seeing the ends of Nora's mouth curl up. "She's smiling. Turn her around so you can see."

But Teru, usually so attentive to the baby, refused to be sidetracked. "Nora's death shames her family," she said.

"What are you talking about?" Caroline asked, confused and still angry with her mother for missing the baby's first smile.

"When you're my age, you'll understand life differently," Teru said. "You still have a lot to learn about faith."

"I have no idea what you're talking about," Caroline said, fearing that her mother had spoken what she'd meant to say and she hadn't understood.

"Everybody has to have faith," Teru explained. "The Yanos have their religion, and I have you. Nora lost faith, and Yukari blames herself because she never had faith in her daughter—never. She believed in her sons, but not in her daughter."

Caroline wanted to tell her mother that she was wrong. Yukari loved her children equally, but she kept what she knew to herself.

Maybe it had been enough to grow up with Yukari's love. And hopefully her mother's faith would be strong enough to extend to her and her baby. That night, she fell sleep with the baby curled in her arms, the sweet scent of Nora's breath expanding in her lungs and becoming the yellow moon rising in her dreams.

Chapter 33

IN THE CENTER of the carnival grounds, Kevin Nishida began drumming from fifteen feet up. He'd grown taller and more powerful since the last time Melissa had seen him, his stance more solid and sure, his control still remarkable for someone his age. Now the sonorous beat of the taiko called the crowd in, told the newcomers that they'd be witnessing something special, and gratified regulars like Melissa with tradition. Promptly at seven o'clock, the koto and shamisen combined with the drumbeat, and piped in feminine voices sang about vanity and loss in minor keys, each syllable of the ancient Japanese wavering as if suffering from a corrupted recording.

Hearing the music as their call to order, dancers in their fancy *kimono* and colorful *hapi* coats formed lines in three concentric tiers around the drum stand, the space around the periphery kept clear for children who darted between bystanders on their way to the next game while balancing cones of shaved ice and plates of char siu bau and teriyaki, their mouths sticky from eating manju. Even though Melissa didn't speak Japanese and had never been to Japan, she'd attended dance practices as a teenager. Starting two months before the carnival, Caroline, Nora, and she would travel across the Valley to the Hongwanji Temple to rehearse, following behind the *obasan* who knew the movements by heart. Nora, though bigger boned than Caroline or Melissa, had been the most graceful. The year before, when she'd gone missing, Melissa had thought for sure she'd show up for *Obon*; she still held out an irrational hope.

Alone this year, without Nora, without Caroline, or Mark, Melissa signed up to work the coffee booth thinking that it wouldn't get busy till late into the evening, when people began to worry about getting home. From her post, a bit removed from the crowd, she could see the dancing better than if she were close up. She watched her mother who together with Caroline's mom was dancing for the first time. The stylish combs and colorful *hapi* coat Melissa had picked out for Asako contributed to her ease as a dancer and Melissa was surprised at her mother's natural gracefulness. She and Teru followed the women in front of them, stopping only occasionally to laugh at themselves when they lost their concentration and tripped over each other's feet.

Earlier in the week, Melissa had helped set up booths while the men hung the Christmas lights. They fanned out from the parapet in spokes, each colored light covered with a thin paper boat. She'd scoured Little Tokyo the week before to find replacements for the torn lanterns and bulbs that had burnt out, and it pleased her to see how each pretty boat floated on the evening breeze. As Melissa stared up at the lanterns, it was Naoko she thought of, hoping Elinore would accept her invitation so that her niece could take part in the festivities that had played such an important role in her childhood, and, selfishly, so that she could see the evening's events through the child's eyes.

Keeping an eye out for Naoko, Melissa was surprised to find Caroline instead. She called to her friend, wondering how Caroline could hear her name over the thick drumbeat and voice over the loudspeaker announcing a raffle winner. "What a nice surprise," Melissa said, seeing the baby curled up asleep against Caroline's chest, and feeling, even if this year's carnival would not be like the others, a sense of fullness.

"It's good to see you," Caroline said, pulling Melissa in for a hug, her baby pressed between them. "I've missed you."

Wade was in a good mood, agreeing to run the coffee booth so that she and Caroline could slip off for a minute to do what they always did together at *Obon*. They watched the dancers for a while, chatted with people they recognized, then wandered off to eat *mochi* ice cream and admire the Japanese doll and *ikebana* exhibits.

"Where's Mark?" Caroline asked when they'd found a quiet place to sit.

"Mark and I broke up," Melissa said dully, chewing on the end of a wooden skewer.

"What?" Either Caroline feigned incredulity well, or she was truly surprised by the news.

"I thought you knew."

"How would I have known?"

"I thought you knew everything about me." Even though Melissa saw her break-up with Mark as serious, she couldn't help but tease Caroline, peeking over the rim of her front carrier at baby Nora, who'd begun to stir.

"Shhhh," Caroline hushed her. "You don't need to wake up."

"Is she a good sleeper?"

"Shhhh." Caroline continued with her white noise, standing up to rock her baby, rolling her eyes at Melissa to show how exasperated she was.

"You're good at that," Melissa told her when she sat down again, the baby back asleep.

"So why on earth did you break up with Mark?" Caroline whispered.

"How do you know he didn't break up with me?"

"I *don't* know," Caroline said wearily. "Except that I saw him the other day and when I asked about you I think he said you were fine."

"Really?" Melissa said, having not seen Mark at church or anywhere else. "Where did you see him?"

"Wade and I had dinner last week at Kyushu Ramen."

"Who was he with?"

"A stack of gyooza," Caroline smiled. "He seemed to be eating alone."

Satisfied, Melissa turned her attention to Caroline. "Why haven't you been at Bible study?"

"It's hard with the baby," Caroline said, stroking her finger across Nora's thick hair.

"Look how her chin quivers," Melissa said, not wanting to discuss Mark. "She must be having a nightmare."

"She always does that," Caroline said dismissively.

Looking from the baby to Caroline, Melissa could see for the first time how worn down her friend looked. Her skin was sallow, her eyes heavily made-up to conceal fatigue. Melissa couldn't remember ever seeing Caroline look less than radiant, and she felt badly about the jealousy that had caused her to assume that Caroline's life with a new baby would be effortless. "I'm sorry I haven't come to visit," she said.

"It's okay," Caroline said, knocking her shoulder against Melissa's. "It's a hassle to have visitors. Not that I count you as a visitor, but really it's okay. My mother has been great about helping me around the house, and Wade's mother drops by almost every day."

"I'm glad," Melissa said, feeling as though she were hearing news of an acquaintance rather than someone she'd been close to all her life.

"I'd better get back to Wade," Caroline said, rising from the bench to walk Melissa back to her post at the coffee booth. "We only came to get out of the house for a bit."

Melissa took the lead, navigating the crowd that had grown thicker in their absence. Back at the coffee booth a line had formed and Melissa stretched her back, waiting for the crowd to thin before taking over for Wade.

"Did you hear that the man Nora was involved with was found dead?" Caroline asked hesitantly.

"What?" Melissa said. "Joaquin Siler?"

"Car wreck," Caroline said.

Watching Caroline shift from side to side, Melissa wondered if her friend had been uncomfortable with the news or whether she was just impatient for Wade to get through the line so she could get her sleeping baby home.

"I guess we'll never know what happened to Nora," Melissa sighed. "Do you still think he killed her?"

"It's likely." Caroline yawned. "Evidently, he had a son, a five-year-old boy."

Tilting her head, pleased with the drop in her shoulders as her neck popped, Melissa knew she should feel bad instead of relieved. "Did Yukari tell you?"

"Yes." Caroline continued to sway, her hips shifting back and forth as she shot fretful glances behind the coffee booth. "And my mother saw a notice in the paper."

As the minutes passed, Melissa began to share Caroline's impatience. Even at the outskirts of the circle, music blared out of the loudspeakers, forcing them to shout at each other as the dancers floated past them, as if in slow motion. When the drum beat let up between songs, a hush fell over the crowd and in the momentary silence Wade ducked under the counter, slipping the apron string from around his neck and handing it to Melissa before pulling Caroline to his side.

"Thanks, Wade," Melissa said, fastening the apron around her waist and rushing to serve the next person.

From the corner of her eye Melissa watched Caroline and Wade walk off, thinking how, even if Caroline wasn't at her best, they looked sweet together. The perfect family of three.

Except for the short interval when she was off, business at the coffee booth never really picked up again, giving her time to watch the crowd. She saw Naoko before she saw Elinore, and it pleased her that the toddler ran ahead of her mom, calling Melissa with her arms outstretched for a hug.

Melissa pointed up at the paper lantern cut-outs, spinning Naoko in circles beneath them, then, leaving the booth to Elinore, she whisked the child off, returning with rainbow shaved ice, a plate of *manju*, and cotton candy, along with a goldfish swimming dizzily in a clear plastic bag, Naoko's prize for playing the ball toss. After Elinore left with Naoko, the sky went totally dark and the faces in the crowd shone in colorful patterns under the lanterns. Melissa tried to remember being Naoko's age, how it felt when the sky went black at *Obon*. Perhaps she'd ask her mother the next time she saw her whether she was talking again by three because looking out at the crowd it occurred to her that she no longer remembered herself as a child. The closest she came was the worried look on her mother's face. As a child she'd watched her mother constantly, believing Asako understood her completely, no words necessary between them.

Chapter 34

SABURO ARRIVED UNANNOUNCED. On a Sunday. With Hideko out back cooling her plants down after a hot day and Elinore inside getting her daughter changed into pajamas, Naoko began flailing her arms, racing down the hall to the front door, causing Elinore to wonder later how she could have known it was him.

Elinore chased after her daughter. Blocking the doorjamb to prevent the toddler from leaving the house, she didn't recognize him at first. His skin was no longer pale the way she'd remembered it, the strawberry scarring along his temples now matching the dark tones of his face. "Saburo?" she said, confused even though Naoko had escaped through the gap between her legs and attached herself to her father.

"I was on my way back to Santa Fe, and I thought I'd stop by," he said sheepishly, rising to meet her gaze after bending down to hug his daughter.

"How did you even know where to find me?" Elinore asked, still confused.

"I didn't," he said. "Until it occurred to me to look up 'Shimizu' in the phone book."

"Why now?" she said, wondering what had taken him so long and needing him to account for his year-long absence. "When I called you Marina answered."

"I was in Bali for the last six months. I sublet the house to her while I was away. She told me you'd called, but that you hung up before she could get a number. I should have told you before I left," he said, tempting her to believe that a full year had not passed between them.

For the moment those words were all they exchanged. Taking her father's hand, Naoko rushed past Elinore and led the way down the hall to her room.

Elinore looked out over the long driveway then walked the path around the house to the spot where her mother stood with the garden hose. "Saburo's here," she announced.

"What?" Hideko said, cupping a hand over her ear.

"Saburo, he just drove up. He's in Naoko's room with her."

"Naoko's father?"

Elinore found it reassuring to see her shock mirrored in her mother's face. It didn't displease her to see Hideko go pale, as if she had moved from the shade of a tall shrub into the sunlight. "Does he want to take Naoko?" she asked.

"I don't know," Elinore said, needing suddenly to return to the house, stunned to think that she might have to fight Saburo for the custody of their daughter.

"You need to work things out," Hideko said sternly.

Elinore stared behind her mother, into the pond. Sensing Hideko's presence, the koi rose to the surface of the water and began circling for food. "Naoko belongs with me," she said decisively, "Saburo knows that."

Hideko's voice rose over her thoughts. "What does he like to eat?"

Elinore smiled. "I don't know. I never cooked for him. He always did the cooking."

"Elinore!" Hideko's chastising tone turned regretful. "I didn't raise you right. A woman should know how to cook for a man."

"What are you talking about?"

"Not that you *have* to do the cooking, but you should know *how* to cook. Everyone should be able to take care of themselves."

Unable to extract the message hidden in Hideko's words, Elinore knew only that her mother's idea of dinner sounded right. Even though Hideko, Naoko, and she had already eaten, Elinore followed her mother's command, rushing around the side of the house to turn off the hose so that Hideko could go directly inside.

When she returned to the house, Elinore found her mother already in the kitchen, pulling leftovers out of the refrigerator, two pots of water already heating on the stove. "He'll never know," Hideko teased, sending her back outside, this time to the garden for arugula to freshen the salad.

In the five minutes that followed Saburo's arrival, Elinore liked her mother more than she'd thought possible in all the time she'd been home. Perhaps she'd known it would be that way when she'd wandered out to the garden in search of her. She appreciated Hideko's certainty, and how it relieved her of the obligation to think things through. Alone in the garden for the first time since her return, she crouched to pick the arugula her mother had asked for, taking in the rich, mustard scent of the earth, damp from having just been watered. The sprigs snapped eagerly between her finger and thumb, a few roots coming up with the leaves, droplets of water and soil clinging to her face. Elinore marveled at the neat, even rows of vegetables. The tomatoes already ripening, tops of carrots poking through the soil, and purple *nasubi* hanging heavy on their stalks. There would be enough to last the entire summer.

"Elinore." Her mother's voice snapped her from her reverie. "I need that lettuce right now!"

"Coming," Elinore called back. After wiping the soil from her fingertips and face, she picked up her basket of salad greens, rising to dust herself off.

Dinner consisted of Japanese noodles and soup served with a bountiful salad. Naoko, who must have sensed the appropriateness of Hideko's gesture, said almost nothing, picking away instead at the contents of her plate, allowing the adults to converse without interruption.

Elinore watched the way Saburo leaned in toward her mother. She loved how friendly he seemed, and polite, using his napkin to dab at his mouth, looking directly into Hideko's eyes when she spoke to him. "Bali is beautiful," he said in response to Hideko's reiterating what Elinore had told her. "The ocean is pristine, and the pace of life is slow. Kind of like Santa Fe, but less subtle because of the ocean, and of course farther away.

"I have several contacts there, people I've been buying from for years."

"Too bad Jun is out of town till Thursday night," Hideko said with a dramatic show of disappointment. "Can you stay long enough to meet him?"

"Please," Naoko chimed in.

"We'll see," Saburo said, and Elinore wondered how purposeful it was that he refused to make eye contact with her, preferring instead to aim his good will at her mother and daughter while she listened in, not catching Hideko's cue to participate.

"You should stay," she said at last, when the table had been cleared and Hideko and Naoko were out of earshot.

"Really?" he said. "I figured there'd probably be someone else by now."

"No," she said, shocked.

He shrugged. "I didn't know what to think."

Elinore bit her lip to keep it from trembling. Struck with the realization that she'd spent an entire year sorting out her feelings about Saburo, she wondered why it hadn't occurred to her that he might be wondering about her. Then her mind settled on Marina, and the call she'd placed to Saburo the night Marina had picked up. "How about Marina," she asked. "Did you and she sleep together?"

"Before, or after you left?"

"Never mind," Elinore said, wanting to take back all the good feelings that had been accruing since they sat down to eat.

"After you left, we hung out for a while," he said. "I'm not saying it to make you angry. But I was lonely, and I think she felt sorry for me."

"She was always attracted to you," Elinore said.

"Apparently she has a new boyfriend," Saburo said. "She's in love."

"And you?"

"No."

"Were you attracted to her?"

"No."

Elinore searched his face for signs of deceit, and, finding none, she thought of the strangers she'd slept with in Saburo's absence. She'd needed each of them, but not because she'd been angry with Saburo. "So, what now?" she asked, pleased as she watched behind Saburo to see that Naoko could load the dishwasher just the way Hideko liked it.

"You left," he said. "Remember?"

"Yes," she said, unable to keep the chronology straight.

After Naoko and Hideko had gone off to sleep, the talk continued. "So what was Bali really like?" she whispered, letting her head rest on his shoulder.

"Very peaceful," he said. "The country there is rich with history."

"Kind of like the Valley," she chuckled to herself. "Did you meet a lot of people?"

"Not so many," he shrugged, casting a sideways glance at her. "Maybe just enough not to be lonely."

"I was lonely," Elinore said, remembering the question Nora had asked her a year earlier. "I had Naoko, of course, and my mother, and on occasion my father. But I was deeply lonely."

"You don't have friends here?"

"No," she said. "But I did meet my half-sister. I found out that my father was married briefly and had a daughter before he met my mother."

"Really?" he said, lowering his chin to look at her. "What's she like?"

"She's Christian, part of a church my father left when he met my mother. She and I don't have much in common, but Naoko's fond of her."

"I was lonely, too," he said after a while. "Feeling connected isn't what you'd think."

"No." She mulled over the strong sense of history she experienced growing up with family in the Valley and how displaced she'd felt since she'd been back. "What is it, then?"

"Interest," he said, decidedly. "Affection." Reaching for her hand he brought it to his lips. "I missed you."

Elinore hesitated when he asked if she'd return with him to Santa Fe. Not that there was much to look forward to in the Valley; only that since her arrival, she'd ceased to believe that a life existed for her elsewhere.

Hideko was unsentimental about her daughter's departure, though she cried for Naoko as Saburo backed the rental car down the driveway. Traveling the highway that led out of the Valley, they fell quiet, the next part of their life together a void like the desert they'd have to cross to get home.

Chapter 35

As the rental car climbed the San Gabriel mountain range out of the Valley, the thermostat rose. Saburo insisted it wasn't anything to worry about, but Elinore, concerned that the car would overheat, recalled a story she'd once heard about her mother's parents. In her mind's eye she saw them just out of the internment camps, their car dwarfed by the wide fields of Central California as they traveled the old highway south, past Bakersfield. The old road still existed. Elinore had noted it out her window along with a few cars traveling it like spiders traversing their spin, imagining the lives of her grandparents. Having spent too long held in by retaining fences, they envisioned, beyond the barbed wire and desert, a home. They longed to be close to the ocean where in the perpetual sound of waves amnesia might be possible, the summer air cool and harmless. They were summoning the courage to imagine their lives as they crested the peak between the Santa Susanas and San Gabriels. Looking beyond the heat to the Valley blossoming below, they swore they could almost see water when their car began to shimmy and sputter, and with barely a dime between them, they were stranded.

There in the beginning lay the Valley, and seeing it their eyes focused quickly on what was familiar. Closer and more reachable than a phone call to relatives, the fields and orchards were a setting to which their eyes were accustomed, the beauty of furrows racing away from long rural roads like the days leading up to Nora's disappearance. But Elinore reminded herself that this was not her story, not her memory. Her grandfather, his thick wrists bent over the steering wheel, sweat dripping down his back, said to her grandmother, *We may as well settle here for a while. We can get work.* And her grandmother looking behind her at her five-year-old daughter said, *Why not?*

Years later, Grandmother Mizuno would recount this moment as a turning point in her daughter's life, summoning the lonely look of the land they left behind in shades of brown, its starkness echoed by the anger in her daughter's eyes that gave a conflicting message— *you are not my real parents; please don't leave me here alone.* Hideko hadn't remembered being present in the back seat of the car. *Though I must have been there*, she once reflected, calculating the years on her fingers. Elinore had listened to both sides until she'd known enough to come to her own conclusions.

After a few months of picking fruit, the Mizunos had saved up enough money to pay for car repairs, only the inclination to drive over the hill to Los Angeles had left them. Their days were hot and full from dawn to midday, and by evening they were too tired. How could they have known then that the love they'd wrought into tomatoes ripe on the vine would vanish, paved streets and rows of houses taking their place? How could they have known about the smog? Or that the Valley would be ten degrees hotter and dryer than Los Angeles in the summer?

Succumbing to the prodding glances cast over his shoulder, Saburo suggested that they turn the heater on, give the engine a chance to cool down, and relieved to be doing something Elinore rolled her window down, surprised at the coolness of the outside air as it rushed into the car. The darkening sky evoked the night not long ago that she'd driven Naoko to meet Melissa at the church carnival. "Isn't the Valley beautiful?" her daughter had said.

Elinore, who couldn't recall ever thinking so, told Naoko 'yes.' She'd come to understand the important connection the child drew between beautiful and home, the short path between love and familiarity. Driving the congested Valley streets along miles of concrete boulevards and strip malls, passing only an occasional flower bed or planter box, she'd told her daughter the story that hardly anyone seemed to know: how beneath the well-polished smoothness of Valley life, the perpetual newness that promised redemption, lay the broken roots of citrus trees, the remains of carrots, tomatoes, and onions. Unsatisfied by her mother's rendition, Naoko had asked to hear about the wedding she'd attended with her mother and grandmother, the one where she'd first met Melissa.

It had taken place the day after their arrival in the Valley, almost half the child's lifetime ago. As Saburo drove, the city lights faded to a single source in the distance, and Elinore recalled standing on the balcony of the old steakhouse where she'd met Nora. That conversation, once so enigmatic, made sense to her given what she'd since learned about the bloodline she shared with Melissa. Nora had recognized her, as had Melissa, and quite possibly Caroline. The knowledge that she and Melissa were related had not much mattered to Melissa. But its lack of effect on Melissa didn't diminish the impact the news had on Elinore. She would miss the Valley this time around, the place where her parents met and she grew up, the place where Nora vanished.

Once past the mountain range, the landscape to the east flattened, allowing Elinore to forget how worried she'd been about possible engine trouble. Saburo drove through the night and early into the next morning, Naoko traveling easier than Elinore thought she would, though she complained that she missed her grandma and her Auntie Miss—ah. From the back seat she chanted Elinore's half-sister's name over and over like the refrain of her favorite song until, suddenly, she stopped. "What rhymes with Auntie Missah?" she wanted to know.

"You do," Elinore told her, and she laughed.

Biographical Note

Julie Shigekuni is the author of two previous novels: *A Bridge Between Us* (Anchor/Doubleday 1995), which was a finalist for the Barnes and Noble Discover Great New Writers Award and recipient of the PEN Oakland Josephine Miles Award for Excellence in Literature, and *Invisible Gardens* (St. Martin's Press 2003). She grew up in Southern California, fled high school for the University of California at Santa Cruz, and subsequently lived in Tokyo and London. She received her B.A. from CUNY Hunter College and her M.F.A. from Sarah Lawrence College. She is currently at work on a novella and short story collection entitled *Beep on Me,* and a 60-minute video documentary, *Manju Mammas & the An-Pan Brigade*, for which she has received funding from the California Council for the Humanities and the Skirball Foundation and sponsorship from Visual Communications, an all Asian media network. She is director of the creative writing program and Development Director of Asian American Studies at the University of New Mexico.

Printed in the USA
CPSIA information can be obtained
at www.ICGtesting.com
JSHW022209140824
68134JS00018B/952

9 781597 091220